Beyond Good and Evil

First Novel of the Series

Michael Hannan

Technical Publishing
Chapel Hill, NC

First Printing: March 2014

ISBN (print): 978-1-890586-36-2
ISBN (ebook): 978-1-890586-37-9

Printed in the United States of America. 10 9 8 7 6 5 4 3 2 1

Library of Congress Cataloging-in-Publication Data
Hannan, Michael, 1944-
Beyond good and evil : first novel of the series / Michael Hannan.
    pages cm. — (A Beyond Good and Evil Novel)
  ISBN 978-1-890586-36-2
  1. Mystery fiction. I. Title.
  PS3608.A715745B49 2014
  813'.6—dc23
                                        2014007041

The text of this book is composed in Warnock Pro using Adobe InDesign®.
Cover image is of Lake Placid with Whiteface Mountain in the background.
Production services by TIPS Technical Publishing, Inc.
Copy edit by J.K. Maxwell.

To Mick and Eric, my sons

Other Beyond Good and Evil Novels

Scrambled Eggs

Louies' Diamonds

The Rolling Stones

Contents

Acknowledgments

While some details of this book are historically accurate, on whole it is a work of fiction. Any similarities between the characters of this story and real people (with the exception of those whose actual names I've used) are either coincidence or an unusual need for recognition on the suspect person's part. The one coincidence I do know is Gun Ek, the *sorcerer's apprentice*. Apparently, there is a Kristin Ek who is now a press officer at the *Moderna Museet*. Since I began writing *Beyond Good and Evil* shortly after the burglary, I cannot account for the concomitance other than Ek is a common Swedish name and I once knew a pretty woman named Gun, though I think she spelled it with two *n*'s. *Beyond Good and Evil* is also a creation of the author's imagination, as well as the title of a philosophical work by Friedrich Nietzsche. The inn's setting, however, was the site – many years ago – of another Adirondack inn that had a marvelous restaurant.

In 1993, thieves did steal six works by Picasso and two by Georges Braques from the *Moderna Museet*; moreover, the thieves entered the museum very much like that described in the 1955 French movie, *Rififi*. While three of the works have been recovered, they were three paintings by Picasso rather than the Picasso statue and the two paintings by cubist Georges Braques that I describe in the novel.

While no fiction is purely imaginative, my characters – especially Mick Keagan, Kelly O'Neill, Niles, and Teal – are my creations. Alas, I sometimes wish they were real because I'm very fond of them. I wonder if writers, especially writers of a series, are adults who haven't been able to discard their childhood imaginary friends.

One

James Campbell had just spent the night crawling through the labyrinthine duct work of Stockholm's *Moderna Museet*, and now knew how he and his brother, Greg, were going to steal six Picasso masterpieces.

Five minutes before the museum opened at ten o'clock, James was in the men's room on the second floor replacing the slip suit he had worn in the duct work with his street clothes. The sketch kit he had with him was just deep enough to accommodate his drawing materials: a thin digital camera, an extra memory stick, a pair of folding infrared field glasses with enough room to spare for the slip suit, and the sketches of the laser security grid that James was hesitant to let the front entrance guard see. He had thought about leaving some of the bulkier items in the duct work, but if they were found they would tip off security of his intentions, and he and his brother would most likely end up in jail. If the guard found them now, he reasoned, what laws had he broken?

He splashed water on his face, patted it dry with a paper towel, and ran a comb through his curly black hair that the slip suit hood had flattened. When he was satisfied with his appearance, he left the men's room and proceeded to the *Reuterswärd Gallery* where the Picassos were displayed. Art students from Stockholm's Royal College were already gathering there when he arrived.

1

He sketched for two hours, then left amid the crowd who either had had enough culture for the day or who were philosophically opposed to institutional food, and thus sought lunch outside the museum in one of the many nearby outdoor cafés, pleasant for this time of the year. The guard at the front entrance asked a question in Swedish, and James told him he didn't understand. The guard repeated his question in English; he was asking if James would open his sketch kit. He examined the contents of the kit carefully, checking the sketches one by one, but because of the its coloration the guard failed to notice that the interior of the kit was shallower than the outside's height indicated.

"These are very nice," said the guard, "you do good work." *Yes,* thought James, *I really do.* He smiled and nodded in appreciation of the compliment, closed the kit, and left the museum.

James met his brother Greg at a café two blocks down and one block over from the museum. He gave Greg the sketches of the laser security system patterns, the memory stick containing detailed photos of the gallery where the Picassos were displayed and of the elevator shafts with the cars resting on the first floor, directions to the location of where they would enter the duct work and several proposed exit routes, and a written schedule of the security guards' rounds that detailed each shifts duration. He double checked that Greg had gotten all the equipment they would need, told him to make prints of all the pictures, and made plans to meet in Greg's hotel room at eight o'clock that night. Then, he went to his own hotel to get some sleep.

They had pretty much decided from previous trips to the museum that they were going to access the *Reuterswürd Gallery* via the duct work. James' excursion the night before was a dress rehearsal of that decision, but there were still details to be worked out, most of which had to do with their escape. While most thieves wanted to get away from the crime scene as soon as they had what they wanted, the Campbells believed that the more obstacles you built for the investigation that would follow the crime, the more complicated the investigation would become, thus you're more likely to get away undetected.

That night they went over the sketches and prints before addressing the options that still remained. When one brother was convinced an option was fool-proof, he defended it to the other brother who looked for flaws. They took a Hegelian approach to art theft. James – who was the more intellectual of the two brothers – believed that if they were going to be thieves, they should be high-end thieves who stole only great art; if they were going to steal great art, they should favor a method for planning their thefts that was as sophisticated and intellectually refined as the artwork they were planning to steal. These brothers were not your typical smash-and-grab art thieves. They were cat burglars, perhaps among the best in the world. Finally, at about 2:00 AM, they had a plan they both liked, which they could both defend. They each had a large cognac and agreed to meet for lunch at 1:00 PM at a different café than where they had met the day before.

At lunch, they established the signals they would use during the theft and went over the details of the plan yet again, looking for flaws. Like many museums, *Moderna Museet* had a cafeteria for its patrons; indeed it had three different eating areas ranging from a fine-dining restaurant, to a quiet café, to an espresso bar. Notwithstanding, the quality of the eating facilities and the provision of food for its patrons and the functions hosted were usually an afterthought in museum design. The *Moderna Museet* was unusual in its design as its fine dining restaurant was located on the top floor to take advantage of the view of the Baltic Sea flowing into Stockholm. Where the *Moderna Museet* did not deviate from the norm in museum design, however, was its food lockers, which were located on the periphery of the building where cafeterias and restaurants took deliveries on a much more regular basis than the museum proper. As a result of this frequent delivery activity, security measures in and around the kitchens were typically more relaxed. The Campbells' plan was remarkably simple. James would again enter the duct work and then, after the museum closed, make his way to the cafeteria, disengage the less-than-sophisticated alarm on the door to the loading dock and open it for Greg, who would have their equipment. Both would then enter an elevator shaft located near the food lockers that would allow them to bypass the security guards' corridor and stairwell patrols and cameras. This would limit their exposure while they hoisted themselves and their equipment into the duct work that would give them access – albeit by different routes – to the gallery where the Picassos were displayed.

As the more cerebral of the two, James was the initiator and strategist of their projects. While he had the intellectual edge on his brother, the difference wasn't great. Greg, on the other hand, had the physical edge on James. Here too though, there wasn't a huge disparity in their strength. Both were extremely well conditioned, as all world-class cat burglars must be. However, James was the trimmer and more agile of the two. He was the real cat of the team and as such would be the one to make the snatches. Greg's job was to make sure that the cat never landed on all fours or at least not while he was suspended above the gallery.

The speed-skater slip suits they wore not only made going through the duct work easier, but also wouldn't leave behind fiber evidence that could later be used against them if they were somehow caught. The slip suit hoods fully covered their hair. They had also taped their eyebrows, assiduously trimmed their nose hairs, and even wore surgical masks to rein in any errant hairs they might have missed or any effusion caused by sneezing from the dusty duct work. And, of course, they wore gloves. They took special care not to snag the suits. In the event that they cut themselves on the duct work seams, they carried tubes of surgical *Krazy Glue* and alcohol wipes. There wouldn't be any trace evidence after the robbery that the Stockholm County Police or the *Rikspolisstyrelsen*, the Swedish National Police, could bring to the National Laboratory of Forensic Science where any that may have been found would be analyzed. They also ensured that there would be nothing for Interpol, which would almost certainly be involved in the investigation. There would be nothing for any law enforcement authority that might be brought into the investigation. Now, all the Campbells had to do was not get caught in the act.

The doorway to the gallery where the Picassos were displayed was equipped with laser-beam security. The beams that covered the entranceway were about four feet from the floor up. James originally thought he could rappel through the top two feet of the doorway, but Greg pointed out that the angle and the sag of their climbing ropes made that approach problematic. Instead, they decided to go through the duct work — not an original idea but surprisingly overlooked because of the museum security's heavy reliance on laser beams in the gallery the Picassos were displayed.

The *Reuterswärd Gallery* was a big room, thirty feet square, with two sets of ventilation ducts. Both sets were located in the north and south side walls of the gallery. The first set was located about eight feet from the gallery's west wall; the other set, about eight feet from its east wall. Greg had worked his way to the nearer north side duct, while James made his way to the corresponding duck on the south side of the room.

They removed the ventilator grills and James backed down the duct about ten feet. Greg, on the opposite side of the thirty-foot wide room, removed a folding crossbow from his Cordura equipment pack and assembled it. He threaded a piece of monofilament fishing line through a hole he had drilled through the flat-headed bolt, just to the rear of the fleche. He tied it off before needling the other end of the fishing line through the end of a slim, but high tinseled-strength climbing rope. When he was satisfied with his work, he concentrated on his breathing and brought his heart rate down to its normal resting rate of forty-five beats per minute. He had to be calm because he would not get a second chance. If he missed the mouth of the duct, he would hit the reinforced wall, which the bolt wouldn't penetrate. Instead, it would fall to the laser-protected floor below and set off the alarm.

Greg was using a 60-pound draw crossbow. It had enough power for the relatively flat trajectory needed for the shot, but not so much that it would penetrate James' *Kevlar* shield, especially since he had replaced the bolt head with a rubber tip. Greg loaded the bolt and braced himself. He aimed, let out a partial breath, held it, and fired. The bolt's impact made very little noise when it thudded into the *Kevlar* shield, rocking James back slightly. James and Greg – at opposite ends of the display room – secured both ends of the rope into the walls behind the duct work with screw bars. Then they waited for the guard to make his rounds.

On schedule, the guard came by. Methodically, he shone his light into the far corners of the room and around the bases of several display pedestals, a feckless gesture since the laser grid that covered the floor would have alerted him if someone were lurking in there. Moreover, checking out the floor to the exclusion of the paintings on the walls and sculptures displayed on pedestals at eye level caused him to miss the taut line across the top of the room; but such is an atavistic limitation. Mammals, human or otherwise rarely look above for danger, which is why predators that strike from above – especially owls, with their silent feathers – are so effective in catching prey.

They had one hour to steal the paintings before the guard returned.

James shone his Mini Maglite at the duct where Greg was, signaling him that he was ready to rappel into the room. Greg positioned his feet on the screw bar anchored into the re-enforced walls, just behind the duct's mouth, and got ready to maneuver the rope. James came out of the duct two feet below the fifteen-foot ceiling. When he was several feet past and above the first Picasso, Greg let out some rope through his Pretzel Figure 8 descender. The slack brought James down and abreast the painting. He signaled Greg, who tied the rope to the screw bar and confirmed that it was secure.

James removed a bundle from his backpack. It was a segmented aluminum pole with shock cord running through it, similar to those used for expedition dome tents, but thicker and sturdier. He unwrapped the Velcro strap that secured it, and cautiously joined the pieces, being careful not to let the pole get too close to the floor's laser beam grid.

After he got the pole fully extended, he screwed on a suction grip — the kind that glaziers use to carry large window panes — to the end of the pole. Extended, it was ten-feet long, but James knew he wouldn't need its full length because he had paced off the floor dimensions while he was here sketching the day before. He wet the suction face with a damp cloth from his pack before raising the pole parallel to the floor and extending it to the east wall. When the suction grip made contact with the wall, he pushed hard against it, locking it in place. Next, he drew the pole towards him, hand over hand. But since it was held fast to the wall, the pole drew him along the wall's length. Greg gave the rope more slack, until he was almost flush with the wall. James attached another suction grip at about the same level, but four feet to the right of the first grip. Using the pole, he pushed himself away from the wall and signaled Greg to lower him three more feet. The two lower grips were slightly different from those above them in that their tops were flat. These lower grips were his foot holds.

Once on the wall, James began removing the paintings, first from the wall and then, using a small pair of needle-nose pliers, from its frame. It would have been much faster to cut the painting from its frame, but it was against the Campbells' personal ethics and they knew that reducing the surface of a masterpiece would reduce its value. James scuttled across the wall like a spider. With each painting, he removed and stowed the framing brads in the belly pack he wore, careful that none fell into the laser grid beneath him. He rolled each painting over the last, put it into his back pack, and re-hung the frame and then moved on to the next painting.

When he had removed and stored the five Picassos, he pressed the illumination button on his Casio watch to see how much time had elapsed. He was slightly ahead of schedule. Then he remembered the two Braques he had seen the day before. Two more placements: a million extra, why not?

He dropped a brad and watched it fall as if in slow motion, knowing it would set off the alarm and bring the guard running, machine-pistol drawn. Suspended five feet above the floor, eight to ten feet from cover, he would never get back to the duct before the guard saw him.

The brad continued to fall to the floor. It bounced ... once ... twice ... James heard the alarm shrieking for the guard's presence, but no guard came. Then, he realized that the room was still quiet: the alarm was sounding only in his head. *Though maybe*, he thought, *the alarms were silent*. Still no guard appeared. He took out his infrared glasses from the pack and saw that the brad had fortuitously fallen between the grid and must not have bounced errantly enough to break the laser beam and set off the alarm.

The mishap shook him. *Quit now*, he thought, *don't push your luck*. The Braques were a pair, though, and he wanted them both. James regained his composure using a QiGong deep breathing technique and performing a simple trick he learned from a scene in *Magnum, P.I.* TV re-runs: "*Work the lock*," he said to himself, "forget the dogs." Whenever Magnum came home to find that Higgins, in a fit of pique over Magnum's irresponsibility, had changed the lock at his apartment, Magnum would have to pick it open. But as soon as he started, he would hear Zeus and Apollo, Higgins' two Dobermans, attacking. He'd look at them once, then turn back to the lock and repeat, *work the lock, forget the dogs; work the lock, forget the dogs*. It worked for the fictional Thomas Magnum, who always picked the lock before Zeus and Apollo tore him apart, thus preventing the ending of a popular series prematurely. This technique had also always worked for James Campbell whenever he needed to refocus. One more placement, five more minutes, and he had the second Braque.

He stowed the painting and made his way back across the wall, removing the suction grips as he retraced his route. At the point where he had first made contact with the wall, he stowed two of the last three grips. He signaled to Greg that he was ready for the final snatch. James pushed away from the wall, using the pole and detached the last suction grip, releasing its hold with the cabled release-trigger he had built into it. When he was in place, he signaled Greg again and simultaneously released his hold. Greg brought him up two feet, where James stowed the last grip and folded the pole, wrapping it again with the Velcro strap — one last piece.

On signal, Greg lowered James to the Picasso sculpture just below him. The sculpture did not have a pressure alarm beneath it, but it was in a locked glass case. The lock was meant to keep average citizens from getting at the sculpture. The laser grid which surrounded the pedestal's base was meant to keep away professionals. He worked the lock very quickly. Four minutes later James was back in the duct on the south wall. The brothers replaced the grills, and removed the screw bars. Seventeen minutes later they were back in the food-service storage area, changing into street clothes.

The guard had reached the room where the Picassos and the Braques were formerly displayed at the same time that the Campbells were stepping through the loading ramp door having just re-armed the door. Again, the guard conscientiously shone his light into each corner and around each pedestal base, and even directly at the glass display case that had housed the Picasso sculpture. He noted once again nothing was amiss.

James gave Greg the two Braques, and the Picasso sculpture. They left Sweden immediately. James drove to Copenhagen, Greg to Oslo, from whence each flew to Ireland where James went to Dublin and Greg to Belfast.

The theft was not discovered until 10:00 AM the next morning when the *Moderna Museet* re-opened for the day.

Two

The police arrived at the museum shortly after the robbery was reported. The *Moderna Museet* was located center-city Stockholm, on Sheppeholmen Island. As soon as the director learned of the theft, he closed the museum. The few early arrivals were given rain checks or refunds and politely ushered out, citing a maintenance problem as the cause for the closing.

"An electrical problem that might compromise the public's safety," said the director.

The museum would re-open tomorrow. He did what so many chief officers and politicians do when faced with a serious situation. He lied, foolishly believing that the public wasn't capable of dealing with the truth, and more absurdly believing that they wouldn't eventually learn the truth. The first tip off — even before the media started poking around — was the arrival of a number of blue and white police cars and a forensic lab van, clearly marked as such, parked directly in front of the museum for several hours. Police don't normally handle electrical problems — not even in Sweden.

Unlike in the United States where crimes in large cities are usually investigated by the police precinct in which the crime occurs, in Sweden — even in the major cities — the county police are responsible for preliminary investigations, similar to rural jurisdictions in America where the county sheriff's department has jurisdiction. However, certainly a theft of this magnitude and of one involving international complications would soon be usurped by the National

Criminal Investigations Department of the *Rikskriminalpolisen.* The officers who first responded to the director's call were from the Stockholm County Police.

Police Intendant Gandalf Dalin and Sergeant Gun Ek, nicknamed *Wizard* and *The Sorcerer's Apprentice* respectively, met with *Doktor* Hjelm, the museum's director, in his office where he frantically attempted to describe the importance of the theft. After several attempts Dalin finally succeeded in calming down *Doktor* Hjelm so he could cogently describe what had happened. Dalin listened carefully without interruption while Ek took notes.

The gist of *Doktor* Hjelm's story was that sometime during the night thieves had broken into the museum from the roof and had stolen five Picasso paintings, a Picasso sculpture, and two Georges Braques paintings, which he said — according to their insurance coverage — were valued at €40 million, approximately $60 million, or kr 257,017,206.

When the *Doktor* Hjelm had finished with his currency exchange calculations, Dalin asked him a few questions to clarify some points that were muddled by Hjelm's over-excited delivery. One of the points that Dalin needed clarified was why the director was so sure that the thieves had entered from the roof top. Hjelm had told him that that's what one of the security guards had reported to him. Satisfied that the director's current version of the *"facts"* of the theft was as accurate as he was likely to get from the man, Dalin asked for Hjelm and the security guard who had reported the break-in site to take him and Ek there.

The modern architecture of the *Moderna Museet* is a reflection of the art it promotes. The main building in Stockholm is long and low, only three floors high, and without the gothic accoutrements of more classical designs. The third floor of the *Moderna Museet* uncharacteristically housed the museum's premier restaurant — curiously called *The Restaurant* — which boasted the *"best view of Stockholm."* Since the museum was located center-city on an island where the

Balkan Sea meets Lake Mälaren, the boast probably wasn't far off the mark. And this is where the security guard, Dag Blixt, led them.

When they arrived at *The Restaurant*, Blixt pointed out the acoustic tile in the ceiling that had been sifted over, apparently so the thieves could gain access to the room and subsequently to the floors below. Ek cited the shifted tile in her notebook. Dalin asked about access to the roof.

The door to the roof was locked and controlled by a security code. Blixt tapped in the code to disengage the alarm, and unlocked the door. Dalin and Ek spent the next thirty minutes scouring the roof looking for how the thieves had broken in. There were no skylights in the roof, and all the exhaust fans and air conditioner covers were secured and bore no tampering marks. More obvious, there were no holes in the roof. The shifted acoustic tile, they concluded, was a red herring.

In 1955, the French film *Rififi*, adopted from a thriller of the same title by French mystery writer Auguste le Breton, had a profound effect on many cat burglars. It was directed by American filmmaker Jules Dassin, who won the Best Director Award for it at the 1955 Cannes Film Festival. The centerpiece of his film was an intricate half-hour heist scene depicting the method of the crime in detail. The scene was shot in near silence, without dialogue or music; the details of the theft alone had to carry it. So explicit was the Dassin's depiction of the fictional theft that his mis-en-scene served as a pattern for many actual high-end crimes subsequently committed around the world. The theft of the Picassos and the Braques, in spite of the askewed acoustic tile, was not one of them. Blixt probably had seen *Rififi* and concluded without the necessary evidence that this was how the museum had been robbed.

"It appears that the thieves have laid out this subterfuge to waste our time and to keep us from looking for where they really broke in," said Dalin as he rejoined Hjelm and Blixt at *The Restaurant*. Ek privately crossed out her notes about the thieves breaking in from the roof.

"Let's take a look at the gallery where the paintings and the sculpture were on display," said Dalin to Hjelm. "I'm assuming that the alarm system has been turned off in that room for opening the museum to the public. If that is still the case, can you activate the internal alarm so that I can understand how the security system works, but not have the alarm sound in our precinct office, the fire department, and the security company's office? The forensic team should be on its way and that will be quite enough people tramping through the scene. We don't need to add to the crowd." Hjelm called down to the Security Department and told the guard on duty there to activate the internal alarm for the *Reuterswärd Gallery*, but keep it turned off from its external sites and stay on the line.

The gallery was on the second floor. It was in the interior of the building, so it wasn't visible from the street or from any buildings in the area. Dalin paused just outside the gallery entrance, taking a pen out of his coat pocket. Holding it by the retractor button on top to get maximum extension of the instrument, he slowly extended the pen through the doorway. The alarm sounded before the pen had cleared the jamb. "OK, you can turn that off now," said Dalin. Hjelm told the guard to disengage the alarm.

Dalin looked quizzically at Hjelm. "Laser beams?"

"Yes, there are five sets of them spaced approximately thirty centimeters apart."

"I didn't get very far, did I?"

"No, you didn't. You might have made it farther, maybe even gotten your whole arm though without breaking a circuit, but the spacing is too narrow for anyone to get through the doorway. You broke a beam right away. You just weren't lucky."

"I guess I better stick to catching thieves rather than trying to start a new career."

Dalin walked into the gallery, and the others followed him. Immediately, he saw where the paintings had been displayed and the sculpture had stood. Ek gazed around the room. Blixt stood mute, his head hanging slightly.

"What other security measures are in place in this room?" asked Dalin.

Hjelm explained that the sculpture was in a locked case, albeit not one with a pressure plate, and the floor was also covered by laser beams, which produced a grid that was too low to crawl under, and too tight to step through even if the thieves could see the pattern with infrared glasses. "Herr Blixt, you were on duty last night in this sector, were you not?" asked Dalin.

Ek left off taking notes and began walking around the room.

"Yes, Intendant. I was."

"How then did you not discover the theft until this morning? Did you skip any of your rounds?" Hjelm starred coldly at Blixt.

"No, sir, I did not. You probably noticed the station check just outside the entrance way. If you examine its log, you'll see that I performed every check within the allotted time, and I did so according to the prescribed method."

Dalin watched Ek wander.

"Still, you must have seen that the paintings were missing. Were you drinking on duty or had you been drinking before you reported for work?"

"No, Intendant, I was not and did not."

"Drugs, then?"

"No, sir. I don't take drugs."

"Then how do you explain the lapse?"

"As you can see, the paintings were on the back wall of this entrance. I cannot see them through the angle the doorway provides."

"Yes, but what about the sculpture? As we can all see," here Dalin ignored the fact that Ek was looking at the very wall that Blixt just referenced, "the pedestal that held the sculpture is in plain sight of the doorway. How do you explain not noticing its case was empty?"

"Intendant, my instructions dictate that I scan the room from a point no closer than one meter from the doorway so that when I extend my arm holding my torch, I don't set off the alarm – that happened quite a bit when the security system was first installed – and shine my light around the room illuminating what is visible from my vantage."

On her own, Ek turned off the gallery's lights. Since the room had no natural light of its own, it was dark. "Shine your torch on the display case, Herr Blixt," said Ek.

Dalin understood at once and moved behind Blixt. The reflection of Blixt's torch blinded him to the case's contents. Ek turned on the lights, unbidden, while Dalin looked askance at Hjelm.

Dalin gazed around the room: no windows, no acoustic tiles, only an unbreached, stucco-coated, drywall ceiling with recessed lighting, and four ventilation registers.

"Dr. Hjelm can you get a rolling scaffold or a very secure and steady ladder up here?" asked Dalin. "Oh, and instruct your personnel downstairs to hold the forensic team there until we've finished here first."

***

The scaffold was a pneumatic one that compressed and extended like a car jack. Dalin told the maintenance man, Anders Haug, who delivered it, just where he wanted it. When it was in place and its wheels locked, he stepped up its three steps and told Haug to raise him to eye-level with the ventilation register. The register bars were too close together to allow an adult's hand to reach though it from the inside, but all four screws were scratched and not fully seated. Dalin shone his small torch through the bars. While they were narrowly spaced, he could still see that the register itself and the duct behind it were wide enough for an adult to crawl through — a trim adult that is. Dalin instructed Haug to lower him and move the scaffold to the corresponding register across the room. The screws there were scratched and also not fully seated.

When he was back on the floor, Dalin asked Haug how it would be possible to remove the screws on the outside of the register while inside the duct when the bars were too narrowly spaced to allow an adult hand to reach between them.

Anders Haug thought for a moment, then his eyes flashed an internal answer and his lips parted slightly in a near smile of appreciation, though very slightly, lest Hjelm see it. "Did you ever see your car mechanic access a nut or a bolt that you couldn't reach with your tool set?" Dalin may have been a crime wizard, but he wasn't much of a mechanic. He had, however, seen a mechanic use a tool that the maintenance man was describing.

"You mean one that's got a kind of floppy joint on it?"

"That's the one. It's called a universal joint. If you were patient or practiced, you could use something like that to do the job. It would also explain why the screws weren't seated all the way. It would be a pretty tedious process even for the patient."

"But wouldn't the screws fall to the floor as they came loose, and set off the alarm?"

"Not with a good magnetic bit head," answered Haug.

Dalin looked up and saw Ek pointing at the floor just in front of her. "What have you got, Sergeant?"

"There's a brad here, sir. I suspect whoever was pulling them from the frames dropped one. Amazing that it didn't break the beam; they must have been luckier than you, which might explain your different vocations. Unlike less patient thieves, these guys didn't cut the canvas from the frames. Check them out." She bent down and marked the spot with a small post-it note she tore from the pack that she routinely carried, but left the brad in place.

Dalin told Dr. Hjelm to tell his people to inform the forensic team that he was ready for them now. He walked over to the wall where the paintings had been displayed. Ek joined him. "What do you think, Gun?" said Dalin.

"My first impression is we're dealing with two very intelligent and athletically talented thieves. I'd say they somehow managed to get a line, perhaps two or more, stretched across the room. One of them performed some very impressive gymnastics while the other controlled the tension of the line, or lines, which controlled the other's position."

"Very good so far. Why two thieves? Why not more?"

"The ducts. More than one person in a duct would form a queue. I didn't see the ducts, but since you asked that fellow about how to get at the register screws from the inside, I'm assuming the ducts are wide enough for one man."

"Why not a woman? You're usually more liberal than that," said Dalin.

"Strength. Maybe the gymnast, but at least one of them had to be a man, unless one was a member of the former East German Women's Weight Lifting Team, and I doubt one of them would fit in the duct. No, had to be at least one man."

"Again, good, as far as you've gone," said Dalin. "But now explain how the gymnast got over to the wall?" "I calculate that the register is almost two-and-a-half meters from the wall where the paintings were displayed."

Ek looked puzzled. She ran through several scenarios. All failed. "I don't know; you've stumped me."

"Look at the wall carefully." Ek stepped up to it.

She was still flummoxed. "Do you see the smudges?" asked Dalin.

"Yes, but I don't know what made them."

"Think glaziers," said Dalin.

"Glass cutters?"

"And installers. How do they carry those large sheets of glass?"

Ek's face registered her understanding.

When the forensic team arrived on the second floor, Dalin led them first to the third floor, where he pointed out the shifted acoustic tile. He told them that it was a false lead, but to check out the area in case they had touched something without gloves, snagged some clothing, or left some trace evidence behind. Dalin held little hope. He didn't like the thieves that he pursued, but he had to admire some of them. So far, these two were way up on his admiration list.

Back in the *Reuterswärd Gallery*, Dalin directed two of the suited-up forensics team members to enter the two ducts, collecting whatever trace evidence the thieves had left behind and to follow the duct work to see if they could discern where the thieves had entered it. Dalin also held little hope of finding anything in the ducts other than where they entered and exited them.

Two hours later, the team was packed up and ready to be released by Dalin. They found nothing in the *Reuterswärd Gallery* that Dalin and Ek hadn't already pointed out. They re-marked the spot where Ek had found the brad, and bagged it for further analysis back at the lab. They also photographed the gallery with a Panoscan camera and the glazier suction smudges with a digital camera.

As Dalin had expected, the two team members – both women – found little in the duct work that lent itself to analysis. The woman in the duct where Greg worked found and photographed the screw bolt indentations, but she didn't see how they would be useful beyond helping to explain how the thieves did what they did. The other woman in James' duct did the same but found nothing else; she missed the small scratch that the crossbow bolt made when it bounced off James' *Kevlar* shield and hit the sidewall.

Both, however, were able to follow the dust trail back to where the ducts joined up and to where the Campbells had, if not entered, at least exited. Anyone who has ever been married, even for the shortest of times, knows that women are far superior at finding dust than even the most perceptive Marine Corps drill inspector. However, the trail died there, at a spot on the second floor corridor across from an elevator door. Nobody on the forensic team was able to figure out where the thieves went from there. They had examined the door, but they found no evidence other than what was left there in the course of its usual use. The thieves wouldn't have used the elevator, they reasoned, because the movement would have alerted security. Also, there were no marks left on the elevator doors suggesting that they hadn't been pried apart, nor was there any indication they had somehow climbed down the shaft. After two hours, all the forensics team was able to learn was the route that two people, probably men, had taken through the duct work.

Three

Swedish National Laboratory of Forensic Science is the government agency under the Department of Justice that is charged with assisting the police in their criminal investigations, specifically by analyzing trace evidence with the purpose of connecting it to people, places, and time. The work of the laboratory is spread among four units: Biological, Chemical and Technical, Drug Analysis, and Documentation. Analyzing the trace evidence of the burglary that occurred in the *Moderna Museet* did not over-tax the laboratory.

One wouldn't expect there would be any documentation to analyze from such a burglary, nor that there would be any drug analysis to be done — unless of course one of the thieves managed to drop a prescription drug of some sort. Better yet for the police, a prescription vial with his name and address on it, but that doesn't happen, even in the cinema. Maybe at a liquor store or a convenience store stick-up, but burglars who focus on high-end art theft are usually of a more practiced sort.

The Biological Unit also did not find itself unduly strained. In fact, like the Documentation Unit and the Drug Analysis Unit, the museum theft had brought it no work at all. Only the Chemical and Technical Unit received anything to analyze from the burglary, and there was precious little, since there was absolutely no trace evidence found in the duct work and nothing to analyze from where the thieves broke in. The police still had no idea how they had gotten in or out for that matter.

The totality of the evidence collected from the museum was the one framing brad Sergeant Ek had found, a Panoscopic film of the *Reuterswärd Gallery*, several swabs and digital photos of the smudges left by the glazier suction grips, several fingerprints from the elevator where the burglars' trail ended, and a button found under a table in *The Restaurant* which turned out to belong to the *maître d'*.

The Swedish National Laboratory of Forensic Science is a very fine forensic laboratory. One needs only to look at Sweden's graduation requirements in mathematics and science for high school students entering university to understand why. But the technicians and scientists there, while highly qualified, were not alchemists or wizards. They couldn't create identities from smudges bearing no DNA, nor could they put together descriptions from dust trails, let alone suspects from shadows.

The laboratory's report sent to the Stockholm County Police, specifically to Intendant Gandalf Dalin, was less than one typed page. After listing the evidence and the scant analysis each bit of evidence underwent, the laboratory concluded: *In the matter of case# 186-449-06-05, submitted to this laboratory on June 21, 2005; viz, the burglary of the Moderna Museet, the evidence submitted revealed no further specifics.* Translation: *we got nothing.*

❋❋❋

The Campbells' plan was for James to play tourist in Dublin for two weeks and for Greg to do likewise in Belfast. Then, they would return home to Boulder, Colorado, where they both lived. James lived in an old ranch house within sight of Boulder Mountain Park that he was remodeling, while Greg lived in a downtown condo. They would go about their normal business, which when they weren't planning or executing burglaries, was composed of enjoying the cultural delights of the university town, researching the art world, organizing new knowledge of various art forms in a database that James designed, and of course maintaining their conditioning, which in this season meant mountain runs and rock climbing.

Ordinarily, the Campbells didn't have to work any more than once every year or two, but sometimes opportunities presented themselves at irregular times, coming in clusters that couldn't be ignored because world-class cat burglars are like world-class athletes: they have short careers. There is a serious difference, however. World class athletes whose careers run too long end up tarnishing their career achievements and their statistics. At worst, they take a humiliating beating like Muhammad Ali did in the Ali-Holmes fight of 1980. If world-class cat burglars stay at their calling too long, they end up in prison. The Campbells had no intention of enduring such an ignominious end to their brilliant careers, so they worked very hard at being up to date in the art world and on advances in technology that affected their careers, such as locks and alarms systems. They worked out like zealots. Moreover, they invested wisely, spent judiciously, and didn't walk away from jobs just because they arrived at inconvenient times. They also didn't hesitate to deviate from their long thought-out plans if the job didn't feel right or if circumstances dictated they do so. The Campbells were very pragmatic. Their first and foremost objective was to avoid capture, followed distantly by scoring big, and finally doing work that was intellectually and physically challenging. The Campbells were puzzle solvers at heart.

Their first objective was why Greg cut and ran.

He had been staying at the Fitzwilliam Hotel on Great Victoria Street for eight days after the burglary. He had checked in using a Canadian passport and had been quietly enjoying the city's attractions: the Grand Opera House that was right next door, Belfast Castle, the Botanic Gardens, and the Ulster Museum — it never hurt to explore new sources. He even played several rounds of golf at the Rockmount Golf Club. He was planning on taking a couple of tours of the countryside during his remaining days in Belfast.

It had rained on the back nine of Rockmount.

***

Even in June the rain in Northern Ireland is cold, so he didn't stop at the bar as had been his practice for the last several days. Instead, he went right up to his room for a hot shower and a change of warm, dry clothes. As he was walking down the corridor, approaching his room, he saw the chamber maid who had been making up his room for the last few days. He smiled hello to her, as she had been very friendly toward him, even flirting a bit the last two times he had seen her. This time, however, she purposely looked away. Greg thought it strange, given her previous openness.

When he got back to his room, he checked his carryall. Neither Greg nor James used the *bureaux* in hotel rooms. They might use a closet if they had a coat, but they kept their bags packed, ready for a quick exit, and used carryalls with zipper and strap closures, always leaving just a few zipper teeth open – specifically five for Greg – and fastened the straps setting the tongues in different holes. Greg's carryall was zippered all the way shut and each buckle tongue was set in the middle hole, not staggered the way he left it. He checked his garment bag; the zipper was closed all the way. He called James in Dublin.

"Get out, now!" James told him. "Call me when you're settled some place safe."

"But the Braques and the sculpture are in a locker I rented at the Rockmount Golf Club."

"Leave them. Get out."

There was nothing missing from his bag but he had three passports in the carryall, in an interior pocket, and he knew the chamber maid had gotten nosey and seen them. She saw something that spooked her; otherwise, she wouldn't have turned away. Greg grabbed his toiletries put them in the carryall, grabbed a towel from the bathroom and wiped down anything he might have touched, which didn't take long because he and James had learned to touch as little as possible in hotels rooms when they were working a job. He took the TV remote with him; too many surfaces to be positive about wiping it *entirely clean.*

He took the stairs down to the parking garage, walked out a side pedestrian exit, hailed a cab, and directed the driver to take him to the Ferry Terminal, where he took the ferry to Liverpool and a train from there on to London's Euston Station. He called his brother when he was settled in London.

⁂

The random forces of the world had conspired against Greg Campbell. The Stockholm Country Police had nothing to do with his near capture, nor did the Swedish National Police or Interpol as they hadn't been asked yet to help with the case, it certainly hadn't. Greg Campbell's near undoing was the convergence of nonlinear dynamics — chaos, if you will.

The chamber maid worked part-time. She was working at the Fitzwilliam because her mother, the regular chamber maid, had a summer cold and needed to take several days off to shake it. The daughter was home for a short break between the end of the spring term at Queens University and an internship at a pharmaceutical company where she would work for the summer gaining practical experience, as well as padding her résumé for medical school. She was very bright, but she had become enamored by Greg Campbell's good looks and strong features. She worked at the Fitzwilliam whenever her schoolwork allowed her so that when her mother was sick, she automatically filled in. She knew the sacrifices her mother made for her.

After seeing Greg several times in passing, she became curious about who he was, what he did for a living, and where he was from. She thought he might be American, but maybe that was because he spoke English well. He was also open like an American, but there seemed to be a certain inner caution to him as well – maybe Canadian or German. She was usually a no-nonsense young woman, but human nature was rife with inconsistency.

She had dawdled a bit in her rounds, just enough so that the other two maids working the floor would finish their work for the day ahead of her. She saved Greg's room for last. She knocked, announced herself, and when there was no answer used her key card. She called out again, announcing herself, and made sure he wasn't there. She made up the room quickly and efficiently. When she was finished, she had gone out into the hall and moved her cart three doors down, then came back to Greg's room and closed the door behind her – something she knew would get her and even her mother in trouble if she were caught, but she'd just wanted to take a quick look at his things to learn something about him. She found nothing in the bureau, and the only thing in the closet was a garment bag with suits, shirts, and ties. *Strange,* she thought, *he had been staying here for over a week, and he hadn't put anything in the bureau drawers or that much in the closet.*

His garment bag was hanging in the closet. She unzipped it. His suits were lovely and the ties were so colorful, unlike the drab ones she saw in Belfast. She wondered if he was gay. She zipped up the bag. The carryall was leather. *Sturdy and expensive,* she thought. She opened it all the way: socks, underwear, casual shirts and slacks, a couple of sweaters. *The usual.* And just like the bag, it was all very nice and expensive looking, as well as very ordered and neatly packed. She saw the inside pocket. It bulged. She wondered if he had a packet of bills in it. She wasn't going to steal them if he did, but she wanted to see how much was there. She unzipped the pocket. Not money – passports, three of them. What was he doing with three passports? What would anyone be doing with three passports?

She put them back, re-zipped the pocket and bag, and set the straps neatly in the center holes. She left the room quickly. *Oh, Jaysus, here he comes.* She couldn't face him. What was he doing with three passports?

The Fitzwilliam is just down the block from the Europia, which during *The Troubles* had the dubious distinction of being the most bombed hotel in Europe. The IRA and the Loyal Unionists had signed the Peace Treaty in 1998. Eimear, the chamber maid, was only ten years old at the time. In spite of the peace treaty, the violence had continued sporadically and nobody living in Ireland during *The*

Troubles ever forgot it. Moreover, she had seen the movie *Omagh* at the University just last month. What if he were a terrorist, planning to blow up the Fitzwilliam or planting a bomb in a stolen car as the *Real IRA* had done in *Omagh*? How could she live with herself?

But if she told anyone, they'd ask how she'd come to see the passports. She could lie and say they were in plain sight, but no one would believe that. She'd lose the job and disgrace her mother who would potentially lose her job, too. If that happened, she'd have to leave the University. She was on a full scholarship, but there were still regular expenses to handle. But what if he killed people? She called her mother.

***

"I'm in London, at the London Marriott."

"Any problems?"

"No, I took the ferry to Liverpool, then the train down."

"How were you thinking about getting home?"

"I'm not sure; I was thinking about Spain."

"Portugal might be better."

"Yes, I think you're right, one more border but it shouldn't be a problem. I'll be French. No hassle between EU countries. I think I'll hunker down here for three or four days, then take the train down. The *Eurostar* to will get me to Paris. I'll have to check on Lisbon. I know there are sleepers that go to Madrid. Any idea what goes to Lisbon?"

"Check out the TVG (*Train á Grande Vitesse*) and the *Sud Express*."

"I'll do that. I'll probably need a week to get back."

"Take your time. Enjoy Lisbon for three or four days, too. Do you have enough money?"

"Yeah, I came away with everything, except for the assignment."

"Don't worry about it. Remember, just like in boxing, the first rule is *to protect yourself at all times*. Give me an update when you know more about your plans. I'll be here for five more days. I'll see you at home."

***

Eimear and her mother, Caoimhe (pronounced *kee-va*) Lynch, were in the General Manager's office of the Fitzwilliam. With them were Chief Inspector Conor Moran and Sergeant James Robinson from the *Special Branch* of the Police Service of Northern Ireland. Mrs. Lynch knew that what Eimear had seen might well be too important to cover up; even if it wasn't, she wasn't willing to take the chance.

Eimear had told the detectives what she had seen, embarrassingly admitting her motivation. When questioned, she told the detectives that she had seen nothing suspicious other than the passports. There were no timing mechanisms, no wiring, no tools or explosives. Nothing but the three passports and the *fine clothes*, but she didn't mention those. She hadn't looked at the names on the passports, but had seen the country names embossed on their covers: Canada, the United States, and France.

The detectives asked more questions, but Eimear had nothing else to add. She had made up his room as she had the past four days, but this time she looked in the closet and the bureau, which were empty – something she thought strange – and then she had briefly looked into his luggage. Everything was very neat, nothing out of the ordinary except the passports.

Moran asked if she could describe the man who was registered as Gregory Hatton. Sergeant Robinson copied down the description, which was unusually detailed. Moran asked Eimear if she were an art student. Eimear said, no, she was in pre-med, so she had advanced knowledge about anatomy. Had the tone in the room been somewhat more relaxed, she might have been tempted to add, "And I was rather interested in studying his in finer detail." But prudence prevailed.

After checking with the concierge, Robinson acquired a list of inquiries that Gregory Hatton had made about tours and entertainments. He brought the list to Moran who honed in on the Rockmount Golf Club. Robinson looked flummoxed. "They have lockers," said Moran. Moran arranged to have a bomb unit meet him at the club and called ahead to let the General Manager know of their imminent arrival. Moran told them that it might be nothing, but that the area should be cleared immediately until the police were certain.

The bomb unit arrived replete with a sniffer dog. The dog, a chocolate lab, checked out the entire clubhouse, ending back at the men's locker room where it started. The golf secretary told Moran that Hattan — if that was his real name — had rented locker #37 until the end of next week. One of the men from the bomb unit cleared the locker for booby traps, and using the key the golf secretary provided him, opened the locker without incident. Well, not entirely.

The sergeant in charge of the bomb unit called the Moran into the locker room and told him – while he had found no explosives or bomb-making materials – he did find something that he thought the Chief Inspector might find interesting. Moran, Robinson, the golf secretary and the club's general manager went into the men's locker room to see what the sergeant had found. When the principles were gathered, the sergeant unrolled the two Cubists paintings by Georges Braques he had found in a carrier tube and unwrapped Pablo Picasso's *Bronze Horse.*

Four

Even before the Braques and the Picasso sculpture were discovered in a golf club locker room in Northern Ireland, the jurisdiction for the burglary, as expected, had passed from the Stockholm County Police to Swedish National Police. When the superintendent in charge of the theft, Hilmar Lampa, learned of the recovery he immediately contacted Interpol. Interpol had no information on any Gregory Hatton. Lampa found it astonishing that not only were no prints found on the sculpture wrappings or on the carrier tube that contained the Braques, but neither were any found on the clubs Hatton had rented. Lampa was not satisfied by Moran's explanation that it was the Rockmount Club's practice to clean and wipe down all rental clubs after use. He would have been more astonished if he knew that both Campbells wiped down whatever they touched in hotels or anywhere that could be traced to them. They did so *de rigueur*.

***

Dalin didn't like that the burglary of the *Moderna Museet* had occurred in his jurisdiction. That the National Police had appropriated that jurisdiction was a technical matter of protocol. Still, that didn't mitigate his displeasure at all.

He had turned over what little evidence he had to the Swedish National Police and had also sent a copy of his initial investigation report, along with a copy of the report Sergeant Ek had provided him, to Chief Inspector Moran in Belfast, Northern Ireland. The matter was out of his hands—officially that is. However, in terms of national, municipal, and personal embarrassment, the burglary of the *Moderna Museet* was at the top of his 18-year career list. He was not going to give it up.

Dalin couldn't work on the case anymore *officially*, but what he did on his own time was – within reason – up to him. He contacted Dr. Hjelm and asked him if he could have access to the museum on the weekend. Hjelm responded to his request by saying that he thought that the case had been turned over to the National Police.

Dalin told him that it had, but that he still had some questions and wanted to take a look at the site again. He promised that he'd be as unobtrusive as possible. He might need a custodian to open up some doors for him so he could access rooms containing windows that might not be normally open to the public, but that's all he could foresee for now. Oh, and he might need copies of the security videos, including those taken while the museum was open to the public, from three days prior to the burglary.

Hjelm said that he would inform the maintenance and custodial staff to allow him access to anywhere in the museum as long as it was during regular operating hours and didn't interfere with the general public. He also reluctantly agreed to provide copies of the archived security videos Dalin requested. Reluctantly, because copying was a tedious process, but Hjelm realized that this was not an occasion to be *öre wise and krona foolish*. If Dalin was willing to bring his talents to the investigation, even though it was no longer his case, Hjelm was willing to deal with small inconveniences and expend a few krona in overtime.

Dalin told Hjelm that he would be there on Saturday and asked that someone be available to him for an hour or two.

Dalin was one of the first people through the doors the next Saturday morning. He even paid the admission fee so that the National Police couldn't complain that he was treading on their investigation.

He checked in at the information desk as per Dr. Hjelm's instructions. A custodian met him there in ten minutes.

The first thing Dalin wanted to do was check out all external entrances to the museum regardless of how secure they were supposed to be. He told the custodian, Jarl Bohl, that he should probably inform the Security Department what they would be up to in case their perusal set off any alarms. Bohl called Security and told them the order in which they would be proceeding. When he finished the call, he led Dalin out to the general entrance.

Dalin had brought a few tools with him. The first one he employed was a 10-power magnifying glass to check for tiny scratches that might indicate a lock might have been tampered with. He doubted that any of the external locks were picked in the traditional sense – they were probably electric – but the thieves had gotten in somehow and as yet the police had no idea how. Dalin didn't want to overlook anything and as his investigation was clandestine. He was under no official pressure to hurry.

First, he checked the external locks of the three doors that comprised the front entrance and they were indeed electric; however, doors that can lock can also always be opened, no matter how sophisticated they are. Dalin checked both sides of the door looking for any indication the locks had been tampered with. He found none. He proceeded clockwise around the building rather than counter-clockwise as there was a large stone outcropping to his left that would have brought him to the second floor. Dalin wanted to be methodical. Along the way, he also examined the windows he could reach and the ground beneath them, looking for ladder leg marks or any indication that suggested how the thieves might have gained entry. Again he found nothing. He really didn't expect to find that they had used a ladder to reach the upper floors, as the outcropping by the front entrance allowed easy access to the third-floor patio for any cat burglar worth his salt. Dalin suspected that even he could have climbed up – unassisted – to the patio.

Dalin and Bohl continued around to the back where there were three entrances: the back entrance for the public, one for maintenance, and a loading-dock entry. Like the front entrance, the doors of the back public entrance showed no sign of tampering, nor did the maintenance entrance, nor the loading-dock door. He didn't bother having Bohl open these two entrances; he'd check them from inside. Something about the loading dock, though, piqued his interest, but he couldn't conjure up what it was. He just had a feeling.

There was an employees' entrance on the far side of the building. It didn't appear to have been tampered with either. He'd check that one inside as well. Dalin and Bohl went inside to examine each window, of which there were many. Most of them were sealed, however, so their inspection didn't take long. Still, Dalin checked each one to see if it had been removed from its casing. He kept going back to: *they got in somehow*.

The patio entrance to the third floor, residing just off *The Restaurant*, was the most logical access, but nothing about it resonated with Dalin, ready access to the red herring shifted ceiling tile aside; perhaps because it seemed so obvious. *If I were a cat burglar*, thought Dalin, *that's where I'd come in. Then again, I'd be a lousy burglar*, Dalin finished. Aside from the red herring ceiling tile, there was nothing there — nothing on the entire third floor that interested him.

He carefully examined the inside of the maintenance, employee, and loading-dock doors. Still nothing. He asked Bohl if he could get a copy of the building's blueprint. Bohl told him that he knew maintenance had the blueprints but that Dalin would have to ask Dr. Hjelm to OK it. He made a mental note to get Hjelm's permission.

Dalin asked Bohl if he had to carry a heavy object to the *Reuterswärd* Gallery what entrance to the museum he would use. Bohl thought about it for a moment – though not a very long moment – before replying "the loading dock." "Why?" asked Dalin.

"Couple of reasons. One, it's the shortest route; two, I wouldn't have to work around the visitors; and three, I'd be able to use the food-service elevator."

"What's that?"

"Well, the restaurants' supplies are brought in from the loading dock. Both the Espresso Bar and Café Blom are located on the first floor, but as you just saw *The Restaurant* is located on the third floor for the view. So they built in a special elevator just for it. We sometimes use it, but mostly it's *The Restaurant's*, and the chef up there gets mighty mad if anyone of us on the custodial or maintenance staff is using it when he wants it. Thinks it's his."

"Does it have a stop on the second floor?"

"Sure, but it's in a storage room."

"Show me," said Dalin.

In less than a week after Dalin requested them from Dr. Hjelm, he received copies of the museum's blueprints and of the videos for not only the day of the theft, but also for the three days prior to it.

Dalin had confided in Ek what he was doing. He told her that if she wanted to help out she was welcome. If she didn't that was fine too, but under no circumstances could she talk to anyone about what he was doing. Dalin said that he would take the lead on every aspect of their clandestine investigation, so that if anyone at National caught on, he'd be the only one hanging out there.

Besides, unless they discovered something that required follow up, all they would be doing would be examining the blueprints and the videos. The blueprints were first. Dalin decided to work the problem backwards. He told Ek a little bit about his thought process and about the *Parable of the Bees*.

"A researcher put five bees into a large-mouth jar, something like a mayonnaise jar," said Dalin. Leaving the lid off, he turned the jar base-first toward an open window. It was a sunny day. When the bees felt the warmth of the day and saw the light, they buzzed straight to where the warmth and the light were coming from, only to smash up against the base of the jar. When the researcher returned in five minutes, all the bees were dead, exhausted and dented from their struggles to escape.

The researcher then duplicated the experiment, this time using ordinary houseflies. At first the houseflies reacted as the bees had, but after smashing into the base once, they tried other approaches: this one going left, that one going right, until one found the open mouth of the jar and led the way out.

The moral of the story is that the bees went to the light and the warmth as bees are wont to do. All the evidence they had suggested that that was their way to freedom, even though all attempts to escape failed. Bees are highly social, so they operate with a group mentality. They operate under conventional bee wisdom. Houseflies, on the other hand, are mavericks; they don't follow the swarm. After only a few failed attempts, they realized that to a fly the way out was not toward the warmth and the light. Interesting, the solution to their escape was 180° opposite the bees' perceived solution.

"A lot of people *talk* about thinking *outside the box*, but I've encountered very few who actually know how. I can't tell you how many problems I've solved by doing the exact opposite – in terms of the parable, 180º opposite – of the conventional wisdom solution."

"So, how are we going to use the bees here?" asked Ek.

"We work backwards, just like the house flies. We know where the theft took place: I don't mean the museum; I mean the *Reuterswärd* Gallery. We also know how they got to the gallery and where they exited the duct work that led them there. Since we don't know how they got into the building, even though the forensic unit has been all over it, and there are five entrance ways and God knows how many windows, albeit sealed, I thought we might — using the blueprints and working backwards — start from the *Reuterswärd* Gallery and work backwards through the duct work to where they exited it. It's as precise as we can get right now."

Dalin had only asked Dr. Hjelm for one copy of the blueprints so if National did catch on to him there'd be no tie to Ek; however, he had had a second set made for him by an architect he had once helped out. He handed the extra set to Ek and showed her how to read them. He had already arranged them so that the top print was of the second floor at the spot where the dust trail in the duct work petered out right in front of the elevator.

"Here's where they came out," said Dalin, pointing so Ek knew where to start. "The question now is where they went from there. The elevator – right here – is the obvious answer, but forensics found nothing there to substantiate that premise – not on the control panel, in the elevator car itself, or even in the shaft. Why don't you find some place where you're comfortable and spend the next hour moving them to some other point in the building that shows us, if not where they exited the building and perhaps entered it, at least the next logical step in their exit? After an hour, we'll create some hypotheses, and then try to blow holes in them."

Ek ran out of possibilities after about forty minutes but had succeeded in coming up with some questions. She gave it another ten minutes, but knew she was just spinning her wheels. She rejoined Dalin at the kitchen table. He had already completed the task before he had gotten together with Ek and of course he had already seen the food-service elevator in the maintenance closet, but he didn't want to prejudice Ek's thinking.

"What have you come up with?" he asked.

"First some questions," answered Ek. "Are we absolutely ruling out the elevator?"

"No."

"I can't remember; are there video cameras in the stairwells?"

"Yes."

"I'm assuming that these little symbols," Ek pointed to an angled line with what appeared to be a rocker beneath it, "are doorways and the rocker indicates which way they open."

"Correct."

"Are there any vertical air shafts or other vertical shafts besides in this elevator?"

"No and yes."

"What does that mean?"

"No, there are no vertical air shafts; yes, there is another shaft."

"Where? I've missed it."

"Here," said Dalin as he pointied at the maintenance storage room.

"How can you tell? I don't see anything that indicates a shaft."

"I wouldn't have either, but Herr Bohl, the custodian who gave me a special tour last Saturday, mentioned it in passing. Then I made him show me."

"So you knew the answer to this exercise before we began. Why didn't you just tell me? Why waste the time I spent looking for the answer?"

"The short answer is that one day you'll be the senior partner. If I don't train you to think for yourself, how will you fare when your partner is a raw rookie? Besides, I didn't know *the* answer: I knew *an answer*. If I told you that, you would have started this investigation as a bee. OK, what have you got?"

"The patrons' elevator that the forensic unit has written off, the stairways at either end of the corridor, and this secret passageway that you kept from me."

"Good start. You didn't automatically discount the patrons' elevator just because forensics didn't find anything there. You were thinking like a housefly, there. Maybe they didn't go far enough. Remember the parable: the first two houseflies – the ones that went right and left – failed too, but they had the right idea."

"Oh good, I'm a housefly."

"So, housefly, you've got four possible answers; where do you go from here?"

"While we can't rule out the patrons' elevator, it's in last place. Since there are videos of the stairways, it should be fairly easy to either validate a stairwell or rule it out by running up the tape to the evening of the robbery and seeing if anyone's creeping down with seven paintings and a sculpture to the first floor."

"Good, with minor flaws."

"What?"

"First, it was a *burglary*, not a *robbery*. Robbery requires at least implied violence. Second, they're DVD's, which have better resolution and they're easier to run up to the starting time, especially if you have a fancy machine like the one I borrowed. And third, maybe they went up the stairwell."

Ek just rolled her eyes.

A little over an hour later, they had viewed both disks for the time periods when the paintings and sculpture had been stolen and saw nothing but the security people making their rounds.

That left the patrons' elevator and the food-service elevator. As forensics had already checked out the patrons' elevator, the food-service elevator now topped the list.

Dalin and Ek came to the museum on the Saturday following their review of the stairwell videos. Jarl Bohl was waiting for them at the information desk to lead them to whatever they needed to see. Dalin told him that he wanted to examine the food-service elevator again, first from the custodial closet on the second floor.

Dalin found no scratches on the lock, but it was a simple lock meant to keep the staff from pilfering the cleaning supplies, not designed to keep out two thieves that had the Stockholm County and National Police forces baffled as to how they even entered the building.

At the back of the closet was the door to the elevator. It was locked. Dalin had brought a fingerprint kit with him and began dusting the elevator door, especially around its control panel and lock. All he found were smudges. He asked Bohl to open the door for him. Bohl pointed out to him that the elevator car was up at the third floor. Dalin told him that's precisely why he wanted the door opened now.

Bohl unlocked the door and stood back from Dalin and Ek. Dalin shone his torch down into the shaft; twenty feet below were the large springs that were meant to limit injuries if a cable snapped and the car plummeted to the bottom. There wasn't anything in the shaft that looked suspicious to Dalin. It was dark, sooty and greasy everywhere near the cables, but he couldn't see any place where the soot had been smudged or the grease smeared. He called Ek over, handed her the torch, and asked her to take a look. Two sets of eyes are usually better than one.

Ek didn't see anything unusual in the shaft, not that she had a lot of experience with elevator shafts, but she had noticed that one of the storage room's shelving sets – one that held the heaviest of the supplies, including five gallon buckets of cleaning fluids and floor wax – was askew. It wasn't tilted much, but it was enough that it caught her attention. She pointed it out to Dalin.

"Herr Bohl, would you go down to the first floor, call the car down to you and wait there for us?"

Bohl did as he requested. Dalin and Ek stepped back from the open shaft and watched the car descend past them. When the car stopped at the first floor, Dalin again shone his torch down the shaft, this time seeing the top of the car instead on the runaway springs.

"There it is, Gun, come see."

Ek looked down at where Dalin was pointing the torch.

"See it?"

She didn't see Dalin's *it* yet. She was about to say *no* when she realized Dalin's torch was aimed at the escape hatch in the elevator car's roof. "Yes, I see it, if you mean the smudges off to the side of the escape hatch."

"That's exactly what I mean, Gun. I'm not sure I would have found it without you pointing out this shelving here," as he spoke he reached over and gripped one of the legs of the shelving set that held the heavy cleaning supplies, and gave it a yank, "Was just a spot out of true. Did you know why when you pointed out to me?"

"No, I didn't."

"Do you know now?"

"Yes, I think so. They fastened a line on to this shelf leg and lowered themselves to the car below, entered the car through the escape hatch – curiously just the opposite of what it was designed for – and somehow pried open the doors, which was how they got to the first floor. The shelving is askew because one of these two probably weighs in above eighty kilos."

"Yes, but probably not above ninety. Remember he had to fit though the duct work."

"I have a question, though," said Ek

"What's that?"

"How did they get their line back?"

"They used a climber's slip knot," answered Dalin.

"Why would a climber want a slip knot? I mean I don't even understand why someone wants to hang off the side of a mountain, but if I found myself doing such a silly thing I'd want the tightest, strongest, most dependable knot ever devised by mankind securing me."

"You'd want such a knot," said Dalin, "for the very same reason that our thieves did – to retrieve your line." Dalin looked around the closet. There was a length of clothesline coiled on a wall hook. He reached up and got it off. "Here, I'll show you." Dalin looped the line so that he had at least two feet of it on each side to work with. Then he folded the looped line under itself to make two loops, one to the right and the other to the left, a little like opposite clover-leaf entrances to a highway.

"These two loops allow you to choose which side of the line you want to slip." Dalin continued, "If you want the left side to slip, you pass the left loop though the right loop." Dalin drew the left loop under the two lines and through the right loop. He then tightened the line that he didn't want to slip. He passed the rope over to Ek while he held the loop.

"Pull on the right line." Ek tentatively pulled. "Harder," said Dalin. She yanked the right line. Dalin held it fast. "Now pull on the left line." Ek did and the line slipped through the knot and Dalin's hands and fell to the floor.

"Don't tell me you rock climb," said Ek, with still a trace of childhood wonder at what she had just witnessed.

"No, but I do sail. Sailors use the same knot."

Dalin and Ek joined Bohl in the food-storage area of the first floor. Dalin examined the car floor. There were no smudges presently on it, nor could they find evidence for any that had been wiped up. They concluded that there had never been any, so there was no trail to follow to their exit. "They wore foot covers," Dalin announced, perhaps to himself, "the kind doctors wear in the operating room."

"How do you know that?" said Bohl.

"They left a smudge on top of the car where they lined down from the second floor, but there's no soot or grease on the car floor. Had to wear covers."

"Or they took their shoes off," said Ek.

"Perhaps, but if I were committing a burglary, I wouldn't want to have to put my shoes back on before I could beat a hasty retreat."

"So, we now know they came this far, but where did they go from here?" said Ek as she turned and scanned the warren of food lockers about them.

"Herr Bohl," said Dalin, "suppose you found yourself at this very spot and a fire broke out on the floor above – a very quick-spreading fire – where would you go to leave the building?"

Bohl thought for a moment before replying, "You mean just take care of myself, don't try to put it out or help others?"

"Right, just get yourself out as quickly and safely as possible."

"The loading-dock door."

"Yes, that's what I thought. Let's go there."

"So, this is where they entered?"

"Not necessarily, Gun, but in all probability this is where they exited. I liked it the first time I saw it, but I had no evidence at the time other than that it required the least movement from the gallery to the outside in terms of the theft. It's the closest thing to a straight line for their exit, with no video cameras, and only a few feet of corridor where they might encounter a security guard making his rounds, although I'm fairly certain they already knew the security rounds schedule."

"I agree," said Ek, "but technically you still have no evidence. We'd need to test that shelving in the closet for fiber traces, and check those smudges on the car roof. And then, technically the line of exit stops there or in the car if we find evidence that the hatch had been opened. Then it ends in the car."

Dalin smiled and said, "Very good, Gun, but rarely are we ever left with a complete set of details in a crime, especially a crime of this caliber. These fellows are quite good. When we come up with gaps in the evidence we have to fill them in with what is most likely given the situation."

Now Ek smiled.

"What?"

"So, I must be precise and not call a *burglary* a *robbery*, not assume that the burglars fled down and not up, even though down is the logical choice, and not assume that video medium is tape."

"Exactly, speaking imprecisely leads one to thinking imprecisely, and assuming they fled down instead of up presupposes that they didn't have an exit there. Suppose they went out onto the patio, with the outcropping. Even I could climb down it and be on my way to a waiting boat perhaps."

"But there are four other exits. I agree with you that the loading dock is the most likely exit, but so was down the most likely direction. How do you make that determination?"

"Simple: I got an expert's opinion. In this case Herr Bohl's, but I had also already checked out all the other exits."

***

On the following weekend, Dalin and Ek were again sitting in Dalin's apartment discussing the next step of the investigation.

"Alright, so we know, or think we know, how they exited the museum, but something tells me we can't assume that's also how they entered it, even though we're way ahead of anybody else in this investigation."

"We don't know where National is; we just know where they were, but you're probably right. Otherwise we would have heard something. They'd be over gloating. And, yes, we can't assume they came in that way. We've both been all over that door and found nothing to suggest they used it to enter the museum. While it's not a Cracker

Jack box lock like the janitorial closet on the second floor, it's still pretty sophisticated, albeit the least so of the five entranceways."

"So how'd they get in?" asked Ek.

"I think they just walked in, or at least one of them did."

Five

They spent the better part of a week reviewing the security videos that Dr. Hjelm had sent them. One by one they had eliminated the various entrances: the loading-dock entrance, the maintenance entrance, the employees' entrance. They started with the entrance that had the least traffic and progressed toward the one with the most traffic – the patrons' front entrance. There were no new hires among their vendors: every delivery was made by the usual route man. There were no new personnel hires at the museum either. Dalin and Ek verified everyone who entered either the employees' or maintenance entrance by their employment photos. Every employee who entered on a particular day, they accounted for leaving.

At this stage of the viewing, Dalin broke the pattern he had established. He skipped the back entrance and began viewing the front patrons' entrance instead.

"Why did you break the pattern?" asked Ek. "Your logic is difficult for me to follow sometimes. You require precise definitions and the elimination of longshot possibilities, but then you fill in the blanks with speculations. Here, you've established a pattern that makes sense to me because by checking out the entrances with the least traffic first, we can eliminate them with certainty. Why break the pattern now when it seems to be working?"

"Remember the bees, Gun."

Gandalf and his goddamn bees, thought Ek, but what she said was, "I think I know what you're trying to say: bees are pattern creatures; flies are individualists. But you started the process as a bee – you followed a pattern and your logic for doing so makes perfect sense to me, but why break away from it? I don't understand what signals you to do that. It can't be just whim. How can I learn your whims? My whims are surely going to be different from yours."

"Not whim, Gun, data."

"I don't understand."

"In the first instance, I had run out of data. I had no other reasonable choice. What else could I do but fill in the blanks with . . . umm, not *speculations*, but *what-if scenarios*. What if the building were on fire? What if one entrance had lighter security than another? What if I were the thief and I found myself in an elevator in the food-locker area on the first floor with five exit choices? What if I could find no reason to not take the nearest exit?"

"In the second instance you mentioned, you were precisely correct about my reasons for choosing the pattern I did: we could rule out those entrances with almost absolute certainty because of their low traffic volume. There is nothing wrong with patterns. Humans are pattern-forming animals. If the temperature is above zero degrees, and we see a grey sky and feel high humidity and notice the wind picking up, we don't have to guess what those signs bode; experience suggests that rain is probable. We'd never learn anything if we didn't establish patterns, but remember what the American philosopher Ralph Waldo Emerson said: *'foolish consistency is the hobgoblin of little minds'*. The bees were foolish because the data proved them wrong, but they ignored the data and persisted out of ignorance until their deaths. Likewise, silly nonconformity is not a better method. In the example that I gave you, the flies' approach was correct because they disregarded the data of the sun's warmth and appearance and proceeded to try three other approaches. Only the third one was successful."

"In our case we've quickly eliminated three of five possibilities, so our pattern has served us well. Now though, we have to choose between two entrances which have much more foot traffic than our first three, although one only has a twenty-five percent greater volume than the other. Now I project – *'What if I were a thief, which would I choose?'* My answer is that *I pick the one with the greater volume and hide among the crowd.*"

"How do you know one has twenty-five percent more volume than the other?"

"I asked Dr. Hjelm."

"Makes sense, Gandalf, now that you explain it, but I don't know if I'll ever be able to make those fine distinctions. I'm not the Wizard."

"Of course you will; that's why I picked you. It just takes practice; besides, while you may not be a wizard now, you are the Sorcerer's Apprentice."

It didn't surprise Ek that Dalin knew what his colleagues called him, but she was surprised he knew her epithet.

When Dalin asked Dr. Hjelm for the security videos, he'd asked him to provide copies of videos for the three days prior to the burglary because he wanted to see if he could spot anyone visiting the museum all three days, or barring that at least twice. However, now he believed at least one of the thieves simply walked in amid the throng of the daily visitors the day of the burglary. He must have hid out – perhaps in the duct work – and, when everyone left for the day, came out of hiding to let in his accomplice. He and Ek started looking at the security video for the front entrance on the day of the burglary.

It took the Wizard and the Sorcerer's Apprentice three more evenings of reviewing the videos before they made a breakthrough. Actually, it was Ek who made the breakthrough. At the time of the year that the theft took place the *Moderna Museet* was experiencing about a thousand visitors a day. If, as Dr. Hjelm had said, the front entrance had twenty-five percent more volume than the back entrance, then approximately 625 visitors used the front entrance.

That's quite a few to keep track of. First, they eliminated children of all ages as Dalin doubted that even teenagers would be sophisticated enough to be able to pull off such a theft, nor did he think they employed an *Artful Dodger*. Next, they eliminated most of the women, noting only the small number who appeared young enough and strong enough to be the gymnast of the pair. Finally, they eliminated quite a few men by virtue of their body type. When they had finished culling outliers, they were left with thirty-seven candidates.

Dalin isolated and copied each one into a file he named "rogues gallery" – not original but appropriate. Then, one by one, they tried to match each of the thirty-seven to a shot of those leaving the museum. The process was tedious, but Ek focused on James Campbell, not only because he fit the body type, but because he was very handsome — not an approach Dalin would have taken but against which he couldn't argue given Campbell's body type.

"Got him," announced Ek on the third night of going through the videos.

"How can you be sure?" asked Dalin.

"Simple. He came in, but didn't leave," gloated Ek.

"But we haven't checked the back way. He could have gone out there. I would if I were he. One more subterfuge."

Of course, Dalin was right; Ek was deflated. Dalin saw her disappointment. "Gun, you've done marvelous work. You've picked out someone who properly belongs on top of the short list. You saw him before I did, but we have to be sure." To that end they spent the next two hours viewing the video of the back exit for that particular day.

"He's not here, Gun; you've got our man. Marvelous work. Marvelous. But we still have one major problem."

"What now, Gandalf?" Ek snapped out, exasperated.

"How are we going to tell National that we've found their man?"

***

Dalin copied James Campbell's picture from the *Moderna Museet* video and sent it along with a request for identification to Interpol. Four weeks later he got a response, which contained a brief file that identified the picture as that of James Crawford of Los Angeles, California, U.S.A. The file said that he had been a *person of interest* in a theft in England concerning a copy of Shakespeare's *The First Folio*. Police not only didn't find the book, they also never found any hard evidence linking Crawford to the theft other than he had attended the viewing. Police questioned him, but let him go the same day.

Dalin then sent James Crawford's picture to Chief Inspector Conor Moran in Belfast requesting him to show the enclosed picture to the young woman who led to the discovery of the two Braques paintings and the Picasso sculpture. Two days later, Dalin got an e-mail from Moran saying that he had shown the photo to Eimear Lynch. While she said there was a resemblance, this was not the man whose bag she'd searched in the Fitzwilliam Hotel; that man was larger, slightly taller and heavier.

Dalin briefly wondered if James Crawford had a brother who might be a little bit bigger than James – big and strong enough to support him as he scurried across a wall of the *Reuterswärd Gallery* and picked off seven paintings – but he had nothing to send Interpol for a further inquiry, so he finally went to his superior, Superintendent Lars Haake, and explained to him what he had learned. Haake was Dalin's superior not because of any intellectual edge, but rather because he knew how to present things in their best light. In other words, he could spin hemp into cashmere.

Haake called Superintendent Hilmar Lampa at National, and told him that he had some good information. He told him that one of his men had done some follow-up on his own time – not to horn in on National's jurisdiction, he didn't want any of the glory; he just did it because he's a very persistent fellow. Anyway, the upshot of it was that the man has identified a picture of someone who came into the *Moderna Museet* on the day of the robbery but that security videos have no record of leaving. Haake said that he'd officially reprimanded the man for stepping on National's jurisdiction and that he was sending the file to Lampa of everything that Dalin had discovered.

Lampa knew that Haake's story about the reprimand was probably bullshit, but he was grateful for the information as he hadn't been able to make any headway in the case himself and decided it would be beneficial to just accept the file and not pursue the infringement. He made a *pro forma* objection to Haake but thanked him for the professional manner in which he had handled the matter.

Lampa did follow up on the Belfast connection by contacting Chief Inspector Moran who filled him in on the curious recovery of the two George Braques paintings and the Picasso sculpture. Lampa was aware – even before Haake had forwarded Dalin's file to him – that those three pieces of the *Moderna Museet* theft had been recovered, but didn't see how any of that information advanced his case.

Moran added that he had managed to track Gregory Hatton, the name the man who registered at the Fitzwilliam Hotel used, from Belfast to London to Paris. After Paris, he told Lampa things got sketchier. A man fitting Hatton's description was seen boarding the TVG, but after that, nothing. Lampa asked Moran where the TVG went. Moran said it stopped at several cities in Spain, most notably among them was Madrid, with the route ending at Lisbon. Moran added that, "Either city could get him to just about any place in the world."

Moran concluded with, "Since it's clear that Hatton has left Northern Ireland, my jurisdiction, I won't be doing any follow-up."

Lampa thanked Moran and rang off, not sure of where to go from here. Unlike Moran, he couldn't just write the theft off because one of the thieves had apparently left the country. The theft was a national embarrassment.

After some thought Lampa reasoned that if the man Interpol identified in the photo provided by Dalin was that of James Crawford of Los Angeles, California, then perhaps Hatton, too, was from the United States. Lampa thought it might be wise to at least contact America's Federal Bureau of Investigation.

Six

NY 73 is a narrow, winding, climbing road that cuts through approximately thirty miles of the pre-Cambrian shield, forming a good deal of the six million acres, which make up the Adirondack State Park; the road runs through two hamlets, ending abruptly at the top of Mill Hill at one of only two traffic lights in the Village of Lake Placid. The road is either unusually gloomy or beautiful, depending on your temperament and the season, as the forest along its sides is thick and the acclivities steep.

Keagan's mood matched the winter darkness of the road. He was suffering one of those black-ass days, to which the Irish are constitutionally prone. His father had blamed them on the rain; his mother, on alcohol, to which the Irish are also constitutionally prone. His father blamed everything on either the rain or on the little people, and everything else that wasn't blamed on the Brits and the Ulster Volunteer Force. His mother, on the other hand, blamed most of the world's ills on male obdurateness, openly acknowledging the redundancy. Those ills, which seemed to defy her single-premise logic with the exception mentioned above, she blamed on religion. However, since religions were male-dominated institutions, and since men had traditionally consumed much more alcohol than did women, perhaps her single-window world view was sufficient after all.

Keagan had sided more with his mother, but wasn't foolish enough to exclude politics as a major factor of human chaos. And politics had more to do with his black-ass mood than did male obdurateness, or religion, or even the lenticular clouds that contoured across the Great Range to his left. He knew that they augured snow, but hoped not too much or too soon.

A storm now would be the play of the little people, he thought. He had come to the Adirondacks to cross-country ski, to camp, to complete a trail he'd been working on for a few years, and to get out of his black-ass mood, but mostly he came to clear his mind so that he could work through a complex problem.

It was December and Keagan had just gone on holiday from the independent school in Boston, where he taught English and on occasion American History for which he had to quick-study, as America was not his native country. He left Boston at about 9:00 AM, planning to spend the night with a friend he had met while interviewing for a position at a boarding school at Lake Placid. The Headmaster of the school offered him the job on the spot, which further convinced Keagan he was the ineffable ass he appeared to be throughout the interview; Keagan told the Headmaster he had other offers, but he would think it over — a fabrication really — and would call him with his decision in a few days. When he had gotten back to Boston, he called the Headmaster to decline the offer. When A full minute after Keagan had declined the offer, the Headmaster — perceptive devil that he was — knew that Kegan wasn't going to accept and hung up. Keagan still thought of him as the manager of the middle station in Conrad's *Heart of Darkness*.

He wished he had accepted the job because he wanted to get out of Boston and his ethnic entanglements there, but he also knew that he couldn't work for someone who, while he may clearly understand the bottom line, knew nothing about education. While he was being interviewed he met several members of the faculty, one of whom stood out. Phil Tucker was a talented man in his sixties who still did a lot of climbing, scrambling, and camping. He had invited Keagan to hike with him the next day. Despite their age difference, they became friends and had climbed together several times since.

Coincidentally, Phil was going to Boston the next day to spend the holidays with friends and told Keagan that he could use his cabin as a base camp, and offered to drop him at the Corey's trailhead on his way out of town in the morning even though it was thirty miles out of his way.

The camp was located about two miles outside the Village of Saranac Lake, just off the main highway, NY 3, which wasn't very main anywhere except relative to the area. Keagan arrived there a bit after 4:00 PM. Not very good time from Boston, but he had stopped at Lake George to see Bill O'Malley, a friend of his uncle's.

Phil came out onto the porch to greet him, wearing hiking shorts and a tee-shirt. Keagan estimated the temperature to be about five degrees above zero. Phil gathered up Keagan's bag, and told him to put his car next to the jeep in the garage and to lower the door because a storm was expected.

The camp was overheated. Phil was familiar with such warm temperatures as he had spent most of his adult life teaching and living in boarding schools. The schools didn't pay much, but they generally provided room and board, of course, and covered utilities. In a convoluted work of mental gymnastics, the teachers, in an attempt to augment their meager salaries, kept their heat turned way up in the winter. When the apartment overheated, they opened windows and, of course, they never turned the lights off until they went to bed. Phil was a recent retiree, and the relationship between ambient temperature and heating bills hadn't fully registered yet.

"I assume you want a drink after your drive," Phil called out – in a Yaley tone – from the kitchen as Keagan entered the camp from the garage.

"I do," Keagan called back. "And none of your cheap stuff either. What do you have?"

"Jack Daniel's. I believe that's one of your preferred poisons."

"Very good, Phil. Yes, on the rocks, and don't desecrate it by adding water," Keagan answered, somewhat startled.

Phil wouldn't know cheap whiskey from good whiskey; he didn't drink alcohol, never had. Keagan's mother would have loved Phil. He was also an agnostic. He was cheap, although not when it came to his friends. He remembered that Keagan liked Jack Daniel's so early that afternoon he laid in a bottle of it and a six-pack of Harp that he guessed that Keagan's heritage would approve of.

"Sit by the fire and warm yourself with this," Phil said as he proffered Keagan a jelly jar filled with ice and Jack Daniel's. Yosemite Sam was painted on the side of the jar. Keagan reflected that the comment sounded like something out of an old movie, but then Phil was like something out of an old movie.

"How are you doing?"

"Reasonably well," answered Keagan, taking a strong pull on the whiskey, his vile mood clipping his response.

"How was the funeral?" Phil inquired tentatively, not wanting to pry, but knowing he couldn't ignore it and might as well get it out in the open right away.

"As funerals go, not bad. Irish funerals seem like gay affairs with all the drinking and toasts, and fine stories that are largely fictional. But the drink and the fine words can't hide the reality of the dead fellow you came to euphemistically *send off*, wherever *off* may be."

"Have the authorities found out who killed him?" asked Phil.

"No, they haven't. The police couldn't care less. As far as they are concerned, David's one less future problem. The prison officials have some interest in determining who killed him, though. An unsolved inmate murder is bad press. However, their pool of potential witnesses has never been much for civic responsibility. We know who did it though."

"We?"

"Yes, *we!*"

"Be more specific."

"Have you ever read Liam O'Flaherty's *The Informer*?" asked Keagan.

Phil knew a great deal about history; he continually astounded Keagan with his breadth of knowledge. True, he had a B.A. from Yale, but he had no advanced degrees. Still he was a historical encyclopedia, who had also taught Latin, Greek, German, and Geology. Never history, though. He hated reading high-school drivel that students tried to pass off as essays or, worse yet, research. Literature was his weak point. The coins of Phil's realm were historical, grammatical, and scientific facts. "No, I haven't." Phil didn't try to fake what he didn't know.

Keagan reflected, what did Mark Twain say? *Always tell the truth. You'll gain the admiration of half of the people and astound the other half.*

"*The Informer*," Keagan explained, "is a story of a fellow who informs on the IRA. Informing — to the Irish — is a more egregious breach of ethics than it is to a Sicilian, *omerta* notwithstanding. The Irish have their own style of retribution. Not surprisingly, we call it a six-pack. Remind me to tell you about it some time. Not now though, I'm only on my first drink. On the other hand, loyalty — and there are still plenty who were loyal to David – is one of the most revered traits of the Irish. Well, after fighting, drinking, and storytelling, of course."

"In any event, there were several other fellows of similar stripe — excuse the pun — in residence who know who killed David, and now we know."

"What does that matter, though?" Phil asked. "I wouldn't think they'd have much credibility with the authorities either."

"That's true, they don't; however, credibility is a component of a logical, not a surreal, system. But we weren't looking for credibility, only an identity. We knew who ordered the kill; we only needed to find out who carried it out. The one who ordered the kill is the same one who is responsible for David being in prison in the first place."

"You're begging the question," Phil chided. "What are you trying to say? That your uncle was framed? You were the one who told me that his Boston bar was a laundry for cleaning money and a conduit for collecting and funneling money to the IRA, and that your uncle was rather serendipitous about his responsibility to that other infamous three-letter organization, the IRS."

Only Phil, reflected Keagan, *could use IRA, IRS, and serendipitous in the same sentence.* "All I'm saying is that we know who killed David, who ordered it, and who carried it out. What they should know is that while David was funneling money to Ireland to a non-violent arm of the IRA that works toward re-unification, the Irish never forget."

"Prisons are like any other society — people talk, *sciencia potentia est*," quoted Keagan for Phil's benefit, translating Sir Francis Bacon's famous quotation, *knowledge is power*, which Phil well knew. "In prison, knowledge is information. Knowing something allows you to sell it or barter it for a favor. To be used when called in. To gain protection and payback — maybe just cigarettes or ice cream from the commissary. The more important the information, the bigger the favor. Of course, the trick is balancing the risks in giving up what you know. In this case the risk was low."

What Keagan didn't say, though, was that the man who killed David, a member of the Aryan Brotherhood, did so to curry the favor of another psychopath, this one on the outside. He also didn't mention that the stop he made at Bill O'Malley's in Lake George ensured that both psychopaths wouldn't live out the week. But he left the latter unsaid because Phil — a life-long academician — could never understand the pragmatism of revenge, nor its visceral satisfaction.

"Are you planning on avenging your uncle's death?" Phil continued, not sure he wanted to know the answer.

"No, Phil, I'm planning on having another drink, and then eating that wretched mess you've been cooking to death in that pot on the stove. Then probably after a third drink I'm going to get a good night's sleep. Tomorrow, I'm going out into this frozen wilderness —wherein you've chosen to live — to cross-country ski and camp and forget about three-lettered organizations, funerals, revenge, and black-ass days."

Seven

The morning was gray, cold, and still. Phil dropped Keagan off at the Corey's trailhead at 7:00 AM. Keagan's original plan was to ski into Shattuck Clearing, camp there for the night, follow the Northville-Lake Placid Trail along the Cold River to Duck Hole, and spend the night there. Then the following night he'd camp at Wanika Falls, come out of the woods on the Averyville road, pick up the defunct Remsen Line, and ski along the old track bed back to Saranac Lake and to Phil's camp.

The stillness and the lenticular clouds that he had seen folding over the Great Range the previous day bothered him, though. So he decided to bypass Shattuck Clearing section, especially because he was almost certain the trail wouldn't be broken. He had hiked or skied all of the Northville-Lake Placid Trail except the segment from Long Lake to Lake Placid. On this trip, he had hoped to complete the trail, first the segment from Shattuck Clearing to Lake Placid and then the part from Long Lake to Shattuck Clearing. But he knew there was no sense in being stupid. His mother would have been proud of him. There would be other trips. He was sure there would be, but he didn't know the degree of truth in his thoughts.

Keagan had an extraordinary sense of his environment. For instance, he would immediately wake if he heard strange steps in the house; however, he would sleep through a familiar step or even a thunder storm.

He also had an intuitive sense of weather conditions. He knew that lenticular clouds foretold precipitation in twenty-four hours, but that was just a logical reinforcement to what he already felt. He could measure distances and times accurately. His coach at the Holy Family Boxing Club in Belfast taught young fighters to approximate distances and then measure off steps to see how accurate they were. Keagan didn't have to count; he just knew the distance and the time needed to get to it. His intuitive sense of his environment was engendered by his experiences growing up in Belfast during *The Troubles*.

Added to his natural instincts was a learned wariness that he referred to as *the cul-de-sac caution:* never get into a situation that doesn't have a way out. He learned that bit of wisdom during his short, but intense and successful stint as an IRA fundraiser.

It was going to snow, and it was going to snow a good deal. The only question was when it was going to start. It made no sense to proceed into the Shattuck Clearing — deeper into the wilderness — when there was a storm coming. Many might argue that going into any part of the Adirondacks alone made no sense, especially in winter. Yet Keagan, in spite of his largely urban upbringing, was comfortable in the wilderness.

Having ruled out Shattuck Clearing, he was left with two choices. He could go back to the road and hitchhike back to Phil's, or he could abbreviate his trip by cutting out Shattuck Clearing and going to Wanika Falls via Duck Hole directly. It would be a long day, but it was doable. The trip was not shaping up as he had planned, but he didn't want to scrap it completely. He needed strenuous physical exercise to get him out of his black-ass mood. *Besides*, he thought, *when the hell did plans ever work out the way you thought they would?*

He started off for Duck Hole. The first three miles were easy because they were on a dirt road that had been packed by a twin-track snow cat. After about a half mile he had the wax right as well as the gliding rhythm down, except for the occasional side-slip on an icy patch. He removed his down jacket, and replaced it with an anorak to keep him from overheating.

The woods were still. The pine needles didn't even ruffle, no tiny snow cyclones rose off the forest floor, and no animals moved. The animals knew it was going to snow and knew better than Keagan; they were digging in and Keagan was gliding on.

After three miles he had to cut over to the hiking trail. The road continued for five more miles, but it was the gated, privileged access to a private park. Keagan toyed with the idea of staying on the road, but he knew that the caretaker regularly checked both it and the camp at the inflow. He also knew that the caretaker would see his tracks, and he couldn't out-race the snow cat, so he took the state trail that skirted the private park.

Progress was slow at first. The trail was unbroken, and the early part of it was through a thick swamp. A mile later, the land began to roll, sometimes sharply. Finally, the terrain leveled out and the trail widened. Keagan got his rhythm back. While no one had been over the trail since the last snow, the last snow had added only three inches to a settled base.

The going got easier after three miles, where the trail merged with the fire service road that took him to Duck Hole. Keagan arrived there just after noon. Duck Hole is a wild place. There used to be a ranger station there, however, the Department of Conservation thought that such a primitive area shouldn't have a station. They ended up burning it down and carting off the ashes. There was still a dam there that had been built back in the '30s by a lumber company to help fight forest fires. The original dam had been replaced, but now the replacement was beginning to rot out and the Conservation Department didn't plan to rebuild it. Keagan had wanted to come here one more time before it washed out and took the Duck Hole with it.

He had lunch: hot coffee from a Stanley thermos with a thick roast beef and raw onion sandwich. There was something wonderful about raw onion in the wilderness. He sat on the log bridge that spanned the outlet of Duck Hole. The bridge was atop the dam, but DOC hadn't removed it along with the ranger station. Keagan wondered why they thought it fit into the primitive area when the ranger's cabin didn't. He was glad, though, that they thought it did since it made crossing Cold River a lot easier.

As he gazed over the frozen pond, he judged the temperature to be about twenty degrees. Even though there was no wind he had switched back to his down jacket from his anorak, having cooled off from being stationary. He looked out over the pond. Something was moving across it. It stopped about mid-way between the outlet where Keagan was having lunch and the far end. He got his binoculars out. There were two coyotes. Mountain coyotes. They didn't look as scraggly as their dry-country cousins. These two had rich, glossy coats. They looked more like young wolves than coyotes. Keagan watched the animals test the air. Almost immediately, snow began to fall, small flakes, sifting straight down. Keagan watched the coyotes rotate their ears. They couldn't hear anything either. There was nothing to hear. They crossed the pond and moved back into the forest, trying to find something to eat — maybe even a deer they could take down in the deep snow — before the storm caused them to hole up too. Keagan had six more miles to go before he could do the same. He finished his now cold coffee, stowed his lunch ware, exchanged his down jacket for the anorak, and pushed off for Wanika Falls. Five minutes along the trail, it was snowing hard.

He arrived at Wanika Falls at about 4:00 PM with just enough light left to set up camp easily. Wanika Falls was only about six miles from Duck Hole, but the trail was narrow and tortuous. Keagan could do little more than shuffle during this stretch. Also, he had skied nineteen miles that day, sixteen over unbroken trails.

Although Wanika Falls is nondescript in winter because it is usually frozen and all but hidden beneath the ice and snow, it can claim two features: a lean-to just off the trail, albeit one half-filled with snow and an ample, flat surface on which to pitch a tent. Keagan made camp quickly. He pitched the tent, unrolled his ensolite sleeping pad (air mattresses are too cold for winter) and shook out his down sleeping bag. After he'd arranged his food and cooking utensils he removed his ski boots and damp socks before he put on dry socks and down booties, over which he pulled nylon mukluk shells. He banged the crusted snow and ice from the ski boots, and put them in a plastic bag in the foot of his sleeping bag. When the camp was arranged to his satisfaction, he got into his tent — a Moss tent that, though it had been discontinued, was top-of-the-line — put on his head lamp, poured himself a large, neat Jack Daniel's, and picked up where he had left off reading Robertson Davies' *The Rebel Angels*.

Eight

Most people think that federal prisons are like country clubs because of the press that some of them get. The ones that house high-profile, white-collar criminals, and some of them are at least in prison terms, but the United States Penitentiary at Lewisberg, Pennsylvania was not one of them. Located in western Pennsylvania and built in 1932, it is grey, cramped, and noisy. The Bush administration's budget cuts and law-and-order posturing hadn't added in any way to its comfort. Notable inmates of Lewisberg have included Al Capone, Jimmy Hoffa, and David Keagan.

What makes prison hell, aside from the Sisyphean routine, is the constant noise. Prison is never quiet. The public thinks that sodomy is the major worry of prisoners. It happens, usually to the weak, but the threat of AIDS has made even the densest of sociopaths circumspect about buggery and blow jobs. But nowhere is there privacy in prison; nowhere is there quiet. Weak and strong alike must endure a constant din. Many prisoners are primal. Prisons are places of screaming: screams of brutality, screams of ecstasy, screams of challenge, and the screams of demonic withdrawal that not even Hieronymus Bosch could have envisioned.

USP Lewisberg was in full cacophony the night when Billy Ray McGuinn — former bad-ass biker, Louisiana shit-kicker, and inept bank robber — was bench pressing 300 pounds. Mick Shaunessy was spotting him, but nobody paid much attention to either Billy Ray McGuinn or Mick Shaunessy. Everyone else in the gym was watching Sweet Connelly give one of the brothers a boxing lesson. Hook, hook, slide to the right; hook, hook, slide to the right. Just before the brother caught on to the pattern, Sweet hooked him three times, once to his ear, twice to his right kidney, slid to the left and then dropped him with an overhand right. The brother hit the canvas just as Billy Ray was locking the seven-foot Olympic barbell that now held 325 pounds directly over his chest. No one heard Mick Shaunessy tell Billy Ray that David Keagan wanted to see him in hell, and no one saw him pinch Billy Ray's trapezius muscles with his thumbs and forefingers. They did, however, hear Shaunessy yell, "Mother of God," as the 325 pound barbell crashed to the floor — first one side, then the other — but by then Billy Ray's wind pipe was crushed. And Billy Ray McGuinn, the murderer of David Keagan, Mick Keagan's uncle, slowly gurgled into a final silence, while Mick Shaunessy, Sweet Connelly, and several not-too-concerned brothers looked on.

Nine

Keagan poured himself another drink after he lit his JetBoil stove, and prepared two cooking pots: one with water he had dipped from a pool in the falls — after chopping a hole through the ice — and the other with a rectangle of frozen sauce he had pried from a Tupperware container. He placed the pots one on top of the other. Water boils slowly when the temperature is only ten degrees Fahrenheit and the altitude is two thousand feet above sea level, but by the time he had finished his drink, the sauce had thawed and the water was boil-ready for the pasta. When the pasta was *al dente*, he drained off as much water as he could and poured the sauce into the pot with the pasta. He lowered the flame a bit, and stirred the mixture so that it wouldn't stick to the pot. In a few minutes, it was ready. He leaned back against the tent wall and enjoyed the meal.

After dinner, he cleaned his utensils, made coffee, and settled back again with *The Rebel Angels*. At 7:30 PM, he changed his knickers and his down jacket for a set of Arc'teryx mid-weight long underwear, before making sure that his head lamp and his Sig P-239 .357 semi-automatic were within reach. He turned off and removed the lamp, and slid into his Eddie Bauer down sleeping bag, one of the great ones before the company went yuppie.

Keagan laughed at himself when he thought about the gun. The first time that he ever camped in the winter he was awakened at two in the morning by what sounded like something plodding slowly around his tent. The temperature was twenty-five degrees below zero, and he was eight miles from the nearest road. Not a typical scene for a mugging. Since it was winter he knew a bear wasn't making the noises. Cerebrally, he knew all this; viscerally, it didn't square with the noises he kept hearing just outside his tent. He finally climbed out of the tent to face whatever it was, only to learn that a slight wind was knocking pods of snow off the spruce, pine and balsam trees surrounding his campsite. The snow-covered area around the tent was cratered, but since the tent was in the middle of a small clearing, none of the clumps had hit it. He laughed at himself, but afterwards never went camping without a gun, be it summer or winter. He was never startled awake in the middle of the night again.

Not until tonight that is.

Keagan wondered at first whether he was having a nightmare, but he rarely had nightmares. Still, the noises sounded very much like *pigs* — the Brit troop carriers that rumbled across Belfast's cobblestone streets when he was growing up. He heard them again, and he was sure he was awake now. He pressed the illumination button of his watch; it was ten o'clock. All was silent now. No, there were the noises, again. The storm filtered the noises, and they phased in and out. There was a loud dull thump, and then the noises stopped.

Keagan got dressed and stepped out of the tent. There was still no wind, but it was snowing even harder now than when he turned in. He reached back into the tent, got his head lamp and the Sig, zipped up the tent door, and started up the falls in the direction the sounds had come from. Fifteen minutes later he acknowledged to himself that what he was doing made about as much sense as the bear episode he had thought about earlier. Despite Keagan's capacity for logic, his intuitive nature told him to continue on. Thirty minutes later he saw the plane.

At first sight, he had no way of knowing whether the plane had just fallen out of the sky or whether it had been there for years. It had gone down in a tangle of spruce and balsam after clipping the tops off them. The wings were sitting on the trees and the snow pack, which at this altitude was four or five feet thick. Keagan had had a fairly easy going trip up to this point because he had stayed on the settled snow that covered the ice of the stream that fed the falls. Now, off in the spruce and balsam tangle, he floundered in the deep snow so that he could only move forward through a series of leaping motions and by pulling himself along stunted tree trunks and branches. It took him ten more minutes to reach the plane. The plane hadn't settled into the snow yet because the surface area of its wings spread out its weight.

If the plane had been there for years, the occupants were remarkably well preserved. Keagan opened the cockpit door to check for signs of life, but he could see from the irreverent angle of their necks that both men were dead.

Keagan reflected that they looked out of place dressed in suits while in the spruce and balsam tangle in the snow. They were in an expensive twin-engine plane that had a pressurized cabin. Keagan's logic wasn't affected. They were flying across the Adirondacks in winter; therefore, they should have been wearing down parkas, wool pants, and pac boots. *Wouldn't have helped them though*, he thought.

In the door pocket, on the pilot's side, Keagan found a copy of the flight plan. They were en route from Montreal to Newark, New Jersey. *Why would they fly this route in this weather*, Keagan wondered? Before he could speculate, though, an inner voice — a homunculus, which he attributed to the little people — questioned the sanity of his own reasons for being out there.

Why, indeed, he continued. He unlocked the door of the luggage well with the keys that he found in the ignition. He shone the head lamp in there; it was empty. He relocked the compartment. He unlocked the passenger compartment, pulled down the stairs, and shone the headlamp inside. All that was in there — other than the two dead men — were a couple of topcoats that lay fallen and crumpled on the floor. He climbed up into the passenger compartment gingerly: he didn't know how stable the plane was, sitting on top of the clipped trees and the snow. There were two single seats forward of the passenger door, a short aisle in between, and a two-person bench seat to the rear of the passenger door.

Keagan sat down on the bench seat to consider what he should do about this problem that had dropped out of the sky on him. The cushions were lumpy and crinkled against his back and under his hips. He stood up, at least as far as the fuselage would allow him. He turned around and pulled the back cushion of the seat forward. There was a zipper along its bottom, which he opened. Inside the cushion was a large green Hefty bag, the kind with *Kevlar* treads that were intended to keep it from tearing.

Keagan opened the bag. "Jesus, Mary, and Joseph," he exclaimed, "will you look at this." Inside the bag were neat bundles of hundred dollar bills. Keagan pulled the seat cushion forward and found that it also had a zipper along its edge. Inside, he found another Hefty bag, also containing neatly wrapped bundles of hundred dollar bills.

"Well, I thought you two looked like a couple of bent-noses, in your shiny suits and pointy shoes, but without looking through your wallets to see if one of you were named Sal or Sonny, I couldn't be absolutely certain," Keagan said to the two dead men. The money also explained the flight plan. *Why would anyone with legal money want to go to Newark?* Keagan thought. *Newark: burned out, chased out, pulled out; it was a sociological, economic, environmental cesspool; and it was about as safe as Belfast or Baghdad or Kabul, and it wasn't anywhere near as pretty as those places.*

Keagan checked the other four seats, finding smaller Hefty bags in the backs of the two passenger seats but nothing in the cockpit seats. Apparently, the brothers Guido had sufficient storage in the bench seat and the two bucket seats that they didn't have to compromise their personal comfort during the flight. They could rest easy. *Well, they were doing that now,* he thought, *or maybe not, depending on your beliefs.*

Keagan swung the Hefty bags outside. He took the cushion covers, climbed out of the plane, and filled them with snow until they fairly resembled their original shape. He placed them back on the seats, carefully wiping the seats' zipper tangs and brushing the snow from the passenger compartment. He knew that his efforts made little sense because once the snow melted, it wouldn't take a savant to realize that the flattened seat cushions once contained something that probably wasn't legal. However, if the plane were found within a few days, maybe the FAA inspectors wouldn't notice, at least not right away. Besides, Keagan reasoned, everything you did to muddy the waters, however trivial, was one more obstacle the opposition –whoever they might be – would have to work through. Accordingly, he locked what he had unlocked and wiped down everything that he had touched with bare fingers, which wasn't much given the temperature. He put his mittens back on, placed the key in the dead pilot's hand, guided it to the ignition and closed the door. He moved the Hefty bags onto the frozen stream and smoothed out the snow surface he had post-holed getting to the plane.

Getting back to his camp was much easier—if not much faster—than climbing up to the crash site. The money was heavy, but he found that he could skid the bags down the frozen stream one-by-one and then slide down to them.

Keagan got back to camp at 12:30 AM. He struck camp and loaded his pack as efficiently as possible, lashing his tent, sleeping bag, and ensolite pad to the bottom extension. He secured the hefty bags of cash with three shock cords to the upper extension. Then, he put his snowshoes on and lashed his skis onto the sides of the pack. Keagan took out his compass (battery-operated GPSs don't always work in the dark, satellite acquisition being already restricted by the snow clouds) and map from one of the pack's side pockets, and put them in the front pocket of his anorak. He shouldered the pack, heaving it upward with a thrust of his knees the way a weight lifter would clean a heavy barbell, adjusting the weight on his shoulders and hips. Damn! it was heavy. He tied off the belly band. With his head lamp guiding him and his ski poles helping him to keep balanced, he started back down the trail toward Duck Hole.

Just after he passed Moose Pond, Keagan left the trail, bushwhacking cross-country to an old logging road that ran from the end of the pavement on the Averyville road almost to the Pine Pond. The going was rough. The forest was thick with undergrowth because it had been logged and burned several times.

Keagan fell twice. Once he had to slip out of the pack to regain his footing. He had put the heaviest item — the cash — on top, which would allow him to efficiently carry the weight on his hips instead of on his shoulders. But the tactic was a tradeoff: carry the weight efficiently but compromise balance. He didn't reach the logging road until 4:15 AM.

Snowmobiles used the road in winter, so the going was much easier than bushwhacking had been. Anything would be. Keagan figured that 10 to 12 inches of snow had fallen since the storm began, and he had had less than three hours of sleep. The pack must have weighed over a hundred pounds. The map told him that he had about three more miles to go before he reached Pine Pond. He had to get there before he could stop because snowmobiles couldn't go all the way to the pond, and if search patrols came out in the morning, he had to be somewhere where they wouldn't run across him.

Keagan arrived at Pine Pond at 6:10 AM, exhausted. He pitched his tent, unrolled his sleeping bag, changed into the dry long underwear, and fell into a deep sleep. He didn't awake until almost 2:00 PM.

He stepped out of the tent in mid-afternoon grey. It was still snowing, but there were holes in the clouds now, signs that the storm had done its worst and was passing on. His snowshoe tracks were mostly covered, it hadn't snowed hard enough to completely cover them. Any decent woodsman could still follow the tracks. He heated some soup in the adjacent lean-to, while he looked at his map and contemplated how he was going to get back to Phil's camp. He could cut southeast through the woods to the defunct Remsen line, but Roger's mountain and a sizeable swamp were in the way. Keagan knew he'd never get through the swamp with his pack as heavy as it was; he'd drown in one of its feeder streams. He could cross Kiwassa

Lake to a side road in the Village of Saranac Lake and walk through town. While he wouldn't be leaving tracks, the way he was weighed down would surely call attention to him.

Finally, he saw that if he crossed Kiwassa Lake to the far end, where it flowed into Oseeta Lake, he could pick up a dirt road at a Franciscan retreat house that led to NY 3, just west of Phil's camp. If he waited till about 4:00 PM to cross Kiwassa, there was a good chance no one would see him. It would be dark by the time he got to Oseeta Lake, and given the time of the year he doubted that anyone would be in residence at the retreat house. He only hoped that the road was plowed.

Keagan snowshoed from Pine Pond to the Kiwassa Lake Landing, and then put on his skis. Balance was more difficult on skis than on snowshoes, but he could glide a little on the lake. The skis spread out the weight better on the shallow lake that had more flow to it than did a deep lake. It was late, the temperature was now about zero and the wind was picking up. The storm was over, but no one was out on the lake,and there were no lighted cabins. The retreat house was dark as well, but the road had been recently plowed. Keagan wondered if the little people had arranged that and, if so, to what end. Perhaps it was the caretaker's usual fire protection. It wouldn't do to meet Saint Peter, with having burned down a Franciscan retreat house in your negative column. He reached NY 3 at 7:00 PM; crossed it without being seen, cut a hundred yards through the woods to Lower Saranac Lake, and skied to Phil's camp. There were lights on at Phil's neighbors, but no one seemed to notice him.

Inside the camp, Keagan stowed the Hefty bags in the sleeping loft.

His immediate inclination was to count their contents, but he thought it best to do what he would normally did upon returning from a ski trip.

Keagan unrolled and hung up his tent in a heated back hall that Phil called the mud room. He washed his cooking utensils, and unrolled and unzipped his sleeping bag to air out his body vapors by the living room fireplace. When he had finished, he poured himself a large, neat Jack Daniel's and sat staring into the fire.

The money was obviously drug money, but even if it wasn't (unless it was bound for a widows and orphans fund) Keagan didn't have much compunction about keeping it. It offered a way out of his personal dilemma. His parents had been killed while he was at Trinity College in Dublin; his uncle David — who had sponsored his United States' citizenship and who had offered some financial security — now, too, was dead. His uncle's Boston bar had been a money maker, and Keagan was David's only nephew. Unfortunately, the bar was seized by the IRS. He could fight the seizure, but the bar was a trap: take it and he'd end up just like David. David had been betrayed to the IRS and killed in prison because of his support of IRA moderation. *Goddamn the dull facility of government abbreviations; goddamn politics that were supposed to have its roots in the needs of people – as if people wanted to die – and goddamn anyone who tried to take the money away from him,* he thought.

Keagan poured himself another drink and counted the money. He didn't count every bill, but took the word of the currency wrappers. "Mother of God," exclaimed Keagan, his tally came to 2.8 million dollars. *No wonder the damn pack weighed so much,* he thought.

The whiskey was getting to him: he had carried a pack that weighed more than a hundred pounds through ten to twelve inches of new snow, slept little and eaten less. What he most wanted to do now was fall asleep, but he needed to stay awake for the eleven o'clock news, and to do that he had to eat something.

Phil's larder was only slightly better provisioned than Mother Hubbard's. Keagan found some potatoes and onions out in the mud room. In the refrigerator, he found three eggs left in a dozen-egg Styrofoam-molded pack, a small block of Monterey Jack, a reasonably crisp bell pepper, and some shallots among the dead, wilting or otherwise decaying vegetable remnants. Keagan silently asked the little people to perform alchemy on the bacon drippings in the refrigerator, and turn the grease into a bottle, a wee bottle would suffice, of extra virgin olive oil. And, as long as they were at it, turn the green bell pepper into a red pepper. Nothing happened, however, for little people are fickle folk who act in mysterious ways, their wonders to behold or in this case withheld.

Keagan fried the potatoes and beat the three eggs in a mixing bowl containing diced cheese, onions, peppers and shallots. As he looked for some paper towels to blot the bacon grease, he discovered a jar of home-made Vermont salsa. Despite what the TV commercials say, good salsa doesn't have to come from Texas. The best in Keagan's experience came from a restaurant in New York City. As he added the salsa to the omelet just before he folded it over, he reflected on his earlier thoughts, "in mysterious ways, their wonders to behold," and broadly smiled thanks to the little people or whoever caused things to happen.

He ate before the TV, alternating spicy mouthfuls of omelet and potatoes with cold gulps of Harp. He watched the last of an ABC shoot-em-up that had started at ten. Keagan liked cop shows. They were mindless, but no more so than a great many other things in life. He finished the last of his dinner as the news was coming on. The station was local – Channel 5 from Plattsburgh – so the commentator led with the plane crash. Details were sketchy. All the newswoman said was that the plane had left Montreal en route to Newark, New Jersey.

Great, thought Keagan, *everybody who owns a pair of snowshoes or cross-country skis in the Tri-lakes area, which means everyone living in the Tri-lakes area between the ages of two and eighty-two, who have heard the route will be searching for the plane tomorrow.*

Lake Placid may be an isolated village, but it is also an international village, having twice hosted the Winter Olympics. Also, many of its residents were extremely knowledgeable in pharmacopoeia. The newswoman added only that the plane had passed through Plattsburgh's radar and then blipped off the screen. No airport to the south, neither Glens Falls nor Albany, had registered any trace of the plane. She concluded her coverage, saying that rescue preparations were underway and, weather permitting, the search would begin tomorrow. Anyone interested in aiding in the search should call the Department of Environmental Conservation in Ray Brook.

Keagan clicked off the television. How should he play it? Join the search, nose around on his own, or just go skiing as he had originally planned? *The storm had pretty much ruined the skiing,* thought Keagan, *and the best place to get information and remain inconspicuous is in the search party.* He decided to call Ray Brook in the morning.

Ten

Brian Mulrooney pulled out of the driveway of the Irish Embassy at 2234 Massachusetts Avenue in Washington, D.C. He drove south to I-395, which would take him to the Beltway. Once on the Beltway he drove north one exit to Fairfax County, Virginia, where he lived. Mulrooney drove a BMW 740i, a car which would normally be out of the range of his published salary of $89,000 a year. However, BMW had put together a deal for certain government agencies — Secret Service, CIA, FBI, ATF, and IRS, and by extension anyone who had a hook into someone in one of those agencies — for a significant discount, and Mulrooney thought the car suited him. He was a functionary in the embassy, well paid, but a functionary nonetheless. What the staff at the embassy, the CIA, and the IRS didn't know was that Mulrooney was also a member of a militant faction of the IRA — The Real IRA, as they liked to call themselves — that had no desire of keeping the Northern Ireland, Easter Sunday Peace Treaty of 1998. It was for that reason that he had turned David Keagan into both the IRS and ATF.

David Keagan was a key figure of a moderate faction of the IRA, by virtue of his being a key fundraiser for them in America. Since he controlled the purse strings that held the contributions of the Boston Irish, David frequently got what David wanted. And what David wanted was a peaceful solution to the re-unification of the six counties of Northern Ireland with the Republic of Ireland, one island nation, free of Britain's control. What Mulrooney and his faction wanted was the conquest of Northern Ireland, and David Keagan's political conquest was getting in their way.

So, Mulrooney provided the IRS with information that led to their finding David's ledger of contributions sent to Ireland. He built a case for ATF, using his own faction's accounting by showing that David's contributions went to purchase arms, ammunition, and explosives for the *Real* IRA. However, in spite of Mulrooney's plan, David's influence had not waned in prison. So Mulrooney had arranged for Billy Ray McGuinn to kill David Keagan.

Mulrooney lived outside the City of Fairfax, not far from the Manassas battleground. He drove without haste or specific intent, very much like the average Washingtonian returning home after a day's work, so he never noticed the pickup truck that had been following him since the embassy.

Inside the pickup were two men who were members of the same moderate IRA faction to which David Keagan had once belonged, although in this case their sense of moderation was closer to Oscar Wilde's *everything in moderation, including moderation* than it was to Aristotle's' *golden mean*. John Horahan was driving the stolen truck. He favored pickup trucks for this kind of work because nobody suspected them; they represented the stuff of which America was made. The government used non-descript boxy cars, the kind Chrysler had made, or huge SUVs; they were so non-descript that the two-block presence of either one in the rear-view mirror caused the driver being shadowed to pick it out faster than Punxsutawney Phil.

Mulrooney's BMW pulled off County 645 onto a narrower country road just south of Clifton. The road was marginally populated with farm houses, several of which had been converted into more genteel living spaces. Mulrooney's house was about three miles in from County 645.

The pickup truck followed, at first keeping back, but gradually reducing the distance between the two vehicles. Mulrooney signaled a left-hand turn into his driveway, a quarter-mile long gravel road. He was about a hundred yards down the driveway when the pickup truck came abreast the turn off. Brendan O'Reilly, the other man in the truck, said to Mulrooney – who could not possibly hear him — *here's a sneak preview of hell, Mulrooney; sorry you can't have more time between the preview and the actual.* He toggled a switch that sent an electrical charge into the C-4 block that O'Reilly had earlier affixed beneath the driver's seat of Brian Mulrooney's beautiful car. Mulrooney and the car now, in truth, became one, engulfed in an orange ball of flame while the pickup truck continued blithely unnoticed down the otherwise quiet country road.

Eleven

Keagan worked with the search teams for three days. Each day he showed up at the Department of Environmental Conservation in Ray Brook, he was assigned to a team, and went out and combed a different area. Twice he climbed mountains, Algonquin out of Adirondack Lodge and Giant near St. Huberts. Curiously, on the third day, his team drew the Northville-Lake Placid Trail from Long Lake, through Shattuck Clearing, Duck Hole, Wanika Falls into Averyville, and along the defunct Remsen Line back to Ray Brook. On the two mountains, he and his team spent an hour on top, scanning everything in their ken through binoculars. Algonquin was one of the few high peaks that had a good view of Nye Mountain. It was right across Indian pass from the mountain where the plane crashed, less than four air miles away. Algonquin was more than a thousand feet higher than Nye. Luckily for Keagan, the crash site wasn't visible from Algonquin because it was on the west side of Nye. There were only four high peaks located west of Nye, but they were too far southwest of them to have the right sight vantage. Nye wasn't even visible from Giant.

While he finally got to complete the Northville-Lake Placid Trail, it galled him that he did so on a snowmobile, which he hated. One advantage, however, was that – since he was the only member of the team that day who was familiar with the trail — he was assigned as team leader, and was able to obliterate what was left of his own ski and snowshoe tracks.

Part of each morning's meeting at the Conservation Headquarters was a briefing, where the searchers learned what the search parties had or had not discovered the previous day. After day three, the searchers still had no idea where the plane had gone down. The search captain even suggested that it could have gone down into one of the more than 2,500 lakes and ponds in the Adirondack Park, in which case they might never find it. The fourth morning, Keagan begged off, saying that he needed to return home. He never mentioned where home was and he had given the Conservation Department a phony name in case anyone — good guy or bad guy — thought to trace the searchers or look into their backgrounds.

After the last briefing, Keagan went back to Phil's camp and spent a leisurely afternoon in front of the fire, scanning *the Montreal Gazette*, the *Albany Times Union*, the *Boston Globe*, and *The Washington Post*, three of which he had to travel into Lake Placid to get.

Keagan scrutinized the Montreal and Albany papers for news of the plane crash. They gave little more information than what Keagan already knew from first-hand exposure and what he had learned each day at the Conservation Department's briefings. He did, however, learn the names and addresses of the occupants, of which he noted.

He scanned the two other papers for verification of the phone call he received when he returned to the Phil's camp after day two of the search. The caller had simply said, "Both problems have been rectified," then he hung up.

Keagan found the story of Billy Ray McGuinn's tragic demise buried deep in the *Boston Globe*. The article mentioned that McGuinn had been a person of interest in the death of David Keagan, who was murdered in the same Federal Prison McGuinn was serving a ten-year sentence for attempted bank robbery. The *Washington Post* documented Brian Mulrooney's passing with more panache, but about as much concern. Keagan was simply glad both problems had been taken care of. He didn't really take any visceral pleasure in avenging his uncle's death in spite of what he thought when he was describing to Phil the Irish penchant of never forgetting disloyalty, and while intellectually he didn't believe that riding the world on these two pieces of moral flotsam would make the world a better place, he did believe at least in making the effort to keep a moral balance, *Manichean Heresy* perhaps, but that's what he believed.

Keagan packed up his gear and put it in the mud room, ready to go in the morning. He also packed the small luggage piece he brought with him, except for two changes of clothes – one for tonight and one for traveling tomorrow – and his toilet kit for the morning. He left the money in the sleeping loft.

Every time Keagan came to Lake Placid, he treated himself to dinner at *Le Grand Cru,* arguably the best restaurant between New York and Montreal. He showered and decided not to have a drink before leaving; he would have enough there. He dressed in cavalry trill slacks, a white turtleneck, a patterned Boston Trader wool sweater, and a pair of Allen Edmonds hand sewn loafers. Keagan knew quality and till now he couldn't afford much of it. All of that was about to change.

He drove over to Lake Placid, but before he went to *Le Grand Cru,* he stopped at a liquor store and picked up four empty cases. Earlier at Ames – a regional discount store, similar to K-mart or Wal-Mart – he bought some 5x8 labels, a magic marker, and a roll of shipping tape.

***

The back bar of *Le Grand Cru* featured stain-glass windows from a church that had been de-sanctified. Keagan wondered *how can that which was holy could be made secular? De-sanctification implicitly called into question the original state of holiness.* It reminded Keagan of George Carlin's routine on *doing eternity on a meat rap.* Carlin's inspiration came from Vatican Council II's finally deciding that while several of the original apostles may have been fishermen, the Catholic Church had carried the metaphor a bit too far.

Keagan sat at the bar. He ordered a Jack Daniel's on the rocks. The drink was served in a nine ounce old fashion glass, packed with money ice. Even with the ice though, the drink must have been four or five ounces. He sipped it slowly, nibbled on some cheddar that he had cut from a five-pound block that sat atop an authentic butcher-block table, and listened to the fireplace behind him pop and crackle.

He had eaten at *Le Grand Cru* three or four times, so some of the staff recognized him and remembered that even though he was alone, he generally ordered from the top of the menu, had a bottle of good wine, and was a solid post-tax, twenty percent tipper. When the other waiters came down the service alley to get their drinks, they asked the bartender whether the single at the bar was having dinner. Waiters in general don't like singles — not enough volume in the check for a decent tip, and sometimes they wanted you to entertain them. The bartender told them that even though he was a single, he was good; he'd probably ask for Jimmy the Gimp.

"Jimmy the Gimp working tonight?" Keagan asked the bartender almost as if he had heard the conversation.

"Sure, you want him?"

"If he's not too busy," said Keagan.

"No problem. It's slow tonight. I'll get him."

A minute later a portly waiter, wearing black slacks, a blue work shirt, black tie, and a heavy leather butcher's apron came through the swinging doors that separated the bar from the restaurant, mopping his brow with a blue cloth napkin. Jimmy the Gimp had waited on Keagan at least twice before when Keagan had eaten at *Le Grand Cru*; he mopped his brow as a matter of course. Whether summer or winter, Jimmy the Gimp perspired.

"Hey, Mick. How are you?"

The Gimp had a very good memory for names and faces.

"Good, Jimmy; how have you been?"

"Joe B. said you'd be having dinner," said the Gimp, and handed Keagan a menu that made up the center pages of a facsimile of a 1932 newspaper, the year Lake Placid first hosted the Winter Olympics.

"What are the specials tonight? Remember, I'm from Boston, so don't tell me about the fresh fish specials. Do you have the Cuban black bean soup?"

"Bowl or cup?"

"Bowl."

"The only other special we have that wasn't swimming two days ago is Veal Oscar."

Keagan loved Veal Oscar, but he was in the mood for beef tonight.

"What's the chance of getting a baby Duke?" Keagan asked.

"Probably good." The Gimp checked his surroundings and said, "the Mad Chef's in a fairly rational mood tonight, so far, and it's slow. Let me check."

The Duke Wellington, like the Chateaubriand, was a two-person entrée at *Le Grand Cru*. The Gimp hurried off to the kitchen to ask the Mad Chef if he'd make a baby Duke for Keagan.

There were three waiters at *Le Grand Cru* named Jimmy. So, to keep them straight, the Mad Chef had given them nicknames. There was Jimmy Hoffman who, whenever there was any extra side work to do, could never be found. He became *Hoffa*. There was *Jimmy Cricket*, who was a Mormon, but who had agreed not to proselytize while working and pretty much kept his promise. Then there was *Jimmy the Gimp*. The Gimp got his nickname when the only thing PC meant was *post coital*. He didn't get it from being handicapped; he got it because he was a handicapper. He loved the ponies and the dogs and all games of chance; in fact, he loved anything that he could place a wager on. In a doldrums, he'd bet on what a customer would order and, while he believed he won more often than he lost, his bank account quietly suggested otherwise.

The Gimp came back into the bar. "I told the Mad Chef you wanted it rare. That OK?"

"How do you remember?"

"It's easy. You're an educated ofay. Right away we're talking medium-rare or less. If you were *African-American* – he mimicked political correctness with obvious sarcasm — or a *Heeb*, you'd want it dead from heat exhaustion. Besides you're a good tipper. I remember good tippers. You still are, aren't you? I don't want to have to go in and tell the Mad Chef you've changed your mind."

The Gimp was an equal-opportunity bigot; he made fun of everyone, without regard for race, creed, color, or religion. He showed no particular rancor to any specific ethic group, except Canadians because they were notoriously bad tippers. The Gimp's parents were from Belarus. Belarus has been marched over more often than the parade ground at West Point. The result was it's citizens were Russian, Polish, Ukrainian, Moldavian, Lithuanian, French, German, and a score of lesser known blood and political strains. The only seminal characteristic Belarus could claim for ethnic purity was the cold. Besides, Jimmy had been born at sea on an unregistered ship a thousand miles east of Fiji, and so he believed he was exempt from the constraints of heritage and political correctness and all their attendant foolishness. He also believed that everyone else should enjoy that same right. Accordingly, The Gimp's logic ran syllogistically thusly:

All ethnicities have their quirks;

My birth at sea on an unregistered ship excludes me from any ethnicity;

Therefore, I can – and will – make fun of others.

. . . Besides, it's fun.

"What else do you remember?" asked Keagan,

"That you like your vegetables as close to raw as possible, and that you're inclined to Bordeaux," he said as he handed Keagan the wine list. "I also remember that you are partial to the alcove and like to sit down to the whole meal. Order another drink, take a look at the wine list, but I'd recommend the Heitz Cabernet."

"Does it come in a half bottle?"

"Yes."

"What's the vineyard?"

"Martha's. And it's an '86."

"Good. Open it now and let it breath."

Keagan ordered another Jack Daniel's from Joe B. and asked, "What do you hear about the plane crash?"

"Only that everybody between the age of eight and eighty is out looking for the plane."

"Why so much interest?" Keagan inquired.

"Well, the geezers are looking for something to do or a way to augment their Social Security checks; the rest are hoping to find drugs."

"What makes them think the plane was carrying money or drugs?"

"Hope mostly, but you tell me what a twin engine plane was doing out there in that storm, flying from Montreal, the East Coast Canadian drug capital, to Newark, major candidate for a nuclear rehab. Nobody willingly goes to Newark unless there they're getting well paid or it's a stopover to someplace else or they're routed there."

Keagan sipped his drink and continued to speculate with Joe B about the plane's cargo and purpose, until the Gimp came in to tell him that his table was ready.

The soup and salad were set, the wine was breathing, and the Gimp was carving the baby Duke. Keagan watched him slice the pastry wrapped, pâté coated, #3 grade prime tenderloin. The Mad Chef had created a masterpiece, and the Gimp was making a show of serving it.

"You need anything else, Mick?" the Gimp asked.

"Not for the moment, thanks."

Just as Keagan started in on the Duke Wellington, he heard a commotion in the kitchen. The Mad Chef was screaming at one of the waiters. Actually, Keagan had never dined at *Le Grand Cru* without the Mad Chef acting out some histrionic or other. The problem this time seemed to center around a customer's concern about the freshness of the fish. Keagan was glad the Gimp hadn't carried Keagan's Bostonian prejudice against fish served more than twenty miles from the sea into the kitchen.

The obscenities from the kitchen stopped as the swinging doors to the dining room burst open, and the Mad Chef banged out into the dining room carrying a twenty pound salmon. He stopped at a table directly across from the alcove where Keagan sat. The Mad Chef turned and smiled at him – a Jack Nicholson smile that Keagan interpreted as a disquieting glimpse into dementia rather than recognition. He stood in front of the table, where the woman who questioned the freshness of the fish sat reading the news about the '32 Olympics.

"Good evening, madam," said the Mad Chef. "Are you the woman who believes we serve frozen, rather than fresh fish?"

Incredulous, the woman stared at him.

The Mad Chef dropped the salmon on her plate, fish slime splashing her face. "Does that look frozen?!" the Mad Chef rhetorically inquired as he turned back to the kitchen, leaving the woman as rictus as the fish in front of her.

Excellence is frequently the by-product of eccentricity, thought Keagan as he enjoyed his meal. After dinner, he had coffee but no dessert.

"Good call on the wine, Jimmy; I enjoyed it."

"You want a Cordon Bleu?"

"I'd love one, but I have to drive over to Saranac Lake, and I want to make some pretense of sobriety as I go past the state troopers' barracks. Just the check, please."

Keagan had to reach into his cash reserves to cover the check because the Mad Chef didn't take credit cards — not just American Express— he didn't take any credit cards. Keagan didn't dare pass one of his new-found bills, yet. At this point, he had no way of knowing whether the money was real or if it was traceable.

Keagan drove back to Phil's camp without incident. He got the empty liquor cases and his earlier purchases from the trunk of his car. Once inside, he laid a fire in the fireplace, then brought the money down from the sleeping loft where he neatly filled the cases with the money, still wrapped in the green hefty bags. He sealed each box, pasted a label on them, and marked the labels *Books*. On the first case, he wrote *Austen to Davies*, on the last *Tolkien to Zamiatin*. Keagan was convinced that in the age of the Internet, satellite TV, iPods, iPhones, X-boxes, Kindles and Nooks no one would steal real books. He took the cases out to the garage and put them in the back seat of his car after putting his camping gear in the trunk. Back at the camp, he lit the fire and poured himself a substantial Martel he had bought at the liquor store while he picked up the empty cases. The effect was somewhat lost because Phil didn't have a snifter — let alone a Waterford snifter — so Keagan drank the Cognac from the same jelly jar Phil had used the night Keagan arrived. His feet up on the coffee table, Keagan stared into the fire in a combination of Proustian reflection and prophetic projection as Yosemite Sam glowered at him in mock menace from the coffee table.

Twelve

Keagan drove back to Boston the next day. On the way, he stopped off at Bill O'Malley's, where he made some discreet inquires about setting up a Cayman Islands account. One of the delights of the tight-lipped Irish are that they respect each other's privacy. Keagan didn't tell O'Malley why he should want to establish a Cayman Islands account and O'Malley never asked.

**

In March, when the school where Keagan worked issued its contracts for the following year, Keagan declined to renew his, saying that the events of the past year — the imprisonment and subsequent death of his uncle — required that he take some time off. The Headmaster was disappointed, as he had seen in Keagan uncommon leadership abilities. He offered him more money, but Keagan declined it, repeating that he needed some time to sort out his life. What Keagan didn't tell the Headmaster was that he had already signed on to crew for a charter boat company that sailed out of Tortola, BVI.

Keagan had learned to sail in Ireland where the waters were wilder than the Caribbean's, unless of course it was hurricane season there. As a result of his early training, his skills were good. He worked for the company for three months, then he started getting offers to ferry boats for rich, novice sailors from one island to another. He liked the freedom, and the work paid well. He still hadn't touched the Cayman account, so he used the delivery fees for his living expenses, which were light as the boats were provisioned. And while he was working, he either slept aboard the boat he was ferrying or at the owner's guest house or at some other accommodation the owner had made for a day or two after delivery.

One night, in Montego Bay, Jamaica, where Keagan had a lay over from delivering a boat from Aguadillo, Puerto Rico to George Town, Grand Cayman, he happened upon two Jamaicans – a man and a woman – arguing. He was staying at the Trade Winds, a resort complex where his client had booked him a room. He, at first, was suspicious that they were setting him up, showing a typical Caucasian apprehension, reinforced to a degree because he couldn't understand what they were saying, as they were speaking patois. Gradually, though he caught the essence of their contention. Apparently, she was a cook, and he was the food and beverage manager. He was telling her if she wanted to be promoted to *sous-chef*, she had better start sleeping with him. She, for her part, was telling him she'd rather sleep with the fishes in the sea. Keagan decided that the confrontation was real and that he should stick around in case the situation got too tense. While the woman was tall and seemed to be well built — it was difficult to tell from the dark and the distance — the man looked to be well over two hundred pounds. Jamaican men are quite muscular. This particular specimen, though, had gone a little too fat.

Just as Keagan decided to approach them — to either shame them into breaking off the row, or be closer if the woman needed his help — the woman put a well-placed left foot just forward and a little above the man's right ear, dropping him to the ground. Keagan ran over to her, but she didn't need his help; the man wasn't getting up for a while.

The woman heard Keagan's approach and thought he had come to help his friend. She shifted her weight to her back foot, raised her knee and threw a kick at Keagan's head exactly where she had planted the one on her boss. Keagan slipped it, caught her ankle in his right hand, and drew her a little forward, toppling her. While Keagan was explaining himself, she jumped up and kicked out again.

And just as before, Keagan caught her ankle — this time in his left hand — but instead of toppling her, he just turned her slowly around in a circle circumscribed by the length of her leg, keeping her off balance.

"I told you I was just trying to help; why did you try to kick me again?"

"I just wanted to see if you could do dat again," she answered.

"Well, now that you've seen that I can, let's say I let your foot down, and you take my word that I can continue to do it. Deal?"

"OK."

"Maybe we should get away from here before someone comes along and notices your friend there," Keagan suggested.

"He is not my friend. He has no honor. Who are you?" the woman inquired.

"Someone who happened upon your argument and a guest at the hotel."

"So you heard what dat peeg said to me?" she asked Keagan.

"Yes," Keagan responded.

"Well, eef I deedn't go with him, my boss, why shoold I go with you, a strange white mon who speaks English, but in an accent I've never heard before?" she asked contemptuously, showing a combination of ethnic and gendric apprehension of white men.

"Because I don't want anything from you," said Keagan. "I could have walked away and not bought into any of this. I still can. If nothing else, you've lost your job and depending on your boss' pull, perhaps you'll be before the magistrate tomorrow morning. My boat's down at the slips. You can spend the night there and figure out what you're going to do tomorrow, or I can leave you to your boss and the magistrate."

"Spend the night, hey? And den what?"

"You can leave in the morning, after you've had time to think about how you're going to deal with this problem."

"No rich mon's hanky-panky?"

"No rich man's hanky-panky," answered Keagan. "Not even a rich man. The boat's not even mine; I'm just delivering it to Grand Cayman."

Keagan and the woman, whose name was Cassie O'Sullivan, first stopped off at her room in the staff quarters, where she collected her belongings. Keagan stood in the doorway watching for the food and beverage manager or the constable. She packed her clothes and a framed picture in a battered solid-side suitcase, which she wrapped with a rope, much like a parcel. Her only other possession was a wooden box, which contents were unknown to Keagan. The packing took five minutes, and then they were off to the slips where the boat Keagan was delivering to George Town in Grand Cayman was moored.

The boat was a Hinkley Sou'wester forty-two foot that had traveled south by degrees from where it was built in Ellsworth, Maine. Keagan unlocked the hatch and turned on the cabin lights. A short ladder led to a large saloon with a wet bar, and a mess area and a galley along its starboard side. There was a chart table and sitting/sleeping area along the port side. Forward were more private sleeping quarters and the head.

Cassie went down the ladder, leading her suitcase ahead of her, cradling the flat wooden box in her left hand. She wouldn't let Keagan help her with her things. He bolted the hatch from the inside and followed her. Inside the saloon, Keagan got his first clear look at her. She stood there in the middle of the cabin, suitcase to the side of her left foot, wooden box under her right arm, secured by her right hand.

Keagan took her in. Her stained kitchen whites and splattered heavy shoes did little to detract from her beauty. She stood there, unsure of her situation, but sure of herself. Six feet tall, lithe and Junoesque all at once. She had the close-cropped natural hair of her race, mocha skin, and bright, skin-contrasting, even teeth, which she tended to conceal. However, by far her most alluring feature was her deep sea-green eyes that startled, intimidated, and intrigued all at the same time. The eyes explained to Keagan her last name and gave a whole new meaning to the term black Irish.

"What's in the box?" asked Keagan.

"My knives."

"Knives?" Keagan questioned, temporarily forgetting that she was a cook.

"These knives costs me over one thousand US dollars. They are the best there is; they are Zwillingswerks," she added as though such additional information were unnecessary for all but the mentally deficient. She delivered the particulars entirely without accent.

"Yes, well, they and you will be safe here, Cassie. Can I get you something to drink? I have bourbon, gin, wine, beer."

"I don't drink spirits," she answered.

Keagan reflected that her green eyes may perhaps be her only paternal legacy. "I'm sorry," Keagan added, "I also have coke, tonic, and Ting."

"No fruit juice?"

"I'm afraid not."

"I'll have a Ting."

Keagan poured her a Ting and poured some Jack Daniel's over ice for himself. As he turned around from the wet bar, he noticed that Cassie was still standing, still holding her knives. He put the drinks on the center table.

"The sleeping quarters are forward. Why don't you put your things in one of the cabins there and wash up if you care to."

Cassie's green eyes bore into him with celibate determination.

"The cabin locks from the inside," Keagan added.

This last detail seemed to settle her. Cassie went forward, stowed her gear, and used the head.

When she returned, Keagan was seated on the couch sipping his drink. He motioned Cassie to one of the two facing padded benches, in front of which was her Ting on the center table. "I put my things in the one on the left," said Cassie. "Both were made up."

"Yeah, I've been sleeping out here during the crossing. How did you come by those green eyes and a name like O'Sullivan?" Keagan asked.

"My mother was a maid for a family on Government Hill in Kingston. Those jobs are hard to come by. Mr. O'Sullivan, the husband of the house, used that fact to seduce my mother. When she became pregnant with me, he fired her. She gave me his name so that everyone would know he was my father," answered Cassie with surprising openness.

"What did your mother do when she lost her job?"

"She did what she had to do to get by. Mostly she cooked and cleaned; she took in wash. She loved to cook, but we had so little food. Finally, things got better. She got a part-time job with a restaurant that also did catering back on Government Hill. White people liked her food and how she served it. Gradually they began to ask for her, and she got some steady customers. When I got old enough, I worked with her. That's where I learned to cook. Two years ago, she died. I could have continued to cook for parties or maybe even become a live-in cook, but my mother wanted more for me, and Kingston is a bad place. So I came to Mo Bay — she slipped back into the vernacular — to work in a big hotel, to get more experience, and to get ahead."

"What will you do now?" Keagan asked.

"I don't know," she answered vacantly.

"Where did you learn to fight like that?" asked Keagan.

"As I said, Kingston is a very bad place. There are many poor there. If you want to keep what little you come by, you learn to fight. A man my mother knew was in the army. He taught unarmed combat. He taught me."

Keagan nodded. While he grew up middle class, *The Troubles* in Northern Ireland brought him to the Holy Family Boxing Club. It was only now that he was away from Ireland, that he understood the oxymoronic humor in the name.

Cassie finished her drink and retired to her cabin. Keagan told her that he hoped to see her in the morning. She didn't answer.

About six o'clock the next morning he heard her leave.

Keagan awoke at 7:00 AM to smells, not sounds. Cooking and baking and brewing smells. When he entered the saloon, Cassie was just setting the galley table. She had prepared a lightly-grilled fish in fresh lime juice and garnished with slices of oteseeta apples, warm mango bread, orange juice, and Blue Mountain coffee. Keagan realized that what he heard earlier was her going to the market, since none of what she had prepared was in his stores.

They sat across from each other without conversation. It was a marvelous meal. Keagan was pouring coffee for both of them when Cassie finally spoke. "I took 150J that I found when I was looking for coffee. I'll repay half if you give me time," Cassie said as Keagan sipped his coffee.

"Half?"

"You ate, too," Cassie said.

"So I did," said Keagan. "And it was marvelous. I haven't had fish for breakfast in a long while. We had it when I was growing up – salmon – but I haven't had it since then. It's a nice difference."

"You should see what I can do with a full kitchen," she bragged. "It is a good way to start the day, fish with fresh fruit. Jamaicans are a funny people. We are surrounded by the sea, but because we came from Africa we are mostly a land-based people. Some fish, yes, and of course we eat fish, but given the choice, we choose meat not fish, even goat; people prefer goat to fish. I guess people don't like to change," said Cassie, opening up now.

"Not in my experience, they don't," said Keagan.

"Where are you from; I don't recognize your accent."

"I'm from Ireland."

"I never met my father, but I have heard Irishmen before; you don't sound like them."

"I'm from Northern Ireland, Belfast, but I can speak in the Republican Tourist Bureau accent as well; our natural accent is generally more clipped, though. Some people say it's more like American Brooklyn than Irish," said Keagan switching back and forth between the more lyrical accent that people identify as Irish and then contrasting the more abrupt northern accent to highlight the difference.

They sat in silence for a while and sipped coffee. Keagan was a coffee drinker. A dear one in Ireland used to chide him, saying that he was the only Irishman she'd ever met who didn't drink tea.

Keagan had never tasted coffee like this. "What kind of coffee is this? It's wonderful."

"Blue Mountain coffee, comes only from Jamaica. It is the world's best," said Cassie with all the assurance of a world traveler.

"Well, I wouldn't know, but I've never tasted any better. Let's clean this up," Keagan said, finishing his coffee. "I've got to go down to the post office, and then we'll see what we can do about getting you employed."

"Dat will be very difficult, without a reference," she said, lapsing into her native accent.

***

Keagan went up to the wicket-work window in the tiny post office to inquire whether there was a general delivery letter for him. The post mistress said there was, if he could verify his identity. Keagan did so with his passport, and took the letter outside to read in the sun.

It was from Bill O'Malley. The last time he had seen Bill in Lake George Keagan had asked him to keep his ears open for restaurant property in the Adirondacks that came on the market. Something out of the ordinary; Keagan hadn't specified what that constituted. O'Malley had told Keagan during a recent phone conversation that he had heard about an inn in Lake Placid with good acreage to expand if necessary, and had asked Keagan how he could get in touch with him if it proved promising. Enclosed with the letter was the realtor's fact sheet of the property. Keagan looked it over before reading O'Malley's letter.

O'Malley thought the inn was a good deal. It needed a bit of work, he wrote, but the structures were all sound. It seems that the previous series of recent owners – of whom there were three – couldn't find a market niche for what once was a solid business, but whose pool of guests had dried up largely because they had gotten old and died. O'Malley thought the inn could be purchased cheaply, and encouraged Keagan to move quickly. He closed the letter, telling Keagan that he'd handle the details if he wanted to buy it.

Keagan read the realtor's fact sheet, again. The inn had a main building with forty guest rooms, a dining room that seated one hundred, several sitting rooms, and a bar with an enormous fireplace. Additionally, it included a boat house, several staff cabins, five guest cabins, and a number of maintenance outbuildings. The price was surprising low, and O'Malley thought it could be gotten for less.

Keagan went back into the post office and asked the post mistress for a Western Union form. He printed, "Buy it" and signed his name. He paid for the transmission, and waited while it was sent. The deal was too good to chance it on the *come soon, mon* philosophy the islands engendered.

When the cable was sent, Keagan hurried back to the boat to tell Cassie he had found her a job.

Thirteen

The *Moderna Museet* theft landed on the desk of Special Agent Mordecai Richter, nicknamed Mordecai the Righteous by his fellow agents for his strict adherence to Mormonism. Richter was in the Stolen Property Unit of the FBI's Wilshire Boulevard office. He was an especially vigilant agent, but he wasn't very well versed in art, let alone Picasso. As the bulk of his work focused on firearms theft (especially from gun shops and armories, from where the weapons eventually found their way into Mexico to arm the various drug cartels operating there) five paintings stolen in Sweden that might have a connection — emphasis on the *might* — to a citizen who lives in Los Angeles wasn't going to find its way to the top of his urgent list any time soon. Richter added the file to his mid-tier priority list. It would have made it to the bottom-tier list except that he thought at least he could check out James Crawford.

He made a note of Crawford's address, or at least the address where he lived at the time of *The First Folio* theft and added it to his do-by-the-end-of-the-week list. Since he received the file on a Thursday morning, he only had two days to check out the address. At 6:30 that evening Agent Richter had learned that James Crawford no longer lived at the address provided, if indeed he ever had. Instead of calling each of the other twenty-nine currently listed James Crawfords in Los Angeles, Richter decided to run his name through NCIC, the National Crime Information Center Database. And while he did find only six James Crawfords listed there, since two of them were black, one was in prison, one was dead, and two were over fifty, none matched the description of the James Crawford he was looking for.

Richter started to put the file with his bottom-tier priorities, but something made him put it back among the mid-tier ones. Maybe it was that the paintings were valued at $60 million or maybe it was that *Title 18, United States Code, Section 668* made it a federal offense to obtain by theft or fraud any object of cultural heritage from a museum regardless of where that museum was located, or maybe it was that the statute also prohibited knowingly possessing or selling such objects. Regardless of the reason, he found himself reviewing the file again on Monday morning.

He had a contact over at ICE, so he gave him a call. In 2003, the investigative and enforcement elements of the U.S. Customs Service and the Immigration and Naturalization Service merged under the control of Homeland Security. The result was the second largest federal law-enforcement agency in the country – ICE (Immigration and Customs Enforcement). Washington loves acronyms, especially cool ones.

"Nathan, this is Mordecai," said Richter when he finally got through to Nathan Wallace at ICE.

"How have you been, Mordecai? I haven't heard from you in a while."

"I've been busy with all the guns going south of the border. How about you?"

"Busy with the torrent of people coming in from there. It's like trying to stop the Deluge with a cork. What can I do for you?"

"Case just landed on my desk about a museum theft in Sweden. I got it because the museum's security cameras picked up a guy coming to visit the museum, but nobody can find a picture of him leaving. Interpol identified him as James Crawford. Scotland Yard was interested in him for another art theft, some Shakespeare book. The guy's address was supposed to be here in L.A., but I can't find him, not even on NCIC."

"I know this is a long shot, but I thought I'd call you to see if there was any way to locate him coming back into the country from Sweden or any place in Europe. I sent his picture to you,."

"Sure, if he used his own name and I knew when and where he re-entered the country."

"Yeah, that's what I thought. I have no idea when he came back or where."

"Best I can do is send a request to the passport division to see if a James Crawford returned to this country from anywhere in Europe in the two-week period after the robbery."

Fourteen

Keagan led the half dozen scarred, grungy, exhausted hikers up the front steps of the inn. All of them wanted drinks, but wanted baths or showers more, so Keagan took their orders and went into the bar to have Niles build the drinks and have room-service deliver them.

"How was the climb, Mick?" Niles the bartender asked.

"Great. I brought 'em all back alive again," Keagan said.

"Not by bloody half, by the looks of them," said Niles.

"Well, there is that. Build these, will you," said Keagan sliding the drink order across the bar. "And maybe they'll come around fully. Who's on this afternoon?"

"Allison," said Niles as an attractive young blond came through the dining room into the bar.

Keagan explained the orders to Allison and told Niles to give him a Budweiser. He swiveled in his seat to look out over the lake and out past Buck Island to Pulpit Rock in the background. Niles put the Budweiser on the bar and placed a glass atop a serviette next to it.

"You in any trouble, Mick?" Niles asked after Allison left with the drink orders.

"It's been a while. Why do you ask?"

"There was a Peeler in earlier asking for you," Niles said, using the Belfast term for cop. "I told him you'd be back between four and five."

"State, local, or federal?"

"Private would be my guess. He could be an insurance investigator. He didn't say he was a cop, but he is."

"How do you know?"

"Cops are like school teachers, no offense, Mick. They get used to having the upper hand, so even in a causal conversation there is an edge to their voice that says, you're going to do what I want you to do, if you know what's good for you."

"Did he say what he wanted?"

"Something about hiring you as a guide," said Niles. "Do you want me to take care of him?"

"No, let's find out what he's after first. Besides, if it's trouble, whoever sent him will just send someone else. It's been my experience that trouble doesn't go away until you deal with it."

"You may be right, but it's been my experience that sometimes I've been able to discourage it."

Niles stood behind the bar: six feet one, 190 pounds, athletically relaxed, feet a little apart, with a smile on his face. Unlike Keagan, who didn't smile often — and if he did it was generally a cynical smile or one of sardonic amusement — Niles frequently smiled, but he had two aspects. The trouble for some people was they weren't much different. They both looked a bit like a cartoon character — a good-natured or even a silly chipmunk. Both were disarming, but there was a subtle difference. Women loved the first one because they saw, whether intuitively or not, that his eyes were in concert with his grin. Reasonably intelligent men understood the second, but the constitutionally self-indulged couldn't look past the facial expression and see that the slope of his shoulders didn't fit with it, nor did the square hands and the thick wrists. The affectation stood alone, unsupported. That's how you knew he was really dangerous. While Keagan was a highly skilled boxer, Niles was lethal.

It was strange that Niles should find himself as a bartender at an American inn, stranger yet that he should be working for Mick Keagan who had been, for several years, a fund-raiser for the IRA, for Niles was an Englishman. No one knew the exact details of the beginning of the Niles/Keagan friendship except Keagan's father, and he was dead now. What was known was that Niles had been a Captain in 14 Int, the intelligence arm of Unit 22 of the elite SAS (Special Air Services) assigned to Belfast, where he led a platoon of men whose chief duty was to hunt down IRA members. Subsequently pieced together was that one night Niles and his men had set up a roadside check point. On this particular night, the Company Commander, a major, had joined the operation — presumably to evaluate the unit's proficiency. He brought with him several replacement troopers for Niles' men, whom he cryptically said had been assigned elsewhere.

Learned later from surviving witnesses was that there wasn't much traffic on the road, but at about 2:30 AM, the unit flagged down a minibus, which was occupied by a band that was traveling home south to the Republic from an engagement at the Castle Ballroom in Banbridge, County Down, Northern Ireland. The band members were ordered out of the van and lined up off the roadside, while one of the replacement troops searched the vehicle. Niles apparently became suspicious of the time the trooper spent focusing on one area and went to check on him. The major attempted to stop Niles, ordering him to stand down. Almost immediately, a bomb exploded prematurely, tearing apart the van and killing the trooper inside and wounding several of those outside. After they recovered, the major and his remaining two troopers attempted to kill Niles and his men and the band members.

It turned out that the major and the replacements he had brought with him that night were also members of the UVF (Ulster Volunteer Force), an illegal paramilitary group, the Northern Ireland counterpart of PIRA, the Provisional Irish Republican Army. Their plan was to plant a bomb and have it explode after the band had crossed over into the Republic, so that the loyalist forces could claim that the band of men were republican bomb smugglers with ties to members of the Republican government.

Less clear was how Keagan's father became involved. Some say he had been attending an IRA meeting and was returning home; others say he was driving a couple of his patrons home after he had closed his pub. Regardless, he came upon the scene witnessing the carnage. Only Niles, the major and two of his men, and two band members were alive. Niles was badly wounded; the major and his two troopers less so; one band member was only dazed by the explosion, but another was seriously wounded by a dum-dum bullet, shot by the Major. The band members and Niles were driven to the County Down hospital in Bangor.

The Major and his men were mysteriously found bound up, outside a police station across the border in the Republic of Ireland where the constable learned of their presence by an anonymous phone call. Keagan's father would later tell that part of the story with a glint in his eye, as if to say they may be here in the service of the Queen, but tis our country, after all.

The surviving band members testified against the Major and his men. The three were later tried and received life sentences.

Niles was decorated, of course; he had to be. He received the Conspicuous Gallantry Cross. However, in keeping with the secrecy code of the SAS, he was listed with the media as a member of his parent regiment rather than as having served with either 14 Int or the SAS. The Ministry of Defence, though, wanted him retired, out of Ireland, and if possible out of England for he was perceived as an embarrassment because of what he had witnessed. He was promoted to Major, and England paid him a full pension at that rank. Mick's father arranged for him to go to Boston to work for David Keagan, Mick's uncle, who had owned a bar in Boston. After the death of his parents, when Keagan first moved to America, he too worked at his uncle's bar, where Niles and he cemented the friendship that started by the kindness that Keagan's father had shown him. When Mick bought the inn, Niles was the first employee he hired after Cassie.

The phone behind the bar rang.

"*Beyond Good and Evil*," said Niles as he answered it. "Who's calling, please? Just a minute."

"Mick, there is a bloke on the phone who says he's Bascombe Treylawne. A proper English name, but there is a decided cast in the lilt of his voice."

"I'll take it up in my office, Niles. Make sure I'm not disturbed, will you."

Keagan went up the steps at the side of the bar. Niles waited for him to pick up the phone then he hung up.

Bascombe Treylawne was Keagan's account manager in the Cayman Islands. "Mr. Keagan, this is Bascombe Treylawne, calling from George Town. Something irregular has happened at the bank that may be nothing, but I should apprise you of it nonetheless."

"Thank you for doing that. What is it, Mr. Treylawne?" inquired Keagan, not impatient, but wanting to get to the point.

"We have had some attempts, merely attempts mind you, of unauthorized access to several accounts; *hacking*, I think you Americans call it. Yours was one of the accounts. Let me assure you though the intruder did not gain access."

"Was this hacking done from inside the bank or outside?"

"Outside, from America actually, but we're not sure where; also, all the accounts that the intruder attempted to access were those of Americans."

"I assume, Mr. Treylawne that your computer system maintains an intruder log."

"Yes, of course, Mr. Keagan."

"Might I ask you for a copy of that log?"

"Well, that would be most irregular, but I suppose we could provide one for you if you allowed us to remove all references to any other accounts. Let me have your e-mail address. I'm sure we have one on file, but you may have a more private one you want me to use."

"I do, but I'd rather you used a parcel service instead. As you may know, e-mail is made up of packets that include a sending and receiving address as well. If the person is accessing your computer, he might also be monitoring your Internet transmissions as well. Do you have access to an overnight carrier in George Town?"

"Yes, we do. We package the document here, then put it on the afternoon plane to Miami so that while it may not be true overnight, you should receive the package in two days' time."

"That will be fine," said Keagan. "Please send it both in printed form or on a PC formatted CD. If there are any problems or technical questions, Mr. Treylawne, please have your systems administrator give me a call. And thank you again for the information and your quick attention to it."

"Trouble?" asked Niles as Keagan came back down to the bar.

"Since I have little belief in coincidence, I'm inclined to think so," said Keagan as he picked up his beer from the bar and turned around to look across the lake.

"Where's Jimmy the Gimp, Niles?"

"He's reading the paper."

Keagan took a sip of beer, and went through the bar past the kitchen where Cassie looked up at him briefly from where she and Anjali, the twelve-year old daughter of the head of buildings and grounds, were basting quail, and into the walk-in cooler. There, amid the frozen juices and meats and bags of ice, sat Jimmy the Gimp, on a folding metal chair, reading USA Today.

"What have we got tonight? Anything special?" asked Keagan.

"One anniversary and one birthday among the house guests. Cassie has already made the cakes. Three parties of Lake People. One is a sixteen, but you already know about them. They are the ones you ordered the quail and oysters for. They did call today for a wine recommendation, though."

"What did you suggest?"

"I said that champagne was the obvious choice, and that we had several grades to choose from. But I also recommended a two-wine course, perhaps a St. Jean Chardonnay with the oysters and one of several Merlots with the quail."

"What did they decide on?" asked Keagan, giving off a slight shiver.

"They said they'd tell me when they arrived. Where did these people get their money, Mick? Not one of them can make a decision. Biff has to talk to Muffy, Muffy has to call Cody, and Cody has to check his wine encyclopedia."

Keagan was always amazed at the discrepancy between what the Gimp said and what he did. In conversation he was sardonic; at work he was the consummate professional, making every effort to ensure that guests were completely satisfied.

"All true, but pleasing them is how we make a living. Anything else?" asked Keagan.

"Niles tell you some flatfoot was asking for you?"

"Yes, he did. Did you see him?"

"Might as well have had a fucking sign pinned to his ass saying, 'I'm a cop; anything you say will be used against you.'

"That obvious?"

"Guy's in the wrong line of work, believe me. He was wearing a L.L. Bean flannel shirt with the packing creases still showing, had it buttoned to the neck. Who but a cop trying to blend in, or a geek would dress that way? The guy didn't have a plastic pocket protector or a pencil neck, so he had to be a cop," said the Gimp, snapping his paper for emphasis. But the effect was lost because the cold humidity of the walk-in had taken the stiffness out of it.

Keagan closed the walk-in door, leaving the Gimp to finish his paper.

Cassie was shaking her head while arranging quail in a basting pan, when Keagan came out of the walk-in. Anjali was helping her. "You and the bigot have a nice conversation in the ice-box?" She used the old term.

"Now Cassie, we've been through this before. The Gimp isn't a bigot, at least not in the usual sense. He makes fun of everybody. Hell, he'd make fun of Eskimos if he ever came in contact with them."

"Maybe he should," she said, shaking her head. "Anybody who reads the newspaper in the ice-box should consider moving to Eskimoland. He certainly wouldn't survive in Jamaica."

"For more reasons than one," said Keagan as he left the kitchen.

Fifteen

"As I live and breathe, tis herself," said Keagan as he came through the entrance from the dining room to the bar. Seated at the bar, talking to Niles, was an enchanting auburn pixie wearing a lime green sun dress and an enormous sun hat. She had her back to Keagan, but he recognized her immediately. Even if he hadn't, he would have known who she was because Niles was leaning on the bar on his forearms, talking with her. Niles only leaned on the bar for two types of people. One, if his intention was to discreetly tell a customer who was making an ass of himself that it would be in his own self-interest and personal safety to the take his act on the road. The other kind of person Niles would lean on the bar to talk with was Kelly O'Neill.

Their relationship was even stranger than the one Niles had with Keagan. While Keagan's father had saved Niles' life and arranged for him to come to America — ironic considering their political affiliations — Kelly had been one of the very IRA members Niles had been charged with tracking down and arresting. He never had, of course, but maybe given more time he would have. It wasn't hard to tell they were both very good at what they did. And of course Kelly and Keagan as partners made an excellent team. But even on his own, so was Niles.

Keagan and Niles' relationship was based on loyalty: a betrayed loyalty by the Ministry of Defence, and an uncanny loyalty towards a former enemy whose father had saved his life. And so the enemies became best friends, and by extension Kelly was part of that friendship. There was something more, though; there was also admiration for an enemy of her consummate skills.

When Keagan walked up behind her, Niles straightened and Kelly, intuiting why, turned to face Keagan.

"Hello," he said with uncharacteristic uncertainty in his voice.

"Hello yourself, boyo," she said as she stood and kissed him.

Keagan held her tentatively, afraid to let himself go into the kiss. After a while, he held her away from him and looked down into her Irish-green eyes, taking in her Celtic beauty. Kelly had a diminutive fanciful beauty: She was 5'4" and 110 pounds with auburn hair, a curvilinear smile that was rare among the Irish, and the most intelligent eyes Keagan had ever seen. There was also mischief in those eyes and in her smile, too, but the mischief only added to her beauty. Keagan had been in love with her since the first time he met her in Belfast when they were fifteen. He was also more than a little afraid of her because he had no escape plan when around her. The *cul-de-sac caution* that he had cultivated from working with the IRA failed him when it came to Kelly.

"God, you stink, have you been wallowing with the pigs, again?" Kelly said as Keagan released her.

"I've been out climbing mountains, scaling peaks, fording rivers, don't you know."

"You might have stopped off at one of those rivers for a bit longer and had a clean-up," teased Kelly.

"What brings you to *Beyond Good and Evil*?"

"Catchy name," Kelly said. "Did you think that up?"

"Yes, I did. Well, actually I borrowed it from a German philosopher, who wrote a book of that title. I had a little trouble with the liquor board, though; they don't like to issue permits to houses that have untoward names. They thought it was a bawdy house, but when I explained that it was a literary reference they gave in, surprising for bureaucrats, but maybe they were tickled to do so, gave them a break in the tedium of saying *no*. I wanted a name that would suggest sybaritic excellence."

"And is that what you provide here?"

"Well, I'm not running a bawdy house if that's what you mean. The kitchen is excellent, the wine cellar extensive, and . . ."

"And the staff's matchless," Kelly added, turning fondly to Niles. Their admiration was mutual.

"Well, if it's so bloody good why hasn't Niles gotten you a drink yet?"

"Because we were catching up on old times, but now that you mention it I'll have some 12-year old Jameson on the rocks, please Niles. I've had a hard travel."

Niles poured the drink and placed it in front of Kelly. Mick motioned to Niles for another beer.

"Niles says you enjoy being an inn keeper and playing Frank Buck."

"I do. It's more enjoyable and better paying than attempting to teach the beauty of language to adolescents in hormonal overdrive."

"But it doesn't pay as well as fund-raising, does it?"

"No," said Mick. "It doesn't. But then if I make a mistake with somebody's reservation or Cassie puts too much spice in the gumbo, I'm not looking at twenty to life; and so far, no one's shot at Niles for making a bad drink or me for recommending a bad wine."

"Well, I know you're both incapable of that," said Kelly, surveying the view. "A place like this must have cost a pretty penny. I thought the IRS got all of David's money." She always moved easily from one topic to another, from banal to private, so that most people found themselves off balance, answering her questions openly without weighing the significance of their replies.

"They got a good deal of it, but only a leprechaun puts all his gold into one pot, and no one ever quite catches a leprechaun."

"I was sorry to hear about David's imprisonment, and sorrier still when I heard of his death. He was a good man," said Kelly.

The sun was behind the inn now. The afternoon blue was inching down the Sentinel Range, and the lake out the front window sparkled in the sun's slant. Keagan loved that view. He loved this time of day in the summer when everything quieted down, flattened out, and was peaceful. He had had a refreshing climb, and he was almost relaxed now. He should have felt good, and he almost did, but the phone call from the Grand Caymans and the insurance cop poking around took the edge off his pleasure. And then there was Kelly. Keagan didn't believe in coincidence, and Kelly's sudden appearance fell into that category. She had a strange and marvelous effect on him. He loved her deeply, but he was afraid of her. More correctly, he was afraid of himself in her presence because he no longer had full control over himself.

Keagan broke out of his reverie, smiled at Kelly, and turned to Niles. "Niles, how about making us two more drinks and having Allison bring Kelly's bags up to my lodge."

"Your lodge?" Kelly smiled from under her enormous hat. "What will the neighbors say?"

"Remember where you are, Kelly dear, *Beyond Good and Evil.*"

"I'll have to keep that in mind," said Kelly, her eyes dancing with her smile.

***

"Make yourself at home while I clean up."

"By all means," said Kelly.

Keagan took his boots off on the porch, and went into his bedroom in the rear of the lodge. As he was undressing, he could hear Allison at the door with Kelly's bags. He let the hot water wash over him, letting it dissolve the caked-on dirt of the day's climb. He then lathered his hair with shampoo, closed his eyes and edged forward toward the shower head. As he did, Kelly stepped into the shower, "Are you clean enough for company?" she inquired as she reached around his waist.

***

"I've got to go down to the inn," Keagan whispered to Kelly. "Why don't you take a nap? I'll give you a wake-up call around eight. We'll have dinner at nine o'clock."

"It's a date," said Kelly.

Keagan kissed her forehead as he slid out of bed.

***

Keagan checked in with Jimmy the Gimp. The Farrington party was just arriving. He welcomed them and let the Gimp lead them to their table. Keagan went into the kitchen to tell Cassie that the sixteen had arrived and to begin the *shuck alert*. He then went over to the Farrington party's table where the Gimp had just finished taking their drink orders.

They sat there arrayed in bright summer colors and chattering away, with snippets of conversation rising above the table. Keagan took them in. Their conversations were so facile, and he suspected they probably had drinks before they had arrived. He judged their collective mood to be about a seven on a scale of ten. It wouldn't take much more than Cassie's cooking to get them up to a nine, maybe even a ten before they left. Keagan did this with all the tables he visited. He always tried to visit each table, not just the big parties. The goal was to have every customer leave *Beyond Good and Evil* as close to ten as possible.

Mr. Farrington called out to Keagan, "Well, Mick, have you got a good meal for us tonight?" He was a heavy man, a football star thirty years ago no doubt, and loud but usually good-natured." Cassie has outdone herself," said Keagan. "She managed to get cultured Damariscotta oysters for you, tonight."

"What are they," asked one of Farrington's quests, the conversations tailing off to hear Keagan's explanation.

"Cultured means that nature had been given a hand in getting everything right; they were raised off the coast of Maine near Damariscotta, hence their name, under controlled conditions. They are very large, and since they are best when served icy cold we've packed them in ice. The oysters won't be opened until just before you are ready for them. They are a special treat. You are really very lucky to have them because the coastal Maine restaurants usually buy up all they can get. Cassie must have been most persistent."

Keagan enjoyed these moments of showing off, a lasting residue of having been a teacher. "Have you decided on a wine?" Keagan asked.

"Not really," said Farrington. "Jimmy suggested champagne or maybe two wine courses, one with the oysters and the other with the quail. What do you think, Mick?"

"Both excellent suggestions, but if I were you, I'd stay with champagne. We have several fine labels, each in two or three different grades of sweetness, but with oysters and quail, I'd recommend a *brut*."

"Which label do you suggest?"

"*Veuve Clicquot*. It's a medium-priced champagne, about half-way between American and *Dom Pérignon*, and for my palette I think it tastes better than *Dom Pérignon*."

"Good, Mick, start us off with six bottles and have about six more ready to go if we need them." Keagan marveled at the decision-making process. He knew Farrington would have gone with the two wines if Keagan had recommended it. The Gimp had told Farrington that champagne was the logical choice, but Farrington wouldn't make the decision until he heard it from the head man.

"Very good, Mr. Farrington, I'll attend to that right away."

Keagan went into the bar and told Niles to ice down sixteen glasses and get six bottles of *Veuve Clicquot* from the walk-in and keep six more in reserve. Keagan glanced around the bar. There was a good crowd tonight with few people waiting for tables. *Beyond Good and Evil* had a good local bar business, too. Keagan nodded to some regulars. Niles suddenly stopped icing glasses and called Keagan over.

"The copper's back," Niles said.

"Which one?" asked Keagan without turning around.

"The one who just came through the porch door, wearing the shark-skin suit."

"If he asks for me, send someone in to find me. If he doesn't, I'll be back in about ten minutes for a progress report," said Keagan.

Keagan went back into the dining room. He told the Gimp about the champagne and went over to the Farrington table where a waiter hovered. Keagan told Farrington to inform the waiter exactly ten minutes before he wanted the oysters served, and went off to the kitchen to see how things were progressing there.

Cassie was busy putting up dinners. Anjali was there helping her. She would also help Cassie with the oysters. Although she was only twelve-years old, she was Cajun and could shuck oysters as well as anyone working in *Vieux Carré*.

The waiter who was working the Farrington party came into the kitchen and told Cassie to start the oysters. Cassie motioned her second cook to take over while she and Anjali turned their attention to the oysters. Keagan went back into the dining room.

He toured the dining room, stopping off at the tables and saying hello to the diners. A waiter came over to him to tell Keagan that a guy in the bar wanted to see him. Keagan looked at his watch; it was eight o'clock.

"Tell him I'll be there in about fifteen minutes." He continued making the rounds of tables. In a few minutes, there was an aggregate gasp in the dining room as three waiters, carrying sixteen half-dozen platters of the very large, very cold Damariscotta oysters, converged on the Farrington table. Farrington flashed his lord-of-the-manor smile at the collective envy of the lookers-on.

***

"I'm Mick Keagan; you want to see me?" Keagan asked the man in the shark-skin suit.

"Yes, Mr. Keagan, I do. My name's Manny Di Ladro," he said extending his business card. Keagan took the card and moved under a light to read it. It suggested that the man who handed it to him was indeed Manny Di Ladro, Chief Claims Adjustor for Fidelity Mutual Insurance Company of Montvale, New Jersey.

"What can I do for you, Mr. Di Ladro?" asked Keagan.

"I need to hire a guide."

"You'll excuse me if I say that you don't look the type."

"I'm not. That's why I need a guide."

Keagan looked at his watch. "You'll have to excuse me. I have a dinner date at nine o'clock, and I have a few things to attend to before then."

"When can we meet? I just need a half hour. How about ten o'clock?"

"Let's say between ten and ten thirty. If you haven't eaten, why don't you have dinner here? You won't find a better place around."

***

"You never answered my question."

"What question was that, Mick?" asked Kelly.

They were sitting in the far corner of the dining room at Keagan's private table, which was situated on a platform, three steps above the dining room floor, surrounded by a banister. Kelly was wearing a white blouse of some suggestive but opaque material, a straight black silk skirt, and a Kelly-green beret. Keagan reasoned that she could travel with about a quarter of her usual baggage if she didn't feel that being hatless in public was analogous to being naked.

"The question of why you suddenly showed up at *Beyond Good and Evil* unannounced," said Keagan in between sips of champagne.

"Why, I came to see you, don't you know," said Kelly mocking him.

"Yes, I know. But why?"

"Because you are my one true love," Kelly beamed.

"How does the poem go? *I could not love thee half so much had I not loved honor more.* Substitute the *Ireland* for *honor*, and we'll be getting awfully close to the truth."

Kelly smiled a wan smile. "Mick, we're more than nine hundred years under their heel. It's been more than nine hundred years since that sham Pope gave Ireland to England to curry favor with the King."

Keagan took her hand. "That's right, Kelly, nine hundred years and what's changed in Northern Ireland? What have the political efforts of Parnell or De Valera or Collins accomplished except grand words for which the Irish are so famous? Do you know why the Irish are famous for their grand words? It's because they've had so much practice. Nine hundred years of talk about the same bloody thing. Any other people would have tired by now. And what has the IRA accomplished in the seventy-odd years of its existence except gratuitous bloodshed? Christ, they can't even shoot straight. They've got to spray a pub to make sure they hit their target."

"You didn't use to think that way," said Kelly.

"No, you're right. I didn't, but then my parents were alive. When they were killed in a stupid random act of violence, the sole purpose of which was to let the Catholics know that the Prods were still in control, was the second my thinking changed. One minute they were sitting down to a pint in their own pub, and the next they were dead, their bodies riddled with bullets from automatic weapons. Then Uncle David was killed. I've seen enough death, thank you."

"Yet, you avenged David's death."

Keagan was surprised that she knew that, but Kelly had a way of knowing things, including what took place three thousand miles away. "What a noble sounding word, *avenged*. I had that scum exterminated. I'm not proud of it, yet I'd do it again under the same circumstances. All I'm saying is that I don't need to go out looking for the circumstances."

The waiter came and cleared their plates. Keagan sipped his champagne. His black mood passed; he smiled over at Kelly. She winked, and she was back to her fay self.

"What I've got in mind, Mick, is that we become partners again."

"You're finally agreeing to marry me?"

The Kelly looked at him sadly, placing her hand over his. "You know I would if I could, Mick, but I've too much work to do. I just can't walk away from it."

"Didn't think so. So nothing has changed?"

"Actually, I've changed my thinking quite a bit. With the Easter Peace of '98, the IRA has got little to do. They're a dangerous pool of angry men, many unemployed. It's worse now with the immigrants coming in and competing for jobs. And the lads sitting around the pubs, no medals or honors for their efforts of the last thirty years and no glorious day of unification to laud, are in a state of suspended animation as it were. They can't fight, celebrate, or get on with their lives. That's a dangerous place for dangerous men to be."

"I'm trying to get the leadership to refocus, adjust to the times, still stay active, still contribute — but now in non-violent ways. Some of the leaders are listening. They know they have a smoldering problem on their hands. Others — like the ones who set up David — see only the old ways. I've got to show them the value of the new ways."

"And what are those new ways, Kelly?"

"I've been shifting my whole focus to information gathering and analysis, and I've put together a plan I believe will move us away from the violence and be a great deal more effective."

"Mick, I've been thinking about this idea for some time now. You're right about the IRA, and you're not the only one who is tired of the violence: the whole world is, and world opinion doesn't differentiate between terrorists. A bomb in Belfast is the same as a bomb in Baghdad or Kabul, and I don't want the Irish thought of in the same vein as those fanatics. The Easter Peace is a godsend, but it's a stalemate, too. We're closer than we've ever been. Soon the Catholics will have a majority, which means we'll have the power of the vote, but we need more than that to get us over this last hurdle. We need world opinion. We win that and it won't be long before Ireland will be united ... "

"No, Kelly, the vote just means we'll switch places with the Prods. World opinion notwithstanding, England isn't going to give up. She isn't going to turn her back on the 800,000 or so Scots-Irish whose progenitors King James I enticed into Ireland in the 17th Century." England isn't going to pack them up and move them back to Scotland, and she isn't going to partition the island the way Mountbatten did in India — Muslims there and Hindus here. She's realized what a fiasco that was. I don't think England knows what to do, so she'll do nothing. Now that the Protestant/Catholic population is about balanced, I have no doubt that there's a chance for a united Ireland, but if it comes it won't be in our lifetime and if it does, we'll be very old. Besides, I'm not going back."

"Well, Mick, I believe that my idea just might speed up the process."

"What, you're going to get Bill Clinton back to charm them again?"

"If we do it right, this information system will allow us to tap into not only what the Unionists are planning, but also what the Brits are up to that affect unification. I'm not talking about official publications, but rather, the back channels of transmissions about their plans."

"I can tell you what the UVF is planning. Just check out their website *No Surrender*. That's what they're planning."

"They may not have a choice, Mick. Think about it. Rather than using information about Brits or the UVF plans to set up an ambush, I propose to use that same information to try them in the court of popular opinion. I know that's a cliché, but clichés are clichés because they contain more than a little truth."

"Information is a two-way street; I want to gather it and analyze its import, but I also want to disseminate it, not just in pubs in New York and Boston and Melbourne and Sydney, but Savannah and Seattle as well as anywhere where the Irish have influence, from their homes to their businesses. Frankly, I don't even know what the potential of this system is; I just know that information is more effective than bombs and bullets. Information shapes world opinion positively; bombs and bullets do so negatively."

"If my idea works and we can keep both sides from breaking the peace, we can focus world opinion on speeding up the process."

"How are you going to do all that?"

"Well, of course it involves hiring experts to put together and design the system and the databases. I've pitched my idea to the IRA leadership and they think it has merit. But before I can do any of that I have to sell the idea — really sell it — if not to the IRA, then to

Sinn Féin. I'm not giving up on this. As I said, the IRA leadership is willing to go along with it, but there's a catch."

"What's that?"

"They'll agree to it as a trial, but I have to finance it. And, of course, to do that I need to raise money. Buckets of it."

"So that's why you're here; you want me to help you seed this project?"

Kelly smiled, "You always were the quick one, Mick Keagan.

"When I said we become partners again I meant like before. Well, almost like before. I've come up with a new wrinkle on our former operation. Remember when you snatched the three Turner landscapes from the old Duke?"

Keagan remembered it well. He had gone to a U2 concert in London, and while there had purchased five posters and a carrying tube just a bit larger than needed to accommodate them. Later that night, he broke into the old Duke's flat on Downing Street and made off with three landscapes by J. M. W. Turner. He taped the landscapes to the back of the three inner posters and painstaking fitted the posters into the tube. He was stopped and searched at customs as soon as he got off the ferry in Belfast. The customs officer pried open the tube and tried to extract the posters. They partially telescoped out, but his frustration prevented him from removing them completely. Exasperated, he threw the tube at Keagan and told him to be on his way. The IRA sold the paintings back to the Duke for one hundred and fifty thousand pounds.

"Dare I ask what the wrinkle is?" Keagan said.

"We go into the recovery business. We recover stolen art work for insurance companies, museums, and rightful owners. For a fee, of course."

"Kelly, what makes you think that you can compete with the various government agencies that track these thieves down? The FBI alone in this country must have whole teams of experts who specialize in recovering stolen art."

"Yes and no."

"What do you mean, yes and no?"

"When the paintings of our first project were stolen, the FBI had one man who specialized in stolen art. Now there is a team of a dozen agents and supervisors based in Washington, D.C. that focuses on art theft. But they are new, only recently trained, and still stumbling around. The sole man who made up the Art Crime Team before the new unit was formed was Robert Wittman. He's based in Philadelphia. When he was alone, he more or less had authority over the investigation, at least as much autonomy as a bureau like the FBI was willing to grant. That distinction is important because Washington is the seat of power, so even though there are more agents working in art theft now, nobody wants to make a decision for fear of making a mistake and jeopardizing their careers. Washington is where the politics happen, not where cases get solved."

"How do you know all that?"

"Because it's my business to know things like that. You don't think I went in to this plan willy-nilly do you? That's not my style."

"No, it's not. Sorry, but one experienced man?"

"America isn't very keen on stolen artwork, Mick. It's got a lot of museums, but oddly enough I suspect they are mostly for the young. The adults seem to prefer sports and NASCAR."

"Aye, and the cultured Irish never frequent the stadia nor the pubs, do they?"

"Well, be that as it may, the Americans don't seem to care much for art once it's stolen. More often than not, the thieves are portrayed in your cinema as sophisticated heroes. Anyway, this fellow Wittman is the only FBI agent who really knows what he's doing. Before this new unit was formed, the rest of the cases were turned over to the agent in queue for property theft. To be fair, the Americans aren't the only negligent ones. A good deal of the world is like that. Italy and France are the only two countries that really take art theft seriously."

"Besides, government agencies are slow to react, and of course don't get involved unless the theft happens in their country or comes to their shores. After September 11th, the national police agencies are too concerned with terrorism. One third of the FBI agents work on terrorism alone, even though forty percent of all stolen art makes its way onto American soil. This is where the money is."

Kelly reached for her bag that hung off the side of the chair. She extracted a small clipping from the July, 2005 edition of *Art and Auction*. Keagan read it: *Belfast police report the recovery of a Picasso sculpture and two Georges Braques paintings, stolen from Stockholm's Moderna Museet. On June 20th, thieves made off with five paintings and one sculpture by Picasso, along with two paintings by the Cubist Georges Braques. The haul was valued at more than forty million pounds. Still missing, however, are the five Picasso paintings.*

"And what makes you think we can recover the paintings, when the police have not even been marginally effective in the last two years?" Keagan asked.

"Because I know who has them and a pretty good idea of who wants to buy them," answered Kelly.

"And how do you know that?" Keagan asked, looking at Kelly and then following her gaze to Di Ladro who was motioning to Keagan that he was going out to the bar.

Keagan looked at his watch — 10:33. "Listen Kelly, I have to meet that fellow in the bar, a problem I have to deal with."

"Why don't you let Niles handle it," said Kelly.

"It's not that kind of problem. Give me fifteen minutes, then come join me. If I haven't wrapped it up by then, I'll get rid of him."

Sixteen

Di Ladro was sitting at the bar when Keagan came in from the dining room. Keagan walked over to him and said, "Sorry I'm late; I was tied up with a very important person."

"Yeah, I'd say so. I saw her."

"Let's sit at a table where we can have some privacy," said Keagan.

Di Ladro picked up his drink, sliding the cash in front of him over to Niles, nodded thanks, and followed Keagan to a far-corner table.

"As I said, Mr. Keagan, I want to hire you as a guide. My company has recently, after over two years of investigation, paid off a multi-million dollar policy. And while we believe the claim is legit, we still feel that the insured merchandise is recoverable."

"After more than two years?"

"Yes, Mr. Keagan, two years in my business isn't long at all. You hear stories all the time about somebody finding an old painting in their attic and it turns out to be a Rembrandt. Anyway, the merchandise in question are diamonds. Are you familiar with a plane crash that occurred somewhere in the mountains around here in December of '05?"

"Only through hearsay. That was before I bought the inn." Keagan watched the answer register in Di Ladro's eyes.

"Yeah, I know. How did you get familiar enough with the area to be a guide in such a short time?"

"I like to hike and climb. When I lived in Boston, I climbed a lot in New Hampshire. The terrain here is a little different, but the skills are the same, and I guess I just have a natural sense of direction," answered Keagan.

"Yeah? Well, right around Christmas in '05 a twin-engine plane crashed somewhere out there." Di Ladro waved his arm at the expanse outside. "It took a little over five months the find the plane. Five fucking months, can you believe it?" Di Ladro was a little looser from his dinner wine and the stinger he was now fondling.

"Yes, I can. There are a lot of empty places out there" — Keagan did not wave at the expanse outside — "where a plane could go down and stay lost for a very long time. If it had dropped through the ice of any number of remote lakes and ponds out there, they'd still be looking for it."

"Anyway, a private pilot finally spotted it one day in May, when the snow had melted enough to uncover part of the plane's wings. May, you believe that? The two men who died in the crash were diamond brokers, returning from Montreal where they had just purchased several million dollars' worth of stones. The search team found the bodies, but they never found the diamonds. Or so they say."

"Mr. Di Ladro . . ." Keagan wanted to tell Di Ladro about the speculations over the empty seat cushions that he heard in the news, but then realized that it would blow his story because he wasn't supposed to know anything about the plane other than it went down."

"Call me Manny, Mick," Di Ladro interrupted.

"Yes. Then, Manny, most of the guiding I do is for guests at the inn. What other clients I take on are usually Lake People who frequent the bar and restaurant. I'm afraid this is out of my line. Besides, I don't see what we could possibly learn from a crash site that is more than two years old. I could take you there, but I'm an inn keeper not an investigator."

"Well, first off, I am a guest of the inn. I'm staying here. Secondly, I am an investigator, Mick, and I want you because you weren't here when the plane went down." Di Ladro made that point a bit more dramatically than he would have cared to. "If I hire some local, how do I know he isn't the very guy I'm looking for?"

"Well, I don't know. I think you're wasting your money." Keagan wanted to get rid of Di Ladro because he was trouble, and he knew that, with very few exceptions, trouble didn't go away by itself. "Let me think about it and check my schedule. Give me a call about four tomorrow."

"No problem, Mick."

"And now if you'll excuse me, I have to check on a few details and then rescue my dinner date from some of the local color."

***

Before Keagan went back to the bar, he went by his office, turned on his computer terminal, and checked on Di Ladro's reservation. After Keagan copied down the credit card information, he turned on his personal computer and called a bar in Belleville, New Jersey. When the phone answered, Keagan asked for the owner.

"Sean, here."

"Sean, this is Mick Keagan."

"Mick, how are you? What are you doing? The last time I heard you were teaching the King's English to rich brats."

"No longer, Sean. Now I sell whiskey and victuals to their parents."

"You bought a restaurant?"

"An inn."

"Where?"

"Lake Placid."

"Aye, in God's country."

"Some might say only God would have it in the winter, but I suppose you are right. It sure beats Boston."

"Try living in New Jersey. What can I do for you, Mick?"

"I need some information. Do you still have your old connections?"

"Some old, some new as well."

"I need anything you can give me on a Manny Di Ladro from Montvale, New Jersey. He says he's an insurance adjustor for Fidelity Mutual, and he may well be, but I'm willing to bet he's got a side line as well. The usual stuff: police record, questionable connections, income, spending pattern, vices."

"Give me a couple of days, and I'll get back to you. Mick, I'm sorry to hear about your uncle David."

"Thanks, Sean. David was a good man. He helped me out a lot. You know he sponsored me to come over."

"Yeah, I did, Mick."

Keagan e-mailed Sean the inn's phone number and Di Ladro's platinum card account number to trace Di Ladro's spending history, and then rang off.

***

When Keagan got back to the bar, Kelly was at the center of a crescent of locals. Some worked at the inn like Jimmy the Gimp and Teal, while others were just regulars who liked the bar because it was quiet, friendly, safe, and poured the largest drinks in town. The group was laughing in response to some story Matt, one of the locals, had just told when Keagan moved next to Kelly and ordered a Martel Cordon Blue from Niles.

"What is all this about?" Keagan asked Kelly.

"Matt here was just telling a wonderful story about some fellow he called a *woodchuck*, though I'm still not sure why. A rustic, I guess." Keagan knew Matt. He was a regular who owned a bar himself. "Anyway, Matt and this woodchuck fellow were discussing buying Matt's lorry, er, truck. The woodchuck was from Wilmington, which I guess is a nearby village, down the mountain somewhere. Apparently, this woodchuck fancied himself quite a haggler who thought he could negotiate a better price, could slicker Matt. *Slicker*, is that the right word? Yes, well, Matt gave him all the specifications of the truck. Oh, I don't know, but all those things you might be interested in if you were buying a used truck such as mileage and model and year. Oh yes, Matt told him it was a '97 Ford something. Matt knew he had him hooked, and indeed the woodchuck fellow was interested, but he misread Matt, thinking he was desperate to sell the truck. So, he told Matt that he was interested but that he wanted to dicker, which I suppose means bargain. So Matt said, 'OK it's a '98 Ford.' This revelation at first seemed to confuse the woodchuck, but apparently made him happy in the end because that was the conclusion of his dickering, and he paid Matt his full asking price."

Keagan laughed at the story as he had many times before. Kelly's version lost a little clarity in her across-the-pond translation, but Keagan was sure that Matt had told the story for Kelly, as the rest of the audience had already heard it. Matt was very witty, and people told and retold his stories. Keagan knew it to be true because he sat right next to the woodchuck from Wilmington when Matt was pitching the sale. Keagan finished his drink in short order and told Kelly to finish hers. He said that it was late and time to go.

"What's the hurry, Mick? Tomorrow's Sunday. You haven't resumed going to mass have you? Besides, I still have to talk to you."

"I know, but it will keep till tomorrow. No, I'm not getting up early for mass; on Sunday I cook breakfast at 6:00 AM for all my dining room and kitchen staff."

"Well, aren't you taking the largesse of the lord of the manor a little too seriously?"

"Quite the contrary, present company excepted of course" — Keagan nodded toward Teal, the Gimp, and Niles — "but many of my employees are prodigious drinkers and roisterers, if you can imagine such a thing in this trade; but if they think they are going to stagger in here with the guests at 7:30 AM looking like the wrath of God, they are greatly mistaken. I want them here at 6:00 AM, sober and fully fed by 7:00. They know I'll be checking them for traces of the shakes and the demons, and if they want to continue working here, they had better arrive looking like clergy for matins."

"Mick Keagan, you are a devious fellow."

"Many have said so, Kelly."

***

When they had returned to Mick's cottage, Kelly seated herself on the couch and said, "Mick, tell me how Teal, a Southerner, ended up here."

Mick sat next to her and put his arm around her. "Teal's from Louisiana. At least I think he is. I know very little about his background.

If I'm right, he's Cajun. The Cajuns are quite a bit different from Southerners. Since they originally came from north of here, the move might make more sense than it appears."

"I know where the Cajuns came from. I don't need to hear another saga of England's sordid colonial history. I want to hear about Teal."

"Ah, well. There isn't a lot to tell; he doesn't talk much about himself and nothing about his previous life. I do know he was in the Air Force at one time and, as near as I can figure, there isn't anything he can't fix. At least I haven't found anything."

"What did he do in the Air Force, work on jet engines?"

"No, he disarmed bombs. I'll never forget his telling me that. I asked him the same question about working on jet engines — it's a natural leap in logic — he paused for a second, then looked up with a curious smile and said, 'no, I dismantled bombs."

What Teal hadn't told Keagan was that he was also occasionally loaned out to the Navy SEALs to set and plant bombs as well.

"Bombs, how quaint. Has he been in jail?"

"Why do you ask, the tattoo?"

"Yes, it isn't as crude as the usual ones I've seen, but it also looks singular, not your run-of-the-mill nonsense many of the young people are decorating themselves with today."

"I have no idea. He showed up one day, asking for a job shortly after I bought this place, he and Anjali."

"Who is Anjali?"

"His ten year old daughter. She was ten then; she is twelve now."

"And where is Mrs. Teal or is Teal his first name?"

"I don't know whether that's his given name or his surname; I make his checks out to Teal, no other name. Nor do I know anything about a Mrs. Teal. I don't know whether she died or she left them or they left her. He never volunteered; and I never asked. What I do know is that you never saw a happier kid. He takes her spelunking and climbing and kayaking. He helps her with her homework; he shows her how to fix things. She, in turn, keeps their cottage for them. She also works here in the kitchen with Cassie, except when the Department of Labor inspectors come around, checking on my employees."

"And, pray tell, who is Cassie?"

"Cassie O'Sullivan, she's the inn's chef."

"Mick Keagan, you have an Irish chef! Are you daft? It's a wonder you aren't bankrupt. The Irish can't cook; you of all people should know that. You know I thought the world of your parents, but what was the house special in your parents' pub – *bangers and mash*? No, the Irish don't even know drink – except for Guinness and Jameson, and they certainly can't cook. They've had nothing to practice on except mutton and cod and potatoes when they could get them. Hardly *haute cuisine*."

Keagan explained Cassie's ancestry to Kelly and assured her that Cassie knew of spices other than salt, of dishes other than mutton stew, and vegetables other than boiled cabbage and potatoes. He reminded her of the marvelous oysters and quail they had had for dinner.

Kelly leaned into Keagan, her eyes smiling. "What a day this has been: Here you are, you and Niles among touts, mysterious Cajuns, and Irish Jamaicans, in a country inn named after a book written by a misogynistic, syphilitic German philosopher, catering to lords and ladies, cheek by jowl with rustics. 'Tis sure a far cry from the rumble of Belfast where we grew up. Speaking of which, we have to talk tomorrow, but right now let us off to bed to have the wonderment continue for a little while longer." Keagan lifted her head and kissed her gently and sadly.

Seventeen

After Keagan had prepared and served to his employees a breakfast of juice, cereal, bacon, eggs, pancakes, and fruit, he cleaned up and checked with Jimmy the Gimp to make sure Jimmy had the guest list, the meal plans, and the guests' happiness ratings.

The happiness ratings were Keagan's idea. Every overnight guest was rated for level of happiness upon entering *Beyond Good and Evil*. The scale was from one to ten, ten signifying near rapture. The ratings were passed or flashed to every department that served the guest. So, for example, if a moderately cranky guest arrived at the front desk — a four say — the front desk would flash the number to the bellman who would do his best to bring up the guest's happiness scale at least one level. Every department thereafter would be alerted of the guest's original happiness rating, and as the guest came in contact with each department, an entry and exit rating would be estimated.

Keagan made sure that one department didn't inflate the exit level to appear better by never blaming anyone for not raising the level. He knew that if inflation crept into the system, it would erode any benefits. He also knew that some guests didn't want to be jollied. Some people were constitutionally incapable of happiness or, more frequently, something in their lives kept them from being happy.

After Keagan checked with the front desk and inspected his staff, he went into the kitchen and had Cassie cook two rainbow trout that one of the guides had caught the night before. He added home-made bread, fresh raspberries, and coffee, then took the tray up to his cabin to Kelly.

***

Keagan entered the cabin, tray slightly above shoulder level and perched on the splayed fingers of his right hand. He placed the tray on the porch table and arranged the dishes. Kelly was still asleep. She was a night person, Keagan a day person. One more incongruity in their romance. Keagan kissed her forehead and she smiled awake.

"Breakfast is served, Milady," he said.

"And what unearthly hour might it be?"

"It's eight o'clock and the troops are fed and there are trout to eat and a full day awaiting us."

"A full day of what? Plans for the project? Or Irish honey cake about retirement, political disinterest, and entrepreneurial concerns?"

"Let's begin with breakfast."

"Aye, still the silver-tongue devil."

They ate on the porch. The lake was flat and gray, reflecting the sky. In the Adirondacks, when the morning is sunny, the day is in the hopper, but if it's cloudy at eight it might clear up by ten. The lakes and the mountains control the weather in the Adirondacks, and in turn the weather controls people's moods.

"I thought we'd take the kayaks up the lake and then climb White-face, let you really see the area."

Kelly ate the raspberries one at a time, by hand, smiling at Keagan. "Will we be able to see anything? It looks like the area around Car-rauntoohil in County Kerry: fifty-three shades of green and the sky the color of lead."

"It will clear. We'll have a high-blue day by the time we get to the head of the lake," said Keagan smiling at Kelly over his coffee.

"What shall I wear?"

"Do you have any soft shoes, sneakers, running shoes?"

"Yes, I have running shoes."

"Good. Running shoes, socks, shorts, a T-shirt, a sweatshirt or sweater, and, of course, a hat."

"Of course. Shall I bring a bathing suit?"

"Yes. Start with one because I want to get you familiar with a kayak and make sure you know how to get out of the boat in case you flip. After the climb, I like to skinny dip if I can, so you can leave the suit here."

"Oh, that sounds wonderfully sybaritic."

"Aye, you're starting to get the idea of the inn's name. Go change and meet me down at the boathouse. I have a few things I still have to attend to if we are to play all day."

***

Kelly had not been in a kayak before, but she took to it easily. Keagan gave her his more stable Phoenix Isère, a moderate volume flat-water boat. He paddled a Phoenix Match II, a twenty-two pound *Kevlar* down-river boat, which tracked well on lakes as long as there wasn't too much wind.

Before shoving off, Keagan had Kelly practice falling out of the boat to show her that she shouldn't feel trapped in the boat by the spray skirt. He rolled her twice to the right and twice to the left. She undid the spray skirt and fell out gracefully each time.

Lake Placid is shaped like an *8* with a curlicue at the top. The lake has two big islands in the middle of it: Buck and Moose; the curlicue is the smaller Hawk Island near the head.

They paddled up the west side of the lake, cutting across the bays and occasionally bracing right to nose through the wakes of power boats. Kelly followed Keagan's lead easily; she was a natural athlete. About three miles up the lake, they cut a northeast angle across the western part of the lake to the tip of Moose Island. They then cut around the northern side of Hawk Island, skirted a beach, and continued on to Whiteface landing, where they shouldered the boats out of the water and carried them off into the woods, out of sight of the Shore-Owners' Trail that circumscribed the lake. Keagan chained them to a tree and hid the paddles in the undergrowth some distance away. The paddles were hand-made Mitchells. The boats were locked up and out of sight of the trail, but the paddles couldn't be locked, so he wanted them away from the boats, just in case. They dried off, changed their footwear and started up the trail.

The woods were warm and dry, and held the smell of dead spruce and cedar needles. Whiteface Brook bubbled over the bedrock to the left of the trail. They crossed the brook and passed the Sunrise Notch Trail on their right, which led to High Falls Gorge in what was locally referred to as the *Wilmington Notch*. About two miles from the landing they came upon a lean-to, which Kelly asked Keagan about it.

"That's an Adirondack lean-to. The Conservation Department," here Keagan used the old name for the department, builds them over in Wanakena about seventy miles from here on the western side of the Park, disassembles them, then brings them in by helicopter and reassembles them. Backpackers use the lean-tos for overnight stays, but years ago Adirondack guides built them so the rich could come out and have picnics and maybe even camp overnight. It made the captains of industry and their friends feel as though they were roughing it, despite the stiff attire they wore — especially the ladies — and the hampers of food the guides transported. The guides did all the work, of course, rowing the gentlemen and ladies across the lake in hand-made guide boats made of cedar — beautiful boats, I'll show you one when we get back to the inn — and hauling the baskets of food over land. But the privileged felt adventurous, and that's what was important. Also, they were escaping the stench of the cities that their industries had created.

"It's very quiet here, isn't it, Mick?"

"Tis, that's why I like it."

"Don't you miss the excitement?"

"What excitement would that be? The excitement of bombs exploding on crowded streets or the excitement of executions carried out by the IRA and countered by the UVF or vice versa, no matter?"

"No, I mean the excitement of challenge, the excitement of being able to get to something valuable that powerful and supposedly intelligent people have taken great pains to keep safe."

"You talk as though it is a game, but it isn't. Your motivation is political, not adrenal or egotistical. You want to be a part of something important, and you want to be in charge of it, at least very much near the center of it."

"What do you want, Mick?"

"I want peace, I want to love and be loved. And I want something else, something that is difficult to explain if you have never felt it. I feel it here, in these mountains, but I first felt it when my parents would take me out of Belfast into the Ulster countryside, and later — much more strongly — when I was sailing the Caribbean. There are philosophical and mystical terms for what I feel, but they seem trite, empty, academic, and coldly clinical; and they are trite and coldly clinical because words fail when attempting to define emotions. I've felt it sailing from Puerto Rico to Jamaica; I've felt it climbing between Algonquin and Iroquois in a thunder and lightning storm when I knew I should have turned back, but couldn't. I needed to experience the raw power of nature. I've felt it once having lunch on the shore of a remote pond, in the quiet just before a snowstorm, when I saw a pair of coyotes cross the ice; some primal connection between us brought about by the imminent storm."

"What you are talking about, Mick, is the excitement of flirting with danger."

"No, Kelly, the trip from Puerto Rico to Jamaica was brisk but safe. And it wasn't the snowstorm, but seeing the coyotes in the pre-storm stillness. Even the lightening wasn't about the danger; it was witnessing at a close range its raw power. Once in November, I felt it kayaking across a broad lake. The lake was flat and cold; the air was still; the fixed, western sun bathed the tamaracks in a forge-drop glow. I was alone on the lake, utterly alone. There were no late-season loons, no droning insects, no rising fish. If I stopped paddling, I would have been deaf. There wasn't a siffle of wind. I was the lone movement in a still life. I didn't dare stop for fear I would be subsumed into the stillness. I experienced, if only a little, elemental power on that silent, immutable afternoon. Not my power, but a power I was somehow apart of, in however small a way."

"What you want seems so egocentric, downright selfish even. I suppose I'm part of what you want, 'to love and be loved,' but the rest seems so self-centered. What about your responsibility to your people and their freedom?"

"Perhaps I was even less clear than I thought I was. What I experienced on that silent November afternoon was a peek into an illusion. The stillness of that day mocked our human attempts. It said to me, 'if humans directed nature, here is how life would be, but it isn't often like this is it?' What difference has four-hundred years of struggle made to Northern Ireland? Do you realize that if you had lived all of those four-hundred years and struggled as so many others had, your whole life would be for naught."

"I once found myself stuck on a rock in my kayak while the river roared around me. I paddled as hard as I could, convinced I was stronger than the flow. I couldn't budge the boat, not even an inch. Finally, I understood that my only hope lay in leaning into the river downstream, which I first thought would capsize me, but it didn't. I came off that rock effortlessly and paddled safely through the white water."

"You think we should give up then?"

"Not give up, relent in our stubbornness. The Irish are trapped in circular logic. They react to what the other side does, who in turn counteracts ignoring the four-hundred-year cycle."

"And Ulster?"

"Well, killing them for the last forty years hasn't brought them into the fold. Maybe peace will confuse them."

"This isn't funny, Mick."

"Don't I know it. But how many funerals do there have to be before both sides understand that killing each other hasn't worked? There have to be more peaceful ways. And even if there aren't, is a united Ireland worth it? I know that's a heretical question, but look at our personal tally: I lost both my parents and my uncle David, and you have lost Liam. My father wasn't a militant, although he did support the IRA financially and provided resources and refuge for wanted members. My mother provided them with medical care, but she hated the violence. She was a nurse, who treated Catholic and Protestant alike. Yet that didn't stop the UVF thugs from walking into the pub she and da owned and machine gunning every soul in the place. Then, of course, IRA thugs had to get revenge, so they blew up a Protestant social club, and so on and so on."

"David was killed, not by the Ulsterites, but by the very organization he funded, a more radical faction perhaps, but the same organization. And Liam, Liam's was perhaps the most senseless killing. He was apolitical."

Liam was Kelly's brother. He was a second-year doctoral student in applied physics at Cambridge when he was killed. He was small like Kelly. The family gene pool wasn't very strong. They seemed to be susceptible to tuberculosis and other diseases that modern medicine has greatly curtailed. Kelly and Liam were the exceptions. It was as though all of the negative genes were filtered out before they got to them: Kelly was a dynamo, and Liam was brilliant.

Liam had come home to Belfast because his mother was dying of tuberculosis. He took the ferry from England. Five miles off the Irish coast, the ferry blew up. It seems there was a rumor that Jerry Adams was on board. Liam was one of eighty-seven people who were killed. Jerry Adams wasn't because he was in Boston at the time speaking and collecting contributions.

Kelly's mother died of tuberculosis. Her father died a month later of despair. Keagan came home from Trinity to be with Kelly, but he couldn't reach her through her grief. She became distant and was even more involved with the IRA. They worked together for a while, stealing artwork, mostly in England. They ransomed the art to their owners, turning over the proceeds to the IRA after a small cut.

After a while, Keagan realized that he, too, had become part of the cycle. What he was doing wasn't bringing about peace, just the opposite. It funded more bombs and bullets that dealt more death. Keagan moved to America shortly after his parents were killed.

"If the dead can't convince you, look to the living," said Keagan. "Your loyalty will be your undoing. Look what happened to Niles. Niles was loyal to his duty with the intensity that matched your commitment to the *Cause,* and where did that get him? He let his focus drift from his duty to what he knew to be right, and that lapse damn near got him killed. He'd done years of service in any number of shitholes around the world, cleaning up messes that few men could, let alone would, all at the bidding of the Ministry of Defence.

And how did they reward him for his bravery and his cunning and his commitment? They thanked him for the risks that he took and for his loyalty to them by kicking him out of the service that he loved and then out of England, his native country. Oh, they gave him a promotion, a pension, and even a medal, but they effectively cashiered him out of the unit he loved and out of the nation he served as few could; then they made his name anathema. They cut him loose from everything he loved because his conscience embarrassed the Ministry.

"The grand irony is that he was saved by his enemies. Well, maybe it wasn't so ironic after all; Niles got into trouble by showing his humanity and my father saved him by showing his. Niles' mates and the SAS and England shunned him and two of his enemies. My father and my uncle David got him to America and started him on a new life.

"You are just like Niles was. Your loyalty to the bloody IRA, no pun intended, controls everything you do. You have no life of your own. You are a fay procurer, with no personal indulgences except for your hats."

"Not true! I live well," said Kelly.

"And what part of your total income goes to the IRA?"

"Immaterial, when you consider the gross. But what about you; you scoff at loyalty but look at the collection of misfits you have gathered around you. Did you have to bring Niles here? Did you have to go to Jamaica to find a chef? And what about Teal and that Gimp fellow, and God knows what other gypsies you have gathered around you. They didn't come from the local employment agency; they aren't just employees to you. You don't fool me about cooking breakfast for them on Sundays. They can get drunk on nights other than Saturday. And don't try to pass it off as a good business practice. Those people aren't just employees to you; they're your family."

"Aye, you're right, Kelly. Now place yourself and your commitment to Ireland, where you put me and my inn. What do you see? I'll tell you what you should see: two of us, our families gone, each of them killed, maybe not your mother, but you can't tell me that your father died of a broken heart at her death. Aye, he had a broken heart, but it was broken when Liam was killed. Loosing Mary drained what little was left, just sped up the process. We're the only ones left and the very thing that killed them off keeps us separated. The difference between us is that I've constructed an artificial family – a poor substitute for the one you and I should have — but still they're people, not a cause or an ideology that's lost in its own cycle."

* * *

They had been climbing steadily for about two hours. The trees were now mostly white birch. There had been a fire here about twenty years ago. The birches always came back first. Whiteface Brook had disappeared underground, and the trail was made more difficult by rocks and the exposed roots in the thin soil. They didn't talk for a long time, yet they continued to contend with each other in the way they climbed. Physical exercise had replaced political sparring. Their pace wasn't casual; it was competitive, stopping just short of being absurd.

Then, they were out of the woods and onto the rocks. Keagan stopped and called to Kelly to turn around. There below them lay

Lake Placid — a still, liquid figure eight. They could just make out *Beyond Good and Evil* on the southwest shore.

Keagan put his arm around Kelly's shoulders.

"It's beautiful, Mick," she said as she leaned into him.

Two Peregrine falcons rode thermals below them. Keagan and Kelly scanned the vista before them. Lake Champlain lay forty miles to the east with Vermont and New Hampshire beyond it. To the southeast were the high peaks, and to the west a vast forest dotted with lakes and ponds, seeming to containing little else.

They continued to the top, but there were too many people there for them. Whiteface Mountain is the only one of the high peaks that has a road to the top, so there are always people there this time of year. There's even an elevator from the parking lot up into the bowels of the weather station at the very top of the mountain.

Mick pointed out to Kelly the distant dome of Mount Royal in Montreal — the promontory that gave the city its name — far to the north. They climbed down just out of sight and earshot of the others, where they had a lunch of mango bread, white grapes, and water.

They sat there enjoying the lunch, the view, and each other without talking much. The falcons rose right up in front of them, riding the thermals in natural amusement.

Finally, Kelly spoke, "Well Mick Keagan, what's it going to be? Are you going to help me raise some money?"

"I'm going to have to know how you came by your information. We're in high season here; I just can't take off to pursue a hunch."

"All right, Mick. As you know, crooks and the IRA sometime run in the same circles. Crooks need passports and other official documents, guns, cars, special tools, and expertise and whatnot; we need many of those same things. As a result, we occasionally run into each other. A byproduct of that association is information. We know who stole the art work, and my network has kept reasonably close tabs on them since the theft. They came to Ireland right after the robbery — one to Dublin and the other to Belfast, where one of the brothers almost got *nicked*. He did, in fact, have to rid himself of the two Braques paintings and the Picasso sculpture."

"Also, the IRA has to move money around the world to finance its operations; we have to smuggle guns and supplies into Ireland while smuggling political fugitives out. And as you also know, a good deal of that operation is funded by Irish-Americans. And, of course, America is the destination of a good deal of the world's dope. Frequently the people who smuggle dope for the drug cartels are the same people who smuggle guns, supplies, and fugitives for us. For better or for worse, we move in the same dirty circles, but those dirty circles are a wonderful source for the type of exclusive information that I need, both to fund my projects and to learn what are political enemies are up to."

"That exclusive information has recently included the name of the two men who stole the art, and a very strong suggestion about a person who would like to buy it. We're also pretty sure where the transaction will take place."

"And where would that be?" asked Keagan.

"Florida," Kelly smiled.

"Ah, what a surprise. You've managed to narrow it down to only one of the fifty states. That "sophisticated organization" you mentioned must have had a difficult time ruling out Iowa, Nebraska, North Dakota, and other high crime areas of this grand land. What a surprise that the state they settled on has the longest coastline in the contiguous United States and a tradition in smuggling that goes back to Ponce de Leon."

"It's not as bad as it sounds, Mick."

Keagan looked at his watch. "We need to get started back. I've got to meet with that fellow you saw me talking to last night."

"I need an answer, Mick; I don't want to drop this conversation. Are we a team again?"

Keagan knew what his answer was going to be, but he dreaded making the commitment. He'd known he was going to accept it when Kelly first made the proposal, but he wished he didn't have to.

Keagan needed the money. While he had gotten the inn for a good price, it needed a lot of restoring. What he needed more though, was a seemingly legitimate extra source of income to make the bent-noses look somewhere else for their lost drug money. If he could make another substantial deposit in his Cayman Islands account, maybe those who tried to hack into his account would interpret such a deposit as the proceeds of a continuous source of income rather than a windfall. But the real reason he was going to take on the project was because he wanted to be with Kelly, if only for a little while.

"Give me until tonight. I've the inn to think of, and, as I've said, this is high season," Mick answered and then fell silent again.

They went back down the trail to the kayaks and paddled back to the inn without skinny dipping.

Eighteen

Righteous Richter's hard work and unquestioned acceptance of authority paid off. He had just been promoted and was being transferred to Washington, which had been his career goal. Mormon males are very focused on success, which isn't limited to spiritual success as many religions are. While a Mormon woman's success is measured by her devotion to her church and to her husband, the size of a man's celestial estate — his personal planet — in the afterlife is partly determined by his professional and material success, which of course is reflected in his tithing.

So, when Richter was cleaning up his files and getting ready for his replacement, he came across the James Crawford file. It had been dormant for almost a year now, since Nathan Wallace over at ICE had gotten back to him that they had no record of a James Crawford entering the country from any place in Europe in the two weeks following the *Moderna Museet* theft. If he left it for his replacement to deal with Richter was sure it would never be seen again. Richter remembered a memo he had received at the end of 2005 detailing a new unit that was to be dedicated solely to the investigation and recovery of stolen art. He called Robert Wittman in Philadelphia, foolishly thinking that because he had been the FBI's sole art theft expert that he would head up the new unit.

When Richter finally reached Wittman, he was in limbo on the Gardner Museum case — a theft that had taken place in Boston sixteen years before — bouncing around among Paris, Barcelona, and

Miami. Richter was surprised to learn that Wittman wasn't in charge of the Art Crime Team, and that in fact it was based in Washington, while he was still in Philadelphia.

Wittman knew the sketchy details of the *Moderna Museet* theft, but as he was trying to wrap up the Gardner case before his retirement, he didn't know that the FBI had had a picture — if not an identity — of the only suspect in the case for nearly a year. Wittman was immediately interested as the Gardner case had been moving in fits and starts for six months. Recovering five Picassos wouldn't hurt his credentials for the consulting business he was planning on starting after he retired from the FBI in 2008.

Richter told him that he had tried to follow up when the file landed on his desk, but was unable to track down Crawford with the information that the Swedish National Police and Interpol had provided for him. He told him that he could not find a James Crawford in the NCIC database, and that he had even contacted a friend in ICE who couldn't find any trace of a James Crawford returning to the U.S. from Europe in the two-week period after the robbery. Richter added that of course maybe Scotland Yard hadn't gotten the suspect's real name when they questioned him in *The First Folio Theft*. Maybe James Crawford was the identity he used for his passport

Richter concluded by asking Wittman for a contact in the new Art Crime Team, saying that as he was being transferred to Washington and that he could pass it on to them when he got there. Wittman knew how those things went, so he asked Richter to e-mail the file to him and noted that after he looked at it he'd pass it on; maybe he'd even recognize the suspect in the photo from one of his earlier cases. Richter assured him that he would as soon as he got off the phone, thinking that doing so would shorten his cleanup list by one.

***

Wittman didn't recognize the photo of James Campbell, but when he saw what Eimear Lynch had discovered in Greg Campbell's luggage in the Fitzwilliam Hotel, he remembered Richter's comment about using an alias on his passport. Fortunately for the Campbells, but unfortunately for both the *Moderna Museet* and Wittman, Dalin's speculation about Eimear Lynch's comment about a resemblance between the photo of James Campbell and the appearance of Greg Campbell never made it into the file and therefore never made it to Lampa, who of course couldn't then pass it on to the FBI, and ultimately for all his diligence and righteousness, Richter couldn't pass it on to Wittman — such are the caprices of investigation.

After he filled in some of the details of the case talking first to Chief Inspector Conor Moran, then to Superintendent Hilmar Lampa, and finally to Police Intendent Gandalf Dalin, what he learned about the case intrigued him even more. He found Dalin to be the most forthcoming and was especially drawn to his confession that it took him and his partner — working on their own time — a little over a month to learn how the thieves had entered the museum. Most museum thefts were either inside jobs or *smash and grab* affairs. Wittman found the Campbell's planning and execution refreshing.

He knew he couldn't keep the case, though. In spite of having founded the Art Crime Team, its supervision had been commandeered from him, ironically by someone with little art-theft experience.

Wittman called the head of the Art Crime Team in Washington and reported what Richter had told him about the case. The head of the team told him to e-mail the file to him immediately. The two men didn't like each other, but their feud had been somewhat contained by Headquarters in Washington who had intervened in an earlier case in order to salvage the operation.

Nineteen

Contrary to popular opinion, not all major South American drug traffickers have homes in Miami. At least one, Alardo Quillaca Cavelya, spent most of his time in the States at his compound on North Captiva Island, not the Captiva that is linked to Sanibel Island via a short bridge over Blind Pass, but rather the island just to north of it. The three islands — Sanibel, Captiva, and North Captiva (officially referred to as Upper Captiva except on nautical charts) — were, prior to the hurricane of 1921, one island.

Before World War II, hurricanes weren't officially named; instead, they were referred to by the year they struck or a combination of the year and the place where they hit. In 1941, the Weather Service began labeling them using women's names. Briefly the naming policy was changed to the military phonetic alphabet – Able, Baker, Charlie . . . Zebra. However, after a few years the Weather Service returned to using women's names for the storms. Then in 1978, in an early move to be more politically correct, the Weather Service began the foolishness of gender equity in hurricane naming.

Political correctness notwithstanding, the *Hurricane of 1921* created Blind Pass that now separates Sanibel from Captiva, and Redfish Pass that separates Captiva from North Captiva. Blind Pass is still spanned by a short bridge, but there is no such land link to North Captiva; consequently, what the few people who live there pay for, other than white sand, blue-green water, and peach-glow sunsets, is privacy; and the few who live there pay a great deal of money and inconvenience for it. While there are about two hundred and fifty homes on the island, only sixty or so people are what might be considered full-time residents. The year-round residents are a varied lot that have only two things in common — money and an inordinate need for seclusion. The rest usually rent their places out and only visit for short stints, which was fine with Alardo Quillaca Cavelya. He liked the idea of a short-staying, rotating population. He also liked the idea of living among fifty-nine other residents who had a deep regard for privacy.

North Captiva was actually Cavelya's second choice for his compound. His first was on Cayo Costa, the next island to the north. About ninety percent of Cayo Costa is owned by the State of Florida, and the idea that Florida was protecting the privacy of one of the biggest traffickers of Bolivian cocaine appealed to his twisted sense of humor. He finally settled upon North Captiva, though, because it had its own air strip. It was a grass strip and could accommodated aircrafts up to twin-engine lights. Cavelya kept a single engine turbo-prop there, which had a top speed of 322 ktas (knots, true air speed), a range of 1,300 nm (nautical miles [approximately 1,500 miles]), and an engine roar that told the island population — transient or permanent — that the Bolivian Red Baron was coming or going. The location was ideal: Cavelya could be in the air within fifteen minutes of hearing the DEA. Accordingly, he kept ample funds at the compound for just such a contingency. After all, when you live on an island, random theft is exceptionally rare.

Alardo Quillaca Cavelya ran his drug empire from North Captiva Island electronically. When he had to leave the island occasionally, he had his captain, who was also the pilot of Cavelya's turbo-prop, fly him to Fort Myers, Tampa, or Miami where he rotated the berthing of his Leer Jet. His wife preferred the company of the other South American drug traffickers' wives who favored Miami. Since she was at an age where the embers of her passion and her fiery beauty had banked, Alardo was content to maintain a high-rise apartment for her there, which he only occasionally visited. When he sought entertainment or companionship, he either brought it to him or motored around the coast where more sociable people gathered.

Alardo Quillaca Cavelya was unlike many of his business associates. He was just as cruel as they, and perhaps even more egocentric, but he thought of himself as a man of discriminating tastes, especially in art. He loved fine art, not for showing off, but for delighting himself. Cavelya believed that exquisite art was wasted on the masses that filed through museums and equally wasted on those dilettantes who wanted to use it in some meretricious display of their vanity. He felt that great art should belong to those who were as great as the art itself (himself for instance) and so when he heard of the theft of the Picassos and the Braques, he had to have them. When the Campbells put out discreet feelers for buyers on the Internet, Cavelya's was the highest bid.

***

Cavelya was very animated. He had motored up to Gasparilla Island to have dinner there with some business associates, distribution men mostly, and one financial analyst. They had a private dining room at the Gasparilla Inn. The food was excellent, a kind of bouillabaisse of Gulf shrimp, oysters, and scallops accented by crisp Moselles. Despite what his associates believed, neither the food the wine, nor the company, was the source of Cavelya's animation. He was ecstatic because he had timed the dinner to coincide with receiving his final instructions for meeting with the Campbells. He wanted to receive the call at a public place rather than at his compound, because the Campbells were not familiar with the sanitized language of drug transactions, and he didn't want to have to worry about the vagaries of telecommunication. The call was scheduled for nine o'clock. At 8:45 Cavelya sent two of his men to the switchboard off the front desk to be in position when the call came in. They made the manager very nervous.

The call came in at exactly 9:00. Professionals are always precise. When the call came in, one of Cavelya's men told the manager to go out on the porch and have a cigarette. The manager replied foolishly that he didn't smoke.

"Take it up," the *bullet-head* said and threw him a pack of Virginia Slims. Cavelya took the call in the manager's office.

"Do you know where Apalachicola is?" James asked.

Cavelya knew where Pensacola was, so he reasoned that Apalachicola might also be in Florida. "Is that in Florida?" responded Cavelya.

"Yes, it's in Florida," James replied, trying to hide his contempt of someone who had the wherewithal to afford rare art, but who had little knowledge of his surroundings. "It's on the Panhandle."

"I'll find it," Cavelya said, vowing to teach the thief some manners, specifically the proper etiquette of dining with sharks.

"Good, you have a reservation at the Gibson Inn next Friday. I assume you'll be bringing friends. If you wish multiple rooms, I suggest you call ahead to reserve whatever extra rooms you need. We'll need a couple of days to arrange the transfer, so plan on staying through the weekend. How will you be arriving?"

"I'll be motoring up on my yacht," answered Cavelya.

"Excellent. Dock at Benson's Marina on St. George Island, just south and east of town. I'll arrange to have a car there, reserved under your name. I'll call you at the Gibson at six o'clock on Friday night."

"The paintings, are you taking good care of them? You are not letting the salt air ruin them, are you?"

"There are only the five Picassos now. We had to leave the Braques and the Picasso sculpture behind, but the five are very well cared for," replied James Campbell.

"What happened to the others?" asked Cavelya.

"Unavoidable, just a fluke, but it was either leave those behind or lose them all."

"Then you made the right decision," said Cavelya, only a little disappointed. "I'll see you in Apalachicola."

The *bullet-head* reclaimed his Virginia Slims; the manager took up his position once again behind the front desk. Cavelya rejoined his associates for obligatory cigars and cognac. He could barely contain himself. His associates thought they had outdone themselves entertaining him tonight with their financial statements and risqué stories.

Twenty

When Keagan and Kelly got back to the inn, Samwise greeted Keagan the way she always greeted him after an extended absence, by following the wagging stub of her tail in circles, smiling as if the ecstasy of the Almighty were upon her, and whining as though Mick were a perfidious master who never took her on hikes. Truth be told, Samwise was as loyal as Niles, but nowhere near as conditioned. If Keagan ever invited her on one of his climbs, she might have plugged on, but would want to turn back in the first mile.

Manny Di Ladro was seated at a table in the bar working on a martini when Keagan and Kelly came in after having placated Samwise who finally curled up on the porch. Di Ladro did not follow the stub of his tail in circles nor did he exude the ecstasy foretold by the prophets; instead, he fawned.

"Mick, how are you? Bring your lovely lady over so I can meet her."

"Is that the fellow you met with last night after dinner?" Kelly asked.

"Tis he."

"I'm charmed."

"Mick, let me buy you and your lady friend a drink."

"It's not necessary, Mr. Di Ladro, I own the place."

"Manny, call me Manny."

"*Barkeep*, give these folks whatever they want."

Niles internally bristled at *barkeep,* but smiled nonetheless. "What can I get you Kelly, Mick?"

"A very large gin and tonic with lime, and not like you Brits make it. I want lots of ice," Kelly teased Niles.

"I'll have a Budweiser, Niles," said Keagan.

Keagan and Kelly walked over to the table.

"Manny, this is Kelly O'Neill. Kelly, this is Manny Di Ladro, an insurance investigator from New Jersey."

"Kelly O'Neill, nice ring to it," said Di Ladro, his eyes and imagination feeling her up.

Di Ladro's imagination had crossed Keagan's line. He was about to tell him he wouldn't guide him to the men's room let alone the crash site, and would instead break his jaw. Kelly knew what Di Ladro had been doing and she was used to it to a degree, but she also sensed what Keagan had in mind, so she put her hand on his arm as if to say, *I'll handle this, Mick.*

"Yes, Mr. Di Ladro, but one of rich historical significance. Names are like that, though they are often significant. Don't you think, Mr. *Di Ladro?*"

Di Ladro tried to think of some response, but he couldn't. He tried to change the subject, but Kelly cut him off.

"I would shake hands, Mr. Di Ladro, but I've been in the back of the beyond all day, and I'm badly in need of a scrubbing. Niles, can you send another just like this up to the cabin in about a half hour? Mick, I'm going to take a bath, will you be long?"

This time it was Niles who cut in, "Mick, I've got a couple of messages for you that might take a bit to answer."

Mick glanced at the messages to see who sent them and then told Kelly that responding to them and dealing with Di Ladro would take an hour or a little more. He insisted that she should take her bath and maybe get in a nap before dinner. He'd be up as soon as he could.

Niles got Mick a Budweiser and gave him the two messages. Keagan scanned the messages. One was a New Jersey phone number, the other a notice of a package that had arrived and had been placed upstairs in his private office. Keagan placed the messages in his pocket and went back to the table where Di Ladro was sitting.

"I have a few business calls to return; they shouldn't take long. If you don't mind waiting, I'll be back shortly."

"Take your time, Mick; I'll be here when you get back."

Keagan went up to his office and dialed the Jersey number. On the third ring the phone was answered, "McGreevy's."

"Sean there? It's Mick Keagan."

"Just a minute."

Keagan could hear a raucous crowd and a Red Sox game on in the background.

"Sean here. That you, Mick?"

"Yes, Sean. What do you have for me?"

"Di Ladro appears clean if not squeaky. He is Fidelity Mutual's chief adjuster. They did underwrite the insurance on the plane that he is investigating. He does live in Montvale, New Jersey in an expensive house, but one he can well afford. He doesn't seem to have any vices. He drinks but less than a publican, plays the ponies, but not excessively so, and doesn't seem to have any romantic activities on the side. At first glance, he is what he appears to be."

"At first glance?"

"I need to go back a bit. Di Ladro started out as an insurance agent in a small town in central New York. He didn't have much money, so he pocketed a percentage of the premiums, playing the actuary tables that those clients would never have a claim. He got away with it for a while too, even made a good deal of money, but he got greedy and took bigger risks. A munitions plant he underwrote in Massachusetts blew up, and he couldn't cover it. He appealed to his wife's family for help. A *connected* brother-in-law, who himself was in the insurance business, solved the problem. He queered the insurance company's computer to show two premium payments and produced a policy. The munitions manufacturer was happy because he got paid; Di Ladro was happy because he didn't do time; the brother-in-law was happy because he made his sister happy and he bought

Di Ladro's loyalty; even the insurance company's executives were happy because they got to keep their families."

"Sean, where the hell did you get all this information?"

"First hand, Mick, we blew up the plant. The blackguards wouldn't sell us munitions."

When Keagan stopped laughing, he thanked Sean for the information and hung up. Next he opened the small overnight package that was sent from Miami. In the mailer there was a CD. He turned on his computer and put it in the D drive. He clicked the computer button, chose Drive D,double clicked the sole file listed, and loaded up the file that Mr. Treylawne had sent him. The file contained a brief message:

July 18, 2007

Dear Mr. Keagan:
Enclosed, please find a phone number. The
person who tried to access our computer managed
to suppress his user identification and tried to
do the same with the phone line from which he
was gaining access. My systems analyst tells me
that our software is sophisticated enough so that
he could not scramble the phone number. It is the
main number at the Fidelity Mutual Insurance Company
in Montvale, New Jersey. Point, counterpoint.
I trust this information serves your purposes.
If I can be of additional help, do not
hesitate to call upon me.

Sincerely,
Bascombe Treylawne

Keagan went back down to the bar, got another Budweiser from Niles, and then re-joined Di Ladro at his table.

"You should have let me buy you a drink," said Di Ladro as Keagan sat down at the table with him. "I know you own the place, but I can still buy a drink, can't I?"

"You can get the next one, Manny."

"Wonderful. Now about guiding me to the wreckage? Are we on for tomorrow? I really need to see that site."

Keagan had made up his mind that shaking this guy might be a mistake, and what he had just learned confirmed his earlier opinion. He said, "yes, meet me down here at 8:00 AM. You'll need comfortable walking shoes — light hiking boots or running shoes — loose trousers, and a shell in case it rains. I'll provide food and drink."

**

Keagan and Kelly were seated at his table in the dining room. They had finished eating and sat silently finishing the last of a bottle of Château Margaux. Mick broke the silence, knowing Kelly would have let it go on for eternity.

"What's the plan?"

"Does that mean that you are going to help?" Kelly asked.

"I have to know more before I commit. Where are the paintings? How secure are they? What resources do we need? How long will we be gone? Remember I have an inn to run."

"Let me address your first question."

"*Address?*"

"Yes, address."

"Why don't you just *answer* it instead? You said earlier that the paintings were in Florida?"

"Probably in Florida or headed that way at least. We don't know for sure. I don't think there is any doubt they are in southeast Georgia or Florida, but we haven't been able to pinpoint the location yet."

"You've managed to narrow it down to one of the five major regions of the nation. How wonderful. The rest should be coffee and cream. Do you realize that the whole of Ireland isn't half the size of one of those states? If, in fact, the paintings are in either."

"It's not as bleak as you make out, Mick. We know the Campbells arrived in Atlanta on July 15th."

"If I'm not mistaken, Atlanta is the busiest airport in the world. If I'm wrong it's the second busiest; Heathrow by comparison serves a million less passengers a year. They could be in Montana or Maine or Arizona. What makes you think they are in the Southeast?"

"Because we've traced their rental car to Jacksonville, Florida."

"Jacksonville? You mean the port city of Jacksonville that, with the exception of Savannah, is the largest port south of New York? Is that the Jacksonville you mean? They're probably in Colombia by now."

"That's what it looks like, doesn't it?"

"Sure does," Keagan answered.

"Then why fly to Atlanta, drive to Jacksonville, and sail to South America? Why not just fly to South America, either from Washington or from Miami? The car rental is a stalking horse. So is Atlanta, other than the fact that it is near where they are going to sell the paintings."

Keagan took a sip of wine and replayed Kelly's logic. He wouldn't buy it from someone else, but Kelly was smart and she knew her business. That she was still alive attested to her understanding of complex situations.

"Okay, since you can't answer my first question, I'll assume you can't answer the others either. How do you plan to proceed?"

"Actually, I can answer one of your questions, but let me hold off for a while. I think we should fly to Atlanta, and talk to the car rental people. Maybe rent a car from them to show our appreciation for the information and go for a drive to Florida."

"Jacksonville?"

"Precisely."

"How do you know the car rental people will be able to give us information?"

"People always give you information, Mick, if you know how to ask them."

"Yes, I can see why you would think so."

"Then, you are in?"

Keagan raised his eyes from the glass he been rotating with his thumb and forefinger and sighed, "Yes, I'll give it a go."

"Wonderful," Kelly said, lighting up. "Now, as for resources I'll cover our expenses. We'll need weapons — at least I will — government identification, and Niles."

"Niles?"

"Yes. The way I see it, we need a third party to do some scouting. Niles will do nicely."

"And what about my inn? Who's going to run it?"

"Oh, you've all sorts of people to run your inn. You have that Gimp fellow, and you've told me how good Cassie is. And Teal can fix anything, remember? No, not Teal we might need him, too. He intrigues me."

***

The bar had cleaned out; Sunday was always an early night, even in high season. Keagan, Kelly, Jimmy the Gimp, Cassie, Teal, and Anjali sat at the bar; Niles stood behind it.

"I need to be away from the inn for a week or so, and I need to take Niles with me, if he is willing," Mick began.

Niles looked at Keagan and nodded slightly. The others didn't know where Keagan and Niles were headed, but they knew they weren't off to a hotelier's convention.

"It's important to me that the inn functions in top form in my absence. In fact, if there is any doubt about the service suffering while we are away, we won't go."

"Jimmy, I know you've got the dining room under control, but can you oversee reservations and housekeeping as well?"

"I won't need to do much, Mick," Jimmy replied. "We've got good people there. All I'll have to do is check in daily to make sure an emergency doesn't develop."

Cassie turned her attention from Keagan to Jimmy the Gimp; she didn't say anything, but the down tilt of her head indicated her surprise at the Bigot supporting others.

"Cassie, how's the larder? Any problems with provisions?"

"No, Mr. Keagan. I don't have any back orders. We're right as rain."

"Niles, can you get Tippler to fill in?"

"Who's Tippler, Mick?" asked Kelly, her interest piqued by the unusual name.

"A distant cousin of yours, Kelly" answered Keagan. "Tippler O'Neill."

"*Tippler O'Neill*?" inquired Kelly. "This place gets more lunatic by the sentence. Who is Tippler?"

Niles answered her. "He is a local who has a bit of a drinking problem."

"And you want him to fill in for you, Niles, while you are gone? Is that what I'm hearing? You want a sot to bartend here at the inn? Is that part of the charm and fabric of *Beyond Good and Evil*?"

"Tippler isn't a sot, Kelly. He just has a drinking problem. He never lets it interfere with his work. If I find him tonight deep in his drams and tell him I want him to open up for me tomorrow, he'll be sober as a Jehovah's Witness and not nearly as annoying when he shows up fifteen minutes early. Myself excluded, of course, he is the best bartender in town. He just doesn't work steady."

"I see," said Kelly. "This really is a fascinating hamlet in which you've chosen to ensconce yourself, Mick."

"Cassie, Anjali, Jimmy will you excuse us; Kelly and I need to talk with Niles and Teal."

Anjali eyed her father silently.

"Mick, you mind if I grab a beer?" asked the Gimp.

"No, help yourself, Jimmy."

"Ladies, can I get you a soft drink?" asked the Gimp.

Cassie eyed him with suspicion, again. "Two Tings; Anjali likes it, too," Cassie answered in disbelief.

The Gimp paid Niles for the drinks. Staff could drink after work and paid discounted prices, but they had to pay. On working nights, they couldn't sit in the bar. The Gimp and Teal were exceptions to that rule.

"Cassie, will you take Anjali to your cabin. I'll come up and get her when we are done. I won't be long," said Teal, looking to Keagan for assurance.

"No, not long, perhaps a half an hour," said Keagan.

When they had gone, Niles made them drinks. Before Kelly could explain the situation, Keagan said, "Teal, I've never asked you about your past and I'm not asking now, but I think you need to be filled in a bit about Kelly's and my background."

"We've known each other since we were kids growing up in Belfast, Northern Ireland during a period euphemistically known as *The Troubles*. We did some work for the IRA, the Irish Republican Army."

"Weren't they terrorists?" asked Teal.

"Perhaps," said Keagan, "in the same way the French Resistance members during World War II were terrorists. If you asked the Germans — they were; the French held a different opinion. Anyway, we raised money for the IRA, and we did that by stealing works of art and ransoming them to their English owners. I guess we were pretty good at it because we never got caught and we raised buckets of money for the IRA."

Teal looked at Niles. Niles nodded and said, "They were very good; otherwise, I would have caught them. Might still have if I had more time. Might have been King of England too, but I doubt it."

"Let's just say, Teal, that neither Niles nor Kelly nor I would have laid long odds on it. We'll never know because I quit for reasons you don't need to know. But Kelly kept working for them, also for reasons you don't need to know. Now, Kelly has a new wrinkle on our old jobs — one where all the net proceeds come from gathering information and not from buying arms and munitions. She can guarantee that because she'll control the money. Kelly wants me to join her again and thinks she has a part for Niles and maybe for you as well."

"I want to be clear about what we're about to get into: we're going to try to recover five stolen paintings — Picassos to be precise. What we'll be doing isn't illegal since we're going to turn the paintings over to the insurance company for a reward. Not illegal, but it is dangerous. While cat burglars aren't usually violent criminals, these paintings are worth millions. Hard to give something like that up without a fight. The real danger will likely be from the buyer. People who are willing to buy stolen art and who can afford to pay even the black-market discounted price for such works of art usually are violent, and frequently are drug traffickers, arms dealers, and other assorted rapacious sociopaths. That being said, I know you have to think of Anjali."

Teal cocked his head at *drug traffickers*.

"On the positive side, Kelly, Niles, and I are all professionals in these kinds of projects. Also, if we are successful, we all stand to make a great deal of money for a week or two's work."

"If you're not interested, you can just say *no* right now and walk away from the offer. If you think you might be interested, I'll need to know the status of the maintenance work. I can't have things fall apart here. Niles has Tippler for a backup, but so far I don't have anyone to cover for you."

"Everything's in order, Mick, the dock project needs to wait until the season slows down, but everything else is pretty much on target. The Uruguayan can handle most of the daily stuff. I can make a list of people to call if an emergency occurs and give 'em a heads-up before we leave. They'll be happy to get on our list."

"You have a Uruguayan?" asked Kelly. "What's his story?"

"Don't ask," said Keagan.

"I'm interested, Mick, but I'll have to think about it and talk to Anjali before I can give you an answer, and of course I'd have to make sure Cassie can take care of Anjali while I'm gone. Can I have a day or two to get back to you?"

Keagan looked at Kelly. She nodded.

"OK, then. I'll let Kelly fill you in on the specifics."

***

Kelly gave Niles and Teal the background on the museum burglary in Sweden and what she had learned about the thieves and their suspected buyer. "I believe the paintings are in either coastal Georgia or Florida, awaiting sale. Ideally, I'd like to intercept them before the sale so that we only have to deal with the thieves, who aren't traditionally violent criminals, as Mick pointed out; however, buyers in this market are. Atlanta is where I think we should start. We know that the Campbells — they're the cat burglars — arrived there and I think it is safe to conclude that the paintings are with them or where they can get at them quickly. Mick and I will begin there. We'll assume some sort of official role, DEA perhaps; however, we'll need at least one of you to do some less official checking."

"That explains Niles, but where do I come in," interjected Teal.

"I'm not sure I can give you a clear answer, Teal; I understand from Mick that you can fix anything, and that you also have other unusual skills, such as rock climbing and spelunking, and that while you served in the Air Force, you dismantled bombs; can I assume from that bit of your *curricula vitae* that you also know how to make them?"

"Sure. Making them is a lot easier," grinned Teal.

"Some time ago a wise person told me if you wanted to be successful, and successful in my line of work means staying alive and out of prison, you should surround yourself with talented people. Eventually, you'll figure out what to do with their talent. Your particular set of skills may come in handy for us, although at this point I have no idea how," said Kelly.

"Who might that wise person be?" asked Niles.

"Why you old rogue, you know very well who said that. You were there. It was Mick."

"Thank you for the adulation, but before we continue," Mick interrupted, "Teal needs to know what's involved. He's not like us; he has Anjali to think of."

"You're right, Mick," said Kelly.

"Teal, seven paintings and one sculpture were stolen from the museum in Sweden; the sculpture and two of the paintings have been recovered at a golf club in Belfast, Ireland. The original value of the seven paintings and the one sculpture was set as $60 million. That figure is somewhat lower now, but the remaining five paintings were the most valuable, so I'd guess that their legal-market value is about $45 million or a tad more. Of course, we'd only reap a percentage of that. Still, it's a lot of money. The people who stole them are professionals. Thieves who steal at this level are usually more cunning than dangerous; nonetheless, they do have a lot to protect. If we can't snatch them before the sale, the real danger will come from whoever purchases the paintings. The suspected purchaser at this point is a Señor Cavelya who is reputed to control forty percent of all the coca that is grown in Bolivia and moved to Columbia to be turned into cocaine that's sent to America." Teal's attention sharpened at that snippet of Cavelya's bio.

"Even if he isn't the purchaser, whoever can afford these paintings probably didn't make his money the old fashion way. He's almost certainly involved in a big-profit illegality. At best, he's an oil sheik. These people are used to getting what they want; that we might stand in their way would be of little consequence to them. So, while the rewards are great, so too may be the risks."

"Kelly, what would be my cut?" asked Teal.

"Nothing if we don't recover them, and nothing if you get killed trying. However, in a more positive vein, if we are successful and recover all five of the paintings, the insurance company will pay a fifteen percent reward of the insured value or roughly six and three-quarter million dollars. Since I brought the project to you, and I will pay all expenses, I get half of the net. Mick has told me that he would then split the other half equally. So, roughly a bit over a million apiece," said Kelly.

Teal smiled.

"Teal, be sure you understand that you could end up dead broke, and I mean that as two separate conditions," cautioned Keagan.

"Mick, people who have never de-activated a bomb usually think those who have are crazy or have a death wish, but the process is a lot like life; it's a chance. Those who take wild chances — free-form climbers, drug dealers, tourists who stray outside Vieux Carré — usually don't live very long. Those who take no risks don't prosper much either, dying of boredom and worse. This is a chance for me to provide for Anjali's future. If Anjali agrees, you can count me in. I'll let you know tomorrow night for sure."

"Good. Niles?"

Niles nodded his reiteration.

"We have a team then," said Kelly. "The plan will evolve according to what we learn in Atlanta. We'll need identification. Mick and I will need the usual, plus some official credentials. Niles and Teal will need drivers' licenses and credit cards. We better keep our identities regional. Mick, Niles, and I should be from Boston, so we don't have to explain our accents. The cover isn't perfect for Niles, but Boston is probably a better choice than Miami. Teal should be from south Louisiana. I'm assuming you're Cajun."

Teal nodded, warily.

"Write down some names and addresses you're fond of and will remember easily. I'll take care of the documents. I'll also make the flight arrangements. Let's plan to leave Wednesday; that should give me enough time to have the documents sent to us. Is that alright, Mick?"

They all agreed Wednesday would be fine.

"Mick and Niles, I'm assuming you still have your weapons."

They both nodded. Mick's favorite was a .357 Sig Sauer model P-239, but ammunition for the weapon was limited because the majority of people who buy the gun prefer the .40 ACP option instead; so, he chose his second favorite, a 9mm Sig Sauer model P-226 with a Bar-Sto barrel. The gun had a double stack magazine that held fifteen rounds with one extra in the chamber. With a rest, the gun was deadly accurate to fifty yards. For backup he carried a .380 Sig Sauer model P-232, for which he had a Lacôn silencer.

Kelly also carried a .380, but preferred the Walther PPK (German abbreviation: *short police pistol*). Mick liked the gun, and in fact had carried one earlier during his fund-raising days, but to carry it safely you had to engage the safety lever, which of course had to be disengaged before firing. Sigs didn't have an external safety; they had a decocking lever. So if you wanted to carry a round in the chamber, the only useful way to carry a defense weapon if it's a semi-automatic after seating a round in the chamber, is to lower the hammer with a decocking lever that would engage an internal safety, which the trigger would disengage. Sigs can be carried safely fully loaded, as long as the hammer is down. While the SAS used PPKs and also various H&K models, Niles was a purest; he preferred revolvers. He did carry an H&K 200SK as a backup because it held fourteen rounds, but he favored the S&W Model 19, the *Combat Masterpiece*, .357 Magnum, with a four inch barrel.

"Teal, what about you? What do you want me to get for you?"

"No, that's all right; I have an accurized .45 Gold Cup I won at Camp Perry while I was in the Air Force," Teal smiled.

They all three quizzically looked at him, evaluating yet another surprise.

***

The following morning, Keagan took Di Ladro to the plane crash site. They drove in as far as possible, about two miles past the end of the pavement on the Averyville Lane, and then walked the four miles into Wanika Falls, where they began to climb. By Keagan's estimate, it took almost twice as long as it should have to get there. Di Ladro was as out of shape as Keagan had guessed he would be.

Keagan found the site easily. Of course, he knew the way, but the trail from the brook that the rescue team had cut made the final approach much easier, especially without the snow. The plane was a shell. Both engines had been removed as had all the instruments; even the seats were gone.

Di Ladro walked around the plane pretending to get a feel for the site, but he was watching Keagan all the time, looking for some reaction. Keagan didn't give him any.

"How far are we from the top of the mountain?" asked Di Ladro.

"Not far, maybe four hundred vertical feet." Keagan pulled out his GPS that he carried on his belt and waited for it to access its satellites. "Yeah, just about four hundred vertical feet."

"Is this the tallest mountain in the area?"

"No, Mr. Di Ladro. By high-peak standards, it's one of the lowest," Keagan responded.

"Why would they be flying so low?"

"I don't know," said Keagan, "especially since the flyway is further south. Perhaps they were off course." He mentioned nothing about the snow storm. Di Ladro weighed Keagan's answers.

"What do you think is the likelihood of someone finding the plane before the search party?" asked Di Ladro.

"I have no idea, but look at this site. Remember that trail from the falls wasn't here then and in winter the brook would be all ice, not terribly inviting."

"What do you think is the likelihood that someone found the plane between when the search was called off and before that pilot saw it from the air, five months after the crash?" asked Di Ladro.

"Again, I have no idea. I don't even know how long the search went on, but look around you. Look how thick the growth is. I'll bet I could walk fifty feet in a straight line from here and you'd never be able to find me."

Di Ladro eyed Keagan cautiously. "You're not going to do that are you?"

"No, Manny," Keagan used his given name to emphasize how dependent Di Ladro was on him at this moment. "You haven't paid me for guiding you here yet, and then there's the matter of your bill at the inn. Nah, you're safe for now."

"OK, Mick, but how come you were able to find the spot? I know you didn't own the inn back then."

"I knew where to look. I checked it out on the Internet, got the general location, and called the DEC this morning for more precise directions. Let me turn your questions back to you. What do you think is the likelihood of someone stumbling upon this site? Not that many people that come in here on the trail to Wanika Falls. Notice we haven't come across any other hikers. The trail is the tail end or the beginning – depending on which way you're headed — of a 130-mile trail through the Adirondacks. Factor in that this mountain is probably the least climbed of all the high peaks, and that virtually nobody climbs it from this side. The other side doesn't have a trail either, but over the years hikers and hunters have formed herd paths, and the deer and bears use them too, keeping the paths defined. Find the right one and climbing to the top is tolerable; miss it and you'll wander around all day, maybe longer. The only people who climb this mountain are people who want to be 46[ers], and virtually all of them climb it from the other side."

"And yet somebody found it because the diamonds are missing."

"I guess I can't argue that. Maybe an earlier private plane spotted it, marked the coordinates, and came back on snowshoes, or maybe they never had the diamonds."

"What do you mean *never had the diamonds*?"

"I'm just speculating. You've got a limited number of choices: they didn't have them for whatever reason, or somebody got here before the authorities. There must have been some attempts made to find the plane soon after it disappeared. You would know that better than I do. Maybe an early search party found it and kept quiet about it."

"Nah, not one of those people has changed their lifestyle since. We are looking for someone who has changed, someone who now has things they didn't have before like cars, houses, businesses." Di Ladro looked at Keagan.

"Well I'm afraid I can't help you. I didn't move here until more than a year after the crash, so I wouldn't know whose life style has changed. Maybe whoever got them is just patient." Keagan didn't offer that the whole area was aswarm with local fortune hunters. Di

Ladro would know that too, but if Keagan knew it, then maybe he was here also.

The deer flies and mosquitoes were eating both of them up, so Keagan suggested they leave. Di Ladro's legs weren't any more nimble on the way out, but his tongue was.

"Mick, what did you do before you were an innkeeper?"

"Believe it or not I taught English in a private school in Boston."

"How does an English teacher afford a place like *Beyond Good and Evil*?" asked Di Ladro.

"Are you checking into my lifestyle, Manny?"

"Nah, I'm just curious, that's all."

"Sure you are. Well, truth be told, I had an uncle in Boston who owned a very successful bar and restaurant. The career change wasn't that dramatic. He died, and I inherited his money."

"How come you moved your operation up here Mick, if the place was so successful?"

Keagan knew Di Ladro knew the answer, so he explained about David's connection with the IRA and his troubles with the IRS.

"The IRS didn't get everything. My uncle was resourceful, and he made sure I was taken care of. I was his only relative. Strange when you consider that the Irish usually have six kids or more. He set up an off-shore account for me, and shortly after he died I bought the inn."

"How do you know I'm not an IRS investigator?" asked Mick.

"I know because I checked you out. You are what your business card says you are, the Chief Claims Adjustor for Fidelity Mutual working out of Montvale, New Jersey. You are not the only one with connections, Mr. Di Ladro."

"Manny, Mick. Call me Manny."

Twenty-One

Apalachicola is a little less than three hundred nautical miles from North Captiva. Alardo Quillaca Cavelya ordered his boat, *Blanca Nieve*, to be ready to leave early on Thursday morning. He could have flown, but Apalachicola had a municipal airport that would have left a log entry at the airport, and while there were three or four airports within an hour's drive of Apalachicola, there were dozens of marinas and mooring spots for boats and also a small gratuity for the dock master that would erase any memory or record that Blanca Nieve had ever been there. He could have driven, but Apalachicola was not near an interstate. It's one of those you-can't-get-there-from-here places. He could have taken the blue highways, but Cavelya was much too impatient to sit in the confined space of a car for the six or seven hours the trip would have taken. Cavelya preferred the easy comfort of his 54' Bertram. He could fish, he could shoot skeet, and he could keep in contact with his distributors. The Gulf was calm and the weather forecast for the next several days was good and, best of all, there were few curious eyes in the Gulf of Mexico. The Coast Guard was there, but mostly to rescue stranded boaters and to intercept night-running boats without lights.

Airports had security personnel who asked questions, and police and DEA agents who were interested in private citizens with planes. Florida's highways were teaming with state police, DEA agents, and cracker deputy sheriffs who took liberties with people they've pulled over for illegal lane changes and drug possession. But on the Gulf, the Coast Guard didn't pull boats over for an improper lane change.

Scheduled to travel with Cavelya were his captain, female companion, and three bodyguards. The captain, John Enright, had graduated from Emory University in Atlanta, where he had also gotten his pilot's license. He was a south Florida native, the son of a shrimper. He loved the Gulf and he loved boats even more than he loved planes, but he was not so quixotic as to believe that he could make a living on the Gulf as his father had. He knew he would need a different kind of boat and that such a boat would cost much more than he could make shrimping. So he signed on with Cavelya with the idea to save enough money in five years in order to make a substantial down payment on a boat he could then charter out. He had been with Cavelya for almost three years now, past the halfway mark. Cavelya paid well and did not require Enright to be directly involved with his drug business. There were, however, two drawbacks to the job as Enright saw it: he could be unemployed without notice because some competitor had removed Cavelya from his business and this world, or he could be blown to bits if a competitor decided to take out his employer aboard the *Blanca Nieve* or aboard *Copo-de-Nieve*, which was what Cavelya named his turbo-prop. The man had a limited imagination.

Like Cavelya, the female companion and the bodyguards were also Bolivian. They were predictable for their roles: the companion was young, lithe, and bosomy; the bodyguards mesomorphic, sullen, and stupid. Enright thought of the bodyguards as the *Three Stooges*, but since among their other attributes they were also very dangerous, he was careful to keep that appellation to himself. Fortunately, he didn't have to deal with them much.

North Captiva didn't appeal much to the woman or to the bodyguards. They preferred the excitement of Miami, but they knew a good thing when they saw it, so the men had to be satisfied with terrorizing the tourists at Barnacle Phil's. The woman was not nearly as fortunate, for Cavelya did not keep her overly occupied; however, she was used to boredom and thought of it as a natural part of existence. She had plans and a full imagination for someone of her station. She knew that her looks wouldn't last forever, so she looked for every opportunity, every advantage.

The woman and the bodyguards had at least one thing in common: they knew that the only means they had of surviving at a level higher than that of the villages from which they had come was their bodies. The woman learned early to be selective with her charms. All the men who saw her wanted her — even her brothers; but her brothers could not pay, and she never gave anything away. The men were bullies, although not the kind in school yards. They were the vicious kind that poverty produces, the kind that experience has taught to take as much as possible because there will be a shortage. They were loyal to Cavelya because he paid them well, but also because they recognized in him an elemental depravity that was far baser than their own. They were uneducated and stupid, but possessed of an instinctive cunning for survival.

Enright felt uneasy that clean Thursday morning as he readied the boat for the trip across the Gulf to the Panhandle; along with the food and drink cases that the bodyguards carried aboard, they also brought three MAC-10s with suppressors, and a pistol-gripped sawed-off 12-gauge, only mildly attempting to hide the guns by draping a blanket over them. Additionally, each man carried his usual Glock 17 in power-side Kydex plastic holsters, albeit shielded from the rest of the Safety Harbor community by the guayaberas that each wore. Wistfully, Enright gazed out into the Gulf and wondered if maybe the charter business was not already a little oversubscribed. Cavelya came aboard carrying two aluminum attaché cases.

The *Three Stooges* had already carried the luggage aboard.

Twenty-Two

Manny Di Ladro spent the day canvassing the banks and real estate offices in the High-Peaks area. He covered the towns that falcate to the east, north, and west of the mountain where the plane went down. It was a large area but there weren't many towns. What he was looking for was someone who had recently made a significant purchase, moved out of the pucker brush and into a camp on Lake Placid, bought an upscale business, paid off a mortgage in one lump sum, or some similar evidence of an unexplained windfall. While several of the banks and realtors had branch offices in the surrounding towns, he only had to check with the main offices. He also eliminated the property management offices and the part-time realtors, which reduced his calls to five banks and a dozen or so realtors. This still left about a hundred-and-thirty-mile area to cover.

He hadn't found what he was looking for by the end of the day. The closest he came was a newly arrived couple from Florida who lived in an affluent area of Lake Placid, though not on the lake, and didn't seem to require employment to keep up their life-style, and a woman — also in Lake Placid — who paid five hundred thousand dollars cash for a quaint lodge that had a beautiful view of the high peaks. It turned out that the couple had strong family ties to old Florida money, the kind of people who look upon work as a curiosity because no one in their recent family history has had to since grandpapa acquired large tracts of coastal Florida, straightened the

177

rivers, and put a dent in the mosquito population. The single woman was recently divorced from a husband who was next in line to the purse strings of old New York money — Mayflower people. Mama, the current purse holder, was only too happy to pay the woman five hundred thousand dollars as an initial settlement just to get her away from her son, her club, her church, and her circle. Simply put, Mama thought of the woman as a pest, something to rid herself of.

The last realtor Di Ladro spoke to was in Long Lake. There were two ways back to Lake Placid from Long Lake: go back the way he had come, or go east for about forty miles before heading north on the I-87 and NY 73 for another forty miles. Di Ladro wasn't much of an adventurer. The route he took was bad enough; the road to the east looked even more desolate, and if the three logging trucks that he saw while waiting at the intersection were any indication as to the traffic pattern, he thought it best to return the way he came. It was long and tortuous, but at least it was narrow.

Di Ladro was thirsty and tired, and he needed to call his employer in New Jersey. Not Fidelity Mutual, but Joey Moccazini, his brother-in-law. Given the topic of conversation, he thought it would be better to call from a public phone than from his cell or from the phone in his room back at the inn. Just before coming into Tupper Lake he saw a roadhouse on his right-hand side. The parking lot made him slightly wary as it was filled with pickup trucks containing racks in the back windows, which held rifles and fishing rods, men for all seasons. Despite his hesitation, Di Ladro spotted a phone booth in the far corner of the parking lot. Plus, he was thirsty.

He sighed, "What the hell." *Christ, I once had a drink in a bar in Bayonne, how bad can this be,* he thought just before he turned in.

The bar was right next to the Raquette River where it flowed into Tupper Lake. The river forked into several channels and there was a back flow there. Di Ladro got out of his car and the mosquitoes attacked. "Christ, this is worse than the Jersey Meadows," he uttered to himself as he swatted his way to the phone booth, happy that it was enclosed.

"Joey, this is Manny," Di Ladro said when he finally got through to Moccazini. "I thought I'd check in with you, let you know what I did or didn't find, and see what you want me to do."

"So, what did you find?" Moccazini asked.

"Nothing. Absolutely nothing. Yeah, I saw the plane, but there is nothing there, even the engines are gone, and there is nothing around the plane but fucking trees. This place is like Alaska. I checked the real estate offices and the banks, another zip. Nobody's moving a lot of cash around. This guy Keagan still looks like the best bet, but he says he got his money from his uncle who was a gun-runner for the crazy, fucking Irish. Says the uncle hid it from the IRS. Not your usual cover story. Plus, the guy looks cool. Runs a nice place, seems to know what he's doing, but I don't know. What do you want me to do, Joey?"

"Stick with this guy Keagan for another couple of days. If you don't pick up anything, come on back. Then have another try at his Cayman account in a week or so."

"Okay, Joey, I'll be in touch."

Di Ladro stepped out of the phone booth, and the mosquitoes attacked again. He got back into the booth and looked at his watch. It was 4:15. He figured he had about thirty, thirty-five miles to go to get back to the inn, which equated to almost an hour on these roads. He looked at the pickup trucks again, with their rifles in their back windows.

"What the fuck," he said, "they aren't going to shoot me in broad daylight; this ain't Newark." He flapped his way across the parking lot into the bar.

The bar was filled with men in green work clothes with cut-off sleeves that revealed dirty, muscular arms. All wore steel-toed boots, and some had toques on their heads in spite of it being summer. They were loggers. Most carried Buck knives on their belts. None of them had shaved in the last two or three days. Few had a full set of teeth, not by half.

Di Ladro went up to the bar; there was one opening, no stool, but there was just enough space to stand at the bar. A fat woman with grey, flyaway hair came over to him. Di Ladro was going to order a Heineken, but he didn't want to push his luck. "Bottle-a-Bud," he said, as he laid a ten dollar bill on the bar. The woman brought Di Ladro his beer; she even brought him a glass. Di Ladro took a long pull on the beer, emptying the glass.

He started to refill it when suddenly he realized that no one in the bar was talking; they were absolutely still. The only sound in the place came from the overhead television. Slowly, he looked around. No one was drinking. No one was shooting pool. No one was playing computer darts. Di Ladro started to get worried before noticing that all of the grizzled faces were staring at the overhead television where a Tom and Jerry cartoon played. Di Ladro looked up slowly, just in time to see Jerry smack Tom in the face with a frying pan as he rounded a corner in yet another of the series' rivalry chases. Suddenly, one of the men, slapped a huge hand down on the bar — Di Ladro thought it would split from the force — and said, "by Gar, I love dat little fellow, izn't he de dickens?"

The rest of the men added their take on the comic duo and were so engrossed in their discussion about the high jinx of the two that no one noticed that Di Ladro left or whether he was even there. No one except the bartender, the fat woman with the grey, flyaway hair noticed he didn't finish his beer and left all his change from the ten dollar bill.

Twenty-Three

Atlanta was hot and humid, especially compared to Lake Placid. Keagan, Kelly, Niles, and Teal flew early out of Saranac Lake to Albany, then onto Atlanta. Niles and Teal traveled very light; each wore jeans and T-shirts and carried small, scuffed, inexpensive looking carry-ons. Their roles didn't call for many costume changes. Keagan and Kelly were dressed professionally. Kelly wore a cream colored blouse and a medium blue skirt and was hatless; Keagan, a tropical-weight worsted grey suit. Kelly also carried a leather shoulder bag. They were on their way to the Avis Rental Car counter across from the luggage carousel when the carousel's red light began flashing, and its obnoxious claxon began sounding, so they detoured for a moment to pick up their luggage before talking with Avis.

They fleshed out a plan the previous Sunday night sitting at the bar at the inn, and then refined it as well as they could each subsequent night after the patrons left. It was a relatively simple plan at this point because they didn't know much. What they did know was that the thieves had arrived in Atlanta two weeks ago, and that they rented a car that subsequently turned up abandoned in the Jacksonville International Airport long-term parking lot. The plan was for Keagan and Kelly to talk to the Avis people, see what they could learn, rent a car, brief Niles and Teal, and decide on the next move.

Niles and Teal stayed upstairs in a coffee shop while Keagan and Kelly went downstairs to the Avis counter. There were two attendants at the Avis counter, one black male and the other a white female. Affirmative action was not going to catch Avis napping.

Keagan addressed the black male who was free, showing the DEA identification that Kelly had gotten for him. He said, "Excuse me, may I speak to the manager on duty?" The counter agent stepped through a doorway that led to a corridor of offices that all car rental companies have behind the partitions that separate them from their service counters. In short order, he returned with a slight man with thinning sandy hair in his late twenties, wearing wire rim glasses, a white shirt with a red tie and the pants of a bad suit.

"May I help you?" he asked as he came out. "I'm Clay Chambliss, the manager."

Keagan held up his DEA ID again, as did Kelly. "I'm special agent Shaw, and this is special agent Kelly. May we speak with you in private?" Shaw was Keagan's mother's maiden name. They had used the names before and were very comfortable with them. They had valid credit cards accounts in those names, although the addresses were post office boxes in Boston held by a member of the IRA. It was a lot easier to use the same names — ones they were familiar with — than to keep changing them and run the risk of lapsing into a former alias, not to mention the time new ID's and credit cards the new identities required.

"Uh, sure, come on in."

The manager asked to see their credentials again, close-up, so Keagan and Kelly handed him their ID wallets. He looked at one, then at Keagan and looked at the other before looking up at Kelly. Satisfied, he handed them back. The compact office was furnished with a desk — most of the surface of which was covered with a computer monitor and a ream of printouts – a castor office chair, and two chrome tubular chairs with nubbly brown seat and back cushions. On the wall to Keagan's left were three coat hooks. Keagan reflected that Atlanta was not always as hot as this. On the wall behind Chambliss were a number of plaques and certificates attesting to the competence of Clayton B. Chambliss. Keagan eyed the name with satisfaction. The manager didn't take himself too seriously; otherwise, he wouldn't have introduced himself as "Clay." In spite of the plaques, the office was clearly a workplace rather than a place to impress clients. Few, if any, clients ever made it back to the office.

"Mr. Chambliss, special agent Kelly and I are investigating a major drug-smuggling case that originated in Boston, and we have reason to believe that two of the principals involved in the case rented a car at this location, a car that was subsequently found in the long-term parking lot of Jacksonville International Airport. We have their names as Pierce and Denis Summerall, although they may have used other names when they rented the car."

"Oh, yes, they certainly did, sir. That case is a continuing headache for me. So much so that I do not even have to look it up in my records for their identities. Actually, that's not correct; I know only the name that the man used who signed the rental agreement for the car. The other one said he would not be driving, so I did not check his license. The car was a blue Ford Taurus, four door. The man who rented it showed identification – license and credit card – indicating his name was Joseph Albright from Chevy Chase, Maryland."

"Do you remember what he looked like, Mr. Chambliss?"

"Well, I gave all that information to the Atlanta Police and also to the Jacksonville Police."

"I'm sure you did, Mr. Chambliss, but they are working a theft-of-services case, and we are working a different case, one involving the smuggling of ten million dollars' worth of cocaine. I'm sure you can appreciate that our concerns run a bit deeper than theirs do. We haven't talked to them yet, but we certainly will be in contact with both police departments. I suspect, however, that a theft of services case won't get a lot of attention from police departments in major cities like Atlanta and Jacksonville. Anyhow, for now we would like to get whatever information you can give us."

Kelly miraculously produced a notebook from the clutter of her bag and just as miraculously produced a ball-point pen, which she clicked on and held poised over the notebook, ready to take down what Mr. Clayton B. Chambliss was about to say.

"Well, both men were in their mid-to-late thirties. Both trim. Mr. Albright, or whatever his name is, is about five foot ten; the other man, a few inches taller, perhaps six feet tall and ten to twenty pounds heavier. While stockier, he looked much more like Mr. Albright's/Summerall's brother than his friend or associate. They were both dressed casually but neatly. The address on Mr. Albright's license was . . . let me double check." He jiggled the mouse to de-activate the screen-saver, clicked an icon, waited a few seconds, then called up the record. "Yes, here it is. Joseph Albright, 4 Oxford Court, Chevy Chase, MD 20815. Police said the address belongs to Supreme Court Justice Sandra Day O'Connor. Seems like those boys had a sense of humor, although I am having trouble seeing it, the mess this has made for me."

"What mess is that? You've recovered the car. Can't Avis at Jacksonville just rotate it into its fleet?" asked Kelly.

"No, the Jacksonville police have impounded the car pending their investigation. As you have already pointed out, Special Agent Shaw, an abandoned rental car does not list high among their priorities. I suspect it's slightly below truancy," offered Clayton B. Chambliss with a sigh of frustration.

"Mr. Chambliss," Kelly asked, "how do you remember so much about the two men?"

"Well, for one thing I waited on them. Lamont out there," he motioned toward the counter, "was on supper break. It got busy, so Mary-Hershall called me out to help her. For another, this is a very boring job; you fill out computerized forms and hand people keys. To allay the boredom, I study the customers. Not everybody, just the interesting ones. If someone comes in from Chicago, wearing sweat pants and a Bulls jacket, I do not give him a second look. These two were different. Remember, I said they were trim. Well, they were more than just trim: they were athletically trim, the kind of trimness that you get only from seriously working at it. I'm not talking about the usual gym buff or jock. Jocks do not dress the way these two did. Everything matched, everything fit. Oh, one other thing: their hands looked much older than their faces and they were marked up, scarred and abraded."

"What, like a workman's or a boxer's?" Kelly asked.

"No, not like a workman...except perhaps like a mechanic's. Most of the damage done to workmen's hands is done on the underside. Not like boxer's hands either. They weren't gnarled. The backs of their hands were scarred and old looking."

Keagan changed the subject. "Mr. Chambliss, can you tell me the mileage the car they rented had on it when it left here?"

Chambliss turned back to the computer, jiggled the mouse again and said, "seven thousand, four hundred and six miles."

"Did they leave here with a full tank of gas?" continued Keagan.

"Yes, all our cars leave here topped off."

"What does Avis calculate that a Ford Taurus gets for mileage?" asked Kelly.

"Twenty-four highway, eighteen city."

"One last question, Mr. Chambliss, *abraded*?" asked Keagan.

"I'm sorry?"

"You said, *abraded*; no disrespect intended, but *abraded* isn't a word I expect from a rental car manager."

"You are right, Mr. Shaw, this job pays the rent. I have a master's degree in English, but I do not want to teach. What I want to be is a writer. Just what the world needs, another Southern writer. I get to see a lot of people in this job, if only for a few minutes, grist for the creative mill. That's why I'm so observant. That's why I can tell that you both have worked hard to eliminate your accents. Yours, Mr. Shaw, is a bit less pronounced than yours, Ms. Kelly. Both are somewhat different from the Irish brogue one usually hears, especially on St. Patrick's Day. And I also noticed, Mr. Shaw that even though you are a DEA agent you are not carrying a gun, but I guess even federal agents, other than the FAA marshals, cannot carry guns on commercial aircrafts."

"You're right on all counts, Mr. Chambliss," said Keagan. "Thank you for your help. Now, I think we need to rent a car from you — government rate, of course – and get instructions on how to get out of the airport." He was somewhat anxious to leave before the next Walker Percy completely catalogued both Kelly and him; Keagan started to wonder how DEA agents from Boston knew about the car rented in Atlanta and abandoned in Jacksonville as it wasn't a usual clue.

***

They rejoined Niles and Teal upstairs and relayed the information Chambliss gave them.

"What's our next move?" asked Niles.

"I think we need to go to Jacksonville to have a look at the car."

"The four of us?" asked, Teal.

"Yes, but in separate cars. Kelly and I will go in one. You and Niles need to rent a separate vehicle, a pickup or a four-wheel drive if you can. Nothing flashy, no yuppie toy. Make sure it is something that keeps with your character."

"Out-of-work construction workers?" offered Niles.

"Precisely," answered Keagan.

Keagan opened his briefcase and took out a hotel directory. "There is a Ramada Inn in Jacksonville, not far from the airport, just off I-10; let's plan on meeting there in the bar at — *he looked at his watch* — seven o'clock. I don't like these chrome and plastic places, but it has a convenient location and we can all stay there. I'll make the reservations."

***

Keagan and Kelly arrived first at the Jacksonville Ramada. They checked in and went down to the bar. Niles and Teal arrived just as the cocktail waitress brought their drinks. Niles must have been driving.

After they joined Keagan and Kelly in the lounge and the waitress brought Teal's and his drinks – two bottles of Budweiser, no Bass, no

Dixie Blackened Voodoo – and another round for Keagan and Kelly, Niles asked, "How do we move from here?"

"Kelly and I need to check in with the Avis people, then talk to the police to see if we can get a look at that car."

"What are you hoping to find?" asked Teal.

"Anything. A gas slip would be too much to ask for, but I need to see the odometer, see how many miles they traveled. How clean the car is. If the outside is dirty that might indicate that they didn't stick to the Interstates, especially if the mileage doesn't square with the direct distance between Atlanta and Jacksonville."

"Niles, I want you and Teal to pick up three cell phones. We're going to have to split up after today, and we need to know what each other is doing. Also, I want you two to spend tomorrow combing the docks along the St. John River – especially the Jaxport – looking for two athletically trim men, mid-thirties, one five foot ten inches and about 170 pounds, the other six feet and about 180-190 pounds, who may have booked passage to South America."

"What about the airport, and bus and train stations?" asked Teal.

"I don't think so. They could have gotten out of Atlanta the same way. Why come to Jacksonville? I'm beginning to agree with Kelly that the car at the airport is a stalking horse, but I want to eliminate it before I'm convinced."

"Who do you plan to visit first, Mick, the Avis people or the police?" asked Kelly.

"The Avis people. The police may be able to add to what we learn from the Avis people, but I don't think the reverse is true."

"Let's finish our drinks, let Niles and Teal get checked in, have something to eat, and wrap up our plans for tomorrow."

***

Keagan and Kelly ran the same scam at the Avis counter at the Jacksonville Airport as they had at the Hartsfield-Jackson Airport. Both were dressed professionally again, except this time Keagan was carrying his 9mm Sig in a Horseshoe crossdraw holster; Kelly still wasn't wearing a hat. Keagan felt in character; Kelly felt naked.

The manager there was far less knowledgeable than Clayton B. Chambliss was in Atlanta, but then he never saw the Campbells. All the information he could provide was the address of where the car was impounded.

***

Keagan showed his identification to the desk sergeant – a caricature of all desk sergeants – at the Leanard Road station house. The sergeant barely glanced at it. Florida and DEA agents, even if they came from Boston, were as common as mosquitoes and just about as pesky.

"Sergeant, who do I talk to get a look at a blue, Ford Taurus, Georgia license number?" – Keagan pretended to check his notebook, "MPH-722, the Atlanta rental you fellows found dumped at the airport."

The sergeant checked his computer and said, "that would be lieutenant Michaelson; have a seat over there, I'll see if he is available."

Forty-five minutes later Keagan and Kelly were seated next to Lt. Michaelson's desk.

"Okay, so why are two Mick DEA agents down here from Boston? It can't be the weather because it's summer," said Michaelson. Michaelson was a large, heavy-set black man, who liked to chew cigars to pulp and was a few lessons behind on political correctness. Keagan liked him right away, although he felt only mildly guilty about deceiving him. Kelly gave him the same story Keagan had given the Avis manager in Atlanta.

"And what do you expect to find in the car?" asked Michaelson.

"We don't know. It's a lead like any other lead. You never know what it will produce until you follow it," answered Keagan. "Have your people been through the car?"

"They dusted it for prints and came up empty," said Michaelson, emphasizing *empty* by chomping down on his already-masticated cigar stub. "I don't see any reason for doing much more. We'll probably release it in another day or two."

"So, can we have a look at it?" Kelly asked, giving her best impression of *St. Bridget of the Meadow*.

Michaelson answered her by punching a four-digit extension number on his phone with his thick index finger, sliding his cigar to the opposite side of his mouth, and speaking into the mouth piece. "Washington, this is Michaelson. I got two *Mick* DEA agents coming down to have a look at that Atlanta rental. No, *Mick* not *Spic*. Broaden your ethnic horizons, Washington. They'll be down in about fifteen minutes," he said and hung up the phone.

He leaned across his desk, fingered a sheet of paper with his name as a letterhead out of a Plexiglas holder and wrote very neatly, *Show these two ofays the blue, Ford Taurus, Georgia license number MPH-722.* "Washington ain't the brightest light in the world. Without this you'd probably get to see the panel truck we got in from Texas. The impound area is behind the building. Go right when you go out the front door," Michaelson said as he handed *St. Bridget of the Meadow* the folded sheet of paper.

"How the hell do you suppose he remembered that plate number?" Keagan asked Kelly when they were out on the street.

"Didn't you notice the Mensa pin in his coat lapel?"

"He wasn't wearing a coat, Kelly."

"No, but there was one folded over a chair in the corner by the computer." St. Bridget never looked so smug.

***

Washington saw them coming. "You them two *hicks* Michaelson sent down?"

"*Spics,* actually," said Kelly, intensifying her brogue as she handed Washington the note Michaelson gave her.

Washington read the note and led them over to the blue Ford Taurus. "Here she is. Take yo time, but let me know when y'all's finished. You know that lieutenant Michaelson is supposed to be very smart, but sometimes, I think he gets confused," offered Washington as he walked back to his office, "*Hicks?* They ain't *hicks*, ain't even *spics* the way he said they was; they just be *honkeys* who hab been to some fancy school. Shit, regular ole nigga can see that, don' have to be no rocket scientist of a police loo-ten-ent."

Keagan and Kelly went over the car methodically. He popped the hood; she popped the trunk. Keagan looked for anything that would tell him where the car had been, some service record on the engine: coolant, brake fluid, power steering fluid, anything that wasn't regular maintenance and that might have been done on the road.

Kelly checked out the trunk for any telltale scrap that might have fallen out of their luggage: motel, gas, parking, or toll receipt. She removed the trunk mat and turned it upside down on the macadam; she looked in the wheel well, then undid the wing nut that held the doughnut spare in place. Kelly tilted the tire; there was nothing under it. She checked the trunk's hinges because occasionally things got caught on them. Nothing. The trunk was immaculate. Kelly put everything back.

Moving towards each other, Keagan took the front seat, Kelly the back seat. Visors, glove compartment, ash trays, hollow console armrest, seat cushions: nothing. Under the seats: nothing. Under the floor mats: nothing.

They came together in the front seat. "Do you think Washington or one of the police lab folks found anything?" asked Kelly.

"I doubt Washington could find sand on the beach. As for the others, it's possible, but if they did, there isn't much likelihood of our seeing it. They may have even thrown it away. They were looking for prints or something they could turn over to the lab for someone else to follow it up, not some scrap of evidence that would take them a month to run down."

"What next?" asked Kelly.

"Let's just sit here for a moment. I'm trying to get a feel for them. He fastened his seat belt. This seat seems just right for me and yours is way back, so perhaps we can assume that the shorter of the two drove the car, which jibes with what Chambliss said. Let me sit there for a moment," said Keagan.

Kelly got out and walked around to the driver's seat, and Keagan took the passenger seat. "Yes, this seat is further back than I would set it." He reached over for the seat belt but it wouldn't unravel. He pulled again — stuck. He got out of the car, then leaned across the seat to see what was causing the lap belt to stick. As he leaned closer, he saw the lottery ticket. It was wedged, at an angle, into the belt retractor on the backside of the belt. *Must have been a pretty amazing gymnastic*, thought Keagan. Gingerly, he tried to straighten the belt. Keagan got it straight, then tried the lap belt again, and the ticket popped out.

"What have you got there, Mick?" asked Kelly.

"It looks like a Florida Instant Lottery ticket."

"Have we won?"

"I think we may have, but we'll have to talk with Mr. Chambliss again in Atlanta to be sure."

"Why is that, Mick?"

"To find out where this car has been on its last two or three rentals."

"Couldn't Washington or one of the lab people have dropped the ticket?" asked Kelly.

"Nay sayer!"

Before getting out of the car, Keagan copied down the odometer's mileage; the trip meter was set at zero.

"Find anything?" Washington asked them on the way out.

"No, nothing," said Kelly. "But maybe we'll get lucky, yet. You believe in luck, Mr. Washington? You play the lottery?"

"Yes, ma'am. I gets me one of dem lotto tickets every week, but Iz never seems to win."

"Well, wish us luck, Mr. Washington," Keagan said as he took Kelly's arm and led her out of the impound yard.

"What good is the lottery ticket going to do us?" Kelly asked when they were on the street.

"The Lottery Commission keeps track of ticket distribution so they can reward the sellers of winning tickets. It not only boosts sales; it's one of the ways convenience stores, gas stations and other places that sell tickets make money. It's an income stream; otherwise, why handle them? They're a pain. Ever get stuck behind a retiree buying an assortment of them? What we need to do is call on the Lottery Commission to find out where the ticket was sold. If it turns out to be Jacksonville or a nearby town, the ticket is a dead end. If it was purchased somewhere other than in a place that is in a reasonably direct line from Atlanta to Jacksonville, yet within the 622 miles the car traveled, we may get an inkling as to where our art connoisseurs are."

"Mick, you are brilliant. How have you learned so much about your adopted country in so short a time?"

"Intellectual toil. Besides, you don't have someone like Jimmy the Gimp working for you without learning a little about gambling or *gaming* as it's now called. People lose just as much, but the name change makes the losers think that they're paying for entertainment, not trying to beat the odds that were stacked against them."

***

Keagan and Kelly found the Lottery Commission office just before it closed for lunch. They asked for the manager, knowing full well they wouldn't get any information out of a clerk. What was true in Ireland was also true in the United States and probably true in Vanuatu as well. Government functionaries, regardless of agency or nation, caused more obstruction than the Maginot Line ever did.

They presented the manager, a middle-age woman whose clothes were a little too fashionable for her position, with their identification. She glanced at them almost as long as she glanced at the clock on the wall behind Keagan and Kelly. "What can I do for you?" she said with practiced politeness.

Kelly answered the question, realizing the woman would feel more comfortable talking to another woman. Her clothes told Kelly that she was proud of being in her position, proud that as a woman she was in charge of this office. She wasn't likely to give away her secrets to a man, not an in-charge kind of man like Keagan, anyway.

"We have a lottery ticket that we found in a car which we have traced to drug smugglers. What we need to know is where that ticket was purchased. I believe you have the resources to tell us as much."

"Yes, I do," she seemed to take personal credit for the ability. "May I see the ticket?"

Keagan handed her the lottery ticket. She went behind the counter, punched up a terminal, and clacked some keys. In a moment she was back, self-satisfied and ready for lunch. She handed Kelly the ticket. "Your ticket was purchased at the One Corner Stop 'N Fill in Carabelle."

"*One corner*? What an odd name. I thought there had to be a minimum of two corners; otherwise, it's a bend in the road, not an intersection," suggested Kelly.

"You ever been to Carabelle?"

"No, I haven't had the pleasure," answered Kelly, unable to pass up on the cliché.

"Carabelle's police office is a phone booth, one of those red English ones. Got it from there, too, I think. At least that's what they say. They think it adds class to the town. How you going to add class to a town of twelve hundred people?"

"How do you know so much about such a small town?" asked Kelly.

"I grew up in Apalachicola, about thirty miles to the west. The police department, if you don't believe me, is documented in *Ripley's Believe It or Not*," she said with an authority that resonated gospel.

***

Keagan and Kelly met Niles and Teal back at the bar in the Jacksonville Ramada. "What did you find out?" Keagan asked Niles.

"That a lot of ships leave Jacksonville bound for South or Central America, but as far as we could tell none carried our two art thieves there."

"You learn anything?" asked Niles.

Keagan told them about finding the lottery ticket and his subsequent call to the Avis manager, Mr. Clayton B. Chambliss, in Atlanta.

"Chambliss told me that the last two rentals were local: northern businessmen who had come to corporate headquarters — one to Coca-Cola and the other to Georgia Pacific — for two or three day meetings, needed a car to get from the airport to the hotel to corporate. The Coke guy ran up eighty-nine miles, the other one hundred and seven. Not enough to get to Florida to buy a lottery ticket. The date on the ticket rules out earlier rentals."

"The ticket was purchased in Carabelle, a small town southwest of Tallahassee," said Keagan as he unfolded a Florida road map and, after taking a few seconds to locate it, pointed to a small town on the Gulf. "Odds are slim that it came from the impound officers or the police who dusted the car for prints. Carabelle is a long way from Jacksonville."

Teal took the map from Keagan. "Carabelle is also out of the way. It is not a place people find themselves passing through. It is not easy to get there; the Interstate is more than an hour north of it."

Teal folded the eastern edge of the map and unfolded the western edge. Running his finger along the Gulf coast he said, "I think we should concentrate on the area between Carabelle and Panama City, a distance of a little over a hundred miles."

"Why not all the way over to Pensacola?" asked Kelly looking at the map.

"Pensacola has an Air Force base, and security is tight. The bay looks big enough, empty enough, but look how narrow the entrance is. Easy to keep track of who comes in there," added Teal.

"If the ticket's pointing the way, it suggests that the buyer is coming by water. I think that it's a safe assumption that Pensacola is the wrong place. You could make the trade in a McDonald's in Pensacola as easily as anywhere else, but on the water it's crazy. I agree with Teal; it's looking for trouble," added Keagan.

"What about Destin?" asked Niles.

"Destin's a possibility," said Teal. "Somehow, it just doesn't fit for me, though. Destin is the heart of the *Redneck Riviera*. This time of the year, it's filled with Georgia, Alabama, and Mississippi crackers, who come out of the hills and pucker brush to bare potbellies, sagging tits – excuse me Kelly – and cellulite legs to the sun and to turn as red as the clay hills they come from, all while drinking an inordinate amount of beers. If I were an art thief, I wouldn't go there, but since I'm a *coonass* I wouldn't mind an all-expenses paid trip."

"How do you know so much about Destin?" asked Niles.

"Occasionally, some cultured ladies and gentlemen from south Louisiana also go there, but only for the waters," Teal said with a twinkle.

"Why Panama City, Teal?" asked Keagan.

"Good question. It's almost as redneck as Destin, but there is more money there. In Destin, the rednecks arrive in pickups with sixty gallon coolers of beer in the truck bed to rent condos for the week. In Panama City – except for spring break – the tourists own the condos and arrive there in Lincoln Town Cars with cases of bourbon in the trunk."

"It's pretty busy this time of the year, which could be good cover for the thieves. On the other hand, crowds cause problems. Panama City would not be my choice. I just included it because it has some possibilities. But I think it's the western boundary of likely places."

Keagan quietly poured over the map. "I agree with Teal. Panama City doesn't seem to be an ideal place for the switch; however, it is just within the range that the rental car traveled. What about these two areas, Teal? Do you know anything about them?" Keagan pointed first at St. Joseph Peninsula State Park and then to St. George Island.

"I've never been to St. George Island, but St. Joe's is ideal. It's quiet, even this time of the year. The buyer could anchor off shore. The seller could motor out in a rental, make the deal, and be on their way. Or the buyer could Zodiac into making the deal."

"You might be right, Teal," said Niles. "But if I were the seller, I'd want a more neutral site for the switch. Quiet is good, but the site's also good for an ambush. I agree with the perimeter of the search, though. What's our next move, Mick?"

Keagan was staring at the map, tapping his finger on the Apalachicola River. "What did you say, Niles?"

"Where do we go from here, Mick?"

"Well, just before you came in Kelly was on the phone to her contacts. They don't know anything after Atlanta. They are sure the thieves are the Campbell brothers, the ones who rented the car, but they have nothing to offer after that. Our only lead is the lottery ticket. I say we follow it up. Also, I agree with Teal. Kelly and I will go to Carabelle while you and Teal go to Panama City. Work the bars, particularly the hotel lounges, and the boat rentals. The thieves are upscale, so check out the better restaurants. We've got a pretty good description of them. If Teal's assessment of the *Redneck Riviera* is correct, they'll stick out, particularly if they went to the State Park. Also, I don't think I mentioned it, but the Avis manager in Atlanta said they both had old hands."

"*Old hands*? What does that mean?" Niles asked.

"I'm not sure, but that's what he said. He really focused on them. He said they weren't like manual workers' hands or the gnarled hands of boxers." Keagan looked at his own hands in mock self-effacement. "You mean like rock climbers' hands, Mick?" asked Teal.

The three stared at him. "Go ahead," Keagan finally said.

"Rock climbers are always scarring their hands. Look at mine, and I haven't climbed in weeks. Also, their hands are always exposed. They usually don't wear gloves, sometimes not even in the winter. Their nails are cracked, their knuckles are scarred, even the backs of their hands have diggers in them. Climbers' hands always look at least five to ten years older than their faces, good climbers that is. I don't know, but I would think rock climbing is a natural exercise for cat burglars, especially ones who are athletically trim."

"You know, you are a pretty smart fellow for a southern frog," said Niles.

"That's guaranteed. However, I prefer the term *coonass*, though only among friends," smiled Teal.

"What's a *coonass*?" asked Kelly. "Did I hear you correctly?"

"It's a controversial term. There are many ideas about where it came from, but nobody's sure. Depends on who you are. Blue-collar workers look on it as a badge of pride, while rich people hate it; but even the blue-collar crowd doesn't like outsiders to use it. It's kinda like a Cajun redneck."

"But doesn't *redneck* imply *stupid*?" asked Kelly

"Yeah, Kelly, and that's why the rich Cajuns don't like it, but fellas like me think of it more as a special name that tells people we're proud of where we came from."

Twenty-Four

Keagan and Niles got up early and ran seven miles. There wasn't a dry spot on their T-shirts when they returned to the Ramada. Coming through the lobby, they saw Kelly and Teal in one of the dining rooms ordering breakfast. Keagan signaled that they would join them as soon as they showered.

Over a last cup of coffee, the four fleshed out the next leg of the plan. As they had said the night before: Niles and Teal would go to Panama City, and Keagan and Kelly would go to Carabelle. After Keagan and Kelly checked out the One Corner Stop 'N Fill, they would work the bars, restaurants, marinas, and gas stations, eventually moving towards each other. They would meet on Thursday in Apalachicola at the Gibson Inn at 6:00 PM. Keagan knew of the Gibson because *Beyond Good and Evil* and the Gibson were once both featured in the same guide of quaint inns, even if they were in different regions of the country.

Niles gave Keagan one of the cell phones and they set off right after breakfast. They had a full day ahead of them. Niles and Teal had almost a five-hour drive, while Keagan and Kelly had about two hours less.

***

I-10 is an open road once you get out of Jacksonville. Tallahassee is the next biggest city on the route, but its population is only a little over a hundred thousand people. While I-10 is a cross-country route, it doesn't get congested until New Orleans and later in Houston, so the four had an easy drive across the Florida Panhandle.

Niles and Teal were in the lead vehicle, a Ford Explorer. Keagan and Kelly were behind them in a white Ford Taurus. Apparently, Avis was fond of Fords. The two vehicles maintained visual contact despite Teal's tendency to speed. Going across a state whose highest point is only 345 feet above sea level doesn't allow for much strategic speeding. Cresting a rise at the speed limit, checking out the landscape to the next rise, and then running twenty to twenty-five miles over the speed limit before tapering off to the next rise, is a tactic that works well in the West.

They pulled over for coffee at a McDonald's just west of I-75. Keagan hated what McDonald's and the other fast-food franchises had done to regional food in America almost as much as he disliked their food. He could only tolerate their coffee because it generally wasn't any worse than gas station coffee. As Keagan was standing in line, getting coffee for himself and tea for Niles and Kelly, he suggested to Teal – who ordered a sausage biscuit with gravy – that he slow down a bit. They had a lot of miles to cover, but if he got caught speeding the police would probably search the car for drugs and weapons. Florida residents can have loaded guns in their cars, but Florida's legislature has not extended the same courtesy to out-of-staters without a permit; they almost certainly would cast a baleful eye on someone from Boston – with a Limey accent – carrying a .357 Magnum, not to mention a Cajun with a Colt .45 and a shadowy past.

Teal agreed with Keagan's appraisal of the possibility, but five miles later he was driving eighty miles an hour, again. Nationalism produces national myths: the French are deluded that they are the world's best lovers, the English mistakenly think that they are the most level-headed of nations, and the Americans labor under the misconception that they are intuitive problem-solvers. Regionalism does more of the same, perhaps with a finer edge: Northeasterners believe that they are heirs to the Puritan work ethic and that the rest of the citizens are indolent, slow thinkers, and even slower reactors.

Midwesterners believe that they are the salt-of-the-earth, a Biblical phrase they incorrectly associate with farming. Californians believe that everyone else in the nation is tight-assed, whatever that means.

Southerners, on the other hand, believe that they invented gentility (which means they would never think of using such a vulgar term as their Californian cousins), the nation's best whiskey (which many of them religiously avoid more than snakes), and automotive speed. While most cars are made in the upper Midwest, most of the famous race tracks – at least the stock car ones – are in the South, Charlotte, Talladega, and Daytona. Every Southern boy has seen *Thunder Road*, and although the movie is almost fifty-years old, it is part of the Southern myth as well as Southern reality. Teal loved speed. He grew up driving in Louisiana, which is the second flattest state in the union. Teal didn't pretend to have any claim on an insouciant lifestyle, on being the salt-of-the-earth, or sole possession of the Puritan ethic or on any other regional stake – ethnic perhaps, but not regional – he simply knew he liked to drive fast.

Near Greenville, there was an imaginative speed-trap: an unmarked car was parked on an overpass with its radar unit hanging down the overpass side focused on the westbound lanes of I-10, while the chase car was half a mile ahead. Teal had again picked up speed. Keagan saw the trap. Teal saw the chase car, but by then it was too late. The trooper pulled out and flashed him to pull over.

"Kelly," shouted Keagan, as he handed her his cell phone. "Call 911, curb your accent, act hysterical, and report that someone is randomly shooting at cars on I-10 from the overpass east of Greenville." Kelly punched the numbers on the cell phone, affected a cultured Boston accent, identified herself as Kitty O'Shea, gave the dispatcher the message, and said she was driving a vehicle that matched the description and license number of the Alabama car ahead of them.

The trooper, now out of his cruiser, started toward Teal and Niles in the Ford Explorer, but halfway there, hearing the 911 emergency call, spun around, ran back to his cruiser, made a U-turn across the median, and headed east toward the sniper who existed only in Keagan's imagination.

"Kitty O'Shea?"

"It's the only name I could think of and there's a certain logic in it. Kitty screwed up what Parnell was doing; I'm just trying to screw up what that peeler was trying to do to Teal."

"Well, it's a good thing you didn't say Monica Lewinsky."

***

The Gulf was calm. Cavelya was enjoying himself aboard *Blanca Nieve*. In the morning, he conducted business; after lunch. He diddled with his female *companion*, took a nap, and then shot skeet. Cavelya was an accomplished skeet shooter; his female companion was less complimentary about his diddling skills. Shooting skeet gave him great satisfaction. Once he shot 147 clay birds in a row. He liked skeet-shooting because it involved guns, he could keep score, and liked watching his targets blow apart. Skeet was just like business: how much money he made told him how smart he was, and how many clay pigeons he broke authenticated how macho he was.

Cavelya shot skeet with his bodyguards. They were not very good. Shooting skeet takes a good deal of hand-eye coordination and a great deal of concentration. They had good hand-eye coordination, but had they been schooled in America, they no doubt would have been diagnosed with A.D.D. (after all, almost every other kid in America is nowadays). As it was, they were schooled in Bolivia, but only until the third grade. Actually one — Carlos — got as far as the seventh grade before he was expelled for repeatedly exposing himself to his teacher. By the seventh grade, Carlos finally found something he really could concentrate on.

Skeet is usually shot in rounds of twenty-five. The rules are simple: whoever breaks the most clay pigeons wins the round. In the first round, Carlos broke twelve; Cavelya, twenty-five. The other two bodyguards – Luis and Manascotta – fared less well; Luis broke ten birds while Manascotta broke only three. They shot too fast, didn't lead, and didn't follow the clay bird's flight. In skeet, you never take your eye off the target. In their normal work, they used MAC-10's, which held thirty-two rounds. Even the Glocks they carried for closer work held eighteen rounds if you kept one in the chamber, which they did. In either case with thirty-two or eighteen rounds, they were not accustomed to aiming and squeezing; they generally just pointed and sprayed. And in their normal work, their targets were much bigger and much slower moving than clay pigeons. They were also closer.

After Cavelya humiliated the three bodyguards, he had Carlos clean his custom-made over-and-under Franchi featherweight. The gun had a French walnut stock, a twenty-eight inch ventilated-rib barrel with an improved-modified choke on the top barrel and modified choke on the lower barrel. Cavelya would not trust the gun to either of the other bodyguards. Carlos was not bright, but at least he understood the value of things and the consequence of marring one of Cavelya's expensive toys. Also, he had an affinity for the forward and backward cleaning movement.

Luis and Manascotta salved their egos leaning against the transom smoking dope. It was late afternoon, and the sun was over Texas. *Blanca Nieve* was north of Cedar Key, off what are probably the least populated shores of Florida. The shoreline between Cedar Key and St. Mark's National Wildlife Refuge, the substantial elbow-arc of Florida's Gulf coast, is largely grasslands and mangrove.

Dolphins ran along the coast as they usually did in late afternoon at that time of the year. Luis and Manascotta spotted a pod and began to fire at them with their 9mm Glocks. Enright heard the sharp sounds and realized that they were not the dull thuds of long-barreled shotguns. When he saw the dolphins, he realized they were the targets, the sacred friend of fishermen. Enright didn't think. He reacted.

He locked the wheel and leapt from the bridge. Manascotta was doing his best to aim when Enright pulled him straight back from the transom with his left hand on his shoulder, kicked the back of his knees with his right foot, and dropped him to the deck.

Anyone else would have let the gun go clattering across the deck, but Manascotta — who couldn't focus on skeet – had a single-minded focus when attacked. Enright stepped behind Manascotta as he fell, so while Manascotta still held his gun, he couldn't see Enright directly behind him: hard to shoot someone you can't see. Manascotta tried to roll and shoot, but when he did, Enright drop-kicked him in the head.

Luis fired a shot in the air and shouted to Enright to stop. Luis held the gun parallel to the deck, repeatedly flexed his fingers on the synthetic grip of the Glock, trying to impress Enright with his lever-age in this situation, a stupid affectation he had picked up from TV street homies. Enright stood up full stature and turned to face Luis. Looking past him, he told Cavelya, who had responded to the fracas that, "if any of your goons ever fire at another dolphin, I will feed him, tied and bleeding, to the sharks. Does any of what I have just said need interpretation? If not, Señor Cavelya, please instruct them of my intention." Cavelya, knowing that no one else aboard could run the boat – and a little unsure of himself because Enright dared to speak to him like that in front of his men – ordered Luis to put away his gun and to attend to the unconscious Manascotta.

Twenty-Five

Panama City was once beautiful — until the land developers started plotting, a practice that always ends in blight — in that while it wouldn't draw *snowbirds* the way south Florida did in the winter, because it was too far north and still a bit of cold when the *snowbirds* were sick of winter — it, and the surrounding area, did have some of the finest beaches in the nation. In at least one poll, Florida averages four of the top ten beaches in America; the Florida Panhandle usually has three of the four. And so, in typical fashion, the land developers — the term is paradoxical to what they actually do — came in and built cement castles in the sky, as close to the water as greed would allow, and the young, upwardly mobile rednecks swarmed out of the red clay hills and bottom lands of Georgia, Alabama, and Mississippi to snap up the beautiful condos by the sea. Panama City went from a small Panhandle fishing village to a grotesquerie of shoulder-to-shoulder condos, hotels, bars, and quaint restaurants with names like the *Tiki Hut* and *Zapata's*. Developers had no sense of geography or history, nor apparently did people who were attracted to places that had ridiculous names. If they did, maybe they wouldn't flock to drink in a hut named after the penis of the god Tāne, unless of course they had a sense of humor.

Across the road, on the land side of US 98, were tightly packed malls with liquor stores, T-shirt shops, video rentals, fast-food places, drug stores, and supermarkets that the locals could also patronize, though usually only at early morning hours while the young, upwardly mobile rednecks were still fast asleep or nursing their hangovers.

About twenty years ago, Panama City's City Council had gotten unusually creative, imitative actually. The City Council cast its collective eye south and east to Fort Lauderdale to covet its college market. The benefits to the city were incredible. Police and fire hires were up, while construction boomed; the health care market — traditionally focused on the elderly — now found a new niche in setting broken bones from balcony jumping, pumping stomachs distended with alcohol poisoning, and salving blistered skin — a byproduct of passing out on the beach. The liquor stores, T-shirts shops, and the drug stores — though primarily the condom and lotion sections — have shown remarkable profit. There had also been a tremendous boom in waste removal — no easy task where the land is largely limestone with very little top soil.

God regularly demonstrated his displeasure with this seaside Sodom by visiting it regularly with hurricanes. The Panhandle had the highest strike rate in the state. Some of the more judgmental citizens, usually those not profiting from the boom, recoiled at the number of injuries and the odd fatalities during spring break brought on by swimming less than an hour after drinking a 12-pack, balcony leaping, and purple Jesus contesting.

A purple Jesus contest is where young, virile males drink, in one minute, as much high-proof alcohol — usually some water-clear elixir that hasn't aged for years in oaken barrels or touched mineral-free spring water; instead, it's 180 proof. To give the toxin some color, it is mixed with just enough grape or cranberry juice. The winner of a purple Jesus contest is judged to be one *hell of a man*; losers, sometimes to be DOA. While the South has resisted Darwin in the past, such contests demonstrate natural selection clearly.

"Let's see if we can get a beer and a sandwich," said Niles. "We can even nose around a little as we do."

***

Up ahead was a ramshackle, weathered restaurant right on the beach. They found a parking space three blocks away. The restaurant had an interior bar and dining room and two exterior areas with benches and tables. One was an exposed deck; the other, which opened to the beach and Gulf beyond, was covered by the deck overhead. Niles motioned Teal toward the latter.

"I'm too whey-faced to be out there for long."

An attractive, young, blonde woman, wearing shorts and a halter top, greeted them and asked them if they wanted something from the bar. Niles ordered a Bass Ale; Teal asked for a Dixie Blackened Voodoo. The restaurant didn't carry either, so they settled for two Budweisers. About ten minutes later, the waitress came back with two Miller Genuine Drafts and menus. Niles felt that all American beer was inferior to English beer, but he drew the line at absurdity. Draft, by definition and process, wasn't pasteurized and had to come from a keg. He sent the sweet young thing back for what they had ordered.

They drank the beer slowly and watched a group of young women playing volleyball on the beach in front of them. They were comely, but not very athletic and seemed to derive a great deal of satisfaction for only occasionally getting the ball over the net. When the waitress returned, they ordered two more beers and, at Teal's suggestion, a dozen raw oysters apiece with two bowls of gumbo. The Gulf was a flat blue-green expanse in front of them.

The oysters were magnificent, the gumbo mediocre. "Florida has better oysters than Louisiana, but nobody outside Louisiana knows how to make good gumbo. It's the roux. One must be very careful with the roux," said Teal. "Once, I had Enola Prudhomme make gumbo for me. She knew how to make the roux."

When the waitress brought the check, Niles asked her where they could get a room and where the higher class restaurants and the night spots were in Panama City. She said that the town was full, they just had to look for vacancy signs and take whatever was available.

She did, however, have first-hand knowledge about the night spots and pretty reliable heresy about the better restaurants.

The waitress was right: Panama City was just about full. Florida is too hot in summer for northerners, but its coast is cooler than central Georgia, Alabama, or Mississippi. After an hour's search, they found a small mom and pop motel about five blocks back from the beach. They checked in, dumped their gear, and then Niles went out to buy a long-billed hat with a French Foreign Legion neck cover, and some SPF-30 sunscreen. Teal went out too, but Niles didn't know where. He just told Niles he'd meet him back at the room in about an hour. After they met up again, they spent the rest of the afternoon combing the area's marinas.

Their cover was simple: they were supposed to get together with some new friends to do some fishing, but they had forgotten the name of the marina they were supposed to meet at, and they had left the slip of paper with the marina's name on it at the restaurant they had met at to make their plans. Neither could remember the name because the night had been long and the celebration alcoholic. They thought the name of the two men were Campbell though, two brothers. "If they had been here," said Teal, "you'd remember them. They were very fit, trim but not skinny like distance athletes. More like swimmers."

Niles and Teal went to eleven area marinas. No one remembered seeing the Campbells.

Late in the afternoon at the last marina, on the western edge of town, they stopped at a bar named The Dead Pelican. It was a locals' joint, but Teal thought they might learn something there. The Dead Pelican had a long straight bar, lined with heavy-based, backless stools, some tables and booths for food service — sandwiches and burgers — against the Gulf-view wall, a sizable dance floor to the far right, and another room just off the entrance where there were four regulation-size pool tables. Two of the pool tables were in use.

They sat at the bar drinking Budweiser. Niles had ordered a Bass ale, which they also didn't have, so Teal didn't bother asking for a

Dixie Blackened Voodoo. There were only a half dozen customers at the bar, but Teal, eyeing the size of the dance floor, figured the place would be packed by nine o'clock with people drinking, dancing, and fighting: nighttime entertainment in a small southern town. Throw in a local and college spring break mix, you were guaranteed any number of fights.

The barmaid, an attractive but hard-looking young women, probably an oysterman's wife or ex-wife, wore cut-offs and a T-shirt which advertised something across the front. Niles felt a bit circumspect trying to read the advertisement across her ample breasts. Teal, on the other hand, took his time and read every word carefully, no doubt because his cradle language was French, not English. She hadn't seen the Campbells either; but seemed to want to talk to Niles. Niles asked her about the night spots in the area, and she confirmed the waitress' selections, asking him if that was what he was doing tonight. Niles didn't answer.

"I'll probably be at the Chart Room at about nine. Maybe I'll see you there," she said.

"That's entirely possible," said Niles. He ordered another round and a rack of balls, and he and Teal went into the side room where the pool tables were. The first two tables were in use, so they chose the back table in the right-hand corner. Niles racked the balls.

"Straight pool, rack of fifty," he said to Teal.

"Flip or lag for break," asked Teal.

"Lag," responded Niles.

The two players on the table directly in front of theirs gave them a side-long glance and one said something to the other that neither Niles nor Teal could make out. Teal won the lag, so Niles broke, if you could call it that. He hit the corner ball on the right side of the rack, sending two balls out and back to cushions and then back almost exactly where they had been originally racked. What Teal was left with was a rack packed almost as tightly as when he had racked it and a cue ball lodged up against the back rail; all he could do was play safe.

"What kind of candy-ass game is that they're playing," said one of the 8-ball players in front of them. They were both in their mid-twenties, broad-backed and thick armed. The one who spoke wore a football practice jersey that exposed his beer gut. The other one wore a T-shirt advertising The Dead Pelican.

"Probably some Limey game. Y'all hear him talk," said one of the players from the other table. He was tallest of the four and just a little thinner than the two across from him. The last one, the one who hadn't said anything yet, was a fire plug, five feet eight or so and about 220 pounds.

"Bad enough we got to put up with these college assholes and even some niggers who come in here from time to time, now we got us Limeys."

"Now, Bobby Lee," said the one wearing The Dead Pelican T-shirt, "that ain't fair, comparing Limeys to niggers. A lot a good shit came out of England, like Scotch whisky. Limeys ain't bad. They are kinda like our cousins, even if they do talk like a bunch of fucking faggots." The four laughed. "On the other hand, what'd we ever git from Africa other than niggers, AIDS — which came from niggers fucking monkeys — and hurricanes?"

"How about algebra, irrigation, libraries, and our alphabet, which you probably have some difficulty identifying even on an eye chart?" answered Niles.

The tall one stood full height and walked over to the axis of the four tables, blocking Niles' way. The fire plug stood behind him. The football jersey moved to the tall one's right, and The Dead Pelican T-shirt, to his left. The only way out of the room was through them.

Teal knew that Niles had a reputation for being tough, but he had never seen him in action. People who were out of line at *Beyond Good and Evil* never seemed to want to challenge him. All Niles had to do was talk to them. There was something in his look that foretold of a bad ending to their stupidity. Niles stood there stroking the pool cue at chest level, parallel to the floor, with his right hand through the bridge the fingers of his left hand formed. Teal was worried. He had seen plenty of bar fights in south Louisiana, but this was four against two, and the rednecks didn't give Niles enough swinging room for the cue to be an effective weapon in such close quarters.

"You making fun of my friends?" the tall one asked.

Teal could see the barmaid in the other room gradually becoming aware of the situation. She looked like she was deciding whether to call 911 or to try to calm everyone down. Before she could make up her mind, Niles drop-kicked the tall one in the balls, stuck the business end of the cue into the soft flesh at the 'V' at the base of the neck of the redneck wearing the football jersey and rammed the handle of the cue into the right eye socket of the one wearing The Dead Pelican T-shirt.

"The lame, the halt, and the blind," said Niles, "always go for soft tissue."

"What about him," said Teal, referring to the fireplug who was just standing there not knowing what to do.

"Oh, he won't bother us," said Niles. "He knows that if he does, I'll really have to hurt him."

The fireplug backed around the table, hands open in front of his chest and let them pass. Niles went over to the bar and said to the barmaid, "sorry I had to make a mess, love, perhaps I can make it up by buying you a drink at the Chart Room tonight."

The barmaid, too, had seen lots of fights in her time, but none that short. She looked at Niles, smiled and answered, "Have a bourbon and coke waiting for me at nine o'clock."

***

The One Corner Stop 'N Fill in Carabelle was your typical *stop and rob* just west of town, if Carabelle can be called a town. It was comprised of a motel, a bar and restaurant, a couple of seafood warehouses, and a police station that was, indeed, located in a phone booth. It was in the design of Giles Gilbert Scott, just like the ones you used see in London. Apparently, if a citizen needed police help, he went to the phone booth and called the posted number, and within minutes the police chief, the only police officer in the town, pulled up to the booth. The number posted was to the chief's house and the call forwarded to his cruiser when he was not at home.

Keagan and Kelly arrived at the One Corner Stop 'N Fill at about two o'clock. A large, dull-eyed, overweight, teenaged black girl sat behind the counter by the cash register. Keagan showed her his DEA identification, produced the lottery ticket, told her that the state lottery office in Jacksonville had said the ticket had been sold here, and asked her if she were on duty on July 18th, the date printed on the ticket. Keagan might as well have asked her to explain anti-matter.

"Duz you wants to buy a lottery ticket?" she asked Keagan.

"No, I want some information about this ticket."

"The Instant Lotto cost fifty cent. The six number quick-pic ticket cost a dollar."

"No," said Keagan, "I don't want to buy a lottery ticket. I want information about this one."

The girl took the ticket from Keagan and punched some numbers into the lottery computer, mouthing each number as she did. "You din't win no money with this one; might but jest trow hit away."

Keagan reached across the counter and took the ticket back just as another black woman, this one much trimmer and looking infinitely more intelligent, came out of the back room.

"Is there a problem here, Keshia?" she asked.

"No, ma'am, this fella just checking his lottery ticket. He goin' to be workin' yet another day."

Keagan again produced his DEA identification, showed the woman the lottery ticket, and restated what the lottery office in Jacksonville had said.

"Keshia, why don't you go in the back and fill up the beer coolers." The woman took the ticket, went over to the lottery computer, punched in a few numbers, and said, "Yes, this ticket was purchased here. What do you want to know?"

Keagan gave her a description of the Campbells and asked if she remembered them. "Sure, I remember them."

"How can you be so positive?" asked Kelly.

"Most of the people we get in here are dressed in cut-offs and T-shirts. These two were wearing pleated tropical wool slacks and Ralph Lauren polo shirts with the collars up. Even the tourists we get in here aren't dressed like that. The men tend to be pink and bald and fat to one degree or another."

"You sound pretty observant," said Keagan.

"Observant for a store manager?"

"Well, yes," said Keagan apologetically.

"Last year I was working in New York, on the fast track with a six-figure salary, when my father, who owns this place, had a stroke. I came down to take care of him. Now I'm the manager of the One Corner Stop 'N Fill in Carabelle, Florida. It's a good thing I've got an MBA from the Fuqua School of Business at Duke, otherwise I don't know how I would I manage to keep track of the varied inventory we carry," she said as she flourished her arm in a wide arc.

"Do you remember what kind of car they were driving?" asked Keagan.

"Yeah, a rented blue Ford Taurus."

"How do you know it was rented?" asked Kelly.

"It had the sticker."

"The sticker?"

"AV, a lot of states used to have specially designate plates, then they gradually got rid of them because too many foreign tourists are getting killed in Miami. I guess the Miami low-lifes think the tourists are easier pickings. They'll do fine as long as they stick to foreign tourists. Wait till they run into a New York stock trader, though. Then they will wish they were on a boat going south."

"Speaking of going, do you know which way they were headed," asked Keagan.

"Yeah, east."

"You've been very helpful, Ms. . . . " said Kelly.

"Clark, Sassi Clark."

"Oh, one more question, Ms. Clark. Illogical things bother me; how did this place come to be named the One Corner Stop 'N Fill. You can't have one corner, minimum is two."

"See that bar over there," asked Sassi, as she hooked her thumb toward the building next door. "That place was started by a guy named Gilhouly, a retired Irish cop from Hoboken. Ever been to Hoboken?"

"I've been there," said Keagan. Kelly hadn't.

"Well, Gilhouly maintained, and judging from your accents you probably already know this story. Gilhouly maintained *that, among the many other great contributions that Ireland has made to the world, they invented street corners for the sole purpose of being able to put bars on them.* Judging from what I've seen of Hoboken, he may have been right. Anyway, there are no corners on US 98 in Carabelle — even County 67 doesn't really form a corner, the angle it comes in — so he decided to call his place *Gilhouly's One Corner Pub.* My father was, until recently — maybe that's why he had a stroke — a regular customer of Gilhouly's, and so when he built this place, he called it the *One Corner Stop 'N Fill.*"

"Thank you for the local lore and the information; you have been most helpful," said Keagan.

"I suspect there is a certain amount of lore surrounding you two that's a better story than Gilhouly's about the Irish inventing the corner. Have a nice day now, and y'all come back soon."

✳✳✳

"Pretty smart lady in there. Too bad she had to end up in a town that has only has one corner and a Brit phone booth for a police station," said Kelly as they got back in the car.

"I wouldn't worry about her, Kelly. I'll bet if we come back this time next year, she'll own most of the town."

"I wouldn't be a bit surprised," said Kelly. "What next, Mick? Drive east, but where?"

Keagan started the car and turned up the air conditioner before he reached over to get the map out of the glove box. He unfolded it to the section that showed the eastern part of the Panhandle. He found Carabelle and followed US 98 to the edge of the page, where East Point was the last town. He flipped that map over, continuing to follow US 98.

"Not east, Kelly, west. They bought the ticket on their way to Jacksonville, that's clear. Why did they drive from Atlanta to Jacksonville via Carabelle? If they haven't already unloaded the paintings, they must have been scouting for a place to make the exchange. Look at the map. Ten miles east of here is a good road that could take them north to I-10, then to Jacksonville. Heading east, the road bends away from the coast, paralleling I-10, and then dips south. That would be a much longer way to take and doesn't square with either the mileage they racked up or the fuel level that was in the Taurus. No, they have to be west of here."

"Why not north, Mick?"

"Why come through Carabelle, then?"

"Stalking horse?"

"No, Kelly, Jacksonville is the stalking horse. Buying a lottery ticket in Carabelle was a mistake, very uncharacteristic from what we've seen of them so far. The next place I would look is Apalachicola. It's about twenty-five miles from here. I liked it from the time we discovered where they bought the lottery ticket. If the exchange is to be made on the Panhandle, this is the ideal place. It's fronted by a number of barrier islands that extend about twenty-fives miles to the west and fifteen miles to the east, and there is a very large river that runs all the way up into Georgia and Alabama. If I were the Campbells, here's where I would make the switch."

"But if there are forty miles of islands out there and a big, navigable river that runs all the way across the state, how are we going to find them? They could be anywhere on those islands or standing on a bridge for that matter, waiting for the buyer to motor up right under them."

"You heard the lady in there, Kelly. They are still dressed as though they were in Palm Beach, not on the *Redneck Riviera*. Somebody will remember them, even if they change clothes."

Twenty-Six

The Campbells had, indeed, changed their clothes because they were at a fish camp on the west side of the Apalachicola River, just north and west of old Fort Gadsden, tucked in behind a large island that was situated about twenty miles from the mouth of the river. The fishing was excellent, but the cover was even better. There are no towns along the river until Estiffanulga, about fifty river miles to the north. While there are a few towns set back from the river, the closest was Bucks Siding about ten miles inland. The river gets a certain amount of recreational travel in the spring and fall, but there isn't much traffic on it in the high heat of summer.

Just across from the camp, on the east side of the river, is the Apalachicola National Forest. There were a few fire and wildlife roads through the National Forest that provided access to the river from County 65, but far fewer than had the land been developed. Also, since there was an alligator farm on the south side of the forest that occasionally had escapees, even the locals were a little circumspect about fishing in there. To the west of the camp is a swamp, which provides a ten-mile buffer between the river and FL 71.

The Campbells had picked an ideal spot for the exchange, if its remoteness be excepted. They had taken other precautions as well, for they didn't trust Señor Cavelya. Cavelya knew he was buying stolen property, which made him a thief, just as they were thieves. Despite the cliché, the Campbells understood that there was no honor among them. They had four planned escape routes. Their rental car was parked on an Apalachicola National Forest wildlife road, just in from the east bank of the river, north of Fort Gadsden. Additionally, along with the camp that they had rented for five hundred dollars for two weeks, they had also rented the camp owner's old pickup truck and his canoe. The truck wasn't much, but it would get them as far as the Tallahassee or the Mobile airport if it had to; in the meantime it wouldn't look conspicuous parked along County 67. The canoe that they had also rented from the camp owner was equipped with an inboard engine with very little draft. It easily got them through the shallow water of the west side of the island that fronted the camp, but also had enough power and range – with only one extra gas can – to take them north to Blountstown where the first bridge that crossed the river was located. The engine was pitched high enough that it could probably take them west across the swamp to FL 71, if worse came to worse.

They had taken other precautions as well. While they never carried guns when they were stealing because anyone they had reason to shoot during a theft would be innocent, they always carried them when they sold their goods because their clients were not innocent, and the court would probably reduce their sentence commensurately for killing them. Both were very competent with guns. Both carried H&K 9mm's because they had heard H&K made the world's best 9mm's. H&K's price authenticated that claim, even if the guns were patently ugly and had a sloppy trigger pull. Normally, the Campbells would never buy anything that was ugly, and while they briefly considered Sigs, which were also quite expensive but not as much as H&K's, they were lured to the H&K because they believed that "you get what you pay for," which was more often than not true.

James also had an AR-15, the civilian model of the M-16. Greg carried a Remington model 870 Express, a pump-action 12 gauge that held seven rounds after he had removed the magazine dowel. So much for the Federal Migratory Bird Law, disregard of which would probably add another six months to their sentence if they got caught. But then neither James nor Greg planned on getting caught nor were they planning on shooting migratory birds, so it was probably a wash.

Teal had been right: the Campbells were rock climbers. They were also experienced woodsmen, so if they had to cross the swamp to FL 71 or bolt cross-country through the National Forest, they could do so without getting lost, being bitten by a snake, and even being eaten by an alligator. They had the know-how and they had the equipment.

***

Niles and Teal didn't go to the Chart Room that night because the the only thing they'd gain was satisfying a bar maid and making themselves susceptible to the revenge The Dead Pelican toughs could muster from their hospital beds. Niles wasn't afraid of their reprisals; he just thought the risk-benefit ratio wasn't favorable. He didn't want to kill someone just to make a new female acquaintance. Instead, they called Keagan who told him he had reserved a room for him and Teal at the St. George Inn on St. George Island for the following night, and set up a meeting with them at the Gibson at 5:00 that night. Niles was convinced that the Campbells were not in Panama City, but he and Teal decided to spend the night there rather than to head out at this hour. They'd move on to Apalachicola the next morning and check out St. Joseph Peninsula State Park on their way.

***

Niles and Teal had lunch at the *Toucan* in Mexico Beach, across the bay from St. Joseph's Peninsula State Park. No one at the *Toucan* could identify the Campbells, either. Afterwards, they detoured over to the state park and checked out the campsites and the beach. They drove slowly through the park, checking first the camp sites and then the beach accesses. There were no rental cars parked anywhere. The park has the highest sand dunes in the state, so the beach wasn't visible from the campground, meaning they had to get out of the car and walk out to the beach through several access points in order to be sure the Campbells weren't there.

There were few people on the beach because of the July heat, and most of the campsites were empty for the same reason. At mid-day, the tourists were out seeking the air conditioning of restaurants or shops or supermarkets, biding their time waiting for the relative cool of the evening.

Pretending to look for their buddies, they asked the rangers on duty if they had seen anyone fitting the Campbells' description. Neither had. Next, they checked out the convenience stores just outside the park. No one remembered seeing two athletically trim men. This was summer: their customers tended to be pot-bellied, pink, and predictable both in appearance and in what they bought. They bought beer and soft drinks, ice, sunscreen, sandwiches, and ice cream for the kids when they couldn't control them any other way. Both Niles and Teal agreed that the Campbells were not at the state park and never had been. By three o'clock they were on their way to Apalachicola.

***

Apalachicola is a curiosity. It touts itself as the *Oyster Capital of the World*, but other places (some of the towns along Chesapeake Bay, for instance) would dispute their claim. It was once America's fifth largest commercial seaport largely because of the cotton and timber that came down the Apalachicola River on barges from Alabama and Georgia. Today, however, it is contained by its remoteness – remote by Florida standards because it is eighty miles from an Interstate, remote by virtue of the state parks and national forest that flank it, and remote by the long-ago spite of a pulp company that wanted to relocate there in order to harvest the skinny pine that grows in the area and float the trees down river as had been done in previous centuries.

The town fathers, however, rejected the pulp company's bid because the tannin from the logs and the sulfur from the pulp process would ruin the oyster beds, And so the lumber company chose a secondary site, but also bought up as much of the area around Apalachicola as it could, productive or not. Local lore maintains that the lumber company said that if they couldn't have Apalachicola, then no one else would either, an epic production replayed too frequently.

In light of its claim as the *Oyster Capital of the World,* or at least that it is a credible contender to that throne, Apalachicola is a viable small town. Its cotton warehouses are old, and crumbling and timber no longer floats down the Apalachicola River; however, it has a couple of decent seafood restaurants and inexpensive motels, and it was only about twelve miles from St. George State Park, one of the top ten beaches in the country, Hawaii included. Finally, it had the Gibson Inn.

The Gibson Inn had been in Apalachicola since 1890 and prospered until the 1950's. It changed hands at that time and fell into disrepair and even greater disrepute, an appreciable feat considering that it had been a bordello earlier in the century. In the late '70s two fellows from Georgia came through the area and upon seeing the inn's potential, bought it, refurbished it, and turned it into one of the premier inns of the myth that is *Old Florida.*

The most impressive feature of the Gibson Inn was the porch that wrapped around three sides of the building. The bar lay just off one side of the porch and had three sets of French doors that opened to a porch that fronted the dining room, and while the dining room had only an emergency exit to the porch, its windows were large, close together, and let in a lot of light and a view of the main street, which was not particularly picturesque but provided the room with a feeling of openness. The lobby was small and quaint, panelled in bead wood. The rooms were irregularly shaped, in the way all hotel rooms that have been redesigned to accommodate private bathrooms are, and while those bathrooms were modern, they all contained outsized, lion-pawed tubs.

***

Keagan and Kelly were sitting on the porch of the Gibson Inn at five o'clock, enjoying a drink when Niles and Teal arrived. Teal was carrying a large paper shopping bag in his left hand. "Sit down; I'll get you both a drink. Niles, a Bass Ale?" asked Mick.

"Don't tell me this quaint backwater has Bass Ale?"

"Yes, it does; however, given its location on the Gulf of Mexico, calling it a 'backwater' seems a bit of a misnomer."

"I'll apologize to the entire house if you get me a bloody bottle of Bass."

"Teal, a Blackened Voodoo?"

"Yes, otherwise, I'll have a Bass too."

"Kelly, another?"

"Not yet, Mick."

Mick went through the open French doors into the bar. "What's in the parcel, Teal?" asked Kelly.

"A present for you."

"And what kind of present might it be, and why would you be spending your money on me when we have only known each other for a few short days? Are you trying to make Mick jealous?" she teased.

"I may be Cajun, but I'm not entirely crazy, at least not in that way. Mick says you have a thing for hats, but I've only seen the big floppy one you're wearing now, which is fine because being an Irlandaise, you have little natural protection from the Gulf sun, but you need a proper hat for the Gulf. I just thought you might like a change." Teal handed the package to Kelly, who opened it to find a white straw, summer cowboy hat. She was fitting it to her head as Mick came back from the bar with their drinks.

"Mick, look at what Teal bought me. Isn't he thoughtful? How do I look?"

Mick put the drinks down, looked over at Kelly and said, "Like an Irish flying nun."

"Mick Keagan, you have the sensitivity of the shanty Irish. You could learn a thing or two from your gallant French friend."

Teal sat there very smug and a little bit nervous, watching for Keagan's reaction.

"No doubt I could," he smiled, first at Kelly and then at Teal.

"Speaking of learning, what have you learned?" Mick asked as he looked over at Niles and Teal.

"A good deal and nothing at all," responded Niles. "We checked all the marinas and all the up-scale restaurants – such as they were – hotels, and clubs between Panama City and here; no one has seen the Campbells. We checked out St. Andrew's State Park and St. Joe's Peninsula State Park, which has great potential for what they want to do. St. Andrew's isn't accessible by land and since no one has seen them at the marinas, we scratched that off our lists. St. Joe's is accessible by road, but no luck there either. No one has seen them at either spot, and believe me these two would stand out. You do any better?"

"Much like you, Niles, a good deal and nothing at all. We know that they bought the lottery ticket in Carabelle and that they later dumped their rental car at the Jacksonville Airport. I can think of no earthly reason for their being on the Panhandle unless they were scouting a meeting area."

"Of course, they could have already made the exchange," interrupted Kelly.

"I thought that was one of my original premises that you refuted, Kelly."

"Just trying to keep an open mind; see how you influence me, Mick."

"Where does that leave us?" asked Teal, "It's not that I don't appreciate being back where the weather isn't a constant enemy, but I miss Anjali already. If we are going to get rich, let's hurry up and get rich. Otherwise, let's go home. Hmm ... I must be crazy - the land of ice and snow, home? Well, I guess it does have its advantages," Teal momentarily stared off into the far distance. *And Mick does special order a couple of cases of Blackened Voodoo for me a month,* he thought.

"Back to our problem," said Teal. "Judging from the map and from what little I have seen of this area driving in from the west, it strikes me that this is the perfect place to make the exchange. The barrier islands and the big river make it ideal. This part of the Panhandle is a little bit like the coast of Louisiana. Louisiana doesn't have towns that front the coast the way they do here, but the islands and the river make it much more complicated. Mick, can you get me another Blackened Voodoo while I go get the map?"

***

Teal folded the map so that they could see most of the Panhandle - what they couldn't see on one side of the map, he could easily flip over to. "Look at the Panhandle coast. There is some backwater that runs, depending on your perspective, from Pensacola to Panama City; however, there are only two exit points: one through Elgin Air Force Base, and the other at Panama City. From my four years in the Air Force, I can tell you that Elgin would be all wrong. Having just left Panama City, I can tell you that it is all wrong, too. While it also has an Air Force base, Tyndall, there are just too many people in Panama City. Too many boats come though that cut to the Gulf. Too many things could go wrong. I'd never risk it."

"You and Teal seem to be in agreement, Mick," said Kelly. "What do you think, Niles? Where would you look? Isn't this river," Kelly motioned to the arching bridge in front of her, "a bottle neck, too?"

Niles looked at the map and considered Kelly's question for a moment. "Not in the same way. The inland bay by Panama City is self-contained. Essentially, there is only one way in and out. The Apalachicola River is different. They could enter anywhere there's access and float down to the Gulf, or they could enter from the Gulf and motor upstream. Plus, the traffic is different. There you have mostly recreational boats, while here commercial, recreational, and tourists' boats. If they are on the Panhandle, they are within twenty-five miles of here."

Kelly looked at the map, arching her finger back and forth through the area Niles just described. "Great," she said, "twenty-five miles of barrier islands, river backwaters, a national forest, and swamps." For the first time, since she brought up the project to Mick, she saw how the landscape – or more accurately the riparian nature of the area

– complicated locating the Campbells. She realized that this wasn't Belfast or London or even Europe. This was raw America. She quietly wondered how well Mick had adapted to his new country.

"How do we proceed then, Mick?" asked Kelly.

"Niles, why don't you and Teal go over to St. George Island, check in and then nose around the bars out there; there can't be many. Tomorrow cover the marinas and the state park; that's the biggest part of the island. Kelly and I are registered here through Saturday night. We also have a hold on the room for Sunday, depending on what we turn up. There are only a couple of places to check in town here. Tomorrow we'll look at the river: drive up to the national forest and scout around, maybe even take a river cruise. Call us if you turn up anything; otherwise, let's plan on meeting back here at six tomorrow evening. Any questions?"

Twenty-Seven

The Blanca Nieve approached Benson's Marina, St. George Island, Florida at five o'clock on Thursday, July 23rd. Captain Enright secured the boat and checked into the marina office at the land-end of the dock, paid cash for two days' mooring, and picked up the keys to a rental car the Campbells had left for Señor Cavelya. A half hour later Alardo Quillaca Cavelya, his bodyguards with their causally draped weapons, his concupiscent companion, and the two aluminium cases that Enright noticed when Cavelya brought them aboard back in North Captiva, went down the dock to the Chevy Impala that was parked in front of the marina office. Enright reflected that apparently Cavelya's business associates had somehow anticipated his entourage, for the car could accommodate all five of them.

Enright watched them drive away. He was on partial stand-by until Sunday, which meant that he would have to sleep aboard the boat and that he couldn't get too far from it, but he could go out for dinner – as long as he carried his cell phone – and he could go for a run, which was what he was preparing to do five minutes after he lost sight of the Impala.

St. George Island is five miles off the coast from East Point, a town six miles east of Apalachicola. The island is approximately twenty-five miles long, but only about a half mile wide. Like most barrier islands, it follows the coast; that is, east-west in this case. The St. George Inn is a block from the Gulf, where County 300 T's into Gulf

Beach Drive. Benson's Marina is at the axis of the T. Just across the last bridge onto the island, Country 300 becomes a divided road for the half mile width of the island. If you were familiar with St. George Island, you would know that you didn't have to go all the way to the axis of the T and then go back the way you came for a block in order to get to the inn, but that's the way most tourists did it and that's what Niles and Teal did too, so as they stopped at the stop sign at County 300, there was Blanca Nieves straight ahead of them.

The St. George Inn doesn't have the character of the Gibson, but it was much more pleasant than the chain motels. Niles and Teal checked into a second floor room that overlooked County 300 that they had come in on.

"Swim or run?" Niles asked Teal.

"Run," said Teal, "I need to sweat off some weight now that I've found a place that stocks Dixie Blackened Voodoo."

***

They turned east on County 300 and ran toward the state park three miles away. Just as they neared the park entrance, they saw a well-knit man, wearing a fisherman's bill-cap similar to the one Niles wore, running back toward town. He waved a kindred-runner's hello as he passed them, and Niles and Teal waved back. The park gate was open but the office was closed, so they ran on. Within a half mile, there was an access to the beach. Niles and Teal went onto the beach, which was deserted, took off their shirts, their running shoes and socks, and dove into the Gulf. Dolphins were running off-shore, so there were no jellyfish. They swam straight out for a half mile and floated for a while.

"It feels good to be back in the Gulf," said Teal. "There is something I feel in it that I don't feel anywhere else."

"Not even in Lake Placid?"

"The only thing I get from swimming in Lake Placid is blue lips, heart stoppage, and shriveled up balls. You and Mick might feel right at home there, but this *coonass* would rather share the water with sharks than ice floes."

"Bad choice of words," said Niles, "given our present location. Let's get back to shore."

***

On their way back to the inn, they stopped by Benson's Marina to get a close-up of *Blanca Nieve*. She was the biggest thing in the marina. Her registry on her stern, below her name, indicated she was out of Miami. Niles memorized her registration number on the bow.

Back at the inn, they showered and went down to the dining room where they had sea bass and drafts of Bass Ale. "Not Blackened Voodoo, but this stuff ain't bad," said Teal. "Back home I used to drink Blackened Voodoo and Turbo Dog, another dark beer that's brewed by Abita. This stuff isn't real different."

There were few others in the dining room. Overhead, plantation fans whirled and a salt breeze blew through open Bahama shutters. The bar closed with the dining room, so they asked their waitress where they could go for an after-dinner drink. She said that there was a band in the bar in the Buccaneer, a half mile to the west, but the locals mostly went to Harry A's, a block over across County 300. She pointed the direction.

Harry A's was as rickety and ramshackle as the hurricanes over the years could make it without blowing it away, but it was still jumping. The late diners were finishing up their burgers and fries or their fish and fries; the revelers were in the bar, drinking, shooting pool, playing darts, and the lovers were out on a small dance-floor, responding to country rhythms. Niles had been no stranger to pubs in his military career, and of course he worked with Keagan at his uncle's bar before following Keagan to *Beyond Good and Evil*, but Harry A's was Teal's territory. These were his people, three states removed perhaps, but they were Gulf people, and Teal knew Gulf people.

They threaded through the tables and found two seats at the bar. "What can I get you?" asked the bartender.

"I'll have a Remy, straight up," said Teal. Niles started to order a Bass Ale automatically, but thought twice and ordered a Remy also.

The juke box was playing *Boot-Skootin' Boogey*, and the dancers were lining up for slap-leather. Teal was slapping his thigh. Niles looked over at the dart competition and recognized one of the contestants as the man he and Teal saw running back from the state park earlier. The man, whoever he was, was way ahead of his opponent, a young redneck who looked like every other young redneck with his ball cap, long unkempt and unwashed hair, black T-shirt, jeans, boots (in the South, they are cowboy boots; in the North, unlaced work boots), and a crude tattoo that announced to the world – however open-minded that world might consider itself to be – that here was yet another clueless soul.

The runner ended the game with his next dart. The redneck reached into his jeans pocket, pulled out a ball of bills, located a five somewhere near the core and handed it to the runner. The runner looked around, but there were no takers. The redneck's friends had watched the game; they knew they were no match for him.

Niles doubted that any of the rednecks would take on Enright, but he gave them a moment. No one stepped forward, so he went up to Enright as he was putting up his darts. "Are you open for another game?" asked Niles.

Enright was a little suspicious of the English accent. He knew that only the Aussies were better dart players than the English, *but what the hell, I'm American and I can't shoot pool, America's bar game, worth a shit.* "Sure," he said.

"It's your board. What shall we play?" asked Niles.

"I'm open – *301, around the clock*?"

In *301* or any of its derivatives: *401, 501, 601*, etc., the shooter subtracts the number of the wedge where he lands from the game name, *301* in this case. Score a *20* and you're now at *281*, an *11* leaves you at *270*. The object of the game is to reach zero, exactly zero. Sometimes, the player who has the board (that is, who won the last game) might call double out, which means that in order to win the shooter must place his dart in the thin band at the outer edge of the wedge. So if a shot is at 16, he would have to place his dart in the thin outer band of the 8 wedge. A player with an odd number score would first have to lower his score to an even number, then place his dart in the thin outer edge of the number. A *17*, for example, would first require a place to reduce his score to say a *16* or a *14* or a *12* and the double out with an *8* or *7* or *6*. If a number reduces the score to below zero, it doesn't count.

The game was fine if the players were friends or there were scoring beads, but it could too easily lead to a fight among strangers. Bad math or cheating can lead to disagreements among friends.

Niles looked over at the dartboard, but didn't see any scoring beads.

"How about around the clock?" he asked. "I don't see any scoring beads and I'm bad at math."

Standard dart boards are divided into twenty wedges. At the narrow end of the wedges are two small circles. The inner circle is worth fifty points; the outer one, twenty-five points. There are also two sets of narrow bands that circumscribe the wedges. The inner one is the triple band; that is, the player receives three times the numbered value of the wedge if he lands in this narrow slice of the wedge. The outer band is the double-score band. The numbered wedges are separated by thin strips of wire.

The shooter has three darts. The object of a game like around the clock is to progress in succession from one through twenty. A player keeps shooting as long as he continues to score. If a dart lands in a non-scoring area of the board, like the outer circumference, or falls out or sticks in another player's dart, it receives no credit.

The segments or wedges are arranged clockwise as 20-1-18-4-13-6-10-15-2-17-3-19-7-16-8-11-14-9-12-5. The order seems curious at best, and since the game is more than 100 years old no one knows for sure how it got that way. Some have suggested mathematical computations for the sequence, but they are more complex than the originator of the game might have used. The answer probably lies in adding risk to the game. If the wedges were placed in order, say 20-19-18 . . . , then the player could concentrate on a particular area of the board, especially in a game like 301. Miss the 19 and hit a 20 or 18 instead, but in the current order, shoot at 18 and the player might only score a 1 or a 4; the 17 adds the risk of hitting a 2 or a 3, and so on.

While the reason for the order is unknown, the originator of the game is not. The dart board was invented by Brian Gamlin from County Lancashire in England in 1896. Gamlin was a carpenter who may have traveled with a carnival. He made and sold dart boards to augment his income, but if he did indeed travel with a carnival, then the risk explanation makes sense.

Given that there are more than a quadrillion – in this case, exactly 121,645,100,408,832,000 – different possible arrangements of the twenty wedges on a standard dartboard, it is perhaps more than a little surprising that Gamlin's arrangement of the numbers is almost perfect, so perhaps one of the mathematical computations makes sense after all.

"Shoot for first?" asked Niles.

"Sure," said Enright.

Enright was closer to the center bull, so he shot first. He made a one, a two, and a three, but missed the four. Niles shot a one through six, and then missed the seven on purpose. Enright ran through ten. Niles' ego wouldn't let him throw the game, but he didn't want to run out either, so he took it up to sixteen. Enright caught him, but missed the seventeen, and then Niles ran out.

Enright reached into his pocket for the five that the redneck just gave him. "You're good," he said handing the five to Niles.

"Keep it. I didn't think we were playing for money."

"Sure you did."

"Well, then buy me a Bass Ale instead. It will probably cost as much; if it's over, I'll cover the difference."

The two walked over to the bar, where Teal was watching the line dancers regroup. Niles introduced himself and Teal. Enright shook hands with them, introduced himself and ordered a beer for himself and two Bass Ales for Niles and Teal.

"Where are you guys from?" asked Enright, somewhat confused about the English-Cajun team up.

"New York," said Niles, knowing full well that saying New York to anyone who doesn't live there automatically means New York City. Everyone who hasn't been to upstate New York thinks the entire state is skyscrapers and concrete.

"How about you, John? Are you local?" asked Teal.

"Florida, yes. The Panhandle, no. I skipper a boat out of the Fort Myers area." Enright didn't think a couple of New Yorkers – if that's where they were really from – would know where North Captiva is, nor did he want to be that specific.

Niles was disappointed with the answer. He was hoping Enright was the skipper of the big boat they saw at Benson's Marina when they went out for their run, the one with the Miami registry. So far he and Teal had come up with nothing, and he was beginning to get frustrated.

"Business or pleasure?" asked Niles.

"Business," answered Enright. "But not mine. I'm the skipper, not the owner. Oh, the pay's good, but I prefer being my own boss." He looked down at his pager. "I can have one more beer, then I have to go. I never know when I'll get a call to weigh anchor and get under way."

Vince Gill was singing a ballad on the jukebox, so the dance floor was crowded with semi-intoxicated people, pressed together, swaying in glided small circles. Teal was watching them. Cajuns love music. Niles could see that he had transposed himself to some dance hall bar in Lafayette or St. Martinville or some other Cajun town in Louisiana, south of I-10. Niles ordered a round of beers for the three of them.

"What brings you to the Panhandle?" asked Enright, trying to focus the conversation on them, rather than on him. He was a little nervous talking about his employer. He always thought if trouble came it would come from Colombians, Jamaicans, or another Bolivian. Still, a Limey and a Cajun confused and worried him.

"I own an inn in New York, and Teal is my head maintenance man. I'm looking to branch out, have a place in the North for the summer trade and a place in the South for the winter trade. Keep both open all year, fully staffed in high season, core staff in the off season. Connect them with computers."

"Isn't this your busy season up there?" asked Enright.

"Yes, it is, but I have good people, and it's not your busy season here – maybe over in Panama City, but I'll bet spring and fall are better here. People tend to sell more and for a lower price in the off season. Also, I learned a long time ago to visit a place where you think you want to live or where you think you want to own a business in its worst months. Florida and Arizona in the summer, New England in what passes for the spring, and Minnesota in the winter."

"You sound as though you have been around."

"I enjoy your country, and I like seeing different places. I guess it comes from living most of my life on an island. What kind of boat do you skipper?"

Niles used a typical interrogation trick: soften up the person with small talk, then sneak in a question of substance; but Enright was smart and wary, "A power boat, not a sailboat." He finished his beer and begged off. "I've got to get back to my command; I'm on call."

Niles stood and Teal followed his cue; they shook hands all around, and Enright left.

Niles turned to Teal, "I'm going to follow him. You stay here and see what you can find out. You fit in here better than I do. If I'm not back in an hour, call it a night. If I'm not back in two hours, call Mick."

Niles drained the remains of his Bass. He didn't follow Enright, who was walking west when Niles came out of Harry A's. Instead, he cut east over to the St. George Inn, then got into the rented Ford Explorer and – even though he was only a block from the dock – drove over to the parking lot of Benson's Marina and waited. Fifteen minutes later Enright arrived, paused, looked around, then – apparently satisfied – walked down the dock to *Blanca Nieve*.

"Why does it have a Miami registry?" asked Teal, back in their room in the St. George Inn.

"My best guess is that *El Jefe's* chief residence is in Miami, but that he has another place in Fort Myers or maybe on one of those islands just off shore. What are they – Sanibel, Captiva, and North Captiva?"

"How do you know about them?" asked Teal.

"Well, because while you were *besotting* yourself with more Cognac, I was seeing just where Fort Myers was."

"And, weren't you – what was that word – *besotting*?"

"Yes, *besotting*," affirmed Niles.

"Anyway, weren't you *besotting* yourself earlier with Cognac?"

"No, Teal. I was having a postprandial, and that's the difference between the English and the French. The English know how to restrain themselves, but the French don't know when to stop. Louis XIV, Louis XV, Napoleon; French history is rife with examples," Niles said with an unseen smile and turned off the light.

"*Sacra, Mogee, Tupper Lake*," muttered Teal. The expression wasn't Cajun, but it was at least part French. It was the favorite mild oath of French Canadian descendants who lived near Tupper Lake, a town about thirty miles from Lake Placid. Mogee was apparently a mayor there some time or other. The expression leaves doubt as to whether he was a good mayor or a bad mayor, just that he was a memorable one.

Twenty-Eight

Niles and Teal took a two-mile swim in the morning. They didn't see Enright out for a run, but *Blanca Nieve* was still at Benson's. Niles called Mick from the beach at St. George State Park. "Mick, we've found a possible. Met a bloke last night who is the skipper of a boat out of, he says, Fort Myers, Florida, but is registered in Miami. He seemed like a nice enough fellow. He's from Florida, but not a local. The name of the boat is *Blanca Nieve*, which, if I remember what little Spanish I know, means Snow White. The captain is the only life I've seen on board. The size of the boat, its registration, and its cute name suggests a street allusion rather than one to the Brothers Grimm."

"I think you are right, Niles. A Latin type, a woman half his age, and three bullet heads checked in to the Gibson last evening shortly after you and Teal left. I got a look at the inn's registry later, and the Latin type registered as *Alardo Quillaca Cavelya, North Captiva Island, Florida*. Kelly called one of her contacts. It seems the DEA has a great deal of interest in Señor Cavelya, as they suspect him of being the major drug trafficker in southwest Florida. It would appear that the puzzle is finally coming together."

"The third piece, the Campbells, however, is still missing. From what you have said, they don't appear to be on St. George Island. Send Teal back to Apalachicola, but have him meet me at noon in the parking lot of the Red Lion – a supermarket – on US 98, just after it bends past the Gibson. While we were all together in full

237

view at the Gibson last night, none of the principals had arrived yet; for now, I think we would be better served not appearing together. If Señor Cavelya gets suspicious of Kelly and me, he will just be suspicious of two of us; we have an advantage in being four."

"What do you want me to do?" asked Niles.

"Try to get aboard the boat – what did you call it – *Blanca Nieve.* See what you can learn. I'm particularly interested in charts. They could be headed right back to North Captiva — if that is indeed Señor Cavelya's place of residence — or they could be headed for New Orleans or Houston to catch a plane to South or Central America. Look for cash and drugs as well. If you find any, take it. Without cash or drugs they won't be able to buy the Picassos. And look for weapons. If you find any, snap or remove the firing pins. I don't need to tell you what to do; you know better than I. Do anything that will give us the advantage."

"I've got you, Mick."

"Call me when you learn something; otherwise, I'll send Teal back with instructions. I don't want to call you in case you are on the boat at that time. A telephone call during a B&E wouldn't do your blood pressure much good," he said, although both of them knew that a nuclear attack wouldn't do much to alter Niles' blood pressure.

✳✳✳

"Right you are, Mick," Niles said, verifying the lie.

Keagan and Teal met in the parking lot of the Red Lion at noon. They sat in the Ford Explorer and looked at an area map that Mick had purchased at a local sporting goods store. "I think the Campbells are on the river, Teal. Kelly and I are going to take a cruise up it. I want you to canvas the boat rentals, the National Forest Visitors' Information Center, bars, bait shops, sporting goods stores, anything you can think of that might lead us to them. Ask about fishing the river, camp rentals, outsiders. Turn on your Cajun charm and accent. This river is nothing more than a big bayou. These folks are your cousins. Maybe not Cajuns, but you know how to talk with these swampers. We need to find the Campbells."

"Mick, who are these people? The Campbells sound like a couple of high class thieves. Thieves with skills that are not your usual *smash and grab* or *stick-em up and give me all your money* kind, but thieves nonetheless. But the buyer sounds like some fat cat who needs some fancy pictures because his mother never hung up his grade-school art work on the refrigerator. Or is he some drug scum who needs the pictures to prove he's something other than a bottom feeder?"

"Kelly's contact tells her that Señor Alardo Quillaca Cavelya is probably the leading drug trafficker in southwest Florida. I don't think we are going to have a lot of time here. According to the registry at the Gibson, Señor Cavelya – if he is the buyer – is leaving on Sunday. We only have today and tomorrow to interdict the sale."

"Mick, I know you were once an English teacher, so I don't mind you using words I don't understand, but last night Niles told me I was *besotting* myself, even though he drank almost as much as I did. I didn't understand *besotting* last night, and I don't understand *interdict* now. I think Niles was pulling my leg, but I don't think you are. What the fuck does *interdict* mean."

"Sorry, Teal. Let me try to explain. You know how the French believe that they invented cooking?"

"Of course, because we did."

"Well, the English – and even more so the Irish – think we invented language or at least a facility for it. *Interdict* means to fuck up the plans of Señor Cavelya. Keep him from buying the Picassos, ensure that we get them, the reward, and stay alive in the process."

"That I understand, Mick," said Teal. "Are you sure this Cavelya fellow is a drug smuggler?"

"One of the biggest, Teal."

* * *

Keagan and Kelly arranged a river cruise with a realtor. They told her they were professional photographers, had photographed animals all over the world and wanted to experience the riparian wildlife of the Florida Panhandle. The hook was that if they found the right place, the article would bring eco-tourists into the area. The agent was to take them up river about twenty miles or so to look at a number of rental-camps that had observation potential: places where they could see birds and alligators, snakes and raccoons, deer, wild pigs, and maybe even a panther – all at a safe distance, of course.

***

Niles kept watch on Benson's Marina from the porch of the St. George Inn. At a little after noon, he walked past it to a weathered stilt-house restaurant – just west of the marina – for a beer and a bowl of chowder. *Blanca Nieve* was still at dock. From the restaurant, Niles could see Enright working on the boat. No one else was evidently on board.

Niles finished his lunch and walked back to the St. George. Just as he resumed his position on the porch, he saw Enright come out of the marina parking lot and jog toward the state park. *Talk about mad dogs and Englishmen*, thought Niles. If Enright was a creature of habit, he would run to the gate at the state park and turn around. The run was approximately six miles and probably took him about forty-eight minutes.

Niles was already wearing a swimsuit, so he didn't have to change, but he did need something else. When he talked to Mick earlier, he knew he might have to go into the water to get aboard *Blanca Nieve*, so he had gone to the mini-mart that was across the road, bought two apples and triple wrapped them in the roll-off plastic bags that such stores provide. The triple-wrapped bag was waterproof and was ample enough to store a rolled bath towel, which Niles had quickly stuffed into it. He walked toward the marina and entered the Gulf just to the west of the marina.

Niles figured someone at the marina would challenge him if he walked down the dock to the boat, so he decided to board her from the water; however, if he boarded her from the water, he would drip all over her deck, and Enright would know that someone had been aboard. He came out of the water and perched halfway up the ladder on the stern, removed the towel from the plastic bags, and dried himself. What little water did drip on the deck he wiped off with the towel. The Florida sun would evaporate what the towel didn't soak up or what he might have missed. He stepped on the towel, letting it absorb the water on the bottom of his feet, then wrapped the towel around him, patting it to absorb the water from his wet swimsuit, minimizing the drip.

The companion way was locked, but it wasn't a serious lock. Niles picked it in less than a minute, without leaving any scratches. He entered and relocked the door. He checked his watch. Twelve minutes had passed since Enright first emerged from the parking lot. If he were right about Enright's speed and distance, he would have thirty-six minutes left. He set the elapsed-time function on his watch for thirty-two minutes, giving him four minutes to get off the boat. He went into the master cabin and searched the lockers there. He found the Franchi almost at once. Removing or breaking the firing pin on a double barrel shotgun is not as easy as it is on an automatic or pump action gun; however, the trigger assembly is readily exposed on a double barrel, so Niles broke the trigger spring instead. He searched the master cabin carefully, thinking that Cavelya would want to keep any sizeable amount of money close to him. All he found was fifteen hundred dollars, which he left. He couldn't buy the Picassos with that.

Twenty-five minutes left.

He searched each of the other cabins as methodically as he had the master cabin. He found skeet guns there and couple of boxes of 9mms and 12-guage shotgun shells. He left the ammunition as a few more rounds weren't going to make that much difference; besides, his taking them might tip Cavelya that someone had been aboard. He disabled the shotguns. Fifteen minutes left.

The galley didn't take too long to look through: stove, refrigerator, pantry, larder. All predictable and in order. The saloon, however, took more time because of the furniture and the number of lockers it contained. If you don't care about leaving evidence behind, you can go through a place very quickly. But if you want to leave it as you found it, you have to remember how you found it. In Northern Ireland, when he searched a Council House apartment, he carried a digital camera and photographed everything he touched – room by room – so he could leave it exactly as he had found it. Here he had to memorize the layout of whatever he touched.

Nothing in the saloon.

Eight minutes left.

Niles climbed to the bridge from the semi-spiral staircase on deck. He had to be careful searching the bridge because he could be seen there, so it took him longer. He stayed mostly on the deck, below view. He found the charts that Enright had used to get to St. George Island, and he found other charts that plotted the course from North Captiva Island to Miami. Some routes were direct, and some were via Key West. Nothing to Houston or New Orleans.

In a locker below the console, Niles found a pair of binoculars. He took them out of their case. He rose up, just high enough to see out the windows. Everything seemed to be quiet, both in the marina and out to sea. With the binoculars, Niles scanned the road from the state park. Nothing at first, then he saw Enright closer to the marina than he should have been.

"Bugger's running seven and a half minute miles," said Niles to himself. "I've only got one more minute here."

Niles put the binoculars back where he found them and scanned the rest of the charts. Only one interested him. It was an unplotted chart of the Apalachicola River. Niles put it back in place and peeked out the window to see Enright coming down the dock. He left the bridge, re-entered the saloon as Enright came aboard. Enright unlocked the saloon door as Niles slipped into the engine room below decks.

The bilge was as stale, as stagnant, and as hot as July in Florida could make it.

"I hope this son of a bitch goes and takes a shower right away, and is not one to sit around drinking beer after a workout the way Mick and I do," Niles wished.

Thirty minutes and two Budweisers later, Enright took a shower, and Niles took his leave – three pounds lighter – from his sauna in the bilge. Before he left the engine room, he was careful to wipe his feet with the towel wrapped around his waist, so as not to leave oil stains on the deck.

***

Kelly was wearing the new cowboy hat that Teal had bought for her, jeans, and a light long-sleeve cotton pullover. Keagan wore shorts, a Ralph Lauren polo shirt, a manufactured smile, and SPF-30 sunscreen. She and Keagan were at dockside on the river about three blocks from the Gibson Inn. A white Lincoln Town Car pulled up. The car had a realtor's name and logo, Forsythe Realty, affixed on magnetic signs on the car's front doors. A short, mildly plump middle-aged female dynamo, dressed in a Chico's summer dress who carried in one hand a pair of gumboots similar to those worn by commercial fisherman and an enormous straw handbag in the other, got out of the car. She walked straight up to Kelly, thinking that Kelly – as the little woman – was the one she had to convince to get the rental. "Hey, y'all, I'm Sally Mae Mathers with Forsythe Realty. We spoke on the phone earlier; that is, if y'all are the folks who inquired about rentin' a camp for bird-watchin' and such."

"Yes," Kelly answered, "we are they. I am Eileen Kelly, and this is Mick Shaw. We are interested in renting a cabin for two weeks, very near the river, so that we can photograph wildlife for an article we are putting together for *National Geographic*." *If you are going to lie,* thought Kelly, *lie big.*

"Why, honey, y'all sure have a nice way of talkin'. Where you from?"

"We are both from Boston," answered Keagan.

"Well, y'all follow me, and we'll get under way."

Sally Mae Mathers led them down the dock onto a slip-run to a 24' with twin 115 hp Yamaha outboards and a Bimini that bore the same name and logo of the white Lincoln Town Car. From the enormous straw handbag, she produced a set of keys fastened to a chunk of day-glow plastic that might have been large enough to serve as a flotation device, which certainly explained how she had located the keys so quickly. She fired up the engine, asked Mick to cast off, and slipped out of her heels and into the gumboots. She eased out of the marina and into the river channel before she gunned the engine such that Keagan and Kelly almost lost their balance.

Unlike the Suwannee River that also flows out of the north, across the Florida Panhandle and into the Gulf of Mexico, the riparian landscape of the Apalachicola River was less varied. It is a meandering river that flows through flat land and bleeds out to form swamps. It was wider and deeper near the mouth, where it was affected by the estuarine fluctuations of the Gulf. There are no twenty-to-thirty-foot clay and limestone canyons such as those that channel the Suwannee. Mostly, the Apalachicola River threads along scrub and saw palmetto banks all the way to the Gulf. The pines take over where the river loses its influence.

Near shore, egrets and the occasional blue heron stood at crooked attention in the shallows, stabbing at fish as they swam by. Not far up the river, the Gulf breeze ceased to have an effect. The air was heavier here, the sun seemed hotter.

Sally Mae eased back on the throttle. She steered the boat over to the east side of the river. "Over there," she pointed to what appeared to be the west bank, "is an island. It began about two miles back, runs about another three quarters of a mile north. There's great fishing just to the west of that island, and of course good fishing means lots a birds and critters. Hard to see from here because the scrub's so thick. There's a camp over there, but it is rented this week. Now over here on the east side of the river, where the scrub gives way to grass, is a good place to see critters. They come down for water if the tide has just about ebbed. It's the only open spot on that side of the river for miles. The camp's a little rough, but the location is good. Would you like to go ashore to have a look and see?"

"Maybe on the way back," said Keagan. "Let's see what is up ahead."

Sally Mae gunned the boat again, and despite their precautions, Keagan and Kelly tottered. Two miles up the river there was another camp on the west side of the river. They were well past the island now. They pulled in close to look at the camp. It wasn't rented, but the owners were on the dock, just tying off their boat. "Let's look at that one, Sally Mae, or at least, pull up to their dock," said Keagan.

There were two men on the dock. They were busy getting their gear and an impressive stringer of fish from their boat up to the cabin when Sally Mae approached their dock. "Billy and Tommy-Lee Albritain," said Sally Mae Mathers, "I've got a couple of Yankees here who want to see your camp. They might want to rent it. They're good Yankees though, not those Damn Yankees who won't go home," and here she laughed at her own joke.

Billy or Tommy-Lee, Keagan wasn't sure which, laughed and offered them a beer. Both Keagan and Kelly accepted. Kelly wasn't normally a beer drinker and it was early for drinking, but it was also unbearbly hot. The river had gotten warmer every mile they moved away from the Gulf. Sally Mae declined their offer and asked for some sweet tea.

"Now, Sally Mae," said Billy – or maybe it was Tommy-Lee – "you know that if you wuz to come to our home, we would certainly have sweet tea for y'all, but this here's a fish camp, and in a fish camp all there is is beer, maybe a little whiskey."

"Billy Albritain, that beer and whiskey must have rotted out your brain. You know damn well that I am a Baptist, and that I wouldn't drink the *devil's brew* regardless where I was. My clients, on the other hand, bein' Papists I'm guessin', aren't obliged by the same rigorous call to the Lord that I have accepted."

"Now, let's talk business. Is this camp for rent for the next two weeks beginnin' Monday, or are you two going to still be out here violatin' your livers and the Lord's trust?"

"Sally Mae," answered one of them, "we appreciate your thinkin' about us, both our souls and our financial well-being, but we're goin' to be fishin' here through next week."

Keagan and Kelly managed to pass their empty beer cans back to Billy or Tommy-Lee and express their thanks for the *devil's brew* before Sally Mae full throttled away from their dock, which was no mean feat.

"Albritain," Sally Mae said, apropos of nothing that Keagan or Kelly could divine. "That's not their real name."

"Did they change it, Sally Mae?" asked Kelly.

"They didn't, but someone else did."

Keagan sensed that there was a good story here, and what Irishman, especially a former English teacher, could pass up a fine story? "I'd like to hear the story, Sally Mae."

"Y'all might know that in spite of Florida's present-day ethnic makeover, spics, and coloreds replacin' God-fearing folks, Florida's pre-dominate ancestry is still English. However, back in the early 19th Century, Florida, Alabama, and Mississippi belonged to the spics. Well, what happened was that one of them immigrant boats — filled mostly with English and some of your people I suspect — ran aground just off St. George Island. Most everyone survived, but the ship's logs and manifests were lost, so the spic bureaucrats of the time sought an easy solution as all bureaucrats and all spics have done for all time. They processed everyone under a single name. Their ship had sailed from England, so their bureaucratic logic declared them henceforth *all Britons*. Almost two hundred years later, we still have Albritains around here. And they ain't much smarter, by the way, than the day they arrived."

Keagan felt sure that Jimmy the Gimp would be embarrassed in short order in Sally Mae's presence as he sensed she really meant what she said.

"There are two other camps up river that I would like to show you. One is about three miles upriver; the other about, twelve."

"Let's look at the first one. I'm not sure I want to go so far up as the second camp. What about you, Eileen?"

"Not for now, but I do want to see that camp you mentioned earlier, the one on the west side of the island," answered Kelly.

The camp that was located three miles upriver was also on the west bank. It was unoccupied, so Sally Mae pulled up to the dock and had Keagan tie off the boat. She hopped over the gunwale and started down the pine-slat dock. Keagan and Kelly followed her. Suddenly, she reached into her enormous straw handbag, pulled out a Ruger .22 automatic – the accurized one that the FBI uses for pistol training – barely took the time to aim, and fired at something ahead of her.

Keagan carefully placed his hand on the Sig 232 in his belly pack, and Kelly had already slipped the safety off her Walther PPK. They didn't know what Sally Mae had fired at, so they kept their guns concealed.

"I hate cottonmouths," Sally Mae said as she put the pistol back in her bag. "I can tolerate diamondbacks because they eat rats, but I seriously wonder if the Good Lord Jehovah might have had a moment of confusion when He created the water moccasin; they are evil incarnate, plain and simple. They eat fish; they attack without notice; and they smile their white smile all the while they are doin' the evil they are doin'."

At the end of the dock Keagan and Kelly noticed a dark thickness writhing on the pine planks, a small bullet hole in its triangular head. Sally Mae tipped the dead snake into the river with her gumboot, and led them though the scrub, up to the cabin.

"Do you always carry a gun, Sally Mae?" asked Kelly.

"I always do when I come up this river or am otherwise removed from civilization. This here ain't Boston. This is Florida, and Florida is aslither with things that can kill ya or at least make your life unpleasant for a long while. Of course, I do keep a gun in my car and several at home because the state is also infested with low-life white trash, coloreds, and spics, which are usually more dangerous than anything y'all might meet out here."

Something slithered under the cabin as they approached it, too fast for Sally Mae's gun. Keagan privately wondered how many real estate agents carried guns in the Adirondacks when they were showing property.

Sally Mae fetched her enormous key ring out of her bag, found a key with a blue plastic ring on the tab, opened the key box, and in turn the locked door to the camp. The cabin had been vacant for some time. Keagan and Kelly looked around, feigned some interest in the site but left as soon as they could. Sally Mae sensed their disappointment and became even more determined to rent them a camp.

"We'll stop at that place we passed on our way upriver. It's in a great location," said Sally Mae. "They used to make bricks on that island, built Fort Gadsden with them. The British used slaves to make the bricks; coloreds make good bricks. The British had to leave when the Americans won the War of 1812, and damned if them coloreds who made them bricks didn't move into that fort. Took Andy Jackson to rout them out. The island not only gives you privacy from the rest of the river—because the western channel isn't deep enough for the really big boats that come up that far—but also from non-locals who come over from the National Forest, over to the east. They think that the island is the river's western shore. Even if they get above the island, the western channel looks like a backwater to them. It's the best spot on the river for what y'all want to do. Y'all do remember though that it is rented for one more week. But if y'all can wait, this is the place for y'all."

Keagan, remembering Sally Mae's stopping at the Albritains, suggested to her that she not disturb the present occupants. They were more interested in the location, the dock placement, and cover than they were in the cabin itself. Sally Mae throttled down and drifted slowly past the camp. A dock pierced the thick vegetation. There was a canoe at the dock, but no one was in sight. The site was the best one yet that they had seen for the exchange. Anyone coming to it in a large boat would have to be picked up out in the main channel. Even if they came in a small boat, they wouldn't have it easy because outside the channel they were in, this part of the river was more swamp than river.

Keagan recognized the canoe for what it was because he had seen several like it up on the Rideaux Chain, on a fishing trip he and Niles had taken in Ontario. Nonetheless, he remarked on it to Sally Mae. "That's an unusual boat, isn't it?"

"That's a swamper's boat, has an inboard engine in it, can go almost as many places as an air boat can in the Glades. We got more trees here and deeper water, so it's really better around here than an air boat would be."

"But the place is rented, so that's not the owner staying there?" asked Kelly.

"No, it's rented for sure, must have even rented them his boat. I know the owner, and he's right fond of that boat. He's been out of work for a while, and I'd bet them boys must have paid well to have gotten his boat, too," said Sally Mae.

"Eileen," Keagan said to Kelly. "I think this is just right for what we want, and I think we can wait an extra week. Let's go back, call up our editor, and see if we can get an extension."

"I agree," said Kelly.

"Sally Mae, this is the place we want, if we can get approval. Can you hold off until Monday for a deposit?"

"I sure enough can," said Sally Mae.

"Oh, and can you arrange for some boats for us? If we're going to be a week late, we'd like to get a head start locating our shooting sites. We'll need a power boat and a light-weight canoe. Two kayaks would be even better. I can give you a cash deposit for those as soon as we dock," said Keagan.

They were back on the river proper now and Keagan checked his phone: two bars.

Twenty-Nine

After speaking with the rangers at the National Forest's Visitors' Center, Teal concentrated most of his efforts on the surrounding area. He stopped at convenience stores, at gas stations, at bait shops, at cafes or what went for cafes in this area, and at bars. There weren't any boat yards; they were all at the mouth of the river or out on the coast. These were closed-mouthed folks, so Teal took an indirect approach. He turned on the Cajun charm and acted like a swamper on a busman's holiday.

His story was that he was hired by two Yankee dandies he had met while working in Atlanta as a stuntman on a movie set. He thought about being more specific, perhaps saying he worked for a run of *Survivor*, but Teal suspected that these people were probably *Survivor* groupies and he'd just trip himself up. He would tell anyone with information that they were set locators and that they were considering the Panhandle as a location for a big movie about drug trafficking from South America to the United States. Faith Hill was going to star in the female lead. Anyway, they had hired him to guide them along the river and through the swamps because he grew up on the bayous in Louisiana and they didn't want the locals to know what they were up to. As typical with big money guys, they knew how to make multi-million-dollar deals, but they had fucked up how they were supposed to hook up together. That was the long version of the story; Teal cut it down considerably whenever he didn't have to give full details.

He didn't get anywhere with the bait shops. He originally thought that the Campbells might have gone to a bait shop as part of their cover, but it wasn't shaping up that way. He dropped the bait shops from his list in light of that fact. He didn't fare any better with the convenience stores and gas stations. The Campbells had probably topped off their tank down on the coast or only pumped gas themselves and didn't go into the attached convenience stores. The cafes weren't any more productive. A few hours, three pieces of pie, and many cups of bad coffee later, no information of importance was uncovered. In the afternoon, Teal started working the bars. These were the roadhouses of Southern song, cinder block buildings with dirt or shell parking lots, where men and some women (usually never unattended, of course) came to drink beer, shoot pool or darts, listen to the jukebox, and get into fights. The bars were smoky and dark, and the smell of their rest rooms would gag a maggot.

Teal was drinking ponies. *No need to besot myself,* he thought, *running down false leads.* The second bar he visited was across the road from an alligator farm. Teal thought this might be one place where it was safer to drive home drunk than to walk. When Teal came in, the patrons all looked at him, but went right back to their beers and their pool. A woman tended bar. She had once been attractive and, with a little attention to herself, less drinking, and less smoking she could be again. She was braless, probably operating under the mistaken assumption that she would be sexier by doing so. From the sag of her breasts, she had been abused by that belief for some time. Teal ordered a Budweiser pony.

"You take a wrong turn, sugar?" the barmaid asked.

Teal saw his entrée. "I surely did," he said and moved seamlessly right into his story.

"Sugar, y'all the wrong person telling thet story. Thet should be me. I been tending bar here, since before the ABC would let me, waiting for some Hollywood type to come along and take me outta here. All I ever git though are these boys and more like 'em. Sorry, sugar, I can't be no help to y'all."

Teal was about to kick back the rest of his pony, when the door opened and a tall, rangy fellow came in and sat at the bar two stools down from him.

"Hey, Harley, you working again? I haven't seen you in a piece now."

"Naw, Letti, I'm still laid off down to the mill."

"Well, you know I can't give you no more credit till y'all settle up your tab."

"I know that, Letti, that's why I am here. What do I owe ya? I'm here to pay up."

Letti went over by the cash register and opened an antique wall cabinet that advertised patent medicines. It was the classiest thing in the place. She pulled out an envelope, riffled through a number of green guest checks, the kind all cheap diners and bars use, and finally selected a pack. She put the rest back in the envelope, closed the cabinet, and placed the stapled guest checks in front of Harley.

"It says there, thet y'all owe $74.25," said Letti.

"Well, if it says hit, then I do," answered Harley. He unbuttoned the left breast pocket on his denim work shirt, of which the sleeves appeared to have been ripped off, and pulled out a fold of bills. He thumbed back two, then pulled off a hundred and handed it to Letti.

"Mark that *paid*, take ten for yourself, and give me a Jack and Coke."

Letti did all three with surprising swiftness. When she brought Harley his drink, she said, "Harley, I don't understand. You win the lottery or somethin'?"

"Or somethin'."

"You didn't do nothin' stupid, did ya," said Letti, giving Teal a sideways glance.

Teal fixated on the bottle of Jagermeister directly in front of him. *Who drinks that shit?* he wondered silently.

"Naw, Letti. I just got lucky for a change. Ya know that old camp I got over to the river, west of the island?"

"The one yer daddy had when we was in high school?"

"That's the one. Well, two Yankees come out there one day and wanted to know if they could rent hit from me fer two weeks. Said they was doin' wildlife research, needed a quiet place where they wouldn't be disturbed. They even rented my boat, the canoe with the inboard and my old truck. Paid me $750."

"They paid you $750 for that place?"

"Well, they get to use that old truck of mine and my boat, too. Boat's almost worth it by itself."

Letti leaned over the bar, a move that was not missed by Harley. He pretended to cock his ear while she whispered to him, but all the time he was staring at her cleavage. Letti told Harley about the movie people. "They weren't doin' no research. They were scoutin' a movie set, were gettin' paid a fortune for doin' hit I bet, so they had gotten the camp cheap. Thet fella, two stools over from you, might pay for knowin' where the camp is because he was supposta be workin' with 'em. Strike up a conversation with 'im. He doesn't sound like your general-purpose California asshole, sounds more like a Cajun."

Teal knew something was up, so he ordered another pony. "Say, fella, you should try somethin' a might stronger then thet pip-squeak of a beer. Let me buy you a real drink. I'm celebratin'."

"Sure," said Teal, "I'll have a shot of brandy." Teal figured they wouldn't have any Cognac in the place and was more than mildly surprised when Letti reached below the bar and pulled out a dusty bottle of Courvoisier, though it was the VS. Finding VSOP or a bottle of Remy in the place would have been an apparition rivaling Medjugorje.

Harley slid over two stools. "I'm Harley Davidson," he said, holding out his hand.

Teal had just brought the pony up to his lips to finish it off, when he heard Harley's last name. He sent a stream of froth and spray across the bar, just missing Letti —who was bringing Teal his shot — and launching her into an impromptu wet T-shirt contest.

"Sorry about that, Harley, you just caught me by surprise."

"No need to apologize. I get thet reaction lots."

Harley continued, "Letti says you're lookin' fer two Yankees who're scoutin' a movie site. Well, I got two Yankees who just rented my cabin on to the river. They could be yer two. Maybe we could work somethin' out. If they was the two, thet is."

Harley was what Teal's father would call a raw-boned fella, which essentially meant that he was long, tall and strong as a son-of-a-bitch without looking it. But there was a dumb simplicity in his eyes. Teal didn't think he was trying to set him up for a roll.

"What you got in mind, Harley?"

"I show you where they left their car and if thet's their car, I take you over to the camp. Well, no. I already rented them fellas my boat, but I kin show you how to git there."

"How much will you charge me, Harley, for these services?" asked Teal.

"No charge if it's not the fellas y'all lookin' fer. One hundred dollars if they is." Harley seemed to have recently become enamored with hundred-dollar bills.

Teal faked thirty seconds of thought and said, "You got a deal, Harley. When can we go?"

"We kin go jest as soon as I get me another Jack and Coke. I been dry a long time."

Teal drove. He didn't want Harley to have control of the vehicle, just in case this was a setup. They headed north on County 65. After about five miles Harley told Teal to slow down. He had to make a left up ahead on a blind turn. Teal finally saw the dirt road and turned onto it. It was a little sloppy, but basically they were riding on limestone. About three miles off County 65 they came to a turn-around that could accommodate four or five parked vehicles. A blue Ford Taurus with Florida rental tags was there. Y and Z were traditionally reserved as rental car plates in Florida, and were omitted as initial letters on passenger plates. The river and a boat-launching site were just beyond the turn-around.

"I wonder why they rented my truck. They need the canoe to get back and forth across the river, but they got a brand new car right here."

"What kind of truck is it, Harley?"

"'88 Ford pickup, a bit of mileage on her, but it can still haul stuff around. Maybe they didn't want to get their car dirty. Must be nice to be able to pay two hundred dollars so as not to get yer car dirty."

Teal and Harley walked down to the river. "D'y'a see 'cross the river there? Well, thet's not the west bank there. Thet's an island; the camp's behind it. Ya go up river pretty nigh three quarters of a mile, you'll see a bald cypress over there, with an osprey nest in hit. That'll be the north tip of the island. Y'all kin float down the west side of the island; there's enough water if you stay in the channel. If y'all are comin' from down river, there'll be a channel marker—number twenty-four—just south of here. As soon as y'all pass hit, ya'll know you got about a mile to go. Floatin' down to the camp is better than headin' in to the channel at the south end of the island—the channel constricts water flow and hit can get pretty fast if we've had a good rain."

Teal and Harley drove back to the bar. In the parking lot Teal gave Harley a hundred dollars, then he peeled off another hundred-dollar bill and gave it to Harley who was much surprised. "Harley, I'm giving you an extra hundred dollars because I want to surprise them fellas, also to shame them a bit for not arranging to meet me. Don't worry; I'll get it back from the studio. But I'd like you to keep quiet about this, so if you see them don't mention me. I wouldn't even tell Letti or any of your friends. Just tell them they weren't the fellas I was looking for because friends who know a friend just made a quick two hundred dollars usually want that friend to buy them drinks. Then pretty soon the two hundred dollars gone and those friends aren't quiet as friendly. Know what I mean, Harley?"

"I surely do. Thanks fer the two hundred and thanks fer the advice. Hell, I won't even mention hit ta myself again."

Teal let Harley out and drove back to St. George Island, but first he stopped off at a hardware store.

***

Teal didn't go directly to the inn; he needed to do something first. When he finally did arrive at the St. George there was a message from Niles to meet him at Harry A's. Teal left the truck at the inn and walked over. There was a pleasant breeze off the Gulf that reminded Teal of south Louisiana. The air was heavier there, but in spite of this state's name, the air here was not as floral.

Niles was at the bar, drinking beer with Enright. Niles saw Teal as he entered, as though he had been looking for him, and waved Teal over. Harry A's was crowded with those who lived in the sun and those who had didn't need to *ooh* and *ahh* at the sunset as it dropped into the Gulf somewhere to the west, as it had every day since Pangea broke into the present day continents. The others, the ones from the Midwest industrial blights like Chicago and Detroit, or those from polluted Atlanta or Savannah for that matter, gathered each twilight at the *Tiki*, a watering hole on the beach, named for a mythological god (in the sanitized version, a part of his anatomy in the racier version) of a people who were—even by transplant—no nearer than six thousand miles away. There they (the tourists, not the Polynesians) gathered to toast the earth's rotation as though they were witness to some rare celestial phenomenon like the appearance of Kahoutec.

"Teal, you remember John Enright from last night," said Niles.

"Sure, did you think I was so *besotted*, Niles? That I forgot him? How are you, John?" said Teal, nodding at Enright.

Enright, not understanding the private joke, nodded back and smiled. "Niles and I have been whipping all the locals in darts. Niles mostly, but I did pull out the last game. We make a great team."

"Aye," said Niles as he ordered Teal a beer. "We're good enough to be able to walk into most pubs in England."

Enright laughed at himself. "You're right, Niles. The free beers for life we've won in this place have given me a swelled head."

"Free beers for life? Just my luck. Free beers for life in a bar that doesn't carry Blackened Voodoo."

"Just a bit of hyperbole, Teal," said Niles.

"Hyperbole? I assume that means a tall tale," said Teal.

"Right you are, Teal. You Americans are known for your 'tall tales'. We English are known for our hyperbole; it's a matter of sophistication."

Before Teal could respond, Niles moved on. "John here was telling me that he used to be a shrimper, but that it didn't pay well enough, so he signed on as captain of a large private yacht that requires light work. Apparently it pays enough so that in five or so years he'll be able to make a solid down payment on his own boat and run charters. John knows the Gulf well. He's been all up and down Florida, up around Alabama and Mississippi, over to Louisiana and Texas, and even down to Mexico." Apparently, the bonding experience of the dart championship had softened Enright up. Niles seemed to have gotten quite a bit of background on Enright that he couldn't get the night before.

"What brings you to St. George Island?" asked Teal.

"As I said last night: business. Maybe you *were besotted*, Teal," Enright joked. "My employer has business in the area. He doesn't usually discuss his business with me, so I don't really know what it is, and I'm not terribly curious either. He is simply a means for me getting my own boat. He tells me to prepare the boat for a trip and that's what I do. Sometimes it's just a dinner run; sometimes, like now, we are out for several days. He tells me how many days and where, so I can lay in provisions and chart a course, but other than getting the boat ready, I don't inquire into his business."

Enright wasn't so naive as to be won over by several winning rounds of darts. He sensed that Niles and Teal were something other than an inn keeper and a head maintenance man looking to expand their business. They were a strange combination, a Limey and a Cajun with only first names. Enright didn't think that they were in the employ of a rival drug trafficker, unless they were contract men.

He was a native Floridian, and had seen his share of people in the drug trade. Drug traffickers usually employed members of their ethnic group, except for special talent. Cavelya was a Bolivian, and so were his flunkies. These two didn't look like flunkies. They didn't look like DEA either; living in Florida and working the Gulf he had seen plenty of those, too. They could be contract men, especially Niles. He had a smile like a friendly cartoon animal, but his eyes revealed nothing—not fear nor friendship, not impatience nor delight. They seemed as devoid of emotion and as dark as the Gulf's dead zone, yet they didn't seem to miss anything. Teal, on the other hand, at first looked like a career criminal until you looked as his face. The jailhouse tattoo did little to hide Teal's intensely amused countenance. Enright had only met him twice, but Teal's face seemed to reflect a knowledge of some Divine jape, which while he may not have been aware of its proportion, fully approved of the intention. Maybe they were Cavelya's men, checking on his loyalty or on his reticence. Still, these two weren't the typical stupid thugs that Cavelya usually employed. Teal may be playing the dumb *coonass*, but his eyes told a different story. Enright didn't know what these two were up to, but he knew that he couldn't cut and run because he'd never skipper in Florida again. And without Cavelya, or someone like him, he'd never get his own boat, so he decided to see where they would lead him.

Thirty

The investigation file Special Agent Wittman e-mailed to Washington concerning the *Moderna Museet* investigation ended up on the desk of Special Agent Anthony Fugaezi. Fugaezi preferred Tony. He had been assigned to stolen property in Philadelphia and knew Wittman. When he heard that an art crime team was being formed, he spoke to Wittman about applying. Fugaezi loved opera, but operas were rarely stolen these days. He figured recovering stolen art was about as close as he was going to come to anything that really interested him in the FBI. He was a good agent, smart and resourceful, but by far his greatest asset (not unlike Wittman was his personality. Fugaezi loved to be with people and it showed. It was strange that he ended up in D.C. because he didn't fit the mold; he valued results over authority, was a bit loose with procedure, and didn't take himself too seriously. He joined the FBI because his father and grandfather had been in the FBI. Truth be told, Fugaezi didn't know what he wanted to do, so the FBI suited him as well as anything else. If it weren't for the territorial imperatives of the Bureau, he would have worked his entire career with the Bureau and never been assigned here. He just wasn't the type.

It didn't take Fugaezi long to read through the thin file. When he was finished, he called Wittman. "Bob, it's Tony. How you been? I haven't talked with you since my transfer to the city of Brotherly Love."

"I thought Philly was the city of Brotherly Love, Tony?"

"Nah, you should see it here; everybody is looking out to help everybody else. It's amazing. Why just the other day one of my fellow agents told me that our team meeting had been rescheduled for a half hour later but that some people for some reason didn't get the update, so he was making sure I knew about the schedule change. Well, as it turned out, I didn't have much going on, so I decided to make sure I knew where Room 447 was, I mean I figured it was on the fourth floor, but Marone, it's a big floor. Anyhow, I wandered up there just a little early and guess what? The meeting had been rescheduled again for the original time. I sent out a memo informing my superior that somebody should look into the memo system here, because I knew of two already that I hadn't gotten in the short time I've been here. I wonder if he got it. Maybe I should have walked it into his office. What do you think, Bob?"

When Wittman stopped laughing, he said, "Yeah, I think that's a good idea. You know you got to cover yourself there."

"Yeah, thanks, Bob, listen, the reason I called is I caught the Swedish museum case. I was wondering if you knew something that wasn't in the file."

"Not really. For a thin file, it's got a long trail, but the guy you want to talk to is oh what's his name. He's got a Lord of the Rings name."

"Dalin? Gandalf Dalin?"

"Yeah he's the one. He put the most work in. The case pretty much dead-ended after the national guys pulled it from him, but the guy learned a lot working on his own time. Maybe he kept at it. I got it from a Mordecai Richter in L.A., but he's in D.C. now. I don't know which division. He didn't have much to offer though. Listen I got to go, but keep in touch. Let me know if I can help in any way with the case. I would have liked to keep it, but I'm busy with the Gardner case and basically the decision makers in D.C. are holding their breath till I retire. They're not likely to hand me another plum."

"Too many missed memos, huh."

"Yeah, that's it Tony. Good luck with this one. It's a tough way to start."

***

Fugaezi called Dalin in Stockholm, introduced himself and thanked him for all the work he had done on the case. He told Dalin the reason he had called was that he wondered if he had learned anything else about the case since he had to officially pass it on. Before Dalin could answer, Fugaezi was telling him he'd really be nowhere without the information that he, Dalin, had put together and that he really appreciated his extra effort. Dalin wondered if this guy would like to meet him to have a beer together, but then he reminded himself that Special Agent Fugaezi was in Washington, D.C. four thousand miles away. *Too bad*, thought Dalin, *he seems like a nice guy*.

Dalin thanked Fugaezi for his kind words and added that yes, he had continued to work on the case in a limited way on his own. He told Fugaezi that he had discovered a website that offered five masterpieces for sale at a price high enough so that they had to be masterpieces, but low enough to suggest that they couldn't be offered on the open market. He said the seller never specifically identified them as Picassos, but anyone knowledgeable enough about the art world, especially about art that lacked proper provenance, would know what the seller was offering.

Dalin told him that he couldn't follow up the website because he didn't have the skills and couldn't pass it on to the Technical Division of the National Laboratory of Forensic Science; he didn't have the jurisdiction and had already been admonished once for that, but Dain insisted that Fugaezi was welcome to the information. He said he'd e-mail it to him as soon as he got off the phone. Fugaezi thanked him again, and Dalin ended the conversation saying, "Tony, keep in touch; let me know how you're doing and if I can help in any way."

"Sure thing, Gandalf," said Tony.

Fugaezi sent a request to The Operational Technology Division (OTD) — based in Quantico, Virginia — to see what they could come up with on the website that Dalin had sent him. In due FBI course, OTD got back to him with what they had learned, which wasn't much because the website had recently been struck, perhaps suggesting that a successful bid had been tendered. They did learn, however, that several people had responded to the offering after OTD had expended a significant amount of wizardry to learn the names, e-mail addresses, and mailing addresses of those people. At the top of the list—ordered by frequency—was Alardo Quillaca Cavelya.

***

Tony Fugaezi arrived on North Captiva at 9:45 AM and made his way to the Resort Properties where he had a ten o'clock appointment. He introduced himself and presented his credentials and asked Wendy Muller, co-owner with her husband Mark, a number of questions about a Señor Cavelya.

"Ah, the Bolivian Red Baron."

Fugaezi apologized for not understanding and asked for an explanation. Muller explained about his plane and the racket it made taking off and arriving. Fugaezi asked if he were in residence.

"I don't think so, but I didn't see him leave ..."

"Or hear him?" interjected Fugaezi.

"No, actually," Muller corrected, "his plane is still here, but I noticed that his boat is out. Left yesterday."

"Do you have any idea where he went?"

"No, sorry."

"Could you direct me to... " Fugaezi fumbled with his notebook and then read the address to her.

"Sure. Nothing's doing here. I can run you over now, if you'd like."

Muller took Fugaezi over to Cavelya's beach-front property and waited for him to try to raise someone. His ringing of the doorbell prompted no answer and he didn't see anyone on the grounds.

"Any idea what cleaning service he uses? I can't imagine Señor Cavelya or his wife cleans this place themselves."

"His wife doesn't live here, or at least I've never seen her. I've heard she lives in Miami, but I don't know that for sure." Muller didn't mention his companion. "It's not like there are a lot of cleaning services on the island, but I doubt Missy would know where he went. Your best bet is Maggie Mae, John Enright's girlfriend. John captains the Red Baron's boat, also pilots his plane. She'd know."

"Where can I find her?"

"She works at Barnacle Phil's at the dock where you landed. She should be in by now. Hop in, I'll take you over."

Fugaezi learned from Enright's girlfriend that Cavelya was sailing to Apalachicola up on the Panhandle and would be gone at least till Sunday. Fugaezi had no idea where Apalachicola was and only vaguely where the Panhandle was, but he knew he had to get there.

His brief check of commercial flights told him that it would take him at least two days, so he chartered a plane — at a hefty cost to taxpayers — for as direct of a flight as he could possibly get from Fort Myers Airport to Apalachicola. It couldn't be perfectly direct as small planes usually don't fly long distances across open water.

Thirty-One

Alardo Quillaca Cavelya had arranged to meet the Campbells in the Gibson Inn's dining room. When they arrived Cavelya was already seated alone at a table, drinking a rum punch. Cavelya's female companion, Luis, and Manascotta sat at another table close enough to see, but not close enough to hear. She was drinking a margarita but the bodyguards had to be content with cokes; they were on duty.

Keagan and Kelly, having inquired of the hostess earlier that afternoon—an inquiry that only cost twenty dollars—learned that Señor Cavelya had reserved a table for three at eight o'clock and another, some discrete distance away, also for three at the same time. Keagan and Kelly correctly suspected that the sellers and the buyer were meeting for the first time. The same twenty dollars that they used for the inquiry also secured them a table right next to Señor Cavelya's. Despite the fact that it was too great a leap in logic to suggest that full-blown greed had not yet reached the Florida Panhandle, the paltriness of the gratuity for the information and table reservation suggested that it hadn't reached the staff of the Gibson Inn yet. Keagan wondered to what degree it had reached his staff at *Beyond Good and Evil*.

Señor Cavelya's table was in the northwest corner of the room, a step from a French door emergency exit that opened to the porch, three or four steps from the kitchen, and no more than a dozen steps from an emergency exit on the far side of the room. No table in the room had more exit options than where Cavelya sat with his back was against the wall. Perhaps he had read the story of Wild Bill Hickok's demise. Señor Cavelya was nothing if not security conscious. His bodyguards had a clear view of him. Luis could watch Cavelya, the kitchen and the two emergency exits, while Manascotta had a clear view of the rest of the dining room. They were separated from his table by the distance of only two tables and the width of the aisle that led to the emergency exit, porch and the street beyond, but it was far enough away (especially with the street noise) that they wouldn't be able to hear what was said at Cavelya's table.

When the Campbells arrived, Señor Cavelya stood to greet them. He was dressed in a white Armani linen suit; his shirt was open to display the small gold cross on a gold chain that he wore. The Campbells were dressed in Polo shirts, pleated slacks, and tasseled loafers. Only the sole edges of their loafers bore any mark of their trip out of the swamp. They had changed en route. Cavelya greeted them cordially, shook hands, and motioned that they have a seat. He called the waiter and asked him to bring over one of the two bottles of Crystal champagne he had reserved earlier, along with three flutes. Keagan appreciated the panache but thought Cavelya took it too far.

Keagan sat with his back to Cavelya and the Campbells. He wore a cranberry Polo shirt, a pair of Sea Island charcoal blue slacks, and Sperry boat shoes without socks. Kelly wore a blue Laura Ashley sun dress and a silk tam, complete with clan ribbons. Kelly sat across the table from Keagan, and—by shifting herself a little to the right or a little to the left—she had full view of Cavelya's table. Her position also allowed Señor Cavelya to flirt with her a bit.

Cavelya's waiter brought the champagne and the flutes. The Crystal was in a silver ice bucket in a stand. The waiter carried the flutes upside down with the stems between his fingers. The bottle had a white, linen napkin wrapped around its neck in the bucket. The waiter looked very professional. He placed the champagne at Señor Cavelya's elbow and rotated the bottle through the ice, using his palms on the bottle's neck. Satisfied with the quick chill, the waiter lifted the Crystal out of the bucket, sliding the napkin down the bottle to absorb the wetness. He presented it to Señor Cavelya, napkin to the back and bottom of the bottle now so that it would not drip but would also allow Señor Cavelya to read the label. Cavelya nodded, and the waiter undid the foil cover and the wire retainer, tilted the bottle at a 45° angle and, with it in his left, twisted the cork out with his right hand. It was an absolutely perfect performance. He then lay the cork in front of Señor Cavelya to smell. When he did, Kelly winced.

"What's the matter?" asked Keagan.

"The waiter, after a flawless performance of opening the champagne, gave Cavelya the cork to smell, and he did," answered Kelly.

"If one of my waiters did that, I'd have him in rehab."

Keagan leaned across the table in a manner that, to the casual observer, would appear as a gesture of intimacy. He silently told Kelly to call Niles and Teal so they could be ready for whatever might occur after dinner. Kelly excused herself as though she were going to the ladies' room, smiled again at Señor Cavelya, and alluringly left the dining room for the far perimeter of the porch, where she called Niles on her cell phone. Seven minutes later she was back at the table. The waiter who had served Cavelya was at the table, presenting menus and taking their drink orders. Keagan ordered two Beefeater and tonics. After he was assured that the Gibson carried Schweppes' Tonic, he told the waiter to put them in large glasses, 12 oz. at least, fill them with ice, and use only a jigger of gin. Their day on the river with Sally Mae had left them with a raging thirst. Keagan and Kelly both begrudgingly admitted that nothing quenched thirst like good English gin and quinine with fresh lime in large glasses filled with ice. Keagan told the waiter that they would order when he brought the drinks.

The waiter went off to the bar, and Keagan listened for anything worthwhile from Cavelya's table. Cavelya wanted to ensure that the paintings had not been damaged in transport or in holding in the hot, humid climate of Florida. The Campbells assured him that they knew their business and that they had taken every precaution to deliver the merchandise in the same condition as it had been while it hung in the *Moderna Museet*. In fact, the paintings were in hermetically sealed containers. James Campbell took out a small Sony digital camera, handed it to Cavelya and showed him how to view the five paintings. Of course, all of their conversation was non-specific. Anyone else eavesdropping would have thought that these three were simply having a business dinner, negotiating the sale of some goods that were susceptible to damage. James Campbell had taken the photos with a digital camera rather than with his iPhone because he didn't want Cavelya to learn any additional information about his brother and him.

The waiter returned quickly with Keagan and Kelly's drinks; a busboy was in tow carrying the Cavelya party's appetizers and salads. Just as Señor Cavelya had earlier ordered two bottles of Crystal, so too had he informed the kitchen that he and his party would have paella as their entrée. All the waiter had to do was take the appetizer and salad order and bring the second bottle of wine with the entrée.

The waiter served Keagan and Kelly's drinks first, and then attended to Cavelya and his guests. When they were served, he told Señor Cavelya that the paella would be ready whenever he was and asked him if he required anything else at the moment. When Cavelya indicated that everything was fine for now, the waiter took Kelly's order for seafood linguine and Keagan's for a bowl of oyster stew with a dozen raw oysters. Keagan also ordered a bottle of Meursault.

"Very nice wine choice," said Kelly, "but, Mick, we may have a busy night. Can you contain yourself, after consuming a dozen oysters?"

"I can do nothing but try, Kelly."

The conversation at the Cavelya table consisted largely of Señor Cavelya cataloguing his art collection to the Campbells, who were understandably bored by his Mexican hat dance: *I, I, I, I*. But, having known for a long time that most of their clients were legends in their own mind, the Campbells didn't want to queer the deal by not appearing rapt with his every word. The money they would get from this sale would purchase plenty of leisure time in which to deride the many and varied character flaws of Señor Cavelya. For now, they would have to content themselves with the wonderful wine and the fine meal.

Teal arrived at the Gibson Inn just as their waiter served Keagan and Kelly coffee. He made a complete loop of the porch. Keagan saw him as he walked pass the emergency exit. He waited two minutes, then said to Kelly, "My turn." He excused himself from the table and walked toward the men's room, outside the bar. Teal followed him. No one else was there.

"Where is Niles?"

"Drinking beer with the skipper of Cavelya's boat. He thought he should keep an eye on the boat."

Keagan didn't like this development, but he had complete confidence in Niles' judgment. At this moment, Keagan felt that he needed a fighter with him. Teal was a marvelous mechanic and loyal as hell, but he was slight, if muscular. Furthermore, his military training consisted of only four years in the Air Force, even if it *was* diffusing bombs. What Keagan needed now was a strike force, not a technician, however steely-nerved Teal may have been.

"What if Cavelya's boat sails? How will Niles get here?" Keagan asked Teal.

"He said that he would find *contingency* transportation, which I took to mean that he would hot-wire a car," answered Teal. "Listen, Mick, let me tell you what I found out this afternoon..."

"I don't have time now, Teal. I have to get back to the table. I'll need you to follow the Campbells when they leave. They're sitting in there with their buyer against the far wall, a Señor Cavelya." Keagan continued to describe them. "Mick..."

"Listen, I have to get back. I want you to follow the Campbells when they leave. I don't think Cavelya will leave with them. I think this is just a preliminary meeting; the exchange will take place tomorrow, but I could be wrong. Cavelya's got three thugs with him, but there are only two of them in the dining room. They are two tables away from Cavelya and are sitting with his female companion. You can't miss them; they have almost as much muscle as they do gold chains. I don't like that the third one is elsewhere. Keep an eye out for him; I'm sure he doesn't look much different from the other two. The female companion has lacquered hair, permanent-pout lips, and a dress that's painted on. You could see her headlights in a fog. See where they go, but be careful. Kelly and I think we know where they are hiding out, but we need to know for sure. I've got to get back."

Keagan went to rejoin Kelly. He wasn't happy with the events, but there wasn't much he could do about it now, and he implicitly trusted Niles' ability to read complex situations. *Teal is the weak link*, thought Keagan. There was nothing to do but play out the plan. Cavelya, his female companion, and his three bodyguards were registered at the inn through Sunday night. It didn't appear that Cavelya was going to make the exchange tonight, unless he was going to do it right here.

Kelly was talking across the table to Cavelya as Keagan approached. Charo glowered at her. It must be the red hair and the green eyes, thought Keagan, or maybe it was the tam as Bolivian women wore hats but usually bowlers. It also could have been the sassy smile or the lithe body or her presence or the . . . he reached the table before he ran out of possibilities. Cavelya stood and greeted him. Apparently, there was a protocol to seduction.

"I am Alardo Quillaca Cavelya, and these men are my business associates, James and Greg. Your dinner date — please excuse me if I speak incorrectly, but I do not see a ring — has engaged me in conversation that I find most stimulating. Could I invite you two to join us for an after-dinner drink? I'm sure the waiter will gladly push our tables together, so we can be more, ah, intimate."

Keagan could see that the Campbells were uncomfortable with the situation. Under other circumstances, they would be happy to share their dinner table with a woman as beautiful as Kelly, but they hadn't stayed alive and kept out of jail all these years by losing their focus, and their focus now was selling the Picassos. If Señor Cavelya had to further stroke his ego by flirting with a stranger's woman that was his business. They had finished discussing their business concerning the exchange tomorrow; they didn't need to be a part of this. Simultaneously, as though they had telepathically decided what to do, the Campbells rose and excused themselves for the evening, saying that they had a full day ahead of them and needed to retire.

Cavelya and the Campbells were in many ways similar, but in essence quite different. They were all motivated by greed, yet what was important for Cavelya was not how he acquired what he did, but simply that he did. The means didn't matter for Cavelya, only the end. The Campbells focused on the task. They had expensive tastes and celebrated in *gloria mundi*, but would live like Trappists for months to be able to steal something that no one else had the skills to get away with. Cavelya had come to get the Picassos on a fifty-four foot yacht that he needed a broker to buy for him and Enright to captain, because he knew nothing of boats, large or small. Bolivia is landlocked. The Campbells had rented an eighteen-foot canoe to get to the camp and perhaps to make their escape from it as well. They knew not only how to run the boat through those sometimes shallow waters, but they also knew how to make minor repairs, and knew that it was the perfect boat for where they had arranged to make the transfer. Cavelya was motivated by acquisition; the Campbells by skillful execution.

"We'll meet again tomorrow, as we discussed earlier," said James. "Thank you for the wonderful meal, Señor Cavelya, but it is late, and we have much to prepare for tomorrow's meeting."

Cavelya remained seated and simply said, "Yes, we will meet tomorrow as we discussed. Good night, gentlemen."

The Campbells nodded good nights to Keagan and Kelly and left the dining room. Two of the chain-laden bullet heads, Luis and Manascotta, sat where they were. Charo continued to pout, an attitude for which she seemed exceptionally well-suited. Keagan continued to reflect on the turn of events. Niles was out on St. George Island, he and Kelly were anchored to a table with Cavelya, and Teal

— the inexperienced member of the group — was following a pair of professional thieves, and one of the well-muscled thugs was unaccounted for. Keagan thought briefly of Anjali. *What would he tell her if things went wrong?*

Teal watched the Campbells leave the Gibson. He had a pretty good idea of where they were headed, so he didn't rush to follow them. While he was sitting in the Explorer, he noticed a sizeable dark skinned man decorated in gold. The *bullet-head* followed the Campbells, so Teal followed him. Blue Taurus sedan, Chevy Impala, and Ford Explorer. Henry would have been proud: he got two out of three.

"What would you care to drink?" inquired Señor Cavelya.

"I'd like a neat Black Bushmills," said Kelly.

"And you, Mr. Keagan?"

"A snifter of Cognac; Martel Cordon Blue."

Cavelya signaled the waiter, who informed Señor Cavelya that while the Gibson did indeed carry Martel Cordon Blue; however, it did not have Black Bushmills. He suggested Jameson 12 as a possible substitute. Additionally, he mentioned that the inn stocked several single malt Scotches, of which he recommended the McCallum 25-year old as being the best of the lot. Kelly accepted his recommendation. Cavelya inquired as to their selection of Ports. The choices were understandably small, given the location of the Gibson; however, they did happen to have a 1990 vintage *Oporto*, which Cavelya ordered.

"I'm sure the bottle has been decanted, but I'd like you to do it again at the table," Cavelya told the waiter. Turning to Keagan, he said, "A port of that quality throws a heavy sediment."

"Yes. Properly, it should be done two hours before serving; however, if it was done correctly the first time, it will be fine. If not, you will know as soon as he begins to pour it," offered Keagan.

"You seem exceptionally well versed in wine, Mr. Keagan. Most Americans only know of port as something that derelicts drink from paper sacks, a legal requirement for public drinking that I'm at a loss to understand. But are you American? You have a touch of accent in your voice, as does your charming companion. English?"

Kelly internally bristled, but Cavelya never knew it because she beamed at him.

"Irish, actually," said Keagan.

The waiter brought their drinks on a silver tray. Keagan thought that it was real. First, he served Kelly her McCallum 25, then Keagan's Cognac, which he first heated rotating the snifter on a brass yoke. Finally, he began to decant Cavelya's *Oporto*.

"Excuse me," Keagan said to the waiter. "The cheese cloth is unnecessary, but you should have a candle." Both the waiter and Cavelya looked confused. Keagan explained, "place the candle behind the neck of the bottle, pour very gently until you see sediment, then resettle the bottle. You only want to trap the sediment; the cheesecloth will also take up some from the wine's richness and may even add something that will affect the wine's taste."

The waiter went off to get a candle. "Mr. Keagan, you fascinate me. You are very like myself. You have an appreciation for the finer things in life," said Cavelya, striking the chord of a very obvious cliché.

***

Special Agent Fugaezi finally arrived at the Gibson Inn at a little after 9:00 PM. He checked in and asked when the kitchen closed. He hadn't eaten since breakfast. The desk told him 9:30 PM which gave him just enough time to drop his bags off in his room, call his office and leave a message, and come back downstairs. Apalachicola is about equidistant – four hours driving time – between Jacksonville and Mobile, the nearest FBI field offices, so Fugaezi was on his own. It was important to let his office know where he was and what he was doing.

As Fugaezi was about to enter the Gibson Inn's dining room, a number of diners were leaving. Fugaezi's attention was immediately drawn to a stunning auburn beauty. He stepped aside to let the party pass and to continue to watch the beautiful woman with the knowing smile in her eyes, but his view was cut off by the exit of another party, which at first triggered a vague response as they were Ayma-ran Indians. Florida still has a number of indigenous people, even on the Panhandle. It took Fugaezi a moment to realize that he was looking at Cavelya. He never even noticed Keagan.

Fugaezi watched Cavelya and his party go upstairs to their rooms. He went into the dining room, quickly scanned the menu, ordered the seafood linguini, a salad, and a glass of red wine, and told the waiter to bring it all at once; he'd be back in a moment.

Fugaezi went to the front desk, showed the clerk his credentials, and asked about Cavelya. He inquired about Cavelya's arrival time, the length of his registered stay, his room number, and any other related room numbers — his car model and what the plate number on it was. It was not the same clerk Keagan spoke with.

The clerk printed out the registration information for Cavelya's three adjacent rooms and handed the sheet to Fugaezi, who noticed that the vehicle information had been left blank.

"I'm assuming from the room numbers that these rooms are right up those stairs and are adjoining?"

"Well, they are one flight up, but not adjoining. They are, however, adjacent. The Gibson is an old inn, so none of our rooms have connecting doors."

"Why no vehicle registration?" asked Fugaezi.

"I can't say; I didn't register them. I guess Sarah, who is on the day shift, didn't notice it."

Fugaezi thanked the clerk and went in to the dining room just as his waiter was delivering his salad and entrée. "I'll be right back with your wine, sir," said the waiter as Fugaezi sat to his dinner.

Right after dinner, Fugaezi checked in at the local police department that was conveniently located cattycorner from the Gibson. The Apalachicola Police Department didn't have a watch commander so the dispatcher had to call Chief Eubeck at home. Ten minutes later Fugaezi was explaining to the Chief that he was in his jurisdiction, that he was alone, and that he would most definitely need those in his department and his help. Specifically for now, he needed his help to watch the inn and tell him if Cavelya was on the move. Eubeck wondered specifically what else he would need, but kept his curiosity to himself.

As if reading Eubeck's mind, Fugaezi said that he would also need a vehicle, as he had flown to Apalachicola and arrived too late to arrange for transportation. Eubeck arranged for one of his men to bring around an old Ford Expedition, the final draw from the motor pool.

Before leaving, Fugaezi told the Eubeck that he'd ask the desk clerk at the inn to call him if Cavelya appeared to be leaving.

"You better also tell him that he needs to keep his mouth shut under the pain of Homeland Security; that boy likes to talk."

Thirty-Two

Teal was right. The Campbells, with Carlos in tow, were headed to the boat access that led to Harley Davidson's camp. Teal watched one of the henchmen enter the access road. He went about a hundred yards farther, made a U-turn, parked on the right-hand side of the road, and waited.

Teal figured it would take Carlos twenty minutes to get to the river, scope out the boat landing, and come back to County 65 where he waited. He would have to use lights on the way into the river, so he would have to stay well behind the Campbells.

Twenty-two minutes later the Impala pulled back onto the County 65. *He must have found the boat ramp and only stayed briefly to hear the Campbells motor around the island to Harley's camp,* thought Teal. He called Keagan and told him that Cavelya's man was headed back toward Apalachicola and that he would follow him at a leisurely pace. Keagan didn't believe him – he remembered Teal's driving on I-10. Regardless, he told Teal to go get Niles, bring him back to Apalachicola, and meet Kelly and him in an hour at the Nest, a bar/restaurant on the west side of town on US 98. Five minutes later Teal passed Carlos at eighty miles an hour, a scourge and terror of possums, armadillos, and other idlers dazed by his lights.

***

The Nest catered to a mixed crowd. The locals mostly went there to drink, and the tourists went there to enjoy its sea-and-salt atmosphere, on the water location, and fresh seafood. The Nest was a rectangular building. Its front faced the highway and its back was to the Gulf. The bar occupied a third of the right side of the building while the restaurant and kitchen took up the rest. The premier seats of the dining room were along the back wall facing the Gulf. The two areas were separated from each other by a partition, topped with lattice work, and festooned with nautical decorations that blocked all but two isles into and out of the dining area. Niles and Teal arrived first and took a table in the dining room facing the Gulf. The dinner crowd had left, so at this hour the dining room served to handle the overflow from the bar. They were waiting for the waitress to bring them two Budweisers as they did not have Niles' beer of choice like the other local haunts; the Panhandle wasn't making much of an impression on Niles. When Keagan and Kelly arrived, they ordered two tonics with lime in large glasses. They had had enough alcohol staging their meeting with Cavelya.

"What have you got for us, Niles?" Keagan asked when the waitress left.

"Enright told me that Cavelya will be concluding his business sometime tomorrow and that they will be sailing back to port afterwards. He's not stupid. He knows that I'm not what I say I am, which is a hotelier from the frozen wastes looking to branch out in Florida. However, he must have decided that I'm not DEA or Cavelya's competition. Still, he's not sure, so he's hedging his bets, feeding me as little information as he can without stonewalling me or giving away the candy store. Apparently, Cavelya intends to go up the river to conduct his business. Enright is nervous about the trip, he says because he is not a river pilot. I think the real reason is that he usually isn't present when Cavelya conducts business. I do think he is what he says he is, a hired skipper until he can afford his own boat."

"Teal, what did you learn today, and what did you learn later when you followed the Campbells?" asked Keagan.

"Well, what I was trying to tell you at the Gibson earlier was that I found out where the Campbells are holed up, so following them tonight was unnecessary. Well, maybe not. One of Cavelya's men followed them. I'm not sure what that adds because if they met tonight to finalize plans for the switch there, then Cavelya already knows about the camp. Maybe the goon was just trying to see if there was some place to set up an ambush."

Keagan felt stupid. He had violated one of his cardinal rules, which was never assume he knew more about the operation than any of his partners. Teal was new, but that was a weak excuse. He'd try not to make that mistake again.

"Sorry, Teal, I should have listened."

"Anyway, a lot of today went nowhere, but this afternoon I ran into a fellow by the name of Harley Davidson, of all names."

Kelly didn't make the connection and looked confused.

"Harley Davidson was once the sole remaining motor cycle company in America," said Keagan. "Threatened with bankruptcy when its customer pool was reduced to miscreants like Hells Angels, when the flood of imports from Japan arrived. The company made a comeback when President Reagan put a forty–five percent tariff on imported motorcycles. Then, yuppies got interested in them, having become bored with most of their other toys of choice. Now it is something of a cult. Their owners make up a distinct sub-culture in American folklore."

Niles looked at Kelly and shrugged.

"Mick, have you lost your everlasting soul to the demons of this country? How have you learned of such things in so short a time? And why would you want to?"

"Sun Tzu: know your environment, near and far," said Keagan.

"Mick, those were my lines. Well, not the sun part," said Teal.

"You ride motorcycles?" asked Keagan.

"Sure."

Curiouser and curiouser, thought Keagan. He didn't voice his thoughts, smiled and told Teal to resume his story.

Teal filled them in about how Davidson came into some money by renting his camp and boat to a couple of Yankees who said they were doing wildlife research. How Harley had shown him the access to the camp, and how when he followed the Campbells and Cavelya's man he saw that they had gone in the same access road. Finally, he told them about the island that hid the camp from the view of regular river traffic.

"It sounds as though the switch is tomorrow at Davidson's camp," said Keagan.

"Yes, but when and how?" asked Kelly.

"Teal, get the Florida highway map out of my car and the river charts we picked up this afternoon, would you please? They're all folded in the driver-side tuck-in."

When Teal came back, he showed them where the access road was, pinpointed it, and gave Keagan the mileage to it from the bar where he met Davidson and also the mileage from US 98 to the bar that was on Country 65. On the river chart, he showed them the long stretch of island that hid the camp's location, but indicated where Davidson had told him the camp lay. Finally, Teal told them about the old truck the Campbells had rented from Davidson.

"Very good work, Teal," said Keagan. Niles and Kelly agreed. All three had been worried about him, but so far he seemed to have worked out better than expected.

"What you have told us corresponds with what Kelly and I found out today. We even got a look at the camp that you are describing."

"They have a rental car," said Kelly, "why would they need an old truck?"

"Alternate escape route," answered Niles. "I bet it is parked somewhere on the other side of the river or upriver near an overpass."

Teal looked quickly at the map. "FL 71, the nearest road to the west, approximately ten to twelve crow miles from the river at that point."

"Teal, did you ever see any of the bayou folk in south Louisiana use a canoe with an inboard engine for shallow-draft work?" asked Keagan.

"Sometimes, yes," said Teal.

"I've seen them up in Canada where fishing guides need to get in among the reeds and the grasses for northern pike. They can move across very shallow water. The Campbells seem to have very good exit plans," said Keagan.

"What about the switch?" said Kelly. "How do you think that will happen?"

"Good question, Kelly, and perhaps the final piece of the puzzle. Cavelya is a drug trafficker, and people who deal in drugs have a nasty habit of trying to profit from both sides of the sale, getting the merchandise and keeping the cash. Not a major leap in creativity from cocaine to Picassos. I think that's what Cavelya has in mind."

"It makes sense to me," said Niles, "because in this transaction Cavelya not only gets the paintings and keeps the cash, but he also breaks the trail. The Campbells may be very good thieves, but if Kelly and her contacts got on to them, then the authorities can't be too awfully far behind. If Cavelya and his men can bury them in a Florida swamp, then they will have tidied things up nicely, won't they have?"

"Niles, you mention Enright's concern about the river. How deep a draft does that boat require, do you think?"

"I don't know for sure, but I should think about somewhere between five and six feet. I don't know whether that figures in the screw because I didn't see how it was set up, but that's a good ballpark. From the charts I saw on board, I would say that he won't have any difficulty if he keeps it in the channel, but I suspect he'll have limited maneuverability, and that island will present a bit of a problem. When I looked at the charts I was pressed for time so I was only able to check out the main channel on the chart. It didn't help that I was unaware of the island at the time. Also, Enright arrived sooner than I had expected him to, and was about to come back aboard to discover me looking over his charts. As such, I had to sit in the bloody bilge for thirty minutes. Required three extra pints of Bass to top off my body fluids."

Keagan looked at the chart of the river that showed the island. "According to this, the channel west of the island is never more than eight feet deep, and I suspect that depth is constantly changing for the worse. Enright will never bring the boat in there. It's too much of a trap, and he can't maneuver in that narrow channel; once in, he either has to exit the other end or reverse out. Cavelya will have to go to them with an alternate craft, or the Campbells will have to come to him. Niles, did you happen to see if Cavelya had some sort of landing craft?"

"Yeah, it's a Zodiac Pro 400, Mick. I don't know what that means, but it's a sizeable one, probably capable of carrying five or six people."

"How would it be advantageous to the Campbells to go out to the main channel and make the switch on Cavelya's boat?" asked Keagan. "Remember, these two are smarter than they are greedy."

"In the main channel, it is more likely that other boats will pass by, but not much because it's summer," said Teal. "Nobody can see them at the camp site. Better for the Campbells because Cavelya would be less likely to shoot them where someone might see his boat and hear the shots."

"True enough, Teal," said Kelly. "However, on the boat, it wouldn't be difficult for Cavelya's men to subdue the Campbells and dispose of them several hours later when they are miles out on the Gulf. You properly identified them as rock climbers, and rock climbers are at home in the out-of-doors. They rented this Harley fellows' lorry when they already have a rental car. That precaution suggests to me, at least that the switch will take place if not at the cabin then on land. Mick and I got a glimpse of the camp this afternoon. While I don't pretend to know much about the Campbells other than their general profile, it seems to me that they are much more suited to the wilderness than either Cavelya or his men."

"Niles, what do you think?" asked Keagan.

"Going out to Cavelya in the channel gives the entire advantage to Cavelya. As you rightly pointed out, the Campbells aren't stupid; they couldn't have stolen the Picassos if they were. Everything points to the Campbells making the switch at the camp. Cavelya and his men are in control on the boat, less so on land. Also, there is the problem of Enright — he may be on Cavelya's payroll, but unless I am very much mistaken, it's only as skipper. Enright is a complication, and Cavelya needs him, at least to get back to North Captiva and certainly to get off the river."

"I change my vote," said Teal.

"OK, we all seem to agree that the switch is not going to take place on board Cavelya's boat on the river," said Keagan. "If we are correct, how does that prove that the switch will take place at the cabin? Choices come in more than *either-or* varieties; thinking so is the fallacy of dichotomies." Teal rolled his eyes as if to say, *sure it is.* "Kelly, if you were the Campbells, where would you make the switch?"

"I'm not much on swamps, even though the English refer to us Irish as bog stompers when they are being kind. I have little experience with that kind of terrain; however, in general terms, were I the Campbells, I'd want to use the environment to every advantage and maybe the Campbells have read *The Art of War* as well. I don't think that they will make the switch in the cabin either because it would be even easier to dispose of them there in the swamp, behind the island. But at the risk of being one who has been seduced at least partially by the *fallacy of dichotomies,* I see only three possibilities: on the river, in the cabin, and in the swamp."

"Quite right, Kelly, but what are the variations of each? I think we need to get out there before dawn to better understand the terrain."

"Before dawn?" asked Teal.

"I should think so," said Niles.

"Yes, but how are we going to get there?" asked Teal.

"Mick took care of that this afternoon," answered Kelly.

"Let's salvage what we can of tonight and meet on the dock behind Boss Oysters at 4:30 AM," said Mick.

Thirty-Three

It was quiet and still on the river at 4:30 AM. Keagan had lashed the two kayaks to the gunwales of the sixteen foot outboard that Sally Mae had rented for them. It had a semi-enclosed deck, which gave them some cover, and a hundred horsepower Mercury engine. It was a boat used for fishing and for going to camp, nondescript and well-suited to their purposes. The kayaks were low-volume boats and a little dicey on a big river — especially if there were a wind or for paddling cross-current — but perfect for maneuvering in back waters because they were quick to turn and drew only inches of water. The kayaks were bright yellow. Sally Mae may have been a soldier for Christ, but she didn't know squat about covert ops.

Kelly was wearing sneakers, hiking shorts, a T-shirt, and a fisherman's bill cap with a Foreign Legion neck cover. She was about to apply a coating of Skin-So-Soft over her SPF-50 sunscreen that Keagan had applied earlier in their room, when Niles shook his head.

Kelly asked what was wrong and told him that Teal had told her it keeps the bugs away.

"It does," said Niles, "but both the Campbells as well as Cavelya and his Bolivian cutthroats will wonder why there is a French tart out there in the swamp."

"I beg your pardon, Niles."

"Not you, of course, Kelly. The Skin-So-Soft, smell it."

Kelly did. "Aye."

Keagan was dressed similarly to Kelly, but didn't wear a hat. Teal wore sneakers, cycling pants, and no shirt. Kelly examined his tattoo; she had never seen one like it before. Niles looked like a militia man at summer camp in Alabama. Head-to-toe camouflage: canvas Vibram sneakers, cargo-pocket pants, T-shirt, and hat. He wore his S&W Model 19, .357 Magnum in a shoulder holster. Kelly carried her Walther PPK in the right cargo pocket of her shorts. Keagan also wore the Sig 9mm in a shoulder holster. Teal didn't seem to have a weapon.

"Where is your weapon, Teal?" Keagan asked.

"It's in my duffel. I have it if I need it."

Keagan, in spite of his self-admonishment the night before, worried about Teal. He didn't seem to take any of this seriously. Keagan, again, thought of Anjali.

At 5:30 AM they reached the south tip of the island. "Where is that boat access, Teal?"

"It's still a ways upriver, about three quarters of a mile. It's directly across from the camp on the east bank of the river."

As they neared, Keagan told Niles, "slow down and get closer to the east bank. We need to find the boat point."

"Why don't we just go up the river a mile or two and float down?" asked Teal.

"Ever try to get into a kayak from three feet above it?" asked Niles.

"No, but then I would have used a pirogue," said Teal.

A mile up, Keagan spotted it. He told Niles to pull over to an old wooden dock and unlash the kayaks. As he and Teal were getting the kayaks ready, Keagan fished out a Mini-Maglite from his duffle, jumped down onto the dock, and walked down to the clearing that functioned as a turn-around and a parking lot. The only car there was the white Ford Taurus with a Florida license plate. Keagan walked down the access road and scanned the dew-laden sand for tire tracks. There were only the two sets from the night before – the Campbells' and Cavelya's follow car.

Keagan walked back down to the dock. The two bright yellow kayaks rested on it, glowing dully in the false light of pre-dawn. Less than twenty-five miles to the west, the Central Time Zone began. 5:30 AM here was much darker than 5:30 AM in Miami. On the western edge of the Eastern Time Zone, it was still very much night.

Keagan gathered the group on the dock. "We've run out of script. From here on out we are going to have to anticipate what's going to happen and where it will happen. We should keep our phones on; that is if the bloody things work out here. I've got two bars. We'll see what the island does to reception. Put them on vibrate. After 6:30 use them only in an emergency. I don't want the bloody things ringing as we're sitting behind a bush watching these guys make the exchange.

"Niles and Teal, you guys will tow Kelly and me upriver, about a half mile past the northern tip of the island, so we can paddle down the west shore where we can access the camp. One way in which this could play out is for Kelly and I to quietly relieve the Campbells of the paintings while they are otherwise engaged preparing for Cavelya's arrival. A similar scenario would be for us to convince the Campbells that it would be in their personal interests to turn over the paintings to us. The down side of that scenario is that we run the risk of nasty people tracking us down at some later date, and since I already have one group pursuing that possibility, I don't need another. What I want to avoid is Cavelya and his men taking possession of the paintings, and making their farewells in any way they feel appropriate. There are, of course, lots of other minor variations. In any event, our job will be to cover the Campbells' end of the exchange. Niles and Teal, your job is to cover Cavelya's end and to react to his actions. Frankly, your job is potentially the more difficult and dangerous. I'm assuming that the Campbells are armed, but I'm also assuming that they just want to sell the paintings. On the other hand, I'm convinced that Cavelya generally prefers to get things without paying for them, an economic philosophy that would have sent Marx into a catatonic state, and would have intrigued Bush.

Economic philosophy aside, Cavelya's bodyguards aren't just for his personal security; and as you mentioned, Niles, Enright is a complication. Kelly and I have two potentially dangerous professionals to cover, but you have four psychopaths and another unknown entity. Still, I suspect the odds seem worse than they are, for unless something goes awfully wrong and you need to engage Cavelya and his men, we should be able to assist you."

Keagan showed Kelly how to get into the kayak from the dock. He placed the paddle, blade down, across the back deck of the boat, with the other blade flat on the dock. The trick was to put the pressure on the shaft of the paddle, not on the blade. Doing so distributes the stress equally while keeping the boat steady. It would have been easier for her to get in from the boat ramp, but they might not always have such a good place to get into and out of the boats. It was better that she knew how to do it under less-than-ideal conditions. Once Kelly was in the kayak, Keagan handed her a belly pack and then had her fit her spray skirts over the cowling, tighten the skirt, and paddle around near the shore. She did just as well as she had a week ago on Lake Placid.

Kelly came back to the dock, shipped the paddle and waited for Keagan to get into his boat. Keagan stepped off the dock into the water by Kelly's boat, leaned down and kissed her. "That's for luck," he said before leaning down and whispering, "and because I love you."

Keagan was standing upright now next to Kelly's boat.

"Aye, you bloody Irish, you may all profess to be Christians," mocked Kelly in an exaggerated English accent. "But truth be told, you are all pagans from misty bogs and your souls are still with the druids."

"Be that as it may, you take care of yourself. The money, the *Cause*, none of it is worth more than a modest risk. Nothing we do today will alter history more than a jot. On the other hand, getting ourselves killed will alter our personal histories enormously." Keagan turned to Teal with a baleful eye. "You are listening to me, aren't you, Teal? Don't you dare make me tell Anjali that her father died in a Florida swamp."

"*Guaranteed*," said Teal with a bright smile, breaking the tension.

"Okay, off we go then. We need to take advantage of the dark," said Keagan. Niles and Teal boarded the power boat and attached two tow-lines to cleats. Teal tossed the lines to Keagan and Kelly. Keagan told Kelly to ship her paddle across her front deck and hold the paddle with one hand and the line with the other.

"If you flip over," he told her, "pull on the nylon lanyard of the spray skirt and fold out of the boat in an *L*, the way you practiced on Lake Placid. Don't worry about the boat or the paddle. If you do that, your knees won't clear the cowl. Instead, push off the foot brace and float out. You don't have to do anything special: gravity will take care of everything. Once you're out of the boat, I'll come get you."

Niles gently powered the boat forward. Keagan kept close watch on Kelly, or at least as well as he could given the hour. Kelly had a tremendous facility for adaptation, and so she had no problems with the tow. Niles estimated they would reach the northern tip of the island in about five to six minutes at the speed the power boat was traveling. He went a little farther as Keagan had suggested so he could explore the west bank for a place to land rather than having to go behind the island. Keagan didn't want to have to drift very far into the channel behind the island. He didn't know how extensive the Campbells' precautions would be, so he wanted an unprotected buffer to his approach to the camp. They didn't find a good landing spot, so they drifted back toward the island. It was a little lighter now, mostly because the river here was wider. Niles and Teal pulled in the lines, and drew Keagan and Kelly up to the power boat. They were about a half mile above the island.

"If there is anything else to cover, now is the time," said Keagan.

"Mick, you know how these things go. One can only plan so much. What we prepared for and what will actually happen will be much different, yet I think we're OK," said Niles.

"I agree," said Kelly.

"Teal, are you comfortable with all this?"

"Niles is right, Mick. We've planned all we can plan. Now we have to adjust and act."

"Adjust and act," repeated Kelly, as she and Keagan let go of the lines and began drifting downstream backwards. Keagan braced with his paddle, rolled his hip and turned around facing downstream in one stroke. Kelly didn't know how to brace with the paddle, but understood enough physics to know that if she dragged one blade of the paddle, she would come about and be going in the direction she wanted. She was about fifteen seconds behind Keagan. He waited for her to catch up.

"We need to paddle down river until we find a place to come ashore," said Keagan. "I'm guessing that the current here is about three miles an hour. Casual paddling will bring that rate up to about five or six miles an hour, and you shouldn't just drift because you have more control of the boat when you paddle. If we haven't found a place to come ashore before the island, we'll pick whatever is available soon after entering the channel behind it. Remember, Teal said the camp is about three quarters of a mile from the northern tip of the island. I don't think we should come ashore any less than a quarter mile north of the camp. It's getting light. When we find an access we'll drag the boats ashore and stow the paddles under the front deck. I don't think there is any advantage in hiding them. The Campbells have their own escape plans. They don't need our help."

They could see the scrub of the eastern shore now. The western shore was saw grass and palmetto. Keagan and Kelly paddled close to the bank, so as to stay in the darkest part of the channel and to cut down the angle of observation from the western shore. Niles and Teal floated by them out in the main channel.

The river turned east for a few hundred yards, and there was an obstruction in their path.

"Skirt the snag," said Keagan. Then a second later, "Oh, shit, that's not a snag, it's an alligator. Kelly, hard on the left blade!" Keagan cut in front of her, so she couldn't get past him and drift into where the alligator was waiting. The problem now, however, was that both of them were drifting toward the gator.

Keagan couldn't do anything else. He couldn't stroke with his left blade because Kelly's boat was touching his. If he stroked with his right blade, he'd veer directly toward the gator.

"Kelly, listen carefully and get it all quickly. Remember how you turned around a few minutes ago? Extend your left blade flat onto the river, arms high and roll your hips left. Be careful not to allow the blade to edge into the river's current. You'll flip if you do. Use the blade as a brace, and do it now," he muffle-shouted.

The alligator looked to be about ten feet long. One this long could easily weigh as much as 600 pounds. Flipping a kayak wouldn't present much of a problem for it.

They were less than a boat-length from the alligator, which had turned toward them, lazily flipping its tail to maintain its position in the river, its pre-historic brain singly focused on the two large, heat-producing organisms that were headed its way. Keagan thought of shooting the gator, but of course the noise would alert the Campbells, and he didn't have the time anyway.

Keagan leaned over and grabbed Kelly's cowl, and pushed back as hard as he could. She braced left as Keagan had told her and veered sharply toward the eastern bank. When he was clear, Keagan also braced hard left, turning his boat sharply away from the gator. Keagan had braced so hard to the left and at such an angle that he flipped over. Kelly saw him go under and saw the gator turn toward the overturned boat. But Keagan rolled over almost immediately. When he came up, two powerful strokes took him down river away from the gator. Kelly was even further downriver than Keagan was. The gator didn't seem to know where its prey had gone.

"Jaysus, Mick, what the hell was that? I mean, I know what that was, but Jesus, it was huge." They could see the island now in the near distance. Keagan refocused.

He called to Kelly to paddle closer to him. "We need to go ashore now."

Fugaezi got two early calls. The clerk at the front desk called to say that the Cavelya party had just checked out. Fugaezi had just gotten the phone cradled when it rang again. This time it was Officer Jackson informing him that Cavelya and his party were just getting into a late-model, white Chevy Impala. Fugaezi threw on a pair of jeans and fisherman's shirt and grabbed his gear bag.

Officer Jackson called him again, this time on his cell phone just after he closed the door to the Ford Expedition loaned to Fugaezi.

"They just drove down to the public dock," said Jackson. "Looks like they're going to take a boat ride. Cross US 98, go two blocks down, turn right."

"Question is, which way is he going – back home or upriver?" said Fugaezi when he arrived at where Jackson was watching the Deep Water Marina. "I'm assuming the department has a boat readily available."

"Yeah, it's moored right down behind City Hall."

"Is it obviously a police boat? I mean, does it have *Police* in great big letters on it?"

"Oh, yeah, and it's got the light bar. No doubt 'bout what it is."

"Any chance I can rent another one?"

Fugaezi watched Cavelya, his men and a still sleepy woman walk down the Deep Water main dock to the riverside mooring, where a very large boat was waiting.

"Not at this hour. Thompson's doesn't open for two more hours. If you want to go out early, you have to rent the boat the day before. That way he can charge you for another day."

"How about calling the Chief, maybe he can get Thompson to open up."

"I already called him. He should be here any minute. You can ask him," said Jackson.

"How far up is this river navigable?"

"Georgia, Alabama; take your pick. The Chattahoochee forms the lower border between those two states. Used to be major traffic on this river, back before the Civil War. Fifth biggest port in the country. Cotton and timber from Alabama and Georgia were barged down to the Gulf, then off to Europe, England mostly. At least that's what I learnt in school."

"So you're from here?"

"Yep. Born and bred as they say."

"Are there any tributaries that feed it? I'm just trying to figure out how we can follow them if we can't keep them in sight."

"Can't really. The first split is about ten miles up and doesn't dead end for another ten miles. You wouldn't know if you took the wrong fork for at least seven or eight miles. Same with the second one. There are a whole bunch more before you get out of Florida. What are we looking for, anyway?" asked Jackson.

"Five paintings worth $45 million stolen in Sweden about two years ago."

"Looks like one of your questions is being answered."

The *Blanca Nieve* was headed upriver.

"So why do you think he's going upriver?" asked Jackson.

"I think he's buying the paintings from the two men who stole them," said Fugaezi.

"Here, on the Apalachicola River, on the Florida Panhandle? Are you serious?"

Chief Eubeck arrived before Fugaezi could tell Jackson that he was very serious.

"Chief, Officer Jackson has been filling me in on the river. I'm trying to figure out how I can follow Cavelya upriver to wherever he's going to make the exchange. I'd rather not do it in a conspicuous boat, especially a police boat."

"Did he tell you ya can't?"

"Pretty much," said Fugaezi.

"Well, he's right. You were a little sketchy last night so you want to tell me now why exactly you're here," said Eubeck.

Fugaezi told him about the theft of the paintings, Dalin's work, and his belief that Cavelya—a suspected drug trafficker, who collected art—was here to buy the stolen paintings.

"Here? In Apalachicola?"

"Same question Officer Jackson asked. Said it pretty much the same way, too."

"Well, good, means the boy's thinking. Have you thought about probable cause? Because I can't figure out how you have any."

"Yeah, it could be a sticking point, but I'm sure I'm right. This fellow in Sweden, Dalin, has done some amazing work. He led me to a web site where the paintings were offered, and the Bureau traced the inquiries. Cavelya was at the head of the list."

"Well, that sounds too high-tech for me, but if you follow this Cavelya upriver all you're going to accomplish is spooking him and queering the exchange if that's really what he's doing. But, truth be told, I can't think of any other reason he'd want to go up river in a boat that big."

"Here's what I suggest. I'll have Bobby here tow the department's boat up to that last national forest service road. You know the one I'm thinking about, Bobby, the one past the Brickyard Road?" Jackson nodded that he did. "You go with him, of course at least to the river. There are only three other feeders before that that would be deep enough for a boat that size. I'll see if I can get a couple of men up there and they'll call you to let you know if that boat turned off or continued on up. Let me have your cell number."

"Cell phone going to work up there?" asked Fugaezi.

"Iffy. I better get you and the spotters two-ways radios. They'll work, I'm sure."

"Anyway, my guess is that they'll go straight on up. The county line runs right down the river. Our jurisdiction is the west side, so Bobby can't go on the boat with you. Over in the national forest, Agent Fugaezi, well then, I guess that's yours, so he can at least get you launched. The last place where that boat could turn off is at about the half way mark, so you'll have all three reports before you get on the water."

"If you get a call that he's turned off Bobby can take you to the best place to get on the water to be able to get down river and survey the exchange. If you get a call from a spotter saying the boat's already headed downriver, then you know that the exchange has taken place or the whole thing is a bust, because I can't stop him without something more substantial than you've given me. If you're right, these boys sure picked a good place to make the exchange—if they don't get themselves killed that is."

"Let's not complicate things," said Fugaezi.

***

Enright was studying the chart one last time before he entered the marked channel. Cavelya had called Enright the night before and told him to bring the boat over to the Deep Water Marina on the Apalachicola River. They were headed home, but before they left, they had to go upriver for about twenty miles, so he needed to review his charts. Enright asked about the rental car. Cavelya said he was leaving a message with the front desk at the inn that he'd be leaving the car in the marina's parking lot. *Just make sure that the boat's fuel is topped off and be at the dock at 6:00 AM.*

Cavelya and the bodyguards went below decks. His female companion was also below decks, but she was asleep in Cavelya's cabin. Cavelya was giving his men final instructions about the exchange. The instructions weren't very detailed or complicated; they couldn't handle complicated. Essentially, he told them that he wanted the paintings and that he didn't want to pay for them. It was an economic theory they all understood.

Cavelya told his men that the Campbells were tricky fuckers and that they should be wary of them even though they didn't look very tough. He also told them that this was not Miami and that while people here were used to guns, they weren't used to automatic fire. Besides, he didn't want Enright to hear gunfire if it could be avoided.

"Make sure you have the suppressors attached. Use your knives if you can. Only use the Glocks as a last resort," Cavelya told him.

Cavelya wanted the Campbells dead—from the time they first made contact with him, he could sense the Campbells' condescension towards him—but he wanted it done quietly. Finally, he told them that if they damaged the paintings in any way (shot them full of holes, or dropped them into the water or mud) he would personally cut off their dicks, stick them in their mouths, and crazy glue their lips shut. "Try to explain that to the paramedics," ended Cavelya.

Cavelya didn't know anything about employee management theory, but he did know about cultural incentives, and he knew that the various images of what he had just said conjured up fears that were far more menacing than the threat of death. Add to that the unusual preoccupation that Latin American men had for the *pinga*, and you had some idea of how chilling his threat was to them. They knew exactly how Cavelya would deal with failure, and so they were determined to get him the paintings, which was precisely what Cavelya wanted. He was a born motivator of men.

Enright was nervously enjoying the cruise up the river. He was fascinated by the landscape (which was quite a bit different from that of south Florida) but kept looking back at the depth sounder, making sure that the boat had enough clearance. The depth sounder read sixteen feet when Cavelya came onto the bridge.

"How's it going?" asked Cavelya.

"Fine. The channel seems plenty deep enough, and the charts say that it is, but all that depends on the tide and amount of rain they've been having upriver. It's just that this is a very large boat to be on a river, even a large river like this. Also, this part of Florida gets hit by more hurricanes than any other part—people think they all hit south Florida but they don't—and a hurricane can tear the shit out of a river channel. Hell, North Captiva used to part of Captiva, which used to be part of Sanibel until a hurricane in the 1920s, I think we are okay, though; I'd just prefer be out on the Gulf."

Cavelya knew that he couldn't threaten Enright, so he turned on the charm instead, and despite Cavelya's depraved nature, he could be charming, one of his personal characteristics that made him that much more deadly. He put his hand on Enright's shoulder and leaned over the chart. "This island," he said, tapping his finger on it, "is where we are headed. You need to go up near the north tip of it and anchor off it while I conduct some business with two gentlemen who have something to sell me. They have a cabin on the west bank. My *compadres* and I will take the Zodiac to meet with them. I have every confidence in your seamanship and your judgment, Captain."

Cavelya turned and looked into Enright's eyes, which flicked to the depth sounder every fifteen seconds or so. "Up until now I have not involved you in any of my business. I normally use the boat for pleasure only. This trip is different. These men have something very special to sell me, but I fear that the sale will involve great danger. You saw those aluminum cases I brought aboard when we started out from North Captiva. They are filled with money. These men may have lured me here to steal my money, and so I have brought Luis, Manascotta, and Carlos for protection. I wish only to buy what they have to sell and to go home safely. I know you want to get your own boat, and if everything goes well today, I may be able to help you do that earlier than you would have, although I really would hate to lose you."

Enright could smell a rat even on a Southern river. "I'm not going to be interrupted by the Coast Guard, am I?" asked Enright. The depth sounder showed seventeen feet.

"No, of course not. I am not involved in the sale of drugs. These men have procured art work that is very valuable and has been essentially, how do I say, unappreciated."

"Unappreciated?" questioned Enright. The sounder gauge showed fourteen feet, so Enright shaved the wheel to the right a bit.

"Yes, you know how these things go. A painter paints a beautiful work and sells it to a greedy art dealer to buy bread and maybe some wine. The art dealer makes a quick profit, selling the piece to someone who needs to cover a spot on the wall. The buyer moves to a nicer apartment and leaves the painting behind. It ends up back with the greedy art dealer, and these very talented young men come along and recognize it immediately for what it is. That is why we are here on this river today."

Enright smiled at Cavelya. The smile was one of satisfaction and amusement. Enright was satisfied that the sounder gauge now read eighteen feet, and he was amused by Cavelya's tale of struggling artist, manipulating art dealer, near-marvelous find and authentication.

Cavelya seemed to be satisfied by Enright's smile. He patted him on the back. "You'll have your boat in no time," Cavelya said to Enright as he left the bridge to give one last motivational speech to his men. Enright reviewed his options. He could run the boat aground. He could turn the boat around, disembark at Apalachicola, and take a bus back to Fort Myers. He could go along with Cavelya's plan and be the faithful employee. Or he could continue to review his options at each step. The down side of the first two options was that he probably would lose his skipper's ticket. Cavelya would bad-mouth him to the Coast Guard who, under pressure, would pull his ticket, and he'd never get his boat. Without a ticket, it wouldn't much matter anyway. There were two major short-comings with option three: he could get killed or he could get arrested for trafficking in contraband, which would also ensure that he'd lose his ticket. Option four seemed to be the only viable one. He would wait and see.

Thirty-Four

The Campbells had been up since 5:00 AM, getting the site ready for their guests whom they had anticipated would probably arrive earlier than their scheduled 8:00 AM meeting. Greg had moved the canoe to a backwater behind the camp that gave access to a stream, which led through the swamp to FL 71, fifteen water miles away. The canoe held most of their gear. If things went badly, they'd be all set for flight. If things went well, they could cross the river, retrieve their rental car, and drive off into the sunset rich men after the departure of Cavelya and his men. However, they doubted things would go that well or that they would ever be using that rental car again, not once they realized that they were followed the night before from the Gibson Inn, which was a fairly useless exercise, especially when the Campbells told Cavelya they would mark the approach to the camp with surveyors tape. Deceivers are pathologically obsessed with being deceived because they believe others think the same way.

They briefly discussed packing up and leaving, but they had no other buyer on the line, and they had too much time, effort, and expense committed to this sale. Perhaps Cavelya was just covering his end, they thought. So, except for the paintings, themselves, their weapons, and a small shop-keeper's bell, the cabin was pretty much as they had found when they rented it from the impecunious Harley Davidson. James was out in front of the cabin, putting the final touches on the grounds.

Keagan saw a movement in the distance through the trees and scrub, and motioned Kelly to stop. He took out his Zeiss 8x20 folding binoculars, and after a moment, he identified the movement as one of the Campbells he had met the night before. It was James, the trimmer of the two. He handed the binoculars to Kelly and pointed in James Campbell's direction.

"What do you think he's doing?" asked Kelly after she lowered the binoculars.

"I don't know, but I would guess that he was getting ready for Cavelya's visit. Looks like some Rube Goldberg contraption."

"Looks more complicated than that what with the tubes and lines, maybe he's rigging a mechanism for the exchange," said Kelly as she raised Keagan's binoculars again. James was hanging something off a two-by-four that he had nailed to one of the dock pilings on the left side toward the water end. She finely adjusted the focus and saw that it was a pulley. He was running a clothesline through the pulley and then back through the tube that hung from it. She refocused to where he was working now. He had the tag end of a roll of duct tape in his mouth and was taping a sheet of paper to the dock flooring. Next, he took what looked like a cell phone that was actually a cheap two-way radio out of his pocket, wiped it with a rag that was hanging out of his back pocket, and taped it on top of the right-hand piling of the set. Then he began looping duct tape around the next set of pilings, if not effectively closing off the dock, at least suggesting that one should go no farther. The sheet of paper taped to the decking contained the instructions for the transfer. When he was finished—holding the butt-end of the clothesline in his right hand—he placed his left foot on the top of the left-hand piling, which was almost as high as his hip, and with one seemingly effortless movement stood up on it and walked the line of pilings down to the land-side of the dock.

"Jaysus," said Kelly.

"What?" said Keagan.

"Shush, I'll tell you in a bit," whispered Kelly.

In the interim, James had gracefully stepped down onto the dock. He began looping the duct tape back and forth around another set of pilings, this time, however, on the land side. When he was finished taping off this second set of pilings, he ran the line through another pulley he had already fit into place, picked up the butt-end of the clothesline, made sure that it was running freely through the tubes, and walked the line all the way back to the camp and handed it through the open left-hand front window to Greg, who ran the line through several other other lengths of tubing and continued through the back door with it.

"Jaysus, how did he do that?"

"Do what?" asked Keagan.

Kelly handed Keagan the binoculars. "Standing on the dock, flat-footed, James Campbell placed his left foot on top of a piling and effortlessly lifted himself on top of it, and then walked down the pilings to the end of the dock and stepped—not jumped—*stepped* down onto the dock. Look at how high those pilings are. They must be close to thirty inches off the deck."

"I could do that."

"No doubt you could, but the resulting hernia wouldn't do either of us any good," Kelly said with a shameless smile.

Keagan raised the binoculars and slightly adjusted the focus. "Yeah, I could do that." A movement caught Keagan's eye. He swung the binoculars to the back of the camp, catching a glimpse of Greg Campbell just before he disappeared into the woods where a short trail lead to the backwater, where he had stowed the boat, and the backwater in turn led to a stream through the swamp that was their back door escape. Keagan couldn't see what Greg Campbell was doing in the woods, but it wasn't too difficult to fill in his visual gaps. After about ten minutes Greg returned and walked into the cabin through the back door. At about the same time Keagan noticed more movement in the front window of the camp, which turned out to be James running the clothesline back and forth though the tube and pulley system and adjusting the line for minimum sag. Interestingly, the exchange system wasn't much different from the one they had used to steal the paintings.

"They are both in the cabin," said Kelly. "Perhaps we should make our move now, relieve the Campbells of the paintings, and depart before Cavelya and his thugs arrive, because it looks like the paintings are going out the front of the cabin to Cavelya. I'd rather deal with the Campbells than with him and his thugs."

"OK, but let's stay in the woods until we get behind the cabin and then angle across the yard toward its northwest corner. I don't want them looking out the window and see us tiptoeing across the open yard. Stay together. If we split up here, we could end up out in the open and right in the middle of the two—I'm assuming armed—Campbells or worse yet between Cavelya's men and the Campbells in a cross fire."

Also, Keagan reasoned that the Campbells would be looking for trouble to come from the river. Cavelya or even his men for that matter would not be the type to bushwhack very far through the scrub. They might try to come at the camp from the north or south sides, but unless Keagan had seriously misjudged them, they would rely more on muscle and fire-power than on stealth and logistics.

Keagan and Kelly started to make their way to the back of the camp when Kelly abruptly held up Keagan by placing her hand on his shoulder. He looked conused: he hadn't seen anything and he hadn't heard anything. Kelly pointed down just above the base of a sapling that was about three feet in front of them. Keagan was still confused. His angle of sight didn't allow him to see that about two feet above the ground was a line of fine monofilament, probably not more than four-pound test that ran around the perimeter of the cabin and was connected to the shop-keeper's bell inside it, which of course neither Kelly or Keagan could see. The Campbells had set it high enough for possums, raccoons, and other small mammals to be able to walk under without tripping it, but low enough so that most people would miss seeing it, particularly since the line was clear. It was a primitive electronic eye, which the Campbells knew a great deal about, and if it weren't for Kelly, it would have worked.

They carefully stepped over the line and were moving toward the rear of the cabin again when the Campbells came out of the back door. Greg walked off down the trail, but James went around the south side of the cabin.

"Damn," said Keagan.

"What do you make of that?" asked Kelly.

"It would appear that neither of these fellows plan to be in the cabin for the transfer. I suspect that they anticipate that sometime during the exchange, or shortly after it, Cavelya's men will charge it, and they don't want to be trapped inside. They seem to have a keen sense of the type of person they are dealing with. Their preparations, however primitive, seem to be as well thought out as their theft of the paintings. It appears that they seriously mistrust Señor Cavelya and his associates, and have taken a number of precautions to ensure that they get paid for their gain, however ill-gotten it might be. I'm rather impressed with them.

"At first glance what the Campbell's have rigged here looks like a Rube Goldberg security system, but when you think about it, it's really quite effective. In Apalachicola, they'd have to make the exchange face to face, whether it was on Cavelya's boat, in his room at the Gibson, or even out on St. George Island. In any of those places, Cavelya would have the upper hand.

"Here, they do. They've been here for a week. Enough time to scout the area, become familiar with it, and have both an exit strategy and a clear route out. I'll bet they've already done a dry run. I'll also bet that Harley's canoe is behind the cabin on some nearby water course all loaded and ready to go.

"Cavelya may have been born in some remote village in Bolivia, but he doesn't strike me as a woodsman, and neither do his men. Even if they had scouted the area, what are they going to do? Drag the Zodiac across the yard and then plunge off into the wilderness? They'd be lost in five minutes, probably less.

"However, in their caution the Campbells have made our job that much more difficult if we can't get the paintings before Cavelya and company arrive, which was always a potential problem, but now because of the Campbells' crude security system, it's a real one."

"Aye, now I see what you're getting at. If we can't get the paintings before the transfer starts, we've got the money going out the back door and the paintings going out the front door, and we want the paintings more than the money because I can almost definitely get more for them from Lloyds than Cavelya's going to be paying for them. And without all five paintings, I'm not establishing much of a reputation as a finder of stolen art, am I?"

"Exactly right, Kelly."

"Why don't you call Niles and Teal and find out if they've seen Cavelya yet?" said Kelly.

Keagan took out his cell phone from his belly pack and speed dialed Niles' number. Nothing. He looked down at the top, left corner of the display: no bars. The island had cut off what limited reception he had out on the river.

"There's no reception here, Kelly. We must be just out of range. Tell me all that you saw besides James rigging the pulley system when you were being impressed by his physical prowess," said Keagan.

"He was testing a set of pulleys. I didn't understand it before, but now it makes sense. The tape barrier, the pulleys, the phone . . . "

"The phone?" asked Keagan.

"Yes, the phone or maybe it's a two-way radio now that I think about it and realize what cell phone limitations there are in this primitive area. I would guess that the Campbells will attempt to make the exchange with as much distance as possible between them and Cavelya and that they have taken additional precautions to ensure their safety, more than stringing monofilament around the cabin's perimeter. Hand me your binoculars again, Mick. I want to check something out. Yes, there it is." She handed the glasses back to Keagan. "Look at the back of the cabin."

"What am I looking for? Oh, yes, of course. The pulleys and tubing go out the back door. You think that the Campbells will make the exchange from there? Do you think Cavelya will go along with it?"

"He hasn't much choice, not if he wants those paintings. The question is, what do we do now? We're in the wrong spot. Instead of being behind the Campbells or Cavelya and his men, we're in the middle, which is exactly what I wanted to avoid.

"I suspect that James is on the other side of the cabin, probably off in the woods. His job, in addition to making sure that Cavelya's men don't charge the cabin, is to make Cavelya believe that he and his brother are inside, and to act as Greg's eyes for moving the paintings and the cash back and forth. Greg's job is to control the pulley system his brother rigged. The procedure will almost certainly involve a series of exchanges: one painting for one payment, say. Verify each; if everything is as it should be, exchange another painting for another payment, and so on. Very cautious and creative fellows. While they have already reduced their vulnerability by making the exchange here, instead of in town or on Cavelya's boat, they're further minimizing it by keeping the cabin between themselves and Cavelya and his men."

"Yes, well, the question is do we go for the paintings now or do we wait for the exchange to be completed and just take the money?" said Kelly.

"I think the Campbells want Cavelya to believe that they are inside the cabin, so that he will be more likely to part with his money. If he thinks they are inside, he'll more readily make the exchange, because after he gets all the paintings, he can have his men storm the cabin, kill the hapless Campbells and retrieve his cash. But, I suspect the cabin is booby-trapped. However, if you're right, we are in the wrong spot. We need to get as close as we can to Greg. He's got the paintings. Let's get them before Cavelya and company arrive."

"So what, you're going to render him unconscious in that delightful way that you have and take the paintings before Cavelya gets here, gather our other troops, and slip away?"

"I've got to believe it's going to be a tad more complicated than that what with Niles on the other side of the cabin somewhere in the woods, and Teal being who knows where, and James in radio contact with his brother, but yes, that's the plan in a general sense," said Keagan.

Keagan and Kelly angled carefully toward the upriver side of the cabin, mindful of the possibility of more lines of monofilament or some kind of crude but debilitating landmine. Halfway across the open yard, they heard the sound of an outboard engine. The noise couldn't be coming from out on the river proper: the island would have muffled it. "That's got to be Cavelya and his men arriving," Keagan whispered to Kelly. "Keep going."

They didn't run into any landmines, but they almost ran into Greg Campbell as they crept along the cabin's upriver side wall rounding the back corner. He was leaning against a very large oak tree that blocked their view of him, and had he not been talking on a two-way radio to his brother who was announcing Cavelya's arrival, he would have heard them. Keagan and Kelly stepped back around the side wall.

At Greg Campbell's feet was a small variable-speed electronic motor hooked up to a twelve volt car battery. The lines that lead to the cabin and on through down the path to the dock were attached to the drive shafts of the motors. Also, at his feet was a cordura duffle. *So much for the hermetically-sealed storage*, thought Keagan.

Leaning against the oak was the AR-15, and on his hip was an H&K 9mm. Greg Campbell placed one of the paintings into a tubular case—like those used for holding several fishing rods—and hooked a small carabineer through the back of the case. James had earlier attached on to the front. He started the motor, testing the line glide both forward and backward. He spoke into the two-way radio. "James, can you hear me?" James acknowledged that he did, and Greg told him that he was running the bag forward, and to tell him when it came through the front of the camp, which James did after a moment. James then picked up another two-way radio when he heard Cavelya's voice coming from it.

"Señor Cavelya, you're somewhat early."

"Yes, I wanted to make sure I had enough time in case my captain took a wrong turn."

"Yes, of course. Señor Cavelya, I regret these precautions, but we are dealing with a very valuable commodity, and we are in an isolated place."

"I fully understand," lied Cavelya into the radio's mouthpiece.

"If you look up at the cabin, you will see a tube just barely sticking out the open window there. This will be the way we'll make the exchange. The tube contains one of the Picassos. I am sending it to you as a display of trust. When you have examined it and are satisfied, you will place one million dollars in the tube and when I've seen that you have placed the bag back on the line, I will retrieve it. When I have verified the payment, I'll send you the next painting and so on through four transactions. The fifth exchange will require you to trust us. After you have received and verified the fourth painting, you need to put two million dollars in the returning case, then we will send the fifth painting. Are there any questions?"

"No, Mr. Campbell. I understand," answered Cavelya.

"Under no circumstances should either you or your men come any closer to the cabin than where I have taped off the dock. The rest of the dock is mined as are the grounds around the cabin. Also, both my brother and I are armed with automatic weapons and will not hesitate to use them if we feel threatened or cheated. Is that clear?"

Cavelya answered into the two-way radio "Absolutely, Mr. Campbell. You have taken excellent precautions," lied Cavelya, again because he believed that the Campbells had trapped themselves inside the cabin. That's where the tubing led, that's where the case was headed, and that's where a rifle barrel extending from the right-hand, front window of the cabin was. Cavelya, of course, planned on killing them as soon as he had the paintings.

"However, what assurance do I have that you will fulfill your last part of the exchange," questioned Cavelya.

"You have your men with you . . . ," James paused for a second as if remembering something, "and they look very professional. If we tried to cheat you, you would no doubt set them on us. Besides you have the advantage: with all but the last exchange you get to examine the painting before we get to examine the money." James quickly switched radios. "Greg, how many men did you say Cavelya had with him last night?"

"Three. The two seated at nearby table with the young woman and the one who followed us," said Greg.

"You're sure that the one who followed us was not one of the two at the table?"

"I'm positive; I saw him when he got into the Chevy. Why?" asked Greg.

"There are only two men with Cavelya now. The other one may be trying to come in behind us. Keep an eye out and be careful."

"Señor Cavelya, I'm going to send you the first painting." Greg flicked the forward-motion switch on the motor at his feet. "How's the line running, James?" He whispered into the other two-way radio. Keagan couldn't hear the response, but the slight smile that formed on Greg's face indicated that it was running fine.

James came back on the radio and told Greg to stop the line. He flicked the switch stopping it abreast of Cavelya, who disconnected the tube, removed the painting, and examined it. When he was satisfied, he handed the painting to Manascotta who in turn placed it in a water-proof case. Cavelya then opened one of the aluminum cases and began shoving stacks of bills into the tubes. When he had put one million dollars into the tube, he spoke into the two-way radio, telling James that the money was ready for him to retrieve.

Greg ran the line back, through the front window and out the back window, where he disconnected the tube and extracted the money.

Greg scanned the stacks of bound bills, verified their depth with a metric ruler. He knew that if the banded bundles were correct, each $10,000 should be 1.0922 cm thick. He did some quick multiplication, and fanned several stacks at random to verify that Cavelya hadn't tried to cheat them. Then, he put the money into the duffle at his feet.

He picked up James' radio and told him so far so good. Cavelya had sent the first installment. No deception yet. The bills were genuine. Greg told his brother that he verified them, testing ten random bills using an iodine pen, the same method bank tellers use to verify their genuineness. He told James that he was sending the next painting off to Cavelya and to let him know when it partially cleared the front window.

When James told him that the tube was half out the front window, Greg stopped the line. James switched radios again and told Cavelya that the next painting was on its way. He should repeat the process of examining the painting and when satisfied send the next installment. Greg restarted the motor.

The process continued until Cavelya lost patience with the third exchange. When Cavelya had retrieved and examined the third Picasso, he told Luis and Manascotta to charge the cabin. They both resisted, reminding Cavelya that James Campbell had told them that the dock and grounds were mined. Cavelya reminded them about his earlier discussion with them regarding the dismemberment of their pingas and Krazy gluing them in their mouths. They complied.

Thirty-Five

Manascotta sliced through the duct tape with his switch blade and duck walked while cupping his scrotum towards the cabin, fully expecting to be blown to bits at every step, or perhaps mercifully shot. He kept waiting for the explosion or the shot. Nothing happened. After he cut through the second duct-tape barrier and he reached the end of the dock, he ran left toward the downriver side of the cabin and rounded the corner still without being shot. He hadn't even been shot at.

Luis also cut left when he got off the dock toward where Manascotta had gone and where Carlos was already waiting. Luis' move made no strategic sense. He simply didn't want to cross in front of both the camp's front windows. If he were smarter, he might have gone right so that the three of them would have three sides of the cabin covered, but he didn't want to cut across and be in the view of where he thought one of the brothers were stationed.

Cavelya could threaten to cut his dick off all he wanted, but Luis wasn't going to get shot for him. Maybe when all this was over, he'd cut off Cavelya's dick and glue his mouth shut around it. He could do it after he took the paintings away from him. He had the Mac-10; all Cavelya had was his pistol.

"What the fuck you doing? You're supposed to be on the other side of the cabin, on the right side," Manascotta said, irate. "You forget what Cavelya said?"

"Yeah, well, I noticed you didn't go right and cross in front of those open windows. I'm not going to get shot for Cavelya," said Luis with conviction.

Manascotta was not so brave though as to defy Cavelya. He inched around the front of the cabin and stepped up onto the porch. When he did, he realized that the rifle barrel sticking out of the left front window was an old .22, not an automatic weapon and that no one was behind it.

As soon as Manascotta had began slicing through the duct tape, James told Greg that Cavelya's men were charging the cabin. Niles saw James getting ready to fire on Manascotta, but he knew that while Carlos hadn't yet spotted James, he was only about twenty feet away from him. Neither one knew of the other's presence. If James started shooting at Manascotta though, Carlos would cut him down. Niles wanted a less messy *dénouement* to this drama. He crept up behind James and pinched his vagus nerve at the point where the nerve wanders down the neck. The immediate effect of doing this resulted first in the loss of speech before quick unconsciousness. Niles lowered him gently to the ground behind a palmetto clump, as much for his own sake as for James'. Carlos was now about fifteen feet away and moving toward him.

Behind the cabin, Greg was frantically trying to answer his brother's call. When there was no answer, he started to steal over toward the side of the cabin where James had been positioned. Keagan interrupted him. Greg looked dumbly at Keagan and Kelly and then at the gun Keagan held. His own gun was uselessly pointed toward the ground. "Too late," said Keagan. "Even if you managed to get me, which you wouldn't, my lovely but lethal partner here would kill you a second later."

"Shit," said Greg as he handed the AR-15 and the H&K 9mm to Kelly. "You with Cavelya? I didn't think so last night."

"No, we are independent contractors. We..." Keagan didn't get to finish his sentence because at that precise second there was a loud explosion in the front of the building.

After their initial involuntary reflex, Keagan said, "let me guess; you booby-trapped the front door?" Campbell nodded. Campbell's nod was followed by gunfire, first muffled automatic fire, then what sounded very much like the boom of Niles' *Combat Masterpiece*. "Who the hell's that now? Somebody advertise this deal?" Keagan didn't answer. Instead, he hit Greg with a short left, knocking him unconscious.

"You haven't lost your touch, Mick," said Kelly.

Niles had moved to his right a little and waited for Carlos. When Carlos was about six feet from him, the explosion at the front door of the cabin ruined his plans for a quiet solution. Even though stealth was no longer a consideration, he saw no reason to shoot Carlos; however, when Luis recovered from the blast concussion, he saw Niles lying in wait for Carlos. He raised his MAC-10 toward him, nervously firing before he had the gun level. Niles shot him center mass, tearing apart his heart. Carlos was fumbling for his Glock: he had dropped his Mac-10 when the explosion startled him. Niles kicked him in the head, cutting short his intention.

***

When Cavelya recovered from the blast, he grabbed the money that was left in the aluminum case and threw it into the Zodiac. He was reaching for the waterproof case that held three of the Picassos when Luis let loose with his MAC-10. While Luis' MAC-10 was equipped with a suppressor, Niles' .357 Magnum was not. So when Cavelya heard Luis' thut-thut-thut answered by a much louder single boom and then silence, he decided it was best to beat a hasty if ignominious retreat. His men could fend for themselves.

"Let's go see what has happened," Keagan said as he and Kelly hugged the wall over toward the side where Niles was. Keagan didn't see anything when he glanced around the corner.

"I don't see anyone," he told Kelly. Keagan looked again. "Wait, someone's down. Stay here and watch Greg."

Keagan peeked around the corner again, scanning the vegetation. He saw Luis but no one else. Niles called to him from behind a clump of palmettos near the front of the building. Keagan cautiously walked over to him. "Everybody's down over here," said Niles. "How about on your side?"

"Greg's also down, should be for another few minutes."

"One of Cavelya's men is where the porch used to be. He's missing a hand. Another over here is dead, James Campbell is out, and the last of Cavelya's men are napping as well. Where's Kelly?"

"She's fine. She's around the other side keeping an eye on Greg. What happened, Niles?"

"Near as I can figure, Cavelya got impatient with the process. He had one of his men positioned over here before he even got to the dock. As we had expected, he wasn't planning on playing fair. Halfway through the transfer he had had enough, so he sent the other two to rush the cabin. James was over here sending instructions back to Greg. I incapacitated him and was about to do the same to this one," here Niles pointed at Carlos, "when the third one showed up with a MAC-10. I had to shoot him."

"Is he dead?"

"Mick, I shot him."

"Right."

"Anyway, apparently the Campbells had booby trapped the front door. That was the explosion you heard. I've tied off the bloke's stump with his belt, but he's in bad shape. We need to get him some place where we can call 911."

"OK, let me check him out," said Keagan. "You want to take care of the dead guy?" Keagan saw Kelly peeking around the corner. He called to her over, "Can you gather up the paintings and the cash by Greg, Kelly?"

"Sure, Mick."

"Oh, Niles, where's Teal?" asked Keagan.

"I dropped him in the river, not far from Cavelya's boat. He wanted to go aboard for some reason. I thought that might be a good place for him to be in case things got nasty. Like you, I don't think I could face Anjali if I got her father killed."

"Why the boat?" asked Keagan.

Kelly, her arms fully of weapons, had joined them.

"Maybe to warn Enright. He seemed like a good bloke. All Teal said was that he had something to do. What else could it be," said Niles.

"Where's Cavelya then?" asked Keagan.

"He's gone. When the door blew, he was halfway up the dock. The blast knocked him on his ass. When he recovered, he reversed direction fast. I heard a single shot and then the Zodiac taking off, no doubt back to his boat."

"Should you have let him do that, Niles?" asked Kelly.

"I was kind of busy when he left."

"Yes, but if Cavelya's headed back to his boat and Teal was headed there…"

"I wouldn't be too worried. Teal's armed, and judging from the way Cavelya took off, I don't think there's much to worry about. He ain't no Simon Bolivar."

"Not you, too," said Kelly. "This barbarous land has afflicted your speech as well?"

"I'm sorry, Kelly; it's the company I keep."

Kelly gathered up the duffles containing the two installments of money that Greg had collected and the two remaining Picassos that he hadn't transferred yet and carried them down to the dock, where she found Teal just coming out of the water. Their boat was moored at the dock.

"What happened to you?" she asked Teal.

"I was approaching the dock when I saw Cavelya about to climb into his Zodiac. He was reaching for a bag. I didn't know if it was the money bag or the one with the paintings, but I figured it was something we might want, so I took a shot at him. Must have shook him up because he dropped the bag he was loading into the boat. It fell into the river. At that point Cavelya seemed to be more interested in saving his ass than jumping in the water to retrieve the bag. He just took off. Took me a while to find it. The water's more like *Lu-zee-ana* water than Lake Placid water."

Kelly stared at him anxiously.

"Don't worry, Kelly, the bag is waterproof. The paintings are nice and dry."

"Thank you, Teal. That would have seriously crimped the profits had Cavelya been less careful."

"Everything all right, Kelly?"

"More or less. You better go see Mick; he was looking for you. He's up by the cabin," said Kelly.

Teal found Keagan and Niles where the porch had been, attending to Manascotta. "Where the hell have you been," asked Keagan, his voice suggesting more anger than he felt. "Why did you go aboard Cavelya's boat?"

"My mother used to do that," said Teal.

"Do what?" asked Keagan,

"Ask me a question she already knew the answer to. I thought it was a parental thing, but maybe it is a boss thing as well."

"Okay, why did you go aboard Cavelya's boat?" repeated Keagan.

"I hate drug dealers, big or small. Some night I'll get drunk and tell you why, but for now just believe that I have my reasons. Also, I would I urge you all to gather up your things and get the hell out of here. I'll explain, at least partly, after we get under way. The boat's at the dock. I've cleaned up the duct tape and gotten rid of the two-way radio."

"Good, let's get these two aboard, then help Kelly police the area brass and weapons and any other evidence of the gunfight. Not much we could do about the door, though. When you're finished, go get the kayaks with Kelly and bring them down here. I have to deal with the Campbells."

"Where are they, Mick?"

"Napping. One's just over there," Keagan said as he gestured toward the south side of the cabin, "and the other's behind the cabin."

"You're not going to kill them are you?"

"No, Teal, I'm not going to kill them."

Niles roused James from the side of the cabin where he had left him, and when he was able to walk, led him behind the cabin to where Keagan was standing over Greg, who was also showing signs of coming around.

Niles told James to sit down. Keagan checked on Greg.

"Who are you?" asked Greg. He had seen Keagan the night before, but had no idea how he figured into everything that had happened up until the present moment.

"Not important. Just rest easy for a moment," said Keagan. He waited for Greg's head to clear.

Kelly and Teal went off for the kayaks while Keagan and Niles followed the Campbells back through the woods where Harley's boat was packed and waiting. Niles searched the packs for weapons and money. He found no other weapons but did find a little over $3,500 in cash.

"Get-away money?" asked Keagan.

They both nodded.

Niles left it in the pack. "So where are you headed?" asked Keagan.

They hesitated for a second, finally telling Keagan where.

"OK," said Keagan, "but don't trash Harley's boat. It's a good one, especially for this country."

Both looked at Keagan, surprised at Harley's name.

"If you're smart, and I think you will be, you'll forget about your losses, and you'll take the shortest route out of here and live to steal another day. Plan on erasing us from your memory and we'll do the same. We're more or less in the same business, just different ends. If we meet each other again and we're not on a job, we'll buy you a drink; if we're on a job, we'll take from you what you've stolen from somebody else. If you're foolish enough to trade information about us to get out of a jam, we'll kill you. Am I clear?"

The Campbells acknowledged that Keagan was abundantly clear.

"OK, then, off with you," said Keagan.

"You're leaving us our cash?" asked Greg.

"Why not?" said Keagan. "After all, we're thieves just like you, and were the roles reversed, we'd expect the same. It's just professional courtesy."

On the way up river to retrieve the kayaks, Kelly kept a diligent eye out for the alligator because she wanted to show it to Teal. She thought he'd be impressed by the prehistoric behemoth, but then figured he probably had dealt with them a lot given where he was from.

As they paddled back and Kelly recounted the story, Teal told her that being on the water with a gator wasn't such a big deal.

"In fact," he said, "when I was growing up, the local YMCA back in south *Lou-zee-ana* gave kids swimming lessons for free. The YMCA didn't have access to a pool, though, so we had the lessons in the bayou. My group had an odd number of kids and the Y's program used the buddy system, so they paired me up with a gator."

Kelly didn't see the humor in the tall tale, but she probably would in a week or two after the shock of the episode faded a bit.

***

By the time Jackson and Fugaezi had gotten the department's boat loaded up, trailered, and driven up County 65 and down the access road it was almost 8:00 AM. Fugaezi got on the river about a mile upriver from Harley's camp. He might have made better time had Chief Eubeck suggested using the Brickyard Road, which is the one the Campbells had used to get to the camp; in fact, they would have made perfect time, because he would have been right across the river from where all hell had broken lose. He wouldn't have heard Luis' suppressed shots, but he might have heard Niles' in spite of the island. In the mountains you can hear a rifle shot for miles, but a swamp — with its water and vegetation — absorbs noise. Still, the Chief's call was a good one, given what he knew. As it was, Fugaezi was too late for the gunfight.

He had gotten accurate updates from the spotters while he and Jackson were driving up County 65, and so the plan looked like it was working. The third spotter about ten miles down below Harley's camp reported that *Blanca Nieve* was still headed upriver. Fugaezi had every reason to believe everything was running smoothly.

Even if Fugaezi wasn't near enough to hear the door blow off Harley's cabin, he sure as hell could hear the *Blanca Nieve* blow up. However, by that time it was too late. Consequently, he never learned what happened to it, nor did he or any of the other law enforcers involved ever learn what had occurred on the other side of the river.

Thirty-Six

Teal had tied off the kayaks just as they were when they arrived earlier that morning and helped Keagan and Niles load an unconscious Manascotta, a dead Luis, various weapons, the money, and the paintings into the boat. They left Carlos tied up at the camp. Using the boat's depth gauge, (Teal found a deep spot a little ways down the river in a pool formed by an eddy) Niles slid Luis' weighted body over the side into it. Next, he threw the weapons overboard. Niles kind of hated to dump the H&K's overboard, but they had plenty of guns as well as plenty of money if they ever wanted to buy more. Despite the quality of the pieces, prudence said to get rid of them. Prudence always ruled.

Suddenly, they heard another explosion. This one was much louder than the one that took Manascotta's hand. Everyone looked at Teal.

"I hate fucking drug dealers," he said. "Sometime, if you get me drunk enough, I'll tell you about it," he said again. About three miles downriver they saw the burning wreckage of *Blanca Nieve*. The deck was blown off it, and what was left was consumed in flames.

"What happened when you went aboard?" asked Keagan.

"There were two people aboard, Enright and a young woman, who must have been Cavelya's squeeze. When I came aboard, I asked Enright if there was anyone else aboard. He told me that there was a woman below decks, sleeping. I went down with him to wake her, and once we had, I ordered both of them over the side, maybe a little bit pirate, but then Jean Lafitte wasn't Yiddish, you know. I told them to swim to the east shore because with the way things were going on the west shore, it would have been best if they weren't a part of the action. The woman resisted, first trying to seduce me, later saying that she didn't know how to swim, but I threw her over board anyway. It was a sink-or-swim kind of occasion. Enright followed her into the water and was getting her to shore when I went down to the galley."

"Cavelya had two candles on the galley table. When I heard the Zodiac approaching the boat, I turned on the stove, but didn't light the pilot, closed the portholes and lit one of the candles, placing it in the far corner of the galley. I'd shut down the ventilation system by replacing the fuse with one that was the wrong size. Then I closed the companion way and left. Given that he probably didn't know much about running the boat and given the time the gas had been flowing, I'm surprised he got as far as he did."

"But I thought you de-activated bombs in the Air Force, Teal. I didn't realize you also constructed them," said Keagan.

"Bombs are a lot like stories, Mick," said Teal. "You know, after you handle a bunch of them and figure out how they work, pretty soon you want to put one together yourself."

***

They continued on down the river. It was a beautiful day, but heating up fast. When they got about a mile north of Apalachicola, Teal pulled over to a boatless dock with a gazebo. Niles and Teal placed Manascotta under its roof, out of the sun. When they reached town, Keagan made two calls: one to 911, informing the paramedics where Manascotta was and the care he needed, and the other to the Coast Guard out on St. George Island, reporting the explosion of *Blanca Nieve*. The seaman taking the information asked for Keagan's name, but Keagan told him he didn't want to get involved and rang off.

On the rental dock, Keagan told Niles and Teal that it would be better if they were not seen together, and that he would meet them back at the inn in Lake Placid. He wasn't sure exactly when. They agreed and walked off to the Ford Explorer. Keagan and Kelly walked over to the Gibson Inn and went to their rooms to clean up. Just as they were getting out of the shower, they heard a Coast Guard harbor boat go under the bridge, siren wailing. They hadn't eaten any breakfast, but they mutually decided that they were hungrier for each other than they were for food.

***

After brunch, they packed. Keagan transferred the money into his duffel while Kelly checked on the Picassos. They were in perfect condition. At one o'clock sharp, they checked out and drove to Atlanta where Kelly called the Lloyd's America, Inc. office and made preliminary arrangements about returning the paintings for a finder's fee of fifteen percent of their insured value. The process took several days. Lloyd's had to ensure they weren't dealing with the thieves who stole them and that the paintings were authentic. Keagan and Kelly had to ensure that the fee had been deposited in Kelly's Swiss account and then transferred to an account Lloyd's couldn't track just in case they reneged.

Three days later, they were on a flight to Albany where they had arranged for the Lake Placid Flying Service to meet them. They arrived at *Beyond Good and Evil* at 4:30. Samwise met them at the porch, scolding Keagan (in a way only a dog can) for leaving her all alone with nothing but the refuse of the guests' steak dinners to give her solace. She whimpered and furiously shook the nub of her former tail while circling around Keagan. She only ceased when he bent down and hugged her. Then she smiled and all was forgiven. When Keagan released her she danced around him one more time and followed him into the bar where he and Kelly had a drink with Niles. Tippler O'Neill was the only customer in the bar. Keagan bought him a drink and thanked him for filling in.

"No problem, Mick. Anytime. I appreciate the work," and added, after he looked at the fresh gin and tonic in front of him, "as well as the drink."

"Niles, can you get one of the bellmen to carry our bags up to my lodge? They are out on the porch," said Keagan.

"Kelly, why don't you go up to the cabin and relax. I have to check things out here. Let's plan to have dinner at about 7:30, but before you go, you, Niles and I have to talk about Cavelya's bequest to us. I've got a couple ideas I'd like to run by you."

***

Keagan checked in with Cassie in the kitchen. She and Anjali were making the salsa for an appetizer for a Mexican special that was on tonight's menu, *Tinga de Carmaron a la Plancha*. He asked her if everything had gone well in his absence. She said they had gone fine but gave him a look that he should tend to business instead of roaming around, doing God knows what.

Anjali gave him a hug and whispered into his ear, "Thank you for bringing my daddy back to me safe." Anjali finally released him and stood smiling at Keagan. Keagan didn't know what to say, so he just smiled back at her, wondering what Teal had told her. Keagan even caught Cassie smiling at him and asked her if the Gimp were around.

"He's in his office," said Cassie, as she and Anjali giggled.

Jimmy the Gimp was just coming out of the walk-in freezer when Keagan got there. He was glad that he didn't have to go inside to talk with him. A lengthy conversation in a freezer after having just returned from summer trip to Florida could potentially have been too much for his system.

In the dining room they went over the night's menu and reservation list. As usual, Jimmy was on top of everything. Keagan wondered *if he and Cassie couldn't run the inn without him*.

"Mick, do me a favor."

"What's that Jimmy?"

"If you have to be away, can you try not to be away on Sundays? I don't mind filling in for you cooking for the staff; it's just that I have to listen to Cassie carry on for the rest of the day about how *the bigot dulled her knives or scored her pans or rearranged her spices* or whatever."

Keagan laughed because he knew that they couldn't run the inn without him. Surely they would kill each other. Niles came into the dining room to tell Keagan he had a call from Bascombe Treylawne.

"You want to take it upstairs?"

"Yes, Niles. Thanks."

"Hello, Bascombe. How is everything in paradise?"

"Paradisal, Mr. Keagan. I believe someone from the bank has already notified you that we received a sizeable transfer into your account yesterday. Well, it seems that the same party who attempted to access your account records was still monitoring your transactions. As per your instructions, I've set up a shadow account and allowed that person to have some limited access to it, thereby obviating compromising our system's integrity or that of our clients."

"Very good Bascombe; I think the party's curiosity has been satisfied, at least I hope so. I appreciate your help."

"We pride ourselves on our security, Mr. Keagan. Yours was a most irregular request; however, we do try to accede to our customers' wishes whenever we can."

"You've done me a great service, Bascombe. Let me know if there is any more electronic eavesdropping."

"Most assuredly, Mr. Keagan."

"Oh, one more thing, Bascombe. I'll be transferring some additional funds to you. Not as much as the last amount, but still sizeable. Before I make the next transfer, I want you to set up three separate accounts for it. I'll want the transfer divided among the accounts in thirds. Send me the paper work, and I will cover the details in writing."

"I'll be more than happy to attend to that, Mr. Keagan. Is there anything else while I have you on the line?"

"No, Bascombe, that will be all for now."

"Very well, Mr. Keagan, I'll ring off then."

"Good news, Mick?" asked Niles when Keagan came downstairs.

"Very good news, Niles. Remember that guy, Di Ladro, who was nosing around last week? Well, I think I got him off my back."

"I could have done that for you, Mick."

"Yes, Niles, but Mr. Treylawne didn't have to hide the body."

Thirty-Seven

Kelly came into the bar at precisely 7:30. She was wearing a blue print three-quarter length skirt, a white tee, dark blue linen blazer, and an Indiana Jones hat of blue felt. She sat at the bar, had a glass of Jameson 12, and talked with Niles while she waited for Keagan.

Keagan came in a few minutes afterwards and sat next to Kelly. "Marion Ravenwood, is it?" he inquired.

"I was hoping to look more mysterious than she," answered Kelly.

"You may have succeeded at that," said Keagan.

Keagan ordered a Jack Daniel's on the rocks, but before Niles could build it for him Jimmy the Gimp came in to tell Keagan that his table was ready. The Gimp told Niles he'd send a waiter for their drinks and led them to Keagan's usual table. He held the chair for Kelly and handed her and Keagan menus when they were seated. The waiter soon arrived with their drinks. He placed the Jameson in front of Kelly. He made the mistake of trying to serve Keagan and look at Kelly at the same time. Keagan grabbed the drink just as the waiter was about to spill it. "I'm sorry, Mick," said the waiter.

"I know, Peter. How do you think I feel?" joked Keagan, trying to make the waiter feel less embarrassed.

"What shall we have, Mick?" asked Kelly with all the exuberance of a child.

"We've eaten a lot of shellfish in the last few days. I don't know about you, but my body seems to be calling for red meat."

"Red meat sounds fine, but let's make it simple. No sauces, or crusts of dough, or pepper, or anything raw. Just a good old, American steak. Raising and butchering beef is one thing your adopted country knows how to do better than anyone else."

"Is that a compliment? I would have thought you would have said Japanese or Argentine beef was better."

"Oh, Mick, you know I'm just teasing you. I just wish you'd come back to Ireland and get involved again with me. Directly, I mean. You see how good we are together."

"Of course we are, and we could be directly involved here as well."

Peter returned before Kelly could respond. He was trying hard to be on his best behavior. Keagan ordered another round of drinks, two filet mignons – one twelve ounce and one six ounce, both medium rare – new salt potatoes, corn on the cob, and a spinach salad made from Malone spinach delivered that day. The vegetables were all local. The potatoes were almost as good as Maine salt potatoes, and the corn was not quite as good as Jersey corn, but there was no better spinach than Malone spinach, and no better steak than #3 grade, prime meat. Keagan told Peter that Jimmy the Gimp had selected a wine for them earlier and that he should bring it now.

The Gimp brought the wine. He placed the bubble glasses on the table and holding them by the stem, he and Keagan observed the proper ritual. Keagan looked around and tasted the wine.

He uttered a sigh and said, "Oh, no," as he lowered his glass.

"What's wrong?" asked the Gimp, "Has it turned?"

"No, Jimmy, the wine is wonderful, but the Mad Chef is here."

"Oh, don't worry about him; he never acts up in anyone else's restaurant. Consider it a compliment; usually he goes to Montreal to dine out."

The Gimp stopped over at the table to greet the Mad Chef, who was with a woman about half his age, and whose bust size – the Gimp calculated after a brief but careful inspection– threatened to be of greater proportion than her IQ. The Gimp took their drink order and went off to give the order to the section waiter. The Mad Chef looked over at Keagan, smiled broadly and nodded. Keagan nodded back in acknowledgement, hoping the Gimp was right. The dinner was wonderful, and the wine superb. While he and Kelly were finishing up the last of the Margaux, Keagan noticed Cassie and Anjali peeking through the kitchen doors. As soon as Peter had cleared their table, Anjali came out of the kitchen carrying two glasses of Romanoff on a cork-lined tray. She was wearing shorts, a T-shirt, and a splotched kitchen apron. She was beaming brightly, eyes and smile contrasting with her olive complexion. All the customers on their side of the dining room watched her as she approached Keagan's table. She placed one of the glasses before Kelly and the other in front of Keagan.

"It's Romanoff," Anjali told Kelly. "Cassie and I made it special for you and Mick. I made yours with raspberries. They are sweeter and have much smaller seeds. Mick likes blackberries better. Cassie says there are not as delicate as raspberries, but also not as common, although finding ripe, unbruised raspberries is difficult. These were picked this morning. Cassie and I got them over by Black Brook. I hope you like them." Anjali stepped away from the table then came back. "You're very pretty, Kelly," she added before dashing back to the kitchen.

None of the customers knew what had just happened other than that a pretty tomboy had just brought a special dessert to Keagan's table. In spite of this fact, they broke into spontaneous applause before Anjali could get back into the kitchen.

"Why do you think they did that, Mick?" asked Kelly.

"What, applaud?"

"Yes."

"I can tell you it wasn't sentimentality. I've worked too hard to create an unaffected atmosphere."

"One that is *Beyond Good and Evil*?" teased Kelly.

"Precisely."

"Then I think you have succeeded," added Kelly.

"To some degree I have. I think I could do much better if you stayed and became a part of the inn."

"Another refugee?"

"Perhaps, but I was thinking more along the lines of as my wife and partner. Either way, the other refugees seemed to have fared well. We may be misfits out there when alone, but here, we work well together."

"You are very lucky, Mick; you seem to have found what you want."

"Some of it. You could too, Kelly."

"Not yet I couldn't. There is still more that I need to do for Ireland. If I came here, feeling as I do, I'd forever hold the dashing of that dream against you. You know that, Mick."

"Intellectually, I do, but not emotionally."

Peter came back to their table, carrying two sizeable snifters of what looked like cognac. Peter told him that they were on the gentleman just getting up from Table 37 and nodded towards the Mad Chef. "It's Louis the XIII," he added. The Mad Chef beamed an enormous, demented smile at Keagan and left the dining room, handing Jimmy the Gimp a fifty-dollar bill as he did.

* * *

Keagan and Kelly had brought their drinks into the bar. The night had turned very cool as the summer nights can in the Adirondacks. Niles had laid a fire in the large river stone fireplace, so they sat and watched the fire and each other, and sipped their drinks in silence. The dining room cleared out, and soon afterwards, the bar. Niles came over to bank the fire.

"Did you see Teal earlier, Niles?" Keagan inquired. "Yes, I did Mick, and I just called him. He's saying good night to Anjali. He'll be down in a minute."

"Have all the guests left?"

"The dining room has been empty for a half hour. All the tables have been reset. All the waiters have cashed out, and I'm about to do the same."

"Good, Niles. When Teal gets here, we'll talk."

Niles cashed out the bar and put the receipts in the safe in Keagan's office. When he came back down the stairs, Teal had arrived and was sitting with Keagan and Kelly. Samwise must have come in with him. "Niles, before you come over, bring four snifters and the bottle of Louis XIIIth. I think I can finally afford to drink this stuff, at least on special occasions."

Niles brought over the cognac and the glasses, and Keagan placed the heavy glasses near the fireplace bumper. Several of the back bar lights were still on, but the only other light in the room was from the fireplace. Keagan retrieved the glasses, poured a generous dollop into each, and passed them around.

"Here's to a successful operation, and for all of us coming back alive," he said as he raised his glass. The others raised their glasses and toasted silently.

"Kelly and I have already made our split. She has taken her half and I have deposited the other half in my account in Grand Cayman. I was on the phone today with the bank manager there, Bascombe Treylawne, and I have instructed him to set up two new, separate accounts, one for you, Niles, and the other for you, Teal. When the paperwork is done, I will have him transfer one third of what was deposited in my account into each of yours. I would advise you, however, not to begin living lavishly right away, and I hope you won't issue your notices tomorrow morning. We make a very good team here as well as in what we have just accomplished. Somehow, I think that Kelly will bring us more projects, and we'll need you both if you've a mind."

"Anjali and I like it here, so why would we leave?" said Teal. Niles just smiled his silly cartoon chipmunk smile.

"The final matter we need to attend to is what to do with the money that Cavelya brought with him. Kelly has agreed that this is over and beyond what we agreed upon. Teal, I have already spoken with Kelly and Niles about this bonus, and they have given their approval, but one-quarter of that money is yours if you want it. Here is what we would like to do. Niles has told me that he thought that

Enright was not involved in Cavelya's drug smuggling, and that he only skippered for him to earn enough money to buy his own boat. You put an abrupt ending or at least a serious crimp in Enright's skippering career, and while I have no problem with that, perhaps we should buy him that boat he wanted. Niles said he seemed like a pretty good bloke."

"That's fine with me. I kinda liked the fella too," said Teal.

"That's done then," said Keagan. "What I would like to do with the rest of the money is to set up a scholarship fund for the children of inn employees. I haven't worked through all the details yet, but it might even apply to our local prep school. I understand it has a new Headmaster, and he is trying to turn it into a school that's known for academics as well as for its hockey and ski programs."

Niles only smiled once again. The four of them slowly and silently finished their cognac as the fire cast its shadows, and Samwise chased chipmunks in her sleep.

Epilogue

Cavelya: When the propane leak reached critical mass in *Blanca Nieve*, the candle that Teal had planted, ignited the gas and blew the top deck and Cavelya off the boat. Cavelya wasn't dead when he hit the water, but he was unconscious and in very bad shape. So bad, in fact, that he never felt the alligator that had earlier lunged at Kelly drag him down to her lair beneath an overhang on the west bank of the river. After a few preliminary tastes of Cavelya, the alligator decided he was unfit for consumption; however, he would be very good grabbing-and-tearing practice for her brood. Señor Cavelya spent the next month, spun by the current of the Apalachicola River, in the alligator's lair. Eventually, the river made him more palatable, so that the brood, that were now tearing more and larger pieces from him, were also digesting some, and even growing stronger as a result. Finally, when Cavelya had been reduced to bones, the alligator nudged his fully-intact skeleton out of her lair. The skeleton was found two years later by a doctoral candidate from the University of Florida, who was looking for evidence to support his controversial dissertation proposal, which maintained that Aymará Indians once lived as far north as Florida's Panhandle. Carbon 14 was his undoing. The doctoral candidate is still ABD, and Señor Cavelya's bones are folded neatly in a box next to his review of the literature, his proposal, and his preliminary two-tailed t-tests, ANOVA's, and Chi Squares.

Charo: Cavelya's paramour's name wasn't really Charo. It was Isabella Maria Cuevas, and as soon as she got back to Apalachicola, she caught the first bus back to Fort Myers. She would have liked to have flown back, but she figured—and correctly so—that by the time she got to Tallahassee, then flew to Miami, and connected to Fort Myers, she'd arrive a day later than Greyhound could get her there. She was very much in a hurry, so she called Enterprise Car Rental and had someone pick her up at the Fort Myers bus station and then drove to Captiva where she hired a water taxi at South Seas Resort to take her to North Captiva.

Isabella Maria Cuevas was in such a hurry because she wanted to get back to Cavelya's compound before the authorities learned of his death, froze his assets, and sealed off the compound. She knew nothing of the alligator. She removed the two million dollars in cash that Cavelya kept in a fortified wall safe in case he should ever have to leave the country quickly. Isabella had known of the safe for some time, but she had only recently learned its combination.

She gathered the money, and all of the jewelry in the house, both hers and Cavelya's. While she didn't know anything about art, she took what seemed to her two of the most promising paintings, that Cavelya had told her were Gauguins, which meant about as much to her as if he had said they were Otto Schminks. She just liked the colors. She also took two Fabergé Imperial Eggs that Cavelya had in the safe. All of this she put into a Louis Vuitton suitcase—drug traffickers are nothing, if not conspicuous consumers—took one of Cavelya's smaller boats back to Captiva, and drove to Fort Myers. There she rented six months of space at one of those storage facilities that thieves always turn to when they want to hide something but want twenty-four hour access to it.

Isabella Marie Cuevas didn't think she was stealing. She thought she was ensuring her rightful inheritance because, while she went by her mother's name, her mother – Celina Margarita Cuevas – was Cavelya's first cousin, and finally because Cavelya was Charo's father.

Luis and Carlos: Niles had chosen the site for Luis' burial well. It isn't likely to be found for some time, and so far it has not been found, but—of course—no one has been looking.

Carlos finally managed to untie his bonds because Niles had wanted him to be able to and tried to get back to civilization, but since he had no sense of direction, other than the forward and backward motion he had demonstrated repeatedly to his seventh grade teacher, he experienced a great deal of difficulty getting through the swamp. Notwithstanding, he almost made it. He was within a mile of FL 71, when he stumbled out of the swamp at night into a Wewahitchka honey bee farm. Bee farms on the Florida Panhandle produce some of the world's best tupelo honey. Carlos was ignorant of that fact though, so when he blundered into the stacked boxes of hives in the dark, he embraced them with an understandable sense of relief that three days of wandering through north Florida swamp and pine wilderness would produce. The bees did not feel the same sense of affection however, and stung him 541 times. When the bee keeper found Carlos the next day, his face was swollen beyond recognition, and he was quite dead. Since Wewahitchka is a small town, it didn't vigorously pursue how Carlos happened to be there. However, they are good people and buried him, at their expense, in a town grave.

Manascotta: The 911 paramedics had little trouble finding Manascotta. They raced him to the hospital in Port St. Joe, where doctors stabilized him before sending him on to the University hospital in Tallahassee. Since Manascotta—in spite of the gold Rolex he wore, the $3,127 in cash he had in his pocket when he arrived at the hospital, and the twelve gold chains he wore around his neck—was by hospital standards indigent because he didn't have either an HMO or a PPO plan, the doctors at University hospital fitted his stump with a leather cup instead of a prosthesis. And since it's hard to get work as a one-handed thug, instead of protecting the welfare of some new drug trafficker with a MAC-10, he is now flipping big Macs, just off I-10.

Harley Davidson: Teal had had second thoughts the morning after they had divided up the Campbells' money. Manascotta had lost a hand, but he was a bad guy. Cavelya had lost his life, but he was drug trafficking slime. Enright had lost his income, so the team had made provisions to provide for him. Harley Davidson, thought Teal, was just trying to make a few bucks while he was out of work. He may never have gotten his boat back, and he had the front door of his cabin blown off, letting in raccoons, diamond backs, panthers, and the rain. Shouldn't he get something?

Everyone agreed that he should, so Teal sent him a cashier's check for $35,000. Harley thought the movie company had sent it to him because they felt responsible for his camp. Harley really wasn't too bright.

He had already found his boat and fixed the cabin, and got an additional fifty dollars for the eight-foot rattler he found inside the camp. The police in Mobile called him because they had found his old truck in the airport's long-term parking there, but he had already bought a new pickup. He drank up the rest of the money, with the help of Letti.

Tony Fugaezi: Neither Fugaezi nor the FBI ever really learned what happened at the camp. What they believed (partially because it's what the Gulf County Sheriff, Franklin County Sheriff, the Forest Rangers, the Coast Guard and Chief Eubeck believed) was that the exchange was supposed to take place at the camp, but that one party tried to either keep the cash and get the paintings or keep the paintings and get the cash. They believed it was likely the former as it fit Cavelya's profile better.

The theory was partially substantiated by a Gulf County sheriff's deputy finding Harley's canoe near FL 71 and the Mobile Police Department having found Harley's old truck at the airport there. What the theory couldn't explain though was what happened to the bodies. Carlos turned up but as he had been stung 541 times by bees defending their nest and had summarily been buried by the good people of Wewahitchka, he wasn't talking. While Manascotta, handicapped—both legally and literally—was living and working in Tallahassee, he had checked himself out of the hospital unofficially without paying his bill. After all, the hospital had his gold Rolex, the $3,127 in cash he had in his pocket when he arrived there, and his twelve gold chains, Manascotta figured they had been more than paid in full—clearly in addition to being thought an undocumented alien he knew nothing about health costs in the United States. And since the hospital could keep all his possessions off the books and its insurance company would pick up the tab from the hospital's default protection policy (who needs national health care, one way or another everybody's covered anyway), it never reported Manascotta's missing hand or his general lack of English. Finally, since the fast food place where Manascotta worked never asked to see his green card and since his English wasn't much worse than their other workers who had been schooled locally, no one ever put the various connections together.

While the Gulf County sheriff clearly had jurisdiction of Harley's camp, it was unclear which of the four other authorities had jurisdiction of the *Blanc Nieve* explosion as it had occurred somewhere near the middle of the river where two county lines and the boundary of a national forest met. The Coast Guard finally assumed jurisdiction of the *Blanca Nieve'* explosion, mostly because no one else wanted it, but also because the Guard was best equipped to do so. After a short investigation, they rightly assumed that the explosion occurred because of a gas leak. What was not included in their report was that the gas leak occurred because Teal had turned on the stove without the benefit of a pilot light or that Teal did so because Alardo Quillaca Cavelya was a drug trafficker. And we'll never really know, unless Teal gets drunk enough some night and tells Keagan. Tony Fugaezi and the FBI did, however, learn from Gandalf Dalin that the five Picassos had been returned to the *Moderna Museet* by the museum's insurance company. Since there were no bullet holes in Harley's cabin, no spent brass about the camp and no bodies anywhere, they felt that the case had come to a successful conclusion and Tony Fugaezi was credited with his first stolen-art recovery.

John Enright: John Enright was sitting at a table under an umbrella outside The Mucky Duck, an English pub of all things, located on the beach on Captiva, trying to figure out what to do with his life. He had been teaching sailing at the South Seas Resort. It was early December. The hurricane season had just ended, but the winter season hadn't really started yet. He wondered, as he sat there staring out at the Gulf, whether he should take what money he had and make a modest down payment on a boat smaller than he wanted, and hope he could keep up with the payments. But he knew the margin, and the prospect didn't look good. He started to turn around to look for the waitress to order another beer when he saw Teal standing next to him, holding two pints of Bass Ale.

"You!" exclaimed Enright angrily.

"Yes," said Teal, "but before you get up and hit me, let me give you one of these beers and point out to you that little girl who is sitting two tables over. She is my daughter, and while you may not be particularly fond of me, she is. Mind if I join you for a moment?" Enright looked over at Anjali, seeing a resemblance. "No, I guess not. At least this time you're holding a pint of beer. The last time I saw you, you had the bad end of a Colt .45 pointed at me."

Teal sat down at the table with Enright and passed one of the drafts over to him. "I'd like to have my daughter join us, but first you have to promise not to mention anything about .45's or exploding boats."

"Of course, the model father."

"I have something for you, and I'll give it to you now, but you can't mention the details of our meeting on the Panhandle around my daughter."

Enright was confused, but he nodded anyway. Teal took an envelope out of the back pocket of his cut-offs and slid it over to Enright.

Teal waved to Anjali to come over. Anjali walked to the table holding a mug of coke. The Mucky Duck didn't stock Ting.

"Anjali, I want you to meet Mr. Enright. John, this is my daughter, Anjali."

Enright didn't answer right away because he was staring at a cashier's check for $465,000, and he was incapable, at least for the moment, of forming words.

"Hello, Mr. Enright," said Anjali.

"What? Oh, yes, hello," said Enright intuitively extending his hand to Anjali.

"Is it not clear? It's a check," said Teal.

"Yes, and for a very large sum, but I don't understand," said Enright.

"Well, Niles and I, and the fellow we work for, feel responsible for you losing your job. And as we know you took it only to get your own boat, we thought we'd help out a bit."

"This is real, isn't it? I mean," said Enright, turning to Anjali, "your father does have a strange sense of humor."

"Yes, *père* is sometimes *étrange*, isn't he," said Anjali

"*Étrange?*"

"Ah, weird," translated Anjali.

"'*Étrange!*' Say that again and I'll take you to Disney world and make you stay for a week," said Teal.

"No, *père*. Not that, anything but that," japed Anjali.

"I don't understand anything that is going on here," said Enright. "You've just given me a cashier's check, made out for a very large amount and your daughter doesn't like Disney world?"

"Oh no, Mr. Enright, well, I don't know anything about the check, but where *père* works almost no one has ever been to Disney world. It's almost a job requirement. Only Cassie has been there. Why would anyone spend all that money to stand in line half the day just to be hugged by a rodent?"

When Enright finally stopped laughing, he asked Anjali what they were doing in Florida then.

"We came for the sailing school, Mr. Enright. We are your next students."

"And if this thing is real," said Enright as he waved the check, "my last."

The Campbells: The Campbells had to dip into their savings in order to go to Cabo San Lucas to recuperate from their disappointment, and to pay for the two dental caps Greg lost as a result of Keagan's punch. However, while they were there, they got a tip—from a kindred spirit, with the same degree of larceny—about some stashes in a Fort Myers, Florida storage compound. Keagan had thought the Campbells might want to know about this. So with the help of Kelly, they found out the details surrounding the stashes before calling him. Two of the storage compartments proved to be exceptionally lucrative. One of them contained a very impressive comic book collection that a local drug trafficker—Cavelya's replacement—had invested in; in the other they found a Louis Vuitton suitcase, which contained assorted men's and women's jewelry and two Gauguins.

When they had sold the Gauguins, the Campbells wired Keagan a ten percent finder's fee because they were nothing if not honest.